Praise for *The Blackbriar Genesis*

"This worthy addition to the Ludlum enterprise . . .
Gervais delivers the exciting action, colorful heroes and
villains, and seamless plots that readers have come to
expect from this dependable franchise. Ludlum would be
proud." —*Publishers Weekly*

"Gervais blows the doors off the hinges with this series-
starting thriller that introduces a pair of characters that
readers will love. Hands down, *The Blackbriar Genesis* is
the best thing to come out of Ludlum's universe since
The Bourne Ultimatum." —*The Real Book Spy*

"*The Blackbriar Genesis* grabs your undivided attention
from the very first spine-tingling page of gritty paranoia
and propels you through fast-paced, high-energy, action-
boosted chapters that will surely satisfy that itch you're
having for some hardcore espionage-action fusion."

—Best Thriller Books

THE BOURNE SERIES

Robert Ludlum's The Bourne Defiance (by Brian Freeman)
Robert Ludlum's The Bourne Sacrifice (by Brian Freeman)
Robert Ludlum's The Bourne Treachery (by Brian Freeman)
Robert Ludlum's The Bourne Evolution (by Brian Freeman)
Robert Ludlum's The Bourne Initiative (by Eric Van Lustbader)
Robert Ludlum's The Bourne Enigma (by Eric Van Lustbader)
Robert Ludlum's The Bourne Ascendancy (by Eric Van Lustbader)
Robert Ludlum's The Bourne Retribution (by Eric Van Lustbader)
Robert Ludlum's The Bourne Imperative (by Eric Van Lustbader)
Robert Ludlum's The Bourne Dominion (by Eric Van Lustbader)
Robert Ludlum's The Bourne Objective (by Eric Van Lustbader)
Robert Ludlum's The Bourne Deception (by Eric Van Lustbader)
Robert Ludlum's The Bourne Sanction (by Eric Van Lustbader)
Robert Ludlum's The Bourne Betrayal (by Eric Van Lustbader)
Robert Ludlum's The Bourne Legacy (by Eric Van Lustbader)
The Bourne Ultimatum
The Bourne Supremacy
The Bourne Identity

THE TREADSTONE SERIES

Robert Ludlum's The Treadstone Rendition (by Joshua Hood)
Robert Ludlum's The Treadstone Transgression (by Joshua Hood)
Robert Ludlum's The Treadstone Exile (by Joshua Hood)
Robert Ludlum's The Treadstone Resurrection (by Joshua Hood)

THE COVERT-ONE SERIES

Robert Ludlum's The Patriot Attack (by Kyle Mills)
Robert Ludlum's The Geneva Strategy (by Jamie Freveletti)
Robert Ludlum's The Utopia Experiment (by Kyle Mills)
Robert Ludlum's The Janus Reprisal (by Jamie Freveletti)
Robert Ludlum's The Ares Decision (by Kyle Mills)
Robert Ludlum's The Arctic Event (by James H. Cobb)
Robert Ludlum's The Moscow Vector (by Patrick Larkin)
Robert Ludlum's The Lazarus Vendetta (by Patrick Larkin)

Robert Ludlum's The Altman Code (with Gayle Lynds)
Robert Ludlum's The Paris Option (with Gayle Lynds)
Robert Ludlum's The Cassandra Compact (with Philip Shelby)
Robert Ludlum's The Hades Factor (with Gayle Lynds)

THE JANSON SERIES

Robert Ludlum's The Janson Equation (by Douglas Corleone)
Robert Ludlum's The Janson Option (by Paul Garrison)
Robert Ludlum's The Janson Command (by Paul Garrison)
The Janson Directive

ALSO BY ROBERT LUDLUM

The Bancroft Strategy
The Ambler Warning
The Tristan Betrayal
The Sigma Protocol
The Prometheus Deception
The Matarese Countdown
The Apocalypse Watch
The Scorpio Illusion
The Road to Omaha
The Icarus Agenda
The Aquitaine Progression
The Parsifal Mosaic
The Matarese Circle
The Holcroft Covenant
The Chancellor Manuscript
The Gemini Contenders
The Road to Gandolfo
The Rhinemann Exchange
The Cry of the Halidon
Trevayne
The Matlock Paper
The Osterman Weekend
The Scarlatti Inheritance

ROBERT LUDLUM'S

THE
BLACKBRIAR
GENESIS

SIMON GERVAIS

G. P. PUTNAM'S SONS
New York

PUTNAM
— EST. 1838 —

G. P. PUTNAM'S SONS
Publishers Since 1838
An imprint of Penguin Random House LLC
penguinrandomhouse.com

Copyright © 2022 by Myn Pyn LLC
Excerpt from *Robert Ludlum's The Bourne Defiance*
copyright © 2023 by Myn Pyn LLC

First G. P. Putnam's Sons hardcover edition / October 2022
First G. P. Putnam's Sons premium edition / August 2023
G. P. Putnam's Sons premium edition ISBN: 9780593419991

Printed in the United States of America
1 3 5 7 9 10 8 6 4 2

GENESIS: The Greek rendering of the Hebrew *bērē'shith*, the first word of the biblical book, traditionally translated as "in the beginning."

PART ONE

THE GENESIS

ONE

Assistant Deputy Secretary of State Edward Russell maintained a brisk pace as he hurried through Terminal 3 of the Cairo International Airport. He walked past the different stores, seeing flashes of books, overpriced food, and clothes. He wondered for a moment who in their right mind bought clothes at an airport, but seeing that every store was busy with customers, he just shook his head and continued toward the main station of the MiniMetro. Quite familiar with the airport, Russell didn't need a map to find the station, which was located between the freshly renovated Terminal 2 and the slightly older but much bigger Terminal 3. Looking past the bobbing and weaving heads of the other passengers walking in front of him, Russell spotted the red-and-white train symbol. He turned left at the next junction, with the instructions he'd been forced to memorize before leaving Washington playing in his mind over and over.

From Terminal 3, walk to the main MiniMetro station. Take the MiniMetro to Terminal 1, then use one of the terminal's public bathrooms before climbing back into the train to Terminal 3. From there, buy a local newspaper from the gift shop and go to the lobby of the Le Méridien hotel by crossing the pedestrian bridge. Someone will be waiting for you in the lobby.

Though he remembered every word, it failed to boost his confidence. Russell wasn't a spy, but he wasn't a fool, either. He knew he was being watched. He just didn't know by whom. All around him, arriving and departing passengers were hauling not only suitcases and travel bags stuffed to overflowing, but also teddy bears, pillows, and shopping bags filled with consumer goods. As large and nice as it was, Terminal 3 was packed with sweaty travelers, and their hurried footsteps, mixed with the sounds of crying babies, echoed up and down its structure. How anyone could find him in this crowd was a mystery. It seemed that every square inch of the terminal was occupied.

And it suffocated him.

To his left, a porter called out, offering to carry Russell's lone carry-on. Russell dismissed him with an impatient wave of the hand and reserved the same treatment for the two currency exchangers waiting on the Mini-Metro platform.

No. He didn't want to exchange his US dollars or euros for Egyptian pounds.

No, he didn't need a taxi.

And no, he didn't want companionship.

Russell wormed his way around the well-dressed peddlers and battled for position as the bright red train arrived. He squeezed into the car, which was already packed. There was standing room only, but he didn't mind after the thirteen-hour flight.

He had much more important things to worry about.

Russell, who had cultivated and maintained a multitude of contacts throughout Egypt during his thirty-year career at the Department of State's Bureau of Conflict and Stabilization Operations, had been sent to Cairo as the US secretary of state's personal emissary. His job for the next forty-eight hours was to hold discreet talks with what remained of the Muslim Brotherhood leadership. Once Egypt's largest opposition movement, the Brotherhood's political wing had won a plurality of seats in Egypt's lower house in 2011 but had been pushed out by a coup d'état two years later. Following a brutal crackdown, many of the Brotherhood's leaders and thousands of its members were imprisoned or forced into exile. With the Muslim Brotherhood completely cut off from political and civic participation, the CIA had cautioned that the remaining influential members of the Brotherhood were about to splinter into different groups. Without a central leadership, the most radical factions of the Muslim Brotherhood would become much more difficult to track. Not only could this cause significant social unrest in the capital and fuel more terror attacks against government forces in North Sinai, it could jeopardize the fragile but improving relationship between Egypt and Israel.

With the current instability in Libya and Sudan, and the escalating crisis in Ethiopia, the United States government saw the rapprochement between Egypt and Israel as vital for its national interests in the region.

In an effort to truly understand the growing discomfort within the Muslim Brotherhood ranks, the secretary of state wanted a finger on its pulse. Russell was that finger. But there was a problem. With the Egyptian government having designated the Muslim Brotherhood a terrorist organization, the United States couldn't afford to be seen entertaining discussions with them. That meant Russell had to travel to Cairo unofficially and without the contingent of DSS special agents he would normally be entitled to for such a trip.

"But it doesn't mean you'll be alone, Edward," the secretary of state had told him when he had summoned Russell into his office. "A small team of private contractors led by a man named Oliver will be waiting for you in Cairo. They're very, very good at what they do. Follow their lead, and they'll keep you safe. Trust me on this."

As the train began to move, Russell could see a dull gray sky beyond the windows. It must have rained hard earlier because the drains adjoining the airport were flooded. The traffic around the terminals was backed up, thanks in part to the vehicles that were double- and even triple-parked curbside. In the background was a constant sounding of horns by frustrated drivers. Russell's eyes moved from left to right, searching for somebody who might be paying too much attention to him. None of the faces looked familiar.

It took Russell a little less than thirty minutes to reach the final step of the procedures he'd been asked to follow. He was midway through the 250-yard-long pedestrian bridge leading to the hotel lobby when a hand suddenly squeezed his elbow.

Russell froze, spooked.

"Don't stop walking, Mr. Russell. You're clear. Keep your distance, but follow me," a tall man dressed in dark slacks and matching zippered jacket said without stopping.

Russell's heart was pounding. Where had this man come from? He just appeared from seemingly nowhere. And, even more critical, who was he? The instructions had said that someone would be waiting for him in the lobby. There had been no mention of someone accosting him on the bridge leading to the hotel.

Shit.

What was he supposed to do? The man's English was perfect, without a hint of an accent.

And he knows my name. It has to be Oliver.

Russell prayed that he was right.

TWO

CAIRO, EGYPT

Oliver Manton entered the hotel lobby and scratched his right ear, a gesture intended for his partner Trent, signaling that Russell was on his way.

"Good copy," Trent replied, his voice coming through the earbud deep in Manton's ear canal. "The SUV is at the door and ready to receive."

The lobby was spacious and elegant, with dark marble floors and a large reading area, but it lacked any real charm. The reception area was busy with the regular hum of arriving and departing guests, and Manton figured that, on a busy day, the check-in counter might be mistaken for a terminal at Hartsfield-Jackson Airport in Atlanta. A quick look outside through one of the large floor-to-ceiling windows confirmed that the rain had stopped, but the dark, low-hanging clouds promised more very soon, which didn't help lighten Manton's bad mood. Another downpour would only worsen the drive out of the airport.

Moreover, in Manton's opinion, it didn't make much sense to have three Treadstone agents babysitting an assistant deputy secretary in Cairo. Manton had read the ops plan prepared by Treadstone Director Levi Shaw and understood why DSS special agents couldn't be involved. He was in agreement with Shaw as to why Russell needed to be protected.

That wasn't the problem.

What Manton couldn't wrap his head around was why Treadstone had been given the assignment in the first place. These kinds of duties were usually assigned to private military companies who specialized in close protection. Treadstone operatives were hardened assassins, not protectors.

Unless . . .

Was escorting the assistant deputy secretary only a cover for a darker assignment? Having worked for Shaw for years, Manton wouldn't be surprised.

Manton grunted at the thought. Did it really matter? Whatever the real reason he and the other agents were in Cairo, they would do what they were told. Like they always did.

He had never worked with the other two operatives before, and he couldn't even remember the last time he had worked so closely with another agent, let alone two. Still, it was comforting to know he was operating alongside highly skilled individuals who had graduated—survived, really—the same brutal training he had.

Manton crossed the polished floor of the lobby and strode past Trent, who had taken position next to the concierge desk. Manton pushed through the brass-framed revolving door and headed toward the dark gray Audi Q7, his head on a swivel. The stench of gasoline fumes emanating from the idling vehicles parked curbside, mixed with the smell of jet fuel, assaulted his nose. The odor was so powerful that Manton could taste it.

When Edward Russell stepped out of the lobby twenty seconds later, followed ten steps behind by the second Treadstone agent, Manton gave the assistant deputy secretary of state a nod and opened the rear passenger door for the two men.

"You can leave your carry-on here, sir," Manton said. "I'll put it in the trunk for you."

Russell complied and climbed inside first, with Trent following seconds later. Manton closed the door, dropped the surprisingly heavy carry-on in the trunk next to a pair of duffel bags, and scanned the area one last time before sliding into the passenger seat of the SUV. The Audi surged forward and merged into traffic.

"We're going to the alternate safe house," Manton said to the driver.

Manton shifted in his seat so that he could look at the Treadstone agent seated behind him.

"Anyone in the lobby?" Manton asked.

"Can't be sure, but probably," Trent replied, pulling out two MP5 submachine guns and a bunch of spare magazines from a hard-sided Pelican case at his feet. "I'd say there's a fifty-fifty chance they made us."

The agent gave Manton an MP5 with three full magazines. Manton quickly inspected the magazines and inserted one into the submachine gun's well. Manton glanced at the side mirror. Aged vehicles in various states of repair swarmed all around their SUV, and it would only get worse the closer they got to the city center. On their right, an old, horribly beat-up white sedan accelerated past them. Manton tightened his grip on the MP5, but relaxed when he saw two young children seated in the rear. One of the kids looked at Manton and waved, a big smile on her face. Caught off guard, Manton tried to return the smile, but only managed a twitch of his lips.

He turned his attention to Russell and was surprised at the intensity with which the bureaucrat was staring back at him. Although Russell had almost jumped out of his socks when Manton had made initial contact with him on the bridge linking Terminal 3 and the Le Méridien, he certainly didn't look scared now.

"What's your name?" Russell asked.

"Oliver."

"Which PMC are you guys with?"

"Does it matter?" Manton replied.

"Guess not."

"By the way, this is Patrick," Manton said, pointing to the driver. "And the big guy next to you is Trent."

Trent nodded at Russell, then turned his attention to Manton and asked, "You want me to grab the rest of the kit?"

Manton nodded. "Yeah. Why not? And get a vest for Mr. Russell, too."

"Hold on a second, will you? Did I miss something?" Russell asked. "What's with going to the alternate safe house and all the guns? Is something wrong?"

Manton realized he hadn't kept Russell in the loop about his thought process.

"Let me first apologize for the series of detours we imposed on you," he said. "But we needed to see if you were being followed or if someone was waiting for you at the terminal."

"I figured that much," Russell said. "So I'm clear?"

"No."

Russell's eyes widened in surprise. "What? On the bridge you told me I was—"

"I lied," Manton said, cutting him off. "I didn't want you to panic and start looking everywhere."

"Are . . . Are you sure?"

"Very. But I don't know who they are or what their intent is."

"I didn't see anyone. Is it possible you're—"

"I said I'm sure," Manton said, once again interrupting Russell.

The assistant deputy secretary of state was doing his best to maintain a straight face, but Manton could see the concern in the man's eyes. Russell's presence in Egypt and the meetings he was scheduled to lead were supposed to be kept under wraps. Now that the cat was out of the bag, decisions needed to be made.

"I don't know you, Oliver, but my boss told me you're good at what you do," Russell said after a moment. "So, what do you suggest I do?"

"It's up to you, sir. You can go back to DC, or we can try to fix this."

"Fix this? What does that even mean?"

"It means that we have numerous contingency plans for situations like this," Manton said with a hint of impatience.

"Like what?"

"You don't need to bother yourself with that, Mr. Russell."

"Maybe, maybe not, but I'd like you to tell me anyway. If you don't mind?"

Manton did mind, but if giving the chatty bureaucrat a two-sentence answer would shut him up . . .

"I can go into the details later if you insist, but we're going to make a series of detours and stops on our way to the safe house. The second stop will be in an underground parking garage right off Tahrir Square, and this is where you, Trent, and I will switch vehicles."

"Okay. I assume the objective is to get to the alternate safe house unnoticed?"

"That's right. If we believe you're still under surveillance, or that the alternate safe house is compromised in any way, then we'll have no choice but to recommend you call off your meetings."

"I see. And what are the odds of that happening?" Russell asked.

"Hard to say without knowing how the opposition found out you were coming," Manton admitted. "Very few people outside this vehicle knew about your trip to Cairo. It's possible that the people who were waiting for you at the airport weren't hostiles, but members of the Muslim Brotherhood making sure you arrived okay. I think there's a fair chance you'll be able to carry on with your mission."

"You *think*?" the bureaucrat asked with a chuckle. "That's not very reassuring."

"Well, that's all I can offer you. There are no guarantees—"

Manton caught a bunch of flashes at the edge of his peripheral vision and turned his head toward their origin— the parking lot of a McDonald's on El Nasr Road two hundred yards away.

Before Manton could scream a warning, the driver yelled, "RPGs!" as he punched the gas and cranked the wheel right, aiming for the drainage ditch on the side of the road. Few men could have reacted as quickly to the threat as the driver did, but even he wasn't fast enough. Manton saw several trails of smoke, and then the white sedan carrying the two kids flew into the air on a pillar of flame, a vicious explosion splitting the air. A millisecond later, a second projectile struck the pavement and detonated less than one meter from the left rear tire of the Audi, tilting the bulky SUV onto two wheels. The driver lost control and hit the ditch at an odd angle at almost fifty miles an hour. Manton's heart lurched into his throat as the Audi took flight. The SUV flipped twice and landed upside down on the other side of the ditch with a sickening, metallic crunch.

THREE

Edward Russell opened his eyes, aware that his legs were higher than his head. He was completely disoriented. His ears were ringing and there was the distinct taste of blood in his mouth. His seat belt was digging into his chest, and there was a dull but prevalent pain in his back and left side. Trent, who had unfastened his seat belt to reach into the cargo area of the SUV, was lying in a heap on the Audi's ceiling. His eyes were open, but his head was twisted at an obscene angle.

What the hell had just happened? The driver had yelled something Russell hadn't entirely caught, then there was a formidable explosion. That was the last thing he remembered.

"Russell? Russell?" came Oliver's insistent voice, his words like light piercing through thick fog.

"I'm here. I'm okay. Trent's dead, I think."

"Stay there. I'm coming to you." Oliver opened his door and unbuckled his seat belt. Russell watched as Oliver ungracefully fell to the ceiling of the Audi and rolled out of the vehicle, an MP5 in hand.

Oliver hadn't been out of the vehicle for more than a few seconds when a storm of bullets raked the side of the SUV. The engine began to hiss, and black smoke started filling the interior of the Audi.

Oh shit. They killed Oliver.

Russell heard eight distinct gunshots fired in quick succession.

They finished him off. Oh, my God! They're coming here next.

He swallowed hard. He was going to be the next one to die, he was sure of it.

Do something! Don't let them slaughter you like a scared animal. Move!

He had to find a weapon. He saw Trent's MP5 and stretched his arm toward it.

Too far. Russell called out to the driver, who, like him, was still hanging upside down from his seat belt.

"Patrick! Hey! Patrick! Talk to me!"

The man didn't move.

Shit. Shit. Shit.

Then, out of the blue, Oliver appeared outside his door, almost giving Russell a heart attack. His MP5 was slung across his chest. Oliver tugged hard on Russell's door, but it didn't budge.

There was another crackle of gunfire, and Oliver disappeared from view. A series of six individual shots, once again fired rapidly, followed. This time Russell understood who had fired them.

Oliver.

Whatever happened next, at least Russell would die knowing the contractors hadn't run away. He'd heard horror stories about PMC guys abandoning their principals. This Oliver guy was a fighter. State hadn't hired the cheapest ones this time around.

For whatever that was worth.

The black smoke was now hanging heavy inside the overturned SUV, and Russell's next breath caused an agonizing cough that sent bolts of sharp pain throughout his entire rib cage. Behind the wheel, Patrick had regained consciousness and was in the process of unbuckling his seat belt.

Bullets pinged off the Audi's doors and windows. Spiderweb cracks stretched over the glass only inches from Russell's face.

Shit! I need to get out of here.

The rear passenger-side door was suddenly yanked open.

"This way!" Oliver yelled at him. "Hurry up. They're coming."

It took more effort than it should have for Russell to unfasten his seat belt. When it finally disengaged, he fell on his right shoulder, and it knocked the wind out of him. An instant later, Oliver grabbed him by the shirt collar and dragged him over Trent's lifeless body and out of the Audi.

FOUR

CAIRO, EGYPT

Manton saw that Russell was unsettled, but at least he was ambulatory and still in the fight. The same couldn't be said about Trent. Not much Manton could do about it now.

Manton pulled a satellite phone from the inside pocket of his jacket and called Treadstone Director Levi Shaw's direct line. The device was equipped with a chip that held an encryption package that guaranteed only the person at the other end of the line would be able to hear him talk.

Director Shaw picked up right away.

"I'm listening," Shaw said, his voice strained. Agents didn't usually call him when deployed—unless something had gone horribly wrong.

"We were ambushed on Airport Road at the intersection of El Nasr Road."

"What? By whom?"

"Don't know. Trent's down, but the principal, Patrick, and I are fine. For now," Manton told him. "But we're about to get hit again."

"Understood. I'll do what I can. Keep your phone with you."

Manton disconnected the call, then reached inside the SUV and snatched an MP5 from under the fallen Treadstone agent. Trent wouldn't need it anymore.

Manton inserted a fresh magazine into his own MP5 and pocketed the partially spent one for future use. So far, he had fired fourteen well-placed shots at six different assailants. The six bastards had come at him in two waves of three and begun shooting in his direction the moment he had rolled out of the Audi. Clearly the ambush had been well planned and these guys had been the mop-up crew. Had the six men been better shots and coordinated their final assault on the SUV the same way the first phase of the ambush had been orchestrated, it would be Manton lying dead in the street instead of them.

But the fight wasn't over. Far from it. To his right, Patrick had taken cover behind the capsized SUV.

"What do you see?" Manton asked, handing Patrick the MP5 he'd just retrieved from the Audi.

"Two pickups, each loaded with half a dozen fighters heading our way."

Manton grabbed one of Russell's shoulders and looked at the man. The bureaucrat was holding his shit together surprisingly well considering the clusterfuck they'd suddenly found themselves in.

"Have you fired a pistol before?" Manton asked.

"A few times, but never in combat. I was a logistics officer in the army before joining the Foreign Service," Russell said, his eyes sharp, his voice perfectly even.

Manton made a judgment call and reached for the SIG Sauer P365 SAS concealed at the small of his back in a waistband holster. The pistol wasn't an offensive weapon by any means—the P365 SAS was a straight-up close-quarter-engagement handgun—but that's all he had to share with Russell.

"You have eleven rounds of nine-millimeter goodness. Ten in the magazine, one in the pipe. Got it?"

"Yes," Russell said, accepting the pistol.

"Cover our six," Manton said, pointing in the direction he wanted Russell to keep his eyes on.

"Yeah. Okay."

"Just point and shoot," Manton continued. "There's no iron sight on this one, no manual safety, either. And please, don't try to hit anything farther away than fifty feet. You'll only waste ammo. Yell if you see something."

Russell nodded, but Manton had already moved to the other end of the SUV. He glanced over the rear bumper of the Audi. The two pickups were barreling down the side street perpendicular to Airport Road, zigzagging between stopped or slow-moving vehicles.

"If they flank us, we're dead," Manton said to the other Treadstone agent.

Bullets clanged against the SUV and both agents took cover.

"These assholes are taking long-range potshots at us," Patrick said. "They want to keep our heads down."

Manton took another peek. One of the pickup trucks had stopped and fighters were dismounting from its bed, fanning out quickly.

"These guys are the fire base!" he yelled at Patrick.

Manton leaned slightly out of cover, took aim at one of the running men, and squeezed the trigger. The man spun and fell. Patrick fired, too, and another fighter tumbled, dead. Manton searched for a target, but the remaining four had taken cover. He shifted his aim to the pickup's windshield and fired five rounds. His first shot went too low and ricocheted off the hood of the truck, but the next four punched the driver's side of the windshield just above the wipers, two of them hitting flesh and muscle.

The second pickup had banked sharply to their right and was moving into a flanking position, confirming Manton's suspicion.

Shit!

"Patrick, keep the fire base pinned down!"

When Patrick began to fire, Manton stood up, abandoning his cover, and emptied the rest of his magazine at the second pickup. The passenger-side window exploded and the pickup veered left, its tires barely gripping asphalt. The driver lost control and slammed directly into the back of a dump truck parked on the shoulder. Two of the fighters in the bed of the pickup were ejected and flew headfirst into the side of the dump truck.

"We need to get out of the X!" Patrick yelled.

"Check," Manton replied, changing his MP5's magazine. Manton took in his surroundings. It was chaos.

Dozens of vehicles were immobilized on Airport Road, their windows shattered, their tires ripped apart by shrapnel. Fifty feet to his left, a red minivan was on fire. One of its occupants seemed to have successfully climbed out of the burning vehicle but now lay dead in the middle of the road, part of his clothes still alight. Steps behind the minivan, inside a black Toyota Corolla, a driver was slumped over the steering wheel. Here and there, people were sluggishly exiting their damaged vehicles. As appalling as it all was, Manton didn't give the injured men and women a second thought. His priority was to find a vehicle—preferably another SUV, but he'd settle for anything with four unscathed tires and a functioning motor—and disengage from the firefight before the attackers could regroup and continue their assault.

The sudden cracks of a pistol sent Manton spinning on his heels, his MP5 up. It took him half a second to find what Russell was shooting at. Forty yards away, one of the attackers Manton had shot earlier was on his knees, about to fire an RPG. Manton squeezed the trigger twice. The man fell to his side, but the RPG was already sailing right at them. The projectile raced over Manton's head, clearing the Audi by only a couple of feet, and exploded somewhere in the background. Before Manton could nod his thanks to Russell, he heard the high-pitched snapping of bullets hitting the opposite side of the Audi. To make matters worse, the surviving assailants from the second pickup truck were getting into position. Within seconds, Manton, Russell, and Patrick would be caught in the middle of multidirectional gunfire.

They had to move. Now.

"On me!" he called to Russell and Patrick. "We're going to use the drainage ditch that follows the fence to move west toward the stadium."

Manton wished he could pop a smoke grenade to obscure their dash across the fifty feet of open ground that separated the overturned Audi from the ditch, but the grenades were with the rest of his kit inside the Audi cargo compartment. Getting to them would take time they didn't have. Manton glanced over his shoulder. Russell and Patrick had bunched up behind him and were awaiting his command.

"Russell, I want you to stay to the left of Patrick, understood?"

"Yes."

"I'm gonna lay down some covering fire. Then you two go."

Patrick's left hand moved to Russell's back. "You ready for this?" the Treadstone agent asked. "Don't overthink it. Just run, stay low, and don't stop for any reason."

Russell's mouth must have run dry because he only managed to nod, but Manton saw that the man's hands were steady, his eyes fierce. Taking a deep breath, Manton tightened his grip on the MP5 and sprang into action. The moment he broke cover, he knew the timing couldn't have been worse. They had stayed too long at the X, and the enemy had zeroed in their fire.

His instinct told him to get back behind the armored Audi, but Patrick and Russell had already stepped out of cover, so he held steadfast, unwavering despite the withering hail of 7.62-millimeter rounds thumping against and around the SUV. Manton felt a round pluck at his jacket but stayed focused, squeezing shot after shot and downing one man. Another fighter got to his knees and shouldered an RPG just as another round snapped inches from Manton's left ear. Manton engaged the new threat, one of his bullets striking the wannabe rocket man square in the gut. As Manton's 9mm round tore its way through his organs, the fighter dropped the RPG and grabbed his belly in shock. Manton's next round hit him in the throat.

But the bullets kept coming, and the overlapping chatter of AK-47s only grew louder. To Manton's left, Russell dived into the ditch just as Patrick was struck by a bullet and fell—only a few feet short of the ditch. Manton let loose another volley, then sprinted toward Patrick. Steel-jacketed rounds swept the sand around Patrick with at least one of them hitting him in his side.

Manton grabbed the Treadstone agent under his shoulders and dragged him down into the ditch, his body leaving a dark trail of blood in the sand. Russell joined him halfway down and helped Manton the rest of the way.

"He . . . He saved my—"

"Not now!" Manton snapped. "Crawl to the top and tell me what you see. And for Christ's sake, stay low."

Manton turned his attention back to Patrick.

"Hey! Stay with me, Patrick. Stay with me."

The injured Treadstone agent let out a long, painful

groan. His eyes fluttered open as he took in a ragged breath, which immediately led to a wet, bloody cough. Manton patted Patrick's sides and back with his hands, looking for the entry wounds. When he drew his hands back, they were slick with blood. Patrick had been shot numerous times and was bleeding internally. There was nothing Manton could do for him, and Patrick knew it.

"Sorry, brother," Manton said, drawing Patrick's pistol from its holster and handing it to him. "Good luck."

"They're coming from two sides," Russell said, panting as he hurried back down the ditch.

"Tell me."

"Four men. Fifty yards," Russell said, using his left hand to indicate the direction. "And there's five more coming out from behind the dump truck."

"How far is the second group?"

"About eighty yards, but they're closing fast. They're halfway across the road now."

Manton could see the approaching fighters and their locations in his mind's eye. The second group was moving to cut them off farther west. It was going to be a challenge to get out of the ditch alive. Manton would have to move fast, or he and Russell would get walled in on two sides.

Manton took one last look at Patrick, who nodded weakly, his face deathly white.

"Okay, Russell, we're moving," Manton said. "Follow the ditch and run."

Staying low and moving fast, they followed a slight northerly bend in the ditch. The arc was pronounced enough to break direct line of sight from where the dying Treadstone agent was about to make his last stand. Ahead, Russell hadn't slowed down, and Manton was happy to see that the former logistics officer's fight-or-flight mechanisms weren't yet overloaded. Manton had seen civilians become downright paralyzed by much less.

Pistol shots cracked the air behind them. They were promptly drowned out by several long bursts of AK-47s. Russell glanced behind him, and Manton could see dread in the older man's eyes.

It was then that something snapped inside Manton's head, and he stopped running.

"Stay there. I'll be back!" he shouted to Russell.

Before Russell could muster a reply, Manton spun one hundred and eighty degrees, brought the butt of his MP5 tight against his shoulder, leveled the muzzle toward the gap in the bend, and started advancing down the ditch in a combat crouch, his heart thudding in his chest. He had never been one to play defense. It didn't sit well with him. He was Treadstone, and Treadstone took the fight to the enemy—not the other way around. There was only one way to play this if he didn't want to get squeezed out.

I'm gonna run straight down these assholes' throats.

Manton, fully aware he was critically outnumbered and outgunned, charged ahead, visualizing what was about to happen next. He was going to kill them all.

Surprise. Speed. Violence of action.

The lead fighter appeared in front of Manton, not

even five yards away. The man was dressed in a pair of khaki cargo pants and a loose-fitting, faded green T-shirt. His AK-47 was pointed in front of him, but away from Manton.

Manton double-tapped him in the face.

Manton, closing in with lightning speed, fired three rounds at the next fighter, who had been standing less than three feet behind the leader. The three 9mm bullets caught the fighter in the mouth. The man dropped still in the dirt, his body coming to rest almost on top of the other guy. Manton stepped over the two dead bodies and continued to push forward, surprised not to immediately see the two other fighters Russell had spotted earlier.

He understood why five steps later.

The third man lay dead halfway down the ditch, several bullet wounds dotting the front of his shirt. The fourth, though, was very much alive and was applying a tourniquet to his left leg using his belt. With his dying breath, Patrick had killed one of the shitheads, and incapacitated another. The injured fighter just had time to gasp a startled curse before Manton sent two rounds into the side of his head.

• • • • •

Edward Russell hesitated, his mind racing to make sense of what he was seeing. Why had Oliver turned around? Why was he heading straight into the four armed men he'd seen heading toward the ditch? Was he nuts?

Russell flinched when he heard gunfire.

Pop-pop! Pop-pop-pop!

Definitely an MP5. Making his decision, Russell brought his pistol up and headed in the same direction Oliver had taken seconds ago.

Pop-pop! Two more shots. Again from an MP5.

Russell picked up his pace and sidestepped over two dead bodies. As he cleared the bend, he saw Oliver, who immediately spun toward him, the muzzle of his MP5 pointed directly at his head.

Holy shit, this man is fast.

Oliver had just started to lower the MP5 when his eyes opened wide, and that's when Russell knew something was very, very wrong.

FIVE

Manton took four quick, powerful strides and tackled Russell to the ground and out of the line of fire just as two fighters opened up with their AK-47s. Lines of 7.62-millimeter rounds sent rooster tails of dark, wet sand and dirt where Russell had been standing. Manton landed on top of Russell and heard a loud thud as the bureaucrat's head smacked against a rock.

With no time to check on Russell, Manton rolled to his left and came up on one knee. He flipped the MP5 fire selector to fully automatic and yanked the trigger, firing a six-round burst at the closest fighter. The bullets tore through the man's chest. Manton switched his aim three feet to the right of the man he had just killed and emptied the rest of his magazine into the second shooter. The shooter's leg buckled beneath him, and he fell into the ditch. Manton ejected the depleted magazine, tossing it in the sand, and scrambled in his pocket for a fresh one.

Empty. His damn pocket was empty. Even the half-spent magazine was gone.

Fuck.

Before Manton could feel sorry for himself, his brain registered movement right in front of him. Ten feet ahead, the dark shadow of a man had appeared against the sidewall of the ditch. A fighter was about to clear the bend by *slicing the pie*. Manton moved to the opposite side of the ditch and tugged a knife from the sheath at his waist, the blade slipping free with the subtle rustling of steel against nylon. Very much aware that he was bringing a knife to a gunfight, Manton crept forward, bracing himself for the imminent close-quarters fight. The muzzle of the fighter's Kalashnikov was the first thing to materialize in Manton's field of vision. The fighter sensed or heard Manton and took a step back, trying to sweep his AK-47 toward the Treadstone agent, but Manton was already on him. The man was huge, six foot five at least, and close to three hundred pounds, and had a pistol in a drop holster strapped to his right leg. With his left arm, Manton swept the barrel up and knocked it away from him while ducking low enough to plunge his knife deep into the man's inner thigh three times in rapid succession. The big man screamed and his finger squeezed the trigger. Bullets showered the interior of the ditch. Manton wrenched the knife back out, tearing through flesh, muscle, and a main artery, and drove the tip of the blade into the man's groin. An animalistic shriek came out of the fighter's mouth. Seeing movement coming from behind his opponent, Manton pressed on with his advantage and swung the now-off-balance fighter counterclockwise while keeping him close and using him as a shield. With his right hand, Manton grabbed the man's pistol from the drop holster, buried the muzzle into his lower back, and shot him four times through his spine.

The fighter fell forward, and, as he did, bullets fired by a fourth man tore the ground and the air around Manton. Manton ducked left and pulled the trigger as fast as he could. Something slammed into his right hip, then into his left knee. He landed on his left side with a grunt, knowing he'd been shot. His assailant was down, too, though. He lay in the ditch ten yards away, his right hand clutching his throat in a futile attempt to stem the tide of blood oozing from his neck and through his fingers. The man was fighting to keep his eyes open. Manton tried to force himself upright, but only managed to sit. His left knee was shattered, and his right hip was throbbing with an almost unbearable pain. He didn't think he had any arterial damage, but his knee was truly fucked. His eyes moved to the pistol in his hand. The slide was locked back. The handgun was out of ammunition, just like the MP5.

Manton scanned the crest of the drainage ditch and almost smiled when he saw another fighter materialize on the ridge, his AK-47 pointed directly at him. Manton looked at the man—a teenager really—in slow detachment as the newcomer prepared to fire. Manton was vaguely aware of how thirsty he had suddenly become as he stared at the man about to kill him. From the man's skinny, shaking arms, to his dark eyes filled with a mixture of hate and fear, Manton could see every single detail with clarity, even the faint stubble of a mustache growing on the teenager's upper lip, and the remains of *kushari* on his old, dirty white shirt.

A series of gunshots coming from Manton's immediate left startled him. The fighter folded forward, then fell into the ditch, his body jerking with the impact of each additional bullet. Manton angled his head toward the source of the gunfire. Assistant Deputy Secretary of State Edward Russell was on one knee, holding Manton's SIG Sauer P365 SAS in a steady two-hand grip, a thin whisker of smoke curling from its muzzle.

I'll be damned.

"Help me up," Manton said.

But Russell didn't move. His eyes were fixed on the man he had just shot.

"Edward!" Manton said louder, using Russell's given name for the first time.

Russell turned his head toward him. "Help me up," Manton repeated. "Let's go!"

Out of his torpor, Russell rushed to Manton's side.

Leaning on him, Manton got to his feet, gritting his teeth. He couldn't put any weight on his left leg, none whatsoever, and his right hip was growing numb.

Shit.

Manton had no idea how to climb out of the ditch. The angle was way too sharp.

"Put your weight on me, Oliver," Russell said. "I got you."

Manton did as he was told and jumped on his right leg to move forward. He hadn't moved more than three feet when a jolt of pain shot through his leg, a pain so intense that it stole his breath. Manton tried to ignore it, but his leg collapsed under him and he fell, almost bringing Russell down with him.

"We'll try again," Russell said, reaching for Manton.

"Stop," Manton said, swiping Russell's hands away. "Grab a rifle from one of the dead men and steal a car, then drive, and don't stop until you reach the American embassy. You hear me?"

"I'm not leaving—"

"I'm deadweight, you idiot," Manton snapped. "Go! Go before it's too late."

But Russell didn't move. Instead, he locked eyes with Manton and said, "I don't know who the fuck you are, Oliver, or if that's even your real name, and I don't care. But I'm sure as shit that you aren't just a private contractor. No. Freaking. Way. I don't know why these goddamned cockroaches want me dead, but what I do know is that you and your men didn't bail on me. So I'm not going anywhere. We come out of this hellhole together, or we die in it. It's your fucking decision."

There was no fear in Russell's eyes, no emotion, just steel determination and grit. Manton would never forget that look.

"All right, then. Go grab a spare pistol magazine from the big guy's belt," Manton said.

Russell did as he was told and handed the magazine to Manton, who was beginning to feel light-headed.

"Do you know how to do a fireman's carry?" Manton asked, reloading the handgun.

"Shut up, Oliver," Russell said. "I was army logistics, not air force."

Despite the seriousness of the situation, Manton chuckled, but winced in pain as Russell helped him up onto his right leg. Then Russell got low and folded Manton over his shoulders.

SIX

CAIRO, EGYPT

Edward Russell's legs were burning, but he didn't dare slow down. Sporadic small-arms fire coming from outside the ditch kept his adrenaline flowing, but Russell's breathing had become labored. He was getting weaker, each new step harder than the previous one.

Keep going. Don't stop.

Russell quickened his stride, knowing that if he stopped, it would be impossible to start again. Oliver, who had ceased responding to Russell's probes, had lost a lot of blood. If he didn't get Oliver to a hospital soon, he would die. Forty yards ahead was another bend, and the slant out of the ditch wasn't as pronounced. He pushed himself to go faster, his legs screaming in protest.

AK-47 automatic fire erupted to his left, much closer this time, and Russell unconsciously ducked, which caused him to lose his balance. With Oliver still on his shoulders, Russell crashed to the ground in a cloud of wet sand and gravel, with little stones biting into the side of his face and forehead as the air exploded out of his lungs. Agony radiated through his ribs, but he refused to give up. Trembling uncontrollably, he got up, and, summoning the rest of his strength, hoisted an unconscious Oliver onto his shoulders.

Russell managed only a few more steps before he stumbled on a loose rock and twisted his ankle, nearly causing him to fall again. He recovered, but thanks to the extra weight on his shoulders, blew his knee out in the process. He uttered a loud grunt filled with frustration as he crashed against the sidewall of the ditch and landed on his ass next to Oliver, who had slid off his shoulders.

Close by, gunfire continued to rage, but the sounds were somewhat different than they had been only seconds ago. The deep barks of Kalashnikovs were still present, but another weapon had joined the mix. The bursts sounded more controlled. More precise.

M4s?

Then, from around the bend, two figures appeared in front of Russell, approaching in combat crouches, assault rifles steady in their hands. Two more men showed up on the crest.

"Mr. Russell?" one of the figures asked.

But Russell didn't reply. He couldn't speak. He was only aware of the sudden flow of tears in his eyes as he recognized the uniform the men were wearing.

"Sir, I'm Captain Parsons, United States Marine Corps. We got you."

PART TWO

BLACKBRIAR

SEVEN

"ETA one minute," Helen Jouvert said, backing her rental Peugeot 508 down an alleyway seventy yards from her final destination.

"Good copy," came Donovan Wade's reply through the miniature earbud in Helen's right ear. "Our friend came to about three or four minutes ago."

"How is he? Alert enough for a chat?" she asked.

"Not yet. Soon. He's still a bit confused and unfocused, but he's coming around," Donovan said with a chuckle.

I bet.

From the alleyway where she had parked her vehicle, the abandoned one-story car repair shop occupied by Donovan and their guest was visible. Donovan's minivan was by the side entrance of the shop and easily accessible in case they needed to rush out of the building. While the decrepit building could compete with all the other structures in the neighborhood for the status of *most neglected*, the fact that it was still connected to the power grid and had running water almost disqualified it. Helen had chosen Fyli—a small town of less than three thousand souls half an hour's drive from Athens's city center—to conduct the next phase of the operation because she'd been assured by the analysts back in New York that the town's inhabitants weren't the kind to pry into other people's business.

Across the street from the repair shop, an unfinished four-story building and a vacant lot had been transformed into a temporary stage for what looked like a moussaka cook-off. Six old men with bouzoukis—a stringed instrument resembling a mandolin—played music, and at least three dozen people drifted back and forth between eating, dancing, and singing. It gave the street a jovial ambiance Helen hadn't expected to see. She grabbed the backpack she had left on the front passenger seat and climbed out of the Peugeot. She hadn't yet closed the door when the moussaka's heavenly scents—a mix of freshly grilled meat, spices, and vegetables—reached her nose and made her stomach growl.

To avoid anyone seeing her enter the repair shop, Helen walked around the back of the Peugeot and headed deeper into the alleyway. She made a left into a narrow side street that led to the back of the shop.

"Donovan, are you hearing the party going on at the property directly across the street?" she asked.

"Hard not to, but they can't see inside," Donovan assured her. "Most doors and windows are boarded up."

"Understood. I'm approaching the rear entrance of the shop. Is it unlocked?"

"It is now," her partner replied an instant later.

Helen pulled the door open and stepped inside the dimly lit garage. She locked the door behind her and adjusted the backpack on her shoulder. She waited for her eyes to adjust to the sudden change in luminosity, then looked around. Twenty steps away and with his back to her, a thirtysomething man was seated on a metallic chair in the middle of the barren space. His wrists and ankles were firmly fastened to the chair with zip ties. He was naked but for a pair of white socks. He had heard her come in and was now craning his neck left and right in a futile effort to look behind him.

By the look of it, the car repair shop hadn't been used in years, but the smell of stale oil and gasoline still lingered in the air and obliterated the last of the wonderful aromas coming from the cook-off that had slipped through the door with her. Dozens of tires were stacked against the walls, and nearly every surface was covered with discarded tools and small motor parts. Sunlight sieved through a filthy window set high against the concrete wall, angling dusty rays of light down into the room and casting a shadow in front of the bound man. On the opposite side of the room, Donovan Wade was leaning against the wall, one hand holding a phone, the other one deep in the pocket of his dark windbreaker. He acknowledged her with a nod but remained silent.

Helen approached the prisoner and ran her hand across his naked shoulders as she walked in front of him. She turned to face him and moved her eyes to his most private part.

"I mean, yeah, it's cool in here, but it's not *that* cold," she said, shaking her head.

"Fuck you, bitch!" the man spat.

Helen laughed. "With what? That? I don't think so."

The man's face mottled red, and he looked away.

Easily rattled. Easily intimidated. And he speaks English like a champ.

Helen unslung the backpack and set it down at her feet. She dug inside for a roll of duct tape, a pair of headphones, and an old iPod. She grabbed the duct tape and walked to the naked man.

"You stupid whore! What are you gonna—"

Helen shut the man up mid-sentence by delivering two quick, powerful jabs to his nose. Blood poured from his nostrils and broken lips, staining his chest red. Before the man could regain his senses, Helen rolled the duct tape several times tightly around the man's mouth. She then plugged the headphones into the iPod and adjusted them over his ears. She scrolled through the available playlists and selected *50 Best Love Songs of All Time*. She tapped the play button and cranked up the volume as high as it would go. The man's body went as rigid as a steel rod and he let out a muffled yell from behind his gag.

She set the iPod at the man's feet, a mere inch away from his toe. She winked at him.

The man's name was Dimitri Callellis, aka Angelo2013.

He was a mid-level thug in the scheme of things, but an influential member of the Popular Fighters Group. The PFG was a left-wing organization that had come together in 2013 as a response to the austerity measures that had been forced down the throats of the Greek people by the International Monetary Fund and the European Central Bank in exchange for the bail-out money that had saved Greece from a sovereign default.

While most of the Popular Fighters Group's terror attacks since its inception had targeted the government of Greece and German organizations in and around Athens, the group had recently sent a series of letter bombs to the residences of American diplomats living in Greece. One of the bombs had killed the ambassador's administrative assistant, and another had slightly injured a Greek police officer. Dreading additional attacks and enraged at how long it was taking the FBI and the Hellenic Police to formulate a response, let alone ferret out the culprits, Director of National Intelligence Edward Russell had tasked Blackbriar Director Oliver Manton to run a covert but parallel investigation.

Not bound by all the inefficient bureaucratic rules and procedures that prevented the FBI from timely action, Blackbriar analysts had moved fast and quickly zeroed in on Angelo2013. Gutsy Angelo2013 had mentioned on several Tor-based darknet marketplaces that more American pigs would soon feel the wrath of the Popular Fighters Group.

"And next time, it won't be letter bombs," Angelo2013 had promised.

Manton had sent Helen and Donovan to Greece to find out who was behind the Angelo2013 avatar and if that person or group was indeed responsible for the letter bombs. Manton also wanted to know what resources were at the group's disposal and how close they were to launching another attack. To lure Angelo2013 out of hiding, the two Blackbriar agents—posing as Hezbollah operatives—had reached out to him on the darknet and implied that they would be willing to contribute to his war efforts by providing him with enough ammonium nitrate to blow up half a city block—but only if Angelo2013 agreed to certain terms. At first Angelo2013 had been guarded, but the resistance had melted away like snow in the sun when Helen had sweetened the deal by offering him a Bitcoin just to meet with them and listen to what they had to say.

Half a Bitcoin now. Half a Bitcoin after the meeting.

Helen and Donovan had set up surveillance near the meeting place—a small café in Exarcheia, a neighborhood with the reputation of being Athens's historical core of radical political activities and a clear favorite among the anarchist crowd. As per the directives Director Manton had given them, Helen and Donovan's primary objective had been to identify the person or people behind the Angelo2013 pseudonym.

It hadn't taken long.

Just as Donovan had predicted, Angelo2013 had turned out to be a twat, not an accomplished operative like Helen had feared. Walking by the café looking nervously left and right no fewer than four times had been a dead giveaway for the Greek terrorist. Medium height and on the chubby side, the man had dark hair pulled back in a ponytail. Both Helen and Donovan had managed to snap good pictures of him with their phones. Using a facial recognition app linked to the Blackbriar tactical operations center in New York, they had rapidly identified Angelo2013 as Dimitri Callellis.

Just before entering the café, Dimitri had peered intently through the glass doorway for a few seconds, as if he was reconsidering his decision to meet with Hezbollah operatives. In the end, greed trumped sanity, and Dimitri had stepped inside the café.

Once Helen was convinced Dimitri was alone, and Donovan had confirmed he was in position, she had given an errand boy five euros to deliver a note to Dimitri inside the café. Following the directives written on the note, Dimitri had made his way to the bathroom, where Donovan was waiting. A quick jab with a needle had rendered the Greek man unconscious. Donovan had carried him through the café's back exit and into a minivan. Donovan had left with the minivan toward Fyli, while Helen had climbed into her own vehicle and checked for surveillance or any sign that Dimitri had brought backup. He hadn't.

Behind Helen, Donovan cleared his throat. She turned to face him, and he gestured for her to come over.

"Anything?" she asked.

"Kind of," Donovan replied. His voice was deep, with

just a hint of huskiness. He handed her the phone he'd been holding. "I think our hero here is acting alone, or at least without the knowledge of the PFG leadership."

"Is that so?" Helen glanced at Dimitri, waving a finger in his direction, as if he were a misbehaving child. Tears stemming from what she imagined to be rage, pain, and maybe a bit of fear streamed down his crimson face. "That would explain why he showed up alone. Let me see."

Helen scrolled through the email messages Dimitri had received in the last four days. Although the messages had originally been written in Greek, Donovan had downloaded onto Dimitri's phone an app capable of translating text written in a foreign language into English.

"Holy crap, his revolutionary friends at the PFG aren't only looking for him, they want to freakin' kill him," Helen said once she was done skimming through the emails. "Either our buddy Dimitri is working for an element outside of his regular network, or he's become an autonomous terror cell."

Donovan made a face. "*Autonomous terror cell?* That sounds a touch too sophisticated for this guy. He's just a piece of shit who went rogue."

"Maybe, but he's killed an American diplomat and threatened to kill more," Helen reminded her partner, handing the phone back to him. "We'll need to forward all of these to headquarters."

"I'll do it, but there's nothing else on the phone. It's clearly a burner. There are no text messages on it, only the emails you read."

"I still think we should ask Dimitri a few questions. You know, to ascertain his motives and determine if he's been working alone," Helen said. "Care to do it?"

She turned to Donovan to gauge his reaction, but he was too close, and she had to take a step back and look up to find his eyes. At five feet nine inches, Helen wasn't a short woman, but Donovan still towered over her by at least half a foot. It was their third mission together, and she didn't know much about him at all. With the exception of what Director Manton had shared with her—that Donovan Wade was a former CIA officer—Helen had no idea what Donovan's life story was. He was a private man, and he wasn't a big talker. She had probed him a few times about his background, but he had remained vague. Still, he was a good partner. She was the team leader, but so far she had never felt the need to pull rank on him, which told her that he had probably spent time in the military prior to joining the CIA.

When she was working for the FBI's Counterintelligence Division, she had regularly partnered with CIA officers on joint investigations. She'd found most of them to be pricks, full of themselves and quick to dismiss her because she was a woman.

But not Donovan. He was . . . different. And yet, she had a tough time getting a read on the man.

"I'd be happy to get some answers out of him for you," he said, his eyes locking on Dimitri. "I'll only need a minute."

Helen didn't know if it was the subtle change in his demeanor or the speed with which his gentle blue eyes had turned threatening when he had looked at Dimitri, but Helen felt a chill run down her spine—an abnormal occurrence for her.

A little voice in her head urged her to ask Donovan to stand down, to tell him that she would ask Dimitri the questions, but just as she was about to open her mouth to speak, her encrypted phone vibrated in her pocket. She looked at the screen.

Headquarters was checking in.

EIGHT

Donovan Wade was very much aware that his investigating skills weren't as fine-tuned as his partner's. Helen was former FBI. Investigating stuff was *her* specialty, not his. His area of expertise was, well, rather different.

Although disappointed Director Manton had selected Helen to be the team leader, Donovan took the news on the chin and didn't complain. Given the speed and manner in which the CIA had kicked him to the curb, he was lucky Manton had considered him for Blackbriar. Team leader or not, being once again a field operative was a better option than the alternative—working at the CIA Museum at Langley, the only job the almighties on the seventh floor would entrust him with.

Someday, though, he would prove to these shitheads how wrong they'd been about him.

And about my brother.

But for now, he had a job to do, and he pushed the negative thoughts away, focusing instead on Dimitri Callellis. The man was in obvious pain, thanks to the music blasting in his ears. Beads of sweat slicked his forehead despite the cool temperature, and his face was smeared with blood and mucus from the two punches he'd earned himself. Dimitri shook his head, doing what he could to dislodge the headphones, but they remained firmly in place. Donovan stopped one step away from the Greek terrorist. He could almost smell the fear oozing from the man's pores. Donovan picked up the iPod and tapped the pause button before removing the headphones.

"That wasn't very nice of her, was it?" Donovan said. "A few more minutes and your ears could have been permanently damaged. Not cool."

Donovan looked around the filthy floor and spotted a fetid, soiled rag to his left. The rag was crispy to the touch, like an overcooked pita bread, but Donovan used it to not-so-gently wipe the blood off Dimitri's face and chest.

"I'm about to ask you a series of questions," Donovan said, a big grin on his face. "It's really important that you answer them truthfully. Do you understand?"

Dimitri nodded.

"If I feel you're being dishonest, either the headphones are going back on or I'm gonna hurt you," Donovan said.

Dimitri shook his head from left to right several times.

"Okay. Good. I'm glad we had this chat. It's a relief,

really. The last thing I want is to hurt you, but if you lie to me, I will. Fair enough?" Donovan said, his tone jovial, as if he were asking a friend to go out for a beer.

With a single pull, Donovan tore the piece of duct tape from Dimitri's mouth. The Greek terrorist bawled in pain.

"First question, and it's an easy one. What's your name?"

The hesitation lasted less than half a second, but Donovan pounced on the opportunity to assert his dominance. In one fluid motion, he grabbed Dimitri's pinky finger and bent it backward until it snapped. Before Dimitri could even comprehend what had just happened, Donovan shoved the soiled, dirty rag into his mouth, effectively muffling the man's scream.

"My bad, my bad," Donovan said. "I'm so sorry, and I know it's not fair, but I completely forgot to tell you about this one rule."

New tears formed in Dimitri's eyes.

"If you hesitate, I'll punish you the same way as if you'd lied to me," Donovan said, removing the rag from Dimitri's mouth. "I need the truth, Dimitri. Don't think you can lie or sweet-talk your way out of this. You can't."

The man coughed, then swallowed, trying to catch his breath.

"What's your name?" Donovan asked.

"Dimitri."

Donovan frowned, then pursed his lips. Dimitri tensed as Donovan took hold of another finger and stretched it back, almost to its breaking point.

"When I ask you a question, I want you to tell me everything, not the bare minimum or whatever you think you can get away with."

Tears were rolling down Dimitri's cheeks freely now. Donovan took a long breath, then released the finger.

"Don't make me regret this, Dimitri," Donovan warned. "I'm one of the nicest guys around, but if you keep pushing my buttons like you've been doing this last minute, I'm gonna lose it. Capisce?"

"Yes! Yes!"

"The third time's always the charm, right?" Donovan asked with a disarming smile.

Terror flashed across Dimitri's eyes and his whole body began to shake. "What? I . . . I don't understand. I . . . I am . . ."

"Never mind, Dimitri. This wasn't a question. Good Lord, you're a nervous one, aren't you?" Donovan said, giving Dimitri's shoulder a soft, friendly shove with his fist. "What's your last name?"

"Callellis. My name is Dimitri Callellis."

"Do you know why we're here?"

"No . . . I mean—"

Donovan punched him hard on the chin, a quick uppercut that sent Dimitri's lower teeth sawing into his tongue. Again Donovan muffled the man's scream with the rag. This time, though, he also blocked the man's airway. Donovan counted to thirty, and only then did he remove the rag covering Dimitri's mouth and nose, not realizing that the man had started to piss himself. Dimitri was trying to stop the flow but couldn't. Warm urine dripped down the Greek man's legs in streaks, soaking his white socks.

Is this for real?

The sharp reek of Dimitri's piss wafted into Donovan's nose. Disgusted, he turned to look at Helen, but she had stepped farther back into the repair shop and was speaking on the phone.

Dimitri continued to wheeze, sucking in big gulps of oxygen. Just when Donovan was about to repeat the question, Dimitri turned his head away from him and spat a mouthful of blood, and maybe even a tooth, but Donovan couldn't be sure about that last part.

"Do you know why we're here?" Donovan asked, once Dimitri had regained some composure.

"Yes. I know why."

"Please do tell."

"You're not with Hezbollah," Dimitri said. "I was supposed to meet with someone from Hezbollah."

"Oh, really? What makes you say we aren't with Hezbollah?" Donovan asked.

Dimitri seemed to be at a loss for words. "I . . . You . . . You look like Americans."

Donovan didn't appreciate the involuntary scowl on Dimitri's face when he said *Americans*. This piece of shit really had it in for the United States!

"Aren't you clever, Dimitri," Donovan replied, resisting the sudden urge to bash Dimitri's face in. "Why were you supposed to meet with someone from Hezbollah?"

This was the moment of truth. If Dimitri answered truthfully, it meant that he was a broken man and that he had come to the conclusion that his full cooperation was his only play. If he lied, Donovan would have to work a bit more on him to gain his collaboration.

"Hezbollah promised me ammonium nitrate, and a Bitcoin," Dimitri said.

"You're in the agricultural business, Dimitri?"

"No. I . . . It was to build a bomb."

"To kill Americans?"

Dimitri swallowed hard and averted his gaze. "Yes," he muttered.

Donovan took three steps and positioned himself behind Dimitri.

"We both know a lightweight like you isn't capable of pulling off a stunt like that alone. You'd have no idea where to start."

Without notice, Donovan grabbed a fistful of hair on the back of Dimitri's head and pulled back hard. "Who's helping you? Who else is involved? Your friends at the Popular Fighters Group?"

For a moment Dimitri's fear switched to rage as his face twisted with anger. "The PFG? They're nothing anymore! They're scared. They are terrified of the Americans. I'm not."

Donovan couldn't help but chuckle.

"Really? You're not?" he said, letting go of the man's hair and making his way back around to face Dimitri. "Because one of us peed himself, and it ain't me."

Donovan squatted so that he'd be at eye level with the Greek terrorist. "You're a frightened little bitch, Dimitri."

Dimitri's nostrils flared wildly, his eyes blazing with resentment, and in a fleeting moment of bravado, he said, "I nearly killed your ambassador."

"Yeah, I know. Who helped you?"

"No one!"

Careful not to step in the urine that had pooled around Dimitri's feet and already begun to seep into the concrete floor, Donovan reached for the Greek's broken finger.

"No, please! No one helped me. No one! You have to believe me!"

"I do believe you, Dimitri," Donovan said, taking a step back and leaving the broken finger untouched.

Dimitri seemed momentarily confused. "You do?"

"Yes, but that's a big problem for you."

The hope Donovan had just witnessed in Dimitri's face was short-lived. Dimitri's expression morphed into a mask of terror as Donovan pulled his Glock 29 from his holster. He didn't bother checking if there was a round in the chamber since he had already done so earlier. With his left hand, he dug into his left jacket pocket and grabbed a suppressor. He screwed the suppressor onto the end of the pistol slowly, while keeping eye contact with Dimitri.

"I . . . I told you the truth. You promised me—"

"What? What did I promise you?" Donovan asked. "Please refresh my memory."

Dimitri remained silent.

"Yeah, that's what I thought," Donovan said, raising the pistol.

"Wait! Wait! I'll . . . I can give you the PFG leaders. All of them!" Dimitri pleaded. "I know where they live, where they stop for coffee, even where their kids go to school."

Donovan heard footsteps behind him. A hand lightly touched his shoulder. He turned to look at Helen, who gave him a nearly indiscernible *Don't kill him* shake of her head. He unscrewed the suppressor and holstered the Glock while Helen replaced the headphones on Dimitri's head and pressed play on the iPod.

"What's up?" he asked her.

"Headquarters called. The PFG is about to put up a ten-thousand-euro reward for whoever brings them Dimitri's head."

Donovan glanced at Dimitri. "What do you want to do?"

"Did he say anything?"

"Yeah, but it's hard to know if he told me the truth."

"What's your gut telling you?" Helen asked.

"I only spoke to him for a few minutes, but I don't think he lied to me. I have the feeling he's been acting alone and without anyone else's support. The messages we found on his phone seem to confirm this. And so does the prize money they're offering for him. I think it's safe to assume he hasn't gotten any help, at least from the PFG."

"They're furious at him for proceeding without their consent," Helen said.

"The spotlight is back on them, and they don't like it," Donovan said. "I've read that the PFG wants to present candidates at the next election, so if they want to be taken seriously, it's in their best interest to neutralize Dimitri, or at least dissociate themselves from him."

"Agreed, but here's the deal. Headquarters told me the FBI is finally getting its act together and is getting ready to send the Fly Team to Athens to provide support to the Hellenic Police."

"What does that mean for us?" Donovan asked.

"I know one of the Fly Team investigators," Helen said. "We went through the Academy together. Solid, brilliant guy. If the local authorities remove the red tape and let my friend and the rest of the Fly Team loose, there's a good chance they'll have everything figured out within a few days, including our involvement."

Donovan considered what Helen had just said. Since they'd landed in Athens the day before, they'd been discreet and kept a low profile. But they hadn't been ghosts, either, preferring to work fast and neutralize the threat before a possible follow-up attack. They'd been invisible to the local authorities, but a crack unit like the FBI Fly Team would eventually sniff out the clues they'd left behind. The special agents assigned to the Fly Team—a small, highly trained cadre of counterterrorism investigators based at the FBI headquarters and ready to deploy anywhere in the world at a moment's notice—were the best the Bureau had.

"What if we were to muddy the water a little?" Donovan said, a plan beginning to take shape in his head.

"Okay . . . What do you have in mind?"

"I'm thinking that if the Greek authorities are able to

close the case before the Fly Team gets here, they'll revoke their request for assistance, which will make it exponentially more difficult for the Fly Team to move around."

"I don't think reaching out to the Hellenic Police is such a good idea," Helen said.

"Who said anything about contacting the police? Here's what I suggest we do."

NINE

Oliver Manton's aching leg muscles were threatening to shut down, and so were his lungs, but he refused to stop. He pushed the button on the panel until the treadmill maxed out at twelve miles per hour and continued to run. Only after he nearly fell face-first and came within inches of smashing his head onto the console did he grab the handrails and put his feet on each side of the running belt. Breathing heavily, Manton staggered off the treadmill and wiped his face with a towel. The full-length mirror threw his reflection back at him. Despite his exhaustion, he liked what he saw. For a man deep into his forties, his body was still responding well to his daily workouts. Although his hair had started to turn gray at the temples, he still had a full head of thick black hair. His face, though, had aged at a different pace than the rest of him. It was weather-beaten and tanned to leather from years spent under the sun, often in countries hostile to his own.

But, more important, his legs were holding up.

Following the events in Cairo, he had needed a new right hip and a total left knee replacement. His convalescence had been short, and he had recuperated twice as fast as most other patients who had undergone the same surgeries. He had passed all the physicals they had thrown at him and the Treadstone doctors had cleared him for duty.

But not Treadstone Director Levi Shaw.

Shaw had canned him just the same. Or at least that's how it had felt to Manton when Shaw told him he was going to spend the good years he had left training new Treadstone recruits.

Manton had been furious. He was an operator, trained to be dropped anywhere in the world—including in the harshest of environments—and be trusted to complete his assignment. And that's exactly what he had done. He hadn't deserved to be cast aside.

Manton pushed the negative thoughts away and grabbed two sixty-pound dumbbells. He sat on one of the several padded benches, his back straight and the soles of his shoes flat against the rubber floor. As he always did when his mind was troubled, he had attacked the cardio machines and the irons with twice his regular intensity. He had three teams of two agents deployed overseas, and one of the teams—the one in Belarus—had missed its last check-in. The next scheduled check-in was in three hours, and despite having spent the last thirty-two hours at the office and without sleep, there was no way Manton would go home before he had received confirmation that his team was okay and out of harm's way.

He pushed the weights over his head and brought them down slowly. After the twelfth rep, the dumbbells were wobbling in his hands.

Three more. One for each team.

Perspiration streamed down his forehead as he worked the weights. A tight-lipped groan escaped his mouth as he pushed the irons once more and at full stretch above him, his arms buckling under the strain as he lowered the weights with agonizing slowness, his body screaming at him to drop them.

One more. Mind over matter.

With a savage grunt, he forced the dumbbells up, held them steady for a three-count, and only then did he allow himself to bring them down.

Bend your body's software to control its hardware. Treadstone.

Manton felt the pressure inside the gym change. Someone had opened the door. Manton turned to face the newcomer. It was Faith Jackson, a twenty-nine-year-old analyst he had pinched from the NSA. She had long black hair, dark eyes, and an easy smile that lit her whole face.

"What is it, Faith?" he asked, hoping his two-man team in Belarus had made contact.

"Something popped up on a dark web server we're monitoring for the Belarus op, sir."

Manton's stomach clenched. "Have we heard anything from our team?"

"They haven't made contact. Their next check-in isn't slated until—"

"I know when their next scheduled check-in is, Faith," Manton cut in, getting up from the workout bench.

"Yes, sir."

"Lead the way." He grabbed a bottle of water from the gym's cooler.

On Jackson's heels, Manton followed her down a brightly lit corridor and past several windowless offices. They turned left at the first intersection, where hallways led in two different directions. Fifty steps later, the hallway ended in a red wall, which was broken by a large airlock hatch. Manton entered his ten-digit alphanumeric code, then placed his hand on the biometric palm scanner—a device that used infrared light to read the mapping of veins underneath the skin. A small green light blinked twice on top of the scanner and Manton heard the clank of locks springing free. He opened the door for Jackson and followed her into Blackbriar's nerve center.

Blackbriar's TOC—or tactical operations center—was a large room buzzing with activity. There were three tiers of workstations and, even though it was Sunday night, half of them were occupied. Manton had organized his staff of forty analysts and logistic experts into four watches to ensure it was manned around the clock. The wall at the front of the room had four massive flat screens but only one of them was turned on. Manton examined it. Displayed on the flat screen were a bunch of pop-up windows, each containing numerous lines of code.

Jackson sat behind a workstation and angled her screen so that Manton could see.

"This is DNI Russell's entire itinerary for his visit to Egypt next week," she said. "It was uploaded less than one hour ago onto one of the dark web servers we've been monitoring in support of the Belarus operation."

Manton read what was on the screen, growing more alarmed as he went.

"This isn't only his schedule, Faith. The Diplomatic Security Service ops plan is there, too."

"Yes, sir. That was going to be my next point."

"And you confirmed both the ops plan and the itinerary are legit?"

"That's the first thing I did, sir. The itinerary and the ops plans were encrypted email attachments sent by the State Department to key staff members at our embassy in Cairo."

"Was the ambassador on that list?"

Jackson hit a few keys on her keyboard, then said, "He was, and so were the regional security officer, the legal and defense attachés, and the CIA station chief."

"What's the station chief's name?" Manton asked.

"Nelson Campbell."

Manton let out a long sigh.

"You know him?" Jackson asked.

"Yeah, I know him," Manton said through clenched teeth.

What he didn't say, though, was that it had been CIA officer Nelson Campbell's involuntary screwup four years ago that had led to an ambush that had nearly killed

Manton and DNI Edward Russell, who was at the time an assistant deputy secretary within the Department of State. Unknown to Campbell, his workstation had been hacked by a civilian employee of the embassy who had been working for the Iranian Ministry of Intelligence. So, when he'd used his embassy workstation to read a classified email that should have been opened only through his much more secured CIA-issued laptop, Iranian intelligence had learned about Edward Russell's trip to Egypt. Since instability in Egypt was good for Iran, the Ministry of Intelligence had decided that it was in their best interest to shut down the talks between the American emissary and the Muslim Brotherhood. Using Hezbollah assets stationed in Egypt as proxies, the Iranians had financed the rapidly laid-out ambush that had nearly killed Edward Russell.

Manton and his team's actions, as well as Russell's own heroism, had saved the day.

And Campbell's career.

"Is it possible the emails were intercepted, or do we have to assume either the embassy or State's firewalls were penetrated?" Manton asked.

"It's way too soon to say for sure, but we don't think this was a cyberattack, sir."

We. Manton cocked his head in Jackson's direction. She was one of the senior analysts on duty, but she had consulted with her colleagues before she had asked him to come over. This was exactly the type of behavior he encouraged among his workforce. An exceptional judge of talent, Manton had singlehandedly picked every member of Blackbriar, often spending days studying and analyzing a potential employee's file before making his first approach. Ensuring each member had the right background and abilities for the job Manton had in store for them was fundamental. It had taken him more than six months to fill all the positions.

Some things couldn't be rushed.

"Why do you believe this wasn't a cyberattack?"

"Whoever leaked this intel knew exactly how to circumvent all of the embassy's internal filters and security measures," Jackson explained. "If we hadn't been monitoring that specific server on the dark web, we would never have known about that security breach. The leak came from inside the embassy, sir."

This whole thing was pointing to a *Let's Kill Edward Russell 2.0* scenario. Blackbriar's standard operating procedures dictated that Manton shoot this up his chain of command, which meant sending a secure email straight to the DNI himself, and let Russell disseminate the intel to the proper agencies. But that wasn't what Manton intended to do. Since the leak could have come from the regional security officer, the CIA chief of station, or even the ambassador, Manton didn't feel like sharing anything just yet. Unfortunately, his three teams of two field agents were already fully engaged in other operations. Manton didn't have a single operative available. Still, investigating a direct threat to the director of national intelligence wasn't something Manton wanted to push back to a later time. Technology was nice, but there was only so much the analysts could do without having actual boots on the ground. To take a more in-depth look into what was happening in Cairo, Manton would have to pull a team out of their current mission and re-task them. This was far from optimal. With the team deployed in Belarus having missed their last comms check, Manton's options were even more limited.

Three teams aren't enough, he thought, knowing that he was already playing with fire given the tempo with which he was deploying his teams. There was no question about the need to recruit more field operatives, but finding the right individuals was proving to be a challenge of epic proportions.

"Faith, can you show me all of our teams' current locations?" Manton asked.

Jackson pushed a few keys on her keyboard and a world map appeared on one of the big screens at the front of the room. There were two pairs of throbbing red dots, and, to Manton's surprise, one pair of blue dots, each dot representing a Blackbriar operative. Manton hadn't expected to see any blue dots tonight.

Two red dots in Minsk, Belarus. Two more in South Sudan. The blue ones were in Greece.

Helen Jouvert and Donovan Wade. Good.

He had checked on the status of that particular team before heading to the gym, and it had shown red like the other two, which meant the team preferred not to be reached outside the predetermined check-in schedule.

"May I have everyone's attention for a moment?" Manton asked.

When all eyes were on him, he asked, "Who's handling Helen and Donovan tonight?"

One row up, a petite woman in her fifties with tightly curled gray hair and designer glasses raised her hand. Her name was Teresa Salazar.

"I am, sir," Teresa said. "And we literally just received an update."

"What does it say?"

"I'm opening the message now," Teresa replied, her eyes moving left to right as she read.

A former counterintelligence officer with the Defense Intelligence Agency who held a PhD in political science from Princeton, Teresa had been one of the first people Manton had recruited. Her razor-sharp mind and twenty-five years of experience in the intelligence world gave her a depth of knowledge that more than justified the salary she'd negotiated for herself.

"It seems like they're still in Athens, but they boarded a flight to Paris fifteen minutes ago."

"They're on the same flight?" Manton asked.

"Apparently so."

Manton felt the squeeze of tension in his stomach.

"Their exit protocols called for a departure tomorrow morning on separate flights," he said. "Any idea why they hastened the timeline?"

"Not at this time, but since their last update earlier this afternoon, we've been monitoring the local news around the clock for any hint that could suggest they've been compromised. So far there's been no allusion to anything even remotely connected to Helen or Donovan."

"Could it be due to the FBI Fly Team on its way?" Faith Jackson asked.

"You're right, Faith," Manton said. "That's probably it."

Manton chastised himself. He'd been so focused on the Belarus and South Sudan operations that he'd forgotten all about the Fly Team on its way to Athens.

Following the DNI's request to get a Blackbriar team to Athens, Manton had given Helen Jouvert and Donovan Wade the task of finding and prosecuting whoever had targeted the American diplomats—and the two Blackbriar operatives had done it in record time. Not only had they found out the perpetrator's name within twenty-four hours of setting foot in Athens, but they had also determined that he had been acting alone, without the guidance or authorization of the Popular Fighters Group leadership. As it turned out, they had been looking for Dimitri, too. It had been a simple affair—and quite cunning in Manton's opinion—for the Blackbriar operatives to share Dimitri's location with members of the PFG.

Three-quarters of an hour after the two operatives had reached out to the PFG, a bunch of anarchist thugs had stormed the car repair shop, with one of them carrying a rolled-up carpet on his shoulder. Ninety minutes later, they had exited the shop, but this time, the carpet was carried away by two people.

Drone footage taken by Donovan had shown the two

Blackbriar agents witnessing it all from the rooftop of an unfinished building across the street, each sipping a glass of ouzo at what had seemed to be some sort of cook-off party.

While he didn't have all the answers yet, it appeared to Manton that Helen and Donovan had pulled it off. Not only had they neutralized the threat, but they had also done so without leaving too big a footprint in their wake. Letting the PFG take care of Dimitri had been a brilliant idea. In their effort to legitimize their future political candidates, the PFG had leaked to the Hellenic Police a video in which Dimitri Callellis admitted to the letter bombings. His body was found rolled up in a carpet half a block away from the American embassy in Athens.

"Have the Hellenic Police withdrawn their official request for assistance?" Manton asked.

"They have," Teresa confirmed. "But the FBI is still sending the Fly Team to check things out."

"Good luck with that," Manton said with a genuine smile.

Familiar with the way the Hellenic Police and the Greek authorities operated, Manton was confident they would make absolutely sure the Fly Team wouldn't get any farther than the airport's car terminal.

These types of issues were exactly why an organization like Blackbriar 2.0 was needed.

Initially created years ago by the Central Intelligence Agency to replace the problem-ridden Treadstone program, Operation Blackbriar had been summarily shut down by the Senate Oversight Committee before it really had a chance to get off the ground. Somehow, rumors of anomalies with the genetic engineering used to enhance the abilities of its field operatives had reached influential members of the committee. Although the CIA had severed all its ties with the program and reassigned the entire staff to other duties, the US Department of State had assigned a skeleton crew to manage the significant real estate holdings that had been acquired for Operation Blackbriar. Still, unlike the once ultra-secret Treadstone program, almost no one knew anything about Blackbriar. As far as the Department of State and the rest of the federal government were concerned, Blackbriar now appeared as one of the hundreds of subcontractors hired to manage the sixty thousand buildings located overseas that were owned by the United States government.

It was the perfect cover for special access programs.

Blackbriar's resurgence was born out of Directive 71.2 from DNI Edward Russell. The organization's size was classified, and its operating budget was paid through the Department of State's black budget—which meant the expenses weren't itemized and couldn't be traced. For the very select few who knew about the rebirth of Blackbriar, it was clear that the organization was quickly becoming America's last line of defense against foreign influence operations. The FBI might have been the lead agency for preventing and investigating intelligence activities on US soil, but with the recent political turmoil and the polarization of the American voters, it was too busy chasing after homegrown extremist groups to be an effective counterintelligence force overseas. And even when they did manage to send a team overseas, host countries were more and more reluctant to give the FBI the necessary leeway it needed to run a successful operation. The FBI being the FBI, they were terrified about breaking a single rule, petrified that they might offend their overseas law enforcement partners.

Blackbriar didn't have to worry about such trivialities.

Manton touched Teresa's shoulders. "Let me know when Helen and Donovan arrive in Paris. I need to speak with them as soon as they land."

"Will do, sir. Should I cancel their connection to New York and reroute them to Egypt? Both Air France and Egyptair are showing availabilities on their nonstop flights from Charles de Gaulle to Cairo International Airport."

"Yes," Manton said. "And since they're flying together to Paris, make sure to book them on the same flight to Cairo."

"Economy or business?"

Manton opened his mouth to say *economy*—his standard reply for any flight under eight hours—but took an extra second to think it over. Helen and Donovan had been in Greece working continuously for the past forty-eight hours, and, before that, they were in Argentina for almost two weeks. They hadn't had a real day off in a long time, and Manton didn't know how long the operation in Cairo would last.

"Business is fine," he said.

"Good idea, sir," Teresa replied, the barest hint of a

smile tugging at the corner of her mouth. "I'm sure they'll appreciate that."

Manton nodded and headed out of the TOC. He needed a shower. As he walked to his office to pick up his shower kit, Manton couldn't help but think about how crazy and fast-paced the last twelve months had been. Had a full year already gone by since Edward Russell—who at the time had just been named director of national intelligence—had summoned him over to his cottage to discuss his plans for Blackbriar?

Damn. It was hard to believe.

Manton stripped off his workout clothes and hit the shower. He stood with his back to the showerhead and let the steam and hot water work their magic. He could feel the stiffness in his neck and shoulders ease as he let his mind wander to the exact moment when he accepted Russell's job offer.

TEN

From the outside, Edward Russell's log cabin looked like something out of a storybook. Secluded and nestled among huge pine trees, the cabin was surrounded by the majestic Wasatch Mountains. A ten-minute walk down a natural trail led to Silver Lake—which was renowned for its abundance of speckled trout. The interior was chic and well appointed, though a bit more modern farmhouse than the rustic log cabin look Manton preferred. Large windows gave the place a spacious, airy feel, and a massive two-story stone fireplace dominated the living room, the warmth of its fire keeping the evening chill at bay. Beers had followed a day on the lake, and Russell had grilled steaks for dinner. They were now seated in buttersoft leather armchairs facing the chimney, drinks in hand.

"Honestly, Oliver, with its current leadership and an

exhausted workforce, I'm afraid the FBI lacks the decisiveness and the resources required to do what's necessary to protect our nation from foreign threats," Russell said. "And with Treadstone now out of my reach and in the hands of the DoD, my options are even more limited."

Manton, not sure why the newly minted director of national intelligence had suddenly begun to talk shop, swirled the remnants of his single malt around the bottom of his tumbler and said, "Yeah, I'm sure they are."

On the lake catching and releasing fish, Russell had yakked mostly about his wine and cigar collections and his utmost surprise at being named—and then confirmed by the Senate—as the DNI. Manton, who'd stayed mostly quiet, had been happy to listen to him. He liked Russell and respected the man. Three days after the ambush, Russell had returned to his desk in Washington, ready to work. But the reporters wouldn't let him, and he quickly became a media darling. Still, Russell had come to visit Manton several times while he was in rehab, and they had become good pals. In fact, Russell was Manton's only friend.

Three months after he'd nearly been killed, Russell had been named US ambassador to Iraq. If Manton was to believe the news articles he'd read, Russell's ambassadorship had been a good one. Was it because Russell could do no wrong in the media's eyes, or was it because he was a gifted diplomat? Manton thought it was both.

Manton polished off his drink and pointed a finger at the half-finished bottle of Macallan Sherry Oak 25.

"Do you mind? It's the best bourbon I—"

"For Christ's sake, it's a single malt," Russell corrected him. "Can't you taste the difference?"

Manton smiled as he poured himself two fingers of the fine liquid.

"Sure," he said with a noncommittal shrug.

"Unbelievable!" Russell cringed, then grabbed the bottle from Manton and tipped it over his own glass. "Did you know you just poured yourself a two-hundred-dollar drink?"

Manton was incredulous. "What? You can't be serious."

"It's a two-thousand-dollar bottle of single malt whisky."

"You bought that with your new pay raise?"

Russell dismissed the thought with a wave of the hand. "Of course not. It was a gift from one of the principal shareholders of Edrington, the group that owns Macallan."

"Good to know," Manton said. "Now I don't feel too bad about drinking it."

"Some say it's the best whisky ever made."

"Why?" Manton asked, skeptical. "What's so special about it? I mean, it's good, but two grand? That's silly. It tastes just like all the other ones."

The DNI cocked his head in Manton's direction and raised an eyebrow, surely wondering if his guest was pulling his leg or being serious.

"Okay, I'll play," Russell said. He whirled the expensive whisky around his glass, looked into it, and inhaled with reverence. "This isn't your average single malt. When you drink nobility like this, it isn't only about its taste. Of course, the palate is important, but the nose—what it smells like—and the finish also play an essential part in the *experience. Swirl it around your tumbler and tell me what you smell."*

Manton tilted the rim of the glass under his nose and allowed the scent of the Scotch to reach his nostrils. "Honey, maybe a bit of caramel," he said after a moment. "No wait, I definitely smell pears in there."

Russell nodded. "Not bad. What else?"

"Hard to say . . . Maybe spices, and smoke? If that makes any sense."

"All right. Now taste it."

Manton took a sip of the single malt and let it rest on his tongue for a beat before swallowing.

"And?" Russell probed.

"Honey again, and maybe nutmeg. Fruity, too, surprisingly."

Manton brought the tumbler back to his lips but paused before taking another sip. "I taste fig, and smoke again."

"That's what we call the finish, my friend. Nice, isn't it?"

Manton shrugged. "Not sure my last sip was worth fifty bucks, though."

Russell rolled his eyes, but he was smiling. "You're a lost cause. Next time, please stick to cheap beers."

Manton placed his drink on the glass-top coffee table between the two armchairs, then said, "About the FBI, I understand what you're saying, and I agree with you, but is there a reason why you're sharing this with me?"

Russell opened his mouth to say something, but then seemed to hesitate.

"You know that if it's about Treadstone, you'll have to

bring this up directly with Shaw," Manton said. "I was forced to leave Treadstone a year ago, remember? And you know why. The whole thing messed me up. It really did."

"Hmmm," Russell said distractedly. He rose to his feet and walked to the fireplace. He grabbed a log and the fire crackled and sparks flew as the DNI added the dry piece of wood to the blaze.

Manton remained silent, watching the log slowly catch fire.

"I do know why you're no longer with Treadstone," Russell said, poking the fire with a cast-iron log grabber. "At least the official reason."

"Well, then you know everything. There's no other reason than the official one. It's like I said, the trainees' deaths messed me up."

"I'm gonna have to call bullshit on this," Russell said, his voice harder than it had been only a moment ago. "I read the after-action report, and the findings couldn't be any clearer. The trainees' deaths aren't on you, Oliver. You know that. Shaw knows it, too. Contrary to what you told me, you weren't forced to leave Treadstone at all. You could have carried on as an instructor if you had wished to do so. That's what Shaw wanted. You were the best trainer Treadstone ever had."

Caught off guard, Manton reached for his drink and said, "You shouldn't believe everything you read."

Russell replaced the log grabber next to the other fireplace tools and turned to face him. "You don't need to worry about me. I don't believe everything I read in reports. But I know you."

Manton took a long sip of single malt and suppressed a smile.

Jesus! I just swallowed seventy-five dollars' worth of the stuff.

Manton didn't like where the conversation was heading. He put down his drink and wiped his mouth with the back of his hand. Russell hadn't been there when the two Treadstone trainees had died. There was no way for him to know how it had impacted Manton.

"I pushed them too fucking hard, Edward," Manton said. "I might not have killed them with my bare hands, but I was the lead instructor. They died on my watch."

"Ah, c'mon! Get your head out of your ass. It was a goddamn accident."

"An accident?" Manton snapped, his temper rising. "I was negligent. And that's exactly what I told Shaw. But he didn't want to listen. Just like you aren't listening now."

"Oh, I'm listening. But these guys knew what they signed up for—"

"They hadn't slept in ninety-six hours when it happened," Manton said, letting his voice grow louder with each word. "They shouldn't have been handling explosives. They—"

"Stop right there! I'm not buying into your bullshit. You wanna know what I think?" Russell asked, but continued without waiting for Manton's reply. "You, my friend, were pissed off at Levi Shaw for yanking you out of the field after Cairo. You couldn't stand being kept out of operations. From what Shaw told me, you hated being an instructor. Isn't that so?"

"What does this have to do with anything?"

"I'll tell you. You were looking for an out. So, when this horrible accident happened, you played the PTSD card to retire."

"How dare you—"

"Enough!" Russell roared, slapping the palm of his hand against the coffee table. "I'm seeing right through you. Like most Treadstone agents, you're a deceptive sonofabitch, Oliver. You're a high-functioning sociopath. And even if there was a hint, and I mean a minuscule trace, of truth in what you're saying, the men selected to join the Treadstone program aren't your typical special agent or army officer. They weren't being taught how to become peacekeepers. You were training them to become members of a clandestine assassination program, for God's sake."

Manton could feel his face flushing red with anger, but he was smart enough to keep his mouth shut.

"Don't you forget that I was standing next to you when you slaughtered the assholes who were trying to kill us in Cairo," Russell continued. "I understand better than most what is required of our assets in the field. Is the selection and assessment course tough? Is it dangerous? Is it fucking insane? Yes. Yes, on all counts. But you did your job. You followed the curriculum. The same one you had gone through yourself, remember? The job of these two men was to survive the training regimen. They didn't. End of story. Case closed."

Manton was taken aback by Russell's abruptness. Usually composed, it wasn't typical of him to explode as he just had. Russell's heart was in the right place, and, clearly, he was a good judge of character, too. He had indeed seen right through him.

"What do you want me to say?" Manton asked, his blood pressure slowly returning to normal.

"I don't want you to say anything, I want you to move on. Can you do that?"

"Move on? You just said I was a—"

Russell raised a hand before Manton could say more. "If you can't, and you want to continue to feel sorry for yourself, that's fine. I'm one of the very few people in this world who knows everything you've sacrificed for our great nation. I'm not saying this lightly, Oliver. I owe you.

"So the decision is yours. If you prefer to live in the past, then finish your drink, because, frankly, it's just too expensive to go to waste, then head upstairs, get some sleep, and we'll head back to the lake in the morning to catch more trout. But if you think you're still fit for duty, tell me now. I might have an opportunity for you."

Manton was rarely at a loss for words, but this time he didn't know what to say. Russell had stunned him into silence.

Fit for duty? Is he serious?

Manton was in better shape than most men half his age. Four to five hours at the firing range every week kept him sharp. His hand-to-hand combat skills weren't what they used to be, but he sparred three days per week at his local MMA gym. He'd even fought twice in the last six months on the local circuit, winning both his fights.

Did he regret what happened to the two Treadstone recruits? Somewhat. But the DNI was right. He had followed *protocols. The recruits had made a mistake and they had paid dearly for it. They hadn't been the first, nor were they going to be the last Treadstone recruits to die in a training accident. Manton certainly didn't feel sorry for himself, and he had moved on a long, long time ago.*

But he knows that already, doesn't he?

Then what game was the DNI playing at? What did he want?

Push my buttons? That's not his style.

Was Russell trying to manipulate him? If so, to what end? Maybe Russell wanted something out of him. But what? It wasn't like Manton had access to anything Russell didn't. The whole exchange had piqued Manton's curiosity.

Dammit! That's the point, isn't it? And the whole thing about being fit for duty . . . He's giving me an out.

"You got my attention. I'm listening. Spit it out, Edward."

It took Russell a full minute to respond, but when he did, his tone was all business. "I need someone I can trust. I believe you're that person."

"You can trust me, but if you're looking for somebody to whack someone for you, you're knocking at the wrong door. I don't kill people for a living anymore," *Manton said, only half joking.*

Russell frowned and shook his head. "That's not it," *he said, breaking eye contact and sitting back in his armchair.*

Manton crossed his legs and stared at the fire, waiting for Russell to continue.

"I need counterintelligence assets capable of going after

the targets the FBI can't get to, whether it's at home or internationally," Russell said.

Manton glanced at the DNI. "Can't get to?"

"You know as well as I do that the FBI's priority is to bring traitors and foreign intelligence agents in front of a judge. FBI special agents are exceptionally good at building legal cases that will stand up in courts, but this takes time and uses a lot of resources. They can't be everywhere at once."

"Maybe, but the FBI has a significant presence abroad," Manton offered. "Their International Operations Division keeps offices in most countries, does it not? Could strengthening the number of agents posted overseas help the situation outside the United States?"

"Not for what I have in mind," Russell replied.

Manton leaned forward. Now this was getting interesting. "All right. Tell me more."

Russell knocked back the rest of his drink. "Our enemies are adapting faster than ever before," he said. "They're learning from their past blunders and they're taking advantage of our internal divisions. Make no mistake about this, my friend. From the Egyptian pharaohs to the Persians, Romans, and our British cousins, all empires fall. And ours, too, will fall. But I'll be damned if I let this happen on my watch."

Manton conceded the point. The United States was on the brink of imploding. There were plenty of foreign powers who couldn't wait for this to occur, salivating at the mere thought of filling the enormous power vacuum that would result from the collapse of the world's only superpower.

Russell continued. "We're so enthralled at tearing each other apart that we've forgotten to watch out for our adversaries. Russia, China, Iran, North Korea, Belarus, and even Mexico are making moves to accelerate our downfall."

"Mexico?" Manton asked. "You mean the cartels?"

"The cartels, but a shitload of corrupt politicians, too."

"Okay. So, what do you have in mind?"

"Have you ever heard of Blackbriar?"

Manton's eyes darkened and he sucked in a deep breath. "Years ago, the simple mention of this operation could have gotten you killed," he said. "Or so I've been told."

"By whom?"

"Jason Bourne."

"Ha. Yes. Jason Bourne." Russell rubbed his eyes. "It makes sense he would say something like that."

"What about Blackbriar?" Manton asked. "The only thing I know is that it was supposed to replace Treadstone. The last I heard it got canceled early on."

"It did," Russell confirmed. "And it didn't."

Russell filled his tumbler and angled the bottle of Macallan toward Manton's glass.

"One more?" he asked.

"Why not? You didn't pay for it."

When Russell was done pouring, Manton asked, "Is Blackbriar still operational?"

"Yes, but not as a replacement for Treadstone. When the Senate committee cut its funding for Blackbriar, the program was far more advanced than everybody thought. Substantial sums of money had already been spent on infrastructure, and a lot of real estate had been acquired *in preparation for what was supposed to become the biggest black ops program the US government had ever funded."*

"I wasn't aware of that," Manton admitted.

"Not many people are."

"So what's Blackbriar's mission?" Manton asked.

"For the time being, it handles the real estate it acquired years ago. Simple. It's completely under the radar. It's just one of hundreds of other companies handling US government-owned real estate. But it could be so much more."

Manton smiled. "And by that you mean a black ops counterintelligence program?"

"Yes. A small-footprint unit with deniable assets totally funded out of my discretionary budget. Where Treadstone's role is to covertly influence events and decision-making processes in other countries, oftentimes by using violence—"

"Targeted killings, Edward," Manton interjected.

"Whatever," Russell said, then continued. "Blackbriar's focus will be on the detection and deterrence of foreign threats who are actively attempting to infiltrate our defenses. The unit would be intelligence led, meaning that research and analysis would be at the core of the program. That intel would then guide small teams of deniable assets in the field."

"These teams you're talking about, what will they do?" Manton asked.

"Their primary duty will be to neutralize the effectiveness of our adversaries' intelligence-gathering activities."

"How?"

"By any means necessary."

"So Blackbriar wouldn't be solely a defensive operation," Manton said, thinking out loud.

"Correct. The way I see it, the assets in the field would be Blackbriar's teeth and could be called in to play a more offensive role when needed."

"Like striking at the opposition force to prevent it from attacking," Manton said.

The DNI nodded. "Precisely."

"You want me to be one of these deniable assets, don't you?" Manton asked.

Russell let out a dry chuckle. "No. You got it all wrong, Oliver. I want you to lead *Blackbriar*."

The word surprised *didn't* even come close to describing how Manton felt. It took him a moment to find his words. "Are you sure about this?"

"I wouldn't have asked if I wasn't."

"Why me?"

"There isn't a man in this world I trust more than you," Russell replied. "And you have the skill set to pull it off."

"Who else knows about this?"

"No one. Not even POTUS."

Manton let out a long whistle. "Aren't you playing with fire by keeping the president in the dark?"

"Only if I get caught," Russell replied, giving Manton a wry smile. "At some point I'll probably have to tell him something, but I'll do my best to keep a measure of plausible deniability between him and Blackbriar."

"What would the chain of command look like?" Manton asked.

"You'd report to me, and to me only."

"What about the staff? The infrastructure?"

The DNI raised his hands. "I haven't figured out everything just yet," he said. "I wanted to chat with you first and hear your thoughts."

Manton rubbed his face. "This whole thing comes attached to a thousand questions," he said. "I'm gonna have to think this through."

As much as he didn't want Russell to see how excited he was about his proposal, the idea of leading a team of covert counterintelligence operatives had a great appeal to Manton just now. Although it was difficult for him to articulate, there was something missing in his life. After everything he'd been through, it seemed that his life had been idling for the last year. His duties with Treadstone had meant something to him. In fact, his time with Treadstone had been the most fulfilling undertaking he'd ever done. Could Blackbriar provide him with the same sense of accomplishment? Opportunities to jump back into the biggest game of all didn't present themselves every day. He couldn't afford to let it pass.

When he looked back at Russell, the DNI had already rolled up his sleeves. There was a mad sparkle in his eyes, as if he knew he'd won a game only he had been playing.

"What do you say we start working on the details together?"

ELEVEN

Donovan Wade was jolted out of a dreamless doze when Helen touched his shoulder and gave it a squeeze. Having no idea where he was, his right hand moved instinctively to the Glock 29 he kept under his pillow.

"Calm down. It's me," Helen said. "It's four fifty a.m. Your shift starts in ten minutes."

Ah, shit. I'm in Cairo.

Donovan's eyes were thick with sleep, but he managed to open one of them. Through the apartment's lone window, the moon cast a shadowy hue, and, in the dimness, Donovan could see Helen's vague outline. He stretched his six-foot-three frame and ran his fingers through his dark hair. His forehead was slick with sweat, and the back of his shirt clung to his deeply suntanned skin. The third-floor studio apartment they were in had no air-conditioning and, despite the early hour, the temperature was uncomfortably warm. An old battery-operated fan was in one corner, but it was so energy-hungry that it had eaten through Donovan's battery supply in less than sixteen hours. The window had long ago lost its glass and could now only be closed with the help of the two ancient shutters hanging crookedly on either side, so the two Blackbriar operatives had decided to leave it open. In lieu of real window treatments, Donovan had hung a pair of mismatched drapes he'd found in the kitchen cupboard. They were old and stained, but he was happy to have them. Still, the apartment's location was perfect. It was one block away from the Internet café the analysts in New York had identified as the spot from which classified intelligence had been uploaded to one of the dark web servers they were monitoring in support of another team of agents operating clandestinely in Belarus. Although the analysts were yet to confirm it, they believed that this specific server belonged to an Egyptian front company controlled by Russian intelligence. During the last four days, top secret information—including the itinerary and security arrangements for DNI Edward Russell's upcoming visit to Egypt—had been uploaded to the server no less than six times. Whoever was leaking the intel had taken precautions and had been very good at covering their tracks. If it hadn't been for the Belarus operation Blackbriar was running point on, the data dump would have remained undetected.

With Russia's recent ambitious—and sometimes

aggressive—military-geostrategic posture in the Mediterranean, Director of National Intelligence Russell had given Blackbriar the green light to neutralize the leak by any means necessary and to disrupt Russia's intelligence-gathering operations in Cairo. Due to Egypt's strategic location at the crossroads of Asia, Africa, and Europe, and its proximity to the Suez Canal and both the Mediterranean and Red Seas, the United States couldn't allow critical intelligence about its plan to combat Russian influence in the region to fall into the wrong hands—unless it came in the form of carefully curated and crafted pieces of disinformation designed to poison the Kremlin's intelligence ecosystem.

But for that to happen, Donovan and Helen had to first find a way to turn the mole into an asset. And, as of now, they didn't know who it was. But they had an idea. A thorough review of the six data dumps had revealed that only four embassy employees had the required security clearances to leak such high-value intel. One of them was the ambassador.

"Did you manage to get some shut-eye?" Helen asked.

"A bit," Donovan replied, scratching his unkempt beard. "Enough."

Once his eyes had adjusted to the darkness, Donovan rolled out of his cot. The worn, narrow boards of the hardwood floor squeaked under his weight. He tossed the thin pillow aside and grabbed his pistol. He pulled back the slide a half inch to confirm a round was chambered. Satisfied the cylindrical brass round was where it was supposed to be, Donovan let the slide go forward and slipped the pistol into the holster on his hip. He made his way to the bathroom, which was miniature and just large enough to accommodate a tiny porcelain sink protruding from the tiled wall, a toilet, and the smallest standing shower Wade had ever seen. At least the bathroom had a door. At the sink, he squeezed a dab of toothpaste on his finger and rubbed it against his gums and teeth.

"Coffee?" he asked, heading to the coffee machine a minute later.

"No, thanks. I'd like to get a few minutes of sleep before the sun comes up."

The tiny apartment had smelled like wet cigarette butts when they'd arrived two days prior. That hadn't changed. The kitchen was big enough for one, and the dining area had only enough space for the minuscule round table surrounded by two cheap folding chairs. The rest of the space was occupied by Donovan's cot and a single bed, which was half a step from the table, and a wooden stool next to the window on which Helen was seated behind a tripod-mounted pair of Zeiss image-stabilized binoculars and an infrared-capable still digital camera.

At least there was a working refrigerator and a coffee machine. Donovan placed a cup under the spout, threw a pod into the device, and pressed the button. The machine hissed and began to spew the black liquid into the cup. While the coffee poured, Donovan powered up his Panasonic Toughbook laptop and set up his secure satellite uplink. By the time the signal was established, his coffee was ready. Donovan took too big a sip and winced when the hot liquid scorched the back of his throat.

"Was there any activity while I was out?" he asked, setting down the coffee cup next to his laptop.

Helen flipped a page of her notepad and said, "Four men and two women entered the Internet café in the last three hours. None of them stayed inside for more than fifteen minutes. I ran their faces through our facial recognition software but got no hit. Headquarters also tried their luck. Same results."

Donovan took a seat on one of the folding chairs and logged on to the encrypted instant messaging service they used to communicate with Blackbriar's headquarters.

"No new messages were uploaded to the website we're monitoring?" he asked.

Helen shook her head. "Might take a while before we get another hit."

"Maybe not," Donovan replied.

Helen shot him a questioning look.

"The DNI's new travel schedule was sent an hour ago," Donovan told her, angling the laptop so Helen could read the message they'd received from HQ. "Someone liked your recommendation."

It had been Helen's idea to release a fake schedule to squeeze the mole out. If mole there was.

Helen yawned, then asked, "Who's on the recipient list?"

"Most of the senior embassy staff, including the ambassador," Donovan said, scrolling down the list of names.

"Whoever's been leaking the DNI's program is bound to upload the new itinerary, too," she said.

"Let's hope so, but, in the meantime, it's your turn to get some rack time," Donovan told her. "I'll wake you up just before dawn unless something comes up."

Before Helen could rise from the wooden stool, the doorknob of the apartment door rattled violently, startling them both. A series of angry knocks followed. Donovan closed the lid of his laptop and pulled out his phone. He opened the app linked to a network of wireless perimeter security cameras he'd installed in the hallway and staircase leading to their third-floor apartment. Standing just outside the apartment door, a beefy man in jeans and a tight black T-shirt was holding in his right hand what appeared to be a bottle of liquor. Donovan conveyed what he was seeing on his screen to Helen. She immediately shielded the surveillance equipment with a set of towels and moved to the window to take a look at the street and sidewalk below, her hand reaching for the H&K semiautomatic pistol she kept in the concealed paddle holster under her waistband.

Wrong apartment, buddy. Move on, Donovan willed, hoping the man wasn't acting as a decoy for a larger team of operators. Donovan switched back and forth between the cameras and was glad to see that there were no black-clad, assault-rifle-toting figures from the Egyptian Ministry of Interior stacked farther down the hallway or staircase getting ready to storm the apartment.

"Building's clear," he told Helen.

Donovan went back to the camera giving him the best

view of the apartment's door in time to see the man take a big swig from the liquor bottle.

C'mon, asshole. Leave.

Instead, the man rammed his left fist against the door and shouted something in Arabic.

"The street's quiet. Nothing unusual," Helen said, keeping her voice low. "But that's gonna change if this idiot keeps hammering his fists on our door."

Helen was right. Whoever this man was, he wasn't going away anytime soon. Donovan signaled to Helen he was going to the door, which prompted her to move into the kitchen, her H&K pistol at low ready. From there, she'd be able to cover him while remaining mostly out of sight. Donovan glanced at his phone and, seeing no weapons in the man's hands apart from the liquor bottle, he approached the door. He drew his pistol and angled it toward the threat, confident the 10-millimeter round of the Glock 29 would easily punch through the cheap hollow-core door of the apartment if needed. Donovan looked through the peephole and adjusted his aim. Only then did he withdraw the double bolt and open the door a few inches, keeping the security chain in place.

"What do you want?" Donovan said in Arabic, hoping that by seeing his face, the inebriated man would realize he had knocked on the wrong door.

But the man's reaction wasn't what Donovan had wished for. In fact, it was the opposite. At hearing Donovan's voice, the man became livid, and his angry, bloodshot eyes opened wide. He yelled something unintelligible, then smashed the cheap bottle of spirits he had been drinking from against the doorframe and took a step back. Guessing what was about to happen, Donovan closed the door, unlatched the security chain, and swung the door open just as the drunken man's foot sailed past where the doorknob had been a fraction of a second earlier. Having expected to encounter a solid door, the man almost flew into the apartment, his momentum carrying him forward. He nevertheless managed to pivot toward Donovan and came at him with the broken bottle. Donovan twisted his body clear of the sharp edges of the bottle as it made to plunge into the side of his neck. With his non-gun hand, Donovan delivered a sharp fingertip punch under his assailant's overextended arm, hitting him deep in his armpit and deadening the man's arm. As the bottle fell from the man's grasp, Donovan drove his foot into the side of his knee. There was a sickening crunch as the knee gave, but before any scream could come out of the drunk's mouth, Donovan punched him hard in his kidney. The air exploding from the man's lungs made a loud whooshing sound. Donovan cracked the butt of his Glock into the man's head, and he fell to the floor like a wet towel.

Donovan brought his pistol up and quickly cleared the hallway before closing the apartment's door. Helen, who had holstered her pistol, had already shoved a dirty sock into the unconscious man's mouth, and was in the process of duct-taping his hands and ankles.

Donovan peeked out the window to make sure the tactical situation outside the building hadn't changed.

Satisfied it hadn't, he holstered his Glock and began to search the intruder for clues about his identity.

"How's his pulse?" he asked.

"Still there," Helen replied.

In the man's pockets, Donovan found two hundred Egyptian pounds in small denominations, a driver's license, an unopened pack of cigarettes, but no weapons. He tore the cellophane away and opened the pack. He dumped the contents on the floor and examined each cigarette. Nothing was amiss. He then read the name on the driver's license and studied the man's face. Same guy.

"Who is he?" Helen asked.

"Tafiq Eltayeb," Donovan replied. "Born May third, nineteen eighty-two."

"Address?"

Donovan handed Helen Tafiq's driver's license. "See for yourself."

TWELVE

He's on the wrong floor?" Helen asked, reading Tafiq's address off his driver's license. She shook her head in disbelief. "Isn't it illegal to drink booze in public in Cairo?"

"Yes and no," Donovan replied. "Let's just say that the Egyptians have an under-the-table relationship with booze. Egypt isn't a dry country like Iran or Saudi Arabia."

Helen cursed their bad luck. "The fool thought we were in his apartment," she said between clenched teeth.

"Looks like it. He lives in the apartment right below ours," Donovan said. "My guess is that he ran out of cigarettes, walked to the nearest store, bought a pack, and returned home—"

"But missed his floor and panicked when he found that the door he thought was his was locked," Helen said, finishing off her partner's thought.

Donovan nodded.

"If that's what really happened, we're not compromised. At least not yet," she said, considering her options.

Now that the DNI's fake itinerary had been out for more than an hour, it was only a question of time, hours really, before whoever had leaked the previous schedule did so again with the later version. But if the mole had a minimum of training, he wouldn't chance doing it in the middle of the night. No, he'd wait until morning, once most recipients had opened and read the email with the updated itinerary. Moving quicker than that would be too risky. It was common knowledge that the sender had the capability to know who had opened and read the email, and when.

Should she and Donovan stay put? Wait until the mole made his move? That would mean keeping Tafiq sequestered for an indefinite amount of time. Was someone waiting for him in his apartment? Would he be missed? Helen wasn't a fan of hostages. Not only were they a liability, taking care of them was a pain in the ass. They needed to eat, drink, and go to the bathroom.

"What do you want to do?" Donovan asked, pressing her.

She was the team leader. It was her call. Her boss, Oliver Manton, liked to give his agents broad leeway over how to complete their mission. She'd have to get used to it. It hadn't been like that in the FBI, where her chief at the Counterespionage Section—an elite unit within the Counterintelligence Division—had a tendency to micromanage every investigation. It hadn't taken her long to realize that Blackbriar was a different beast. Now she had enough rope to hang herself several times and then some.

She looked at her partner, who was staring back at her with his bright blue eyes, waiting for her response. Donovan had dark brown hair, a taut jawline, and the lean, ripped physique of an avid mountain climber. Although this was their fourth mission together, it was the first time she'd seen him knock someone out. As a former Team USA judoka, she appreciated how easy he had made it look.

At least he didn't shoot the man, she thought, thankful Donovan knew how to exercise good fire discipline. Back in Greece, she'd been surprised when he'd aimed his pistol at Dimitri's head. Would Donovan have shot him if she hadn't intervened? Or was he messing with Dimitri's mind?

"We can't stay here," she finally said, pocketing Tafiq's driver's license. "We have to relocate to our secondary observation post."

"Agreed," Donovan replied. "What about our friend Tafiq? I'm afraid leaving him here isn't an option."

Donovan had a point. It was best not to attract undue attention to the apartment.

"He reeks of booze," Helen said. "He's not going to remember what happened to him. I say we carry him outside and leave him in the alley at the back of the building. We'll keep his cash and driver's license. With any luck, he'll think he got beat up by a bunch of street thugs."

THIRTEEN

PRAGUE, CZECH REPUBLIC

John Dixon couldn't remember the last time someone had actually called him by his given name. The
scuffed Swiss passport he carried in his pocket was
made out in the name of Raphaël Feldmann—an identity
Dixon had assumed three decades ago. To most people,
Feldmann was a well-liked and respected senior investment banker who had the reputation of providing hefty
returns to his exclusive clientele. Within certain shady
circles, though, Feldmann was also known as a man capable of rinsing the dirt off your treasure. While managing his wealthy clients' money provided him with the
necessary income to pay for his luxurious penthouse
apartment in Zurich, his wine collection, and the Bentley
Bentayga he was currently driving on his way to Prague,
it was his central position within the bank's web of money-

laundering operations that paid for his four-million-euro yacht in Saint-Tropez and lavish ski chalet in Verbier.

Dixon, a tall, well-built, and clean-shaven man in his mid-fifties, had been washing money and expanding his contacts with arms smugglers, Russian oligarchs—especially since the recent, wide-ranging sanctions against them—and even the treasuries of some corrupt governments, for more than two decades. The complexity of his illicit transactions—all of them deftly interwoven with the bank's legitimate dealings—had fooled the half-dozen international regulators who had attempted to unmingle them.

But to the handful of people who knew his true identity—Dixon estimated the number at less than five—he was much more than just another astute banker. John Dixon was an American deep-cover intelligence asset.

John Dixon was an assassin.

John Dixon was Treadstone.

Thirty years. Eighteen missions. Twenty-two sanctioned kills.

Dixon loosened his tie, then stretched his arms one by one before rolling his head in an effort to loosen the tension in his neck and shoulders. For a moment, he wished he had flown to Prague by taking the bank's Cessna Citation CJ4 instead of driving the Bentley. The flight from Zurich would have lasted less than ninety minutes, but the long-distance journey from Switzerland's largest city to Prague was too good an opportunity to pass up. Very rarely did a genuine occasion to conduct a long and thought-out surveillance detection route present itself.

Over the years, SDRs had become second nature to Dixon, but as much as he tried to remain vigilant in Zurich, there were simply too many static locations where watchers could hide and remain unseen. To anyone watching him, this road trip would be so unexpected, and departed so clearly from whatever pattern of life they'd been able to attribute to him, that they would have no choice but to follow him.

And that's exactly what Dixon wanted.

An ordinary road trip from his office to Prague should have taken no more than eight hours, but his SDR had stretched his travel time to almost twenty hours and he was yet to cross into the Czech Republic. The Bentley's luxurious cabin with its rich-smelling leather seats and real wood trim didn't do much to appease the increasing stinging in his back. Keeping his eyes on the road, Dixon reached into the breast pocket of his suit jacket and pulled out a small orange plastic bottle. He popped the lid with his thumb and shook two painkillers into his mouth. He grabbed the can of energy drink snugged into the cupholder of the center console and guzzled half of it to wash down the pills. He grimaced at the flavor. It tasted like sewage water mixed with two pounds of sugar.

Thanks to the degenerative arthritis in his back, he doubted he would ever be able to get off those damn painkillers. His rheumatologist had explained that the throbbing in his lower back was caused by the breakdown of the cartilage between the facet joints in his spine, which in turn limited his overall range of motion. Not a good ailment for anyone, but especially precarious for an assassin. Treadstone agents had a tendency to die young, and while he had no way to validate this, Dixon believed there was a good chance he was the most senior one still operating in the field.

He sighed, wondering if he'd ever be allowed to retire with his head still attached to his shoulders. As compartmentalized as Treadstone was, Dixon had nevertheless heard whispers that Adam Hayes—a fellow Treadstone operative—had managed to do it for a while before being sucked back in. Would the same happen to him?

Dixon pushed the thought out of his mind. Now wasn't the time to get complacent.

So far, he had made nine stops during his surveillance detection route, all of them at predetermined locations, and each time scanning for watchers. His longest stop had been in Regensburg—one of the best-preserved medieval cities in Europe—where he had lingered over a double espresso and biscotti at a twenty-four-hour coffeehouse in an attempt to draw out potential surveillance assets. He hadn't spotted any.

When Dixon finally entered the Czech Republic, he did so through the Rozvadov border crossing via European route E50—a 3,200-mile route that connected the key naval port of Brest, France, with Makhachkala, a major Russian seaport on the Caspian Sea. Dixon stopped two hundred yards later at a large gas station for fuel, a bottle of sparkling water, and cellophane-wrapped banana bread. The gas station doubled as a truck stop, and it was busy with the early breakfast crowd. There were a dozen or so dining tables, and they were all occupied.

The convenience store area was packed with travelers stocking up on munchies, bottled soft drinks, and cigarettes. While in line to pay for his water and banana bread, Dixon compared each face and vehicle to a mental catalog of the people and cars he'd seen since departing Zurich the day before. Although conducting countersurveillance at night had its challenges, the darkness also forced potential watchers to move closer to their target than they would normally do so during daytime, which made it easier for Dixon to spot them.

At the moment, Dixon didn't feel watched, and there were no nagging voices at the back of his mind telling him he was under surveillance.

He was in the black. For now.

After decades living and working as Raphaël Feldmann, it wasn't being outed as a Treadstone operative that had Dixon on edge—it was the perpetual threat of being betrayed by the criminals he worked with. These people weren't the kind of *clients* who liked loose ends. They usually preferred clipping the loose threads. Dixon understood that more than most. Over the course of his distinguished banking career—but mostly during the initial stage when he was still building up his felonious clientele—he had on a few occasions preemptively clipped loose threads himself. Treadstone had taught him a valuable skill set in this regard, and Dixon hadn't hesitated to shed blood to solidify his cover or to protect the bank's reputation.

As his standing in the criminal world grew, he had become more selective regarding who he did business with, preferring to concentrate on accounts worth more than twenty million Swiss francs—approximately twenty-one million United States dollars. Dealing with bigger accounts brought in substantially more income for him and the bank, but it also allowed Dixon to share enhanced intelligence reports with his masters over at Treadstone, which kept them happy and off his back. Although Dixon had never personally been ordered to assassinate one of his clients, five of them—four men and one woman—had died over the years in ways that could be described as suspicious only a few short weeks after Dixon had sent Treadstone detailed accounts of their financial involvement with organizations or governments deemed hostile to US interests. While the authorities had declared all their deaths either accidental or naturally occurring, Dixon knew otherwise. His clients had been targeted and then killed by Treadstone operatives.

Dixon was surprised to hit traffic a few miles west of Prague, and his eyes automatically darted between the Bentley SUV's mirrors. In the passing lane, four cars back, a white panel van came to a stop behind a blue sedan. Dixon had seen one just like it drive past the gas station while he was fueling up. The panel van he remembered seeing earlier had red decals on its sides, showing that it belonged to an electrical company, and had two ladders fastened to its roof. This one didn't, but if the van was one of several surveillance vehicles, its driver could have easily taken an exit off the highway and ditched the ladders to change the van's profile. Dixon adjusted his side mirror so he could see the van's right side.

No decals.

Dixon drummed his fingers on the leather-wrapped steering wheel while he considered his options. The two men he was on his way to meet in Prague had been referred to him by one of his trusted clients—a wealthy former French soccer player who had legally immigrated to Switzerland to escape his home country's high and somewhat punitive taxation rate. The footballer had told Dixon that the two men, whom he had known for years, had recently sold their tech start-up to a large media conglomerate for nearly four hundred million euros. They were now conducting interviews hoping to find the right private banker through whom they could invest their newfound wealth. As he did for any potential clients, Dixon had spent a considerable amount of time doing his due diligence on the two men and their business.

Jakub Svoboda and Tomáš Málek had founded Frontal six years ago. Frontal, a Prague-based software company that developed commercial database management systems, had a rocky start, but, thanks to the disruptions caused by the worldwide pandemic, Svoboda and Málek had been able to capitalize on the unprecedented acceleration of digital transformation. They had pushed through by securing high-interest loans from nontraditional lenders and had bet it all on Frontal. Within months, they had managed to distinguish themselves by providing a cheaper way for enterprises to store their secondary files, like backups and analytics data, over a single cloud platform. The company's workforce quickly jumped from fifty to more than four hundred employees. The two founders' work ethics and resilience, combined with the next-level consistency of their software, had made Frontal one of the fastest-growing tech start-ups in Europe. In Dixon's professional opinion, if Svoboda and Málek had stayed at the helm of their company for another twelve to eighteen months, Frontal had a fair shot at achieving unicorn status—a privately held start-up valued at more than one billion dollars. With the prospect of a selling price much higher than they had obtained from the media conglomerate, Dixon couldn't help wondering why they had sold.

He had asked the question of his French footballer client, but his answer had been vague and inconclusive, leading Dixon to believe that Jakub and Tomáš had something to hide. This didn't mean Dixon wouldn't do business with them. On the contrary. But it prompted him to do additional research into the two men.

As easy as it had been for Dixon to find information about Frontal's capitalization, revenue streams, profit figures, and even its competitors, it had been quite a challenge to do the same with Jakub Svoboda and Tomáš Málek. Except for a few mentions in business journals, it was as if the two men didn't exist on the Internet. The few blurry pictures he'd been able to dig up were too dark and out of focus for a positive identification. Dixon thought it was strange, but not as unusual as some might think. Most of his clients, even the ones who had acquired their wealth legally, weren't active on social media and cherished their privacy. They didn't want their faces splashed all over magazine covers. As far as Dixon was concerned, if Jakub and Tomáš's strategy had been to focus on growing their company instead of posting useless stuff online, it had worked really well for them. With the financial resources they had at their disposal, it was possible they had hired a private security firm to conduct their own due diligence on the private banker they knew as Raphaël Feldmann.

The traffic started to move again, but only in sporadic spurts. Looking at his side mirror, Dixon couldn't tell what was inside the cargo area of the van, but the driver—a stocky man sporting a full beard—seemed to be the only occupant, seated at the front. With the vehicles in the passing lane going a bit faster, Dixon stayed in his and allowed the white van to slowly pass him. Without turning his head, he examined the van.

Damn.

It was the same one he'd spotted earlier. He was sure of it. The decals had been peeled off, but their outlines were still visible against the van's grimy side panels. Having established that the white van was a surveillance vehicle, Dixon's next move was to determine if he was indeed the mark, and, if he was, how many more vehicles were part of the surveillance package. Then he'd have to figure out the "why" and the "who." Like Jakub and Tomáš, Raphaël Feldmann's online profile was minuscule. It was understandable that the two men he was about to meet were guarded about sharing proprietary information with him and wanted to learn more about him before moving forward.

But wasn't that why they were meeting in Prague?

The get-together was meant to be an introduction. There was only so much one could do via emails and texts. Face-to-face meetings were important in his business. There was nothing like being in the room to get a read on somebody. And that went both ways. Sharing a meal with the two Czech businessmen would give them the opportunity to ask him any question they wanted, and Dixon was sure they had already pressed their footballer friend for everything he knew about Raphaël Feldmann.

So why would they feel the need to hire a firm to conduct physical surveillance on him prior to their first encounter?

A wry smile spread across his lips. *They wouldn't.*

Somebody else had ordered him followed, and Dixon was going to find out who it was.

He considered calling off his rendezvous with Jakub and Tomáš but decided otherwise. It wasn't every day he had the opportunity to meet clients with a nine-digit portfolio. Depending on the type of investment or stratagem they wanted him to build for them, his commission could be worth millions. He checked his watch. He had another four hours before he had to show up for the brunch reservation he had made at a trendy restaurant located right in the heart of Prague's Old Town.

Four hours. More than enough time.

Whoever was tailing him, Dixon was about to turn the tables on them.

FOURTEEN

Seated behind the wheel of her rental car—a Mitsubishi Lancer—Helen Jouvert was driving through the morning traffic of Cairo, looking for a spot to park from which she could observe the entrance of the Internet café.

The dashboard clock read 8:20 a.m.

The car in front of her came to a sudden halt for no obvious reason, and Helen had to stomp on the brakes. A horn blared behind her.

This shit is crazy!

The never-ending noise coming from horns, and the complete chaos reigning on the roads, made driving through Cairo a dangerous adventure. It seemed like every motorist thought they had the ultimate right to drive and turn whenever and wherever they wanted. Apparently, the concept of "right of way" was unfamiliar to

Cairo's drivers. They did, however, create their own local version in which large vehicles had the right of way over pedestrians and smaller cars alike. It was madness.

After leaving a still unconscious Tafiq squeezed in between garbage bags in the alleyway behind their last OP, they had made their way to their secondary observation spot. The new apartment had turned out to be less than ideal. A large tree blocked the view from the only window with a direct line of sight to the café. Helen didn't blame the analysts who'd rented the place. They had done their best to find available apartments around the café at a moment's notice, and it had been impossible for them to verify every detail. She'd sent Donovan on foot to keep an eye on the café while she drove around.

Her partner's voice crackled in her earbud. "I'm heading toward the bagel shop we spotted earlier."

"Good copy," Helen replied. "I'm still looking for a parking spot, but I don't think I'll find one with a direct line of sight."

"Understood. Why don't you leave the vehicle farther away and join me on foot? How does an omelet-stuffed bagel sound?"

"No, thanks. I never eat grains for breakfast," she said.

"Of course you don't. My bad."

She couldn't see Donovan's face, but Helen imagined him rolling his eyes as he said that.

"I wouldn't say no to a smoothie, though," she said, making a right into a narrow one-way side street.

"Well, I'm sure they'd be happy to prepare one of those green smoothies you like to gorge on so much."

"Then it's a date," she said.

A small, dented old car with a mountain of suitcases and bags on its roof zoomed out of an alleyway right in front of Helen, turning the wrong way into the one-way street.

Stupid is headed straight at me!

Helen swerved to her right to avoid a head-on collision, barely missing a parked motorcycle and a pedestrian. The reckless driver honked and waved as he sped past her, a big smile on his face. A woman seated in the front passenger seat was holding a phone against her ear, laughing hard at whatever the person on the other end of the line was saying. At least four children were squeezed into the rear seat of the small car. The luggage on the roof was strapped to the vehicle with frayed ropes that seemed as threadbare as the car's tires.

Shit! That's business as usual for them.

Helen ended up leaving the car in an outside parking lot much farther away than she had wanted. As she walked toward the bagel shop, she came to the conclusion that Cairo was an out-of-control city. For a megacity with a population of more than twenty-one million people, it was remarkable how few functional traffic lights there were in the metropolitan area.

No surprise the streets are always congested.

Helen was beginning to wonder if the endless honking had become a form of communication between motorists. She turned left on a residential street and was appalled at the amount of free-roaming detritus floating around. Littering was another problem. She could see it, but she could smell it, too. The lack of a trash collection system was apparent. To her right, a street seller yelled something at her, probably thinking she was a local.

She didn't blame him.

Perhaps her best asset as a Blackbriar operative was her ability to blend in. Within minutes and with a few touches of makeup, she could morph from street thug to Fortune 500 executive. After leaving the previous apartment, she had changed into a pair of loose-fitting brown capris and a white button-up shirt paired with a light gray scarf, white sandals, and a broad-brimmed tan hat to hide her short blond hair. She'd always kept her hair short, mostly because she liked it that way, but also because in a fight, long hair tended to be a disadvantage. Her pistol was within easy reach, secured in a small cross-body bag.

The diesel roar of buses and cars intensified as she neared the outdoor terrace of the bagel shop, where her partner had taken up the eye—a position from which a watcher could observe his mark. The bagel shop's tables, which lined the sidewalk and overlooked a small fountain and a jewelry shop across from it, were covered with red-and-white plastic cloths. Early morning or not, the terrace's six tables were packed with customers.

Helen pulled up a chair, its metal feet grating dissonantly against the cement, and took a seat next to Donovan. Seated at the table directly behind them, two old men were playing dominoes, each with a cigarette dangling from the corner of their mouth.

"Green smoothies aren't a thing here," Donovan said, bringing an espresso cup to his lips.

A waiter arrived, and, speaking Arabic, Helen ordered a coffee and a bowl of fresh fruit.

"Your Arabic is better than mine," Donovan noted once the waiter had retreated.

"Your Arabic is nonexistent," Helen replied.

Donovan dipped a biscotti in his cup. "That doesn't invalidate my statement," he said.

Helen had a working knowledge of four languages beyond English, three of which she spoke with fluency, including Arabic and French. Her German needed some work, but she could speak Spanish almost like a native.

Helen stretched her neck and sighted the Internet café. It was one hundred yards to their left, and Donovan had a direct view of the entrance.

"We're a bit far, aren't we?" she asked him.

Donovan pushed his phone toward her. "Not really," he said.

She took the phone and looked at the screen. There was a live video feed of the café's entrance.

"It has audio, too, but I muted it," Donovan said.

"You just did this?" she asked.

Donovan sank his teeth into the biscotti and swallowed the rest of his espresso.

"About thirty minutes ago," he said, raising his empty cup and signaling the waiter he wanted another. "I set up two of our wide-angle video cameras, but I lost connection with one of them."

Helen was familiar with the wireless spy cameras. They were half the size of a sugar cube and weighed less than five grams. One side was self-adhesive and could effortlessly stick to most surfaces.

"What happened?"

"It worked fine for a minute or two, then it fell off, and a pedestrian stepped on it," Donovan said. "I actually saw the sole of the shoe that crushed it."

"Where did you attempt to affix it?"

"To a streetlamp twelve steps away from the café. I guess the surface was too dirty and the adhesive didn't hold."

"That's too bad, but the one still transmitting is positioned perfectly."

"Would have been nice to have redundancy," Donovan said. "We won't be able to stay here and sip coffee all day."

Helen pushed the phone back toward Donovan. The waiter came, skillfully balancing four plates of food on one arm and holding a tray with their coffees. He set two plates in front of Donovan—one with an omelet, bagel, and potatoes, the other a large bowl of steaming oatmeal—and almost dropped Helen's smallish bowl of fresh fruit into her lap before leaving a plate of delicious-looking golden French toast in the middle. The rich aromas of cinnamon, strong coffee, and freshly baked bread perked up her appetite.

"You should eat," Donovan said. "Dig in."

The amount of food he had ordered was staggering. "How can you eat all that and still look the way you do?"

she asked, regretting the words the moment they came out of her mouth.

Donovan was about to take a bite from his bagel, but it stopped inches from his lips. He put the bagel down and looked squarely at her in a playful, roguish way. "What do you mean?"

"Certainly not what it sounded like," Helen replied, her mouth suddenly dry. She lifted the glass of water to her lips and took a long sip, then stabbed a piece of strawberry with her fork.

She could feel Donovan's eyes on her, studying her, his gaze unwavering. He didn't know a thing about her, and she didn't know much about him, either. And that was perfectly fine. The last thing she wanted was to give Donovan the impression she was attracted to him—because she wasn't. He was handsome enough, with faint but genuine laugh lines at the corners of his liquid blue eyes, and she'd bet a paycheck that he'd be one of those annoying men who'd only get better looking with age, but that wasn't the point.

They worked together.

Her phone vibrated, making a humming noise against the tabletop.

"Headquarters," she mouthed to Donovan.

She put her fork down and took the call.

"Jouvert," she said, just loud enough to be heard.

"This is Oliver," Director Manton said. "Can you talk?"

"Yes. I'm with Donovan."

"We have you and Donovan pinged at a bagel shop just east of the café. Confirm."

"Confirmed," she replied, her eyes on her partner as he washed down a huge bite of French toast with a gulp of water.

"Okay. I need to speak with Donovan, too. Transfer the call to your Bluetooths."

Helen gestured for Donovan to connect his earbud to her encrypted phone. She did the same with hers.

"We're both on the call," she said once Donovan had given her a thumbs-up.

"We might have caught a break," Manton started. "We hacked into the Egyptian Ministry of Internal Affairs and combed through the data coming from the RFID chips installed on the embassy vehicles and the personal cars of the staff."

Helen was vaguely aware of the Egyptian traffic police department's plans to modernize their law-enforcement technologies. In an effort to enforce regulations, all vehicles plated in Egypt had to be equipped with an RFID chip on their windshield. Radio-frequency identification chips consisted of a minuscule radio transponder, a radio receiver, and transmitter. Every time the RFID chip was triggered by an electromagnetic interrogation pulse, the tag attached to the windshield transmitted the identifying inventory number associated with that particular vehicle. The government used the data to charge motorists for highway usage, and the police planned on launching a new initiative that would see them combine RFID data and traffic camera footage to scan vehicles and automatically fine car owners for any traffic violations.

Clearly, this was still a work in progress.

"What did you find?" Donovan asked.

"We focused our search on the days the data dumps took place," Manton said. "We determined that RSO Steven Cooper's wife's car was in the vicinity of the Internet café on all those days."

"Steven Cooper?" Donovan said. "I served with a Steven Cooper."

"Same guy," Manton confirmed. "We cross-referenced his file to yours. Cooper was a Force Recon marine and was one of your instructors at Camp Pendleton during your basic reconnaissance course."

"Cooper was hard-core," Donovan said. "I'm surprised he left the Corps."

Helen smiled to herself, realizing she'd been right about Donovan. He had indeed served in the armed forces.

A United States Marine. Force Recon, no less.

"He was honorably discharged nine years ago, then finished his degree in business administration at the University of Oregon," Manton said. "He joined the US Diplomatic Security Service a few months later."

"But you said it was Cooper's wife's car that got tagged, right?" Helen asked.

"Correct, but we're scouring through the video footage to see if we can find out who was driving. We're also doing a deep dive on Cooper and his wife. I'll get back to you with the results."

"Thanks for the info, sir. We'll keep you in the loop about our progress, too," she said.

"I know you will," Manton said, ending the call.

Helen glanced at Donovan. Her partner's face was unreadable.

"How well do you know Cooper?" she asked.

"I haven't spoken to him in years," Donovan said, digging a spoon into his oatmeal. "We weren't friends, but the guy had a solid reputation. An exemplary marine, I'd say."

"Not the type of guy who'd betray his country?"

Donovan snapped his head in her direction, his blue eyes turning to ice, his gaze piercing right through her.

She didn't like the feeling.

"What?" she asked, suddenly on the defensive without knowing why.

"How should I know? I told you I haven't spoken to the guy in years," Donovan said, his voice hard as steel and harsher than she'd ever heard it. "Do I look like I have a crystal ball?"

Helen was taken aback, but she wasn't the push-around type. "What the fuck's gotten into you?" she asked, matching his tone but keeping her voice low. "I asked you a legitimate question based on your personal relationship with Cooper. So cut that marine macho shit right the fuck now."

Donovan flattened his lips and held her gaze for a moment. And then, as quickly as it had appeared, the unguarded anger she'd witnessed in his eyes vanished.

"You're right, of course. I'm sorry," Donovan said.

She didn't know why, but her instinct told her to probe further. Why had Donovan jumped at her like that? She could tell by his reaction that her question had touched a nerve. A very sensitive nerve. But why?

"Well, shit," Donovan said, before she could speak again.

He angled his phone so that she could see the screen. Regional Security Officer Steven Cooper had just entered the café.

FIFTEEN

John Dixon accelerated past two vehicles immobilized on the side of the road—a minor traffic accident, but clearly the cause of the massive traffic jam he'd been stuck in for the last twenty minutes. Between the damaged vehicles, two men were arguing loudly. In his side mirror, Dixon saw a pair of police officers driving their motorbikes on the shoulder of the road and slowly heading toward the scene.

Fifty yards ahead, the white panel van he had tagged earlier as a potential surveillance vehicle had also driven past the fender bender. The van was now traveling slightly above the speed limit, which told Dixon there was probably at least one other vehicle tailing him. If the white van had been the only vehicle, surely its driver would have driven below the speed limit to ensure that Dixon passed him.

Time to test the theory.

Dixon activated his blinker and took the next exit toward Stříbro, a small town a couple of miles north of the E50 highway renowned for its stone five-arched bridge spanning the Mže river. Dixon made a left onto Route 230, making sure to follow the posted speed limit. He didn't want to give potential watchers any hint of what he was about to do next. Three cars had left the highway via the same exit, but only two took a left onto Route 230. Dixon couldn't discern the make or model of the cars, but one was a dark blue sedan, the other a silver midsize SUV. Half a mile north of the E50, Route 230 turned into a two-lane country road surrounded by dense forest on either side. Dixon looked at his in-vehicle navigation system and spotted a bend in the road less than one mile ahead. A quick check in his rearview mirror confirmed that the two vehicles were still following roughly three hundred yards back. Traffic was light, but the occasional semitrailer whizzed by in the opposite direction. Reaching the bend, Dixon used the paddles to select the proper gear and flexed his right ankle, the Bentley's 4.0-liter turbocharged V8 instantly going to work. A deep purr swelled through the cabin and the speedometer jumped from fifty-five miles per hour to more than ninety in the blink of an eye. The tires held firm, and Dixon smiled despite himself.

This is fun.

Dixon lifted his foot off the gas pedal the moment the car behind him came around the bend, approximately six hundred yards back. For the next few minutes, Dixon did his best to maintain the same distance between him and the vehicles behind him. If the lead car got closer, Dixon accelerated. If it seemed to fall slightly behind, Dixon slowed down. When he reached Stříbro, he continued on the main drag and scanned the side streets until he found the perfect spot.

Dixon parallel parked in front of a small grocery store nestled between a sports shop and a pharmacy. He turned off the engine, then looked in his side mirror. In order for the driver of the car behind him to see him climb out of the Bentley and enter the grocery store, Dixon had to time his exit perfectly. When he caught the dark blue sedan's reflection in his side mirror, he opened the door and took his time exiting the Bentley. From the corner of his eye, he saw the silver SUV make a sudden left on a side street. The blue sedan continued on its way and drove past the Bentley just as Dixon entered the grocery store.

Basic surveillance procedures for such a scenario dictated that one of the vehicles had to be positioned to allow the watcher to see the target's vehicle. The other surveillance vehicles had to set themselves in a manner that would permit them to monitor the different routes the target could take and to efficiently transition back into mobile surveillance. Although it was always possible that the surveillance team would send a man inside the grocery store to see with whom he interacted, Dixon thought this was unlikely.

The grocery store wasn't big, but it was large enough so that people living in Stříbro could buy almost anything they wanted without having to drive to a bigger town. The store was busier than Dixon expected, but no one paid much attention to him. Two gray-haired clerks were busy stocking shelves, and a dozen shoppers were browsing the aisles, pushing trolleys or carrying blue plastic baskets. Dixon headed to the back of the store, looking for the back room. He found it through a set of double swinging doors next to the dairy section. The back room was filled with pallets of cereal boxes, chocolate candies, potato chips, and jars of jellies. Cardboard boxes waiting to be thrown out were stacked next to the open door of the loading dock. An older man wearing a green apron was sweeping the elevated portion of the dock.

The man didn't say a word, nor did he stop sweeping the floor, when Dixon jumped off the loading dock and sprinted to a big, green movable waste container ten yards away. Dixon examined his surroundings. He didn't see the silver SUV or the dark blue sedan. He opened a mapping app on his phone to get his bearings and to study the nearby streets. There weren't that many, making it easy for Dixon to pinpoint the few spots where the surveillance vehicles could have parked.

He had walked into the grocery store less than two minutes ago. Dixon figured he had at least another eight to ten minutes before whoever had eyes on the Bentley decided to risk sending someone on foot to determine if Dixon was still inside. Dixon tugged his .45-caliber HK USP Compact Tactical free from the holster at the small of his back, checked it had a round chambered, and returned the pistol to its holster. He patted the interior breast pocket of his suit jacket and felt the weight of the suppressor. Dixon took another look at the map and zoomed in on one specific spot. If he had been running a two- or three-car surveillance detail, this is where he would have positioned one of the vehicles. He visualized what he wanted to do, and then carefully picked his route.

Dixon walked south one block before turning west into a street parallel to the spot he had identified on the map. He was still twenty yards from the main road when the white panel van rolled past, its speed low enough for Dixon to see its driver looking in the opposite direction from where he was standing. The presence of the white van didn't change anything tactically for Dixon, but it did confirm that at least one of the vehicles that had followed him off the highway and into Stříbro was a surveillance vehicle. Dixon slowed his pace and waited for the van to move farther north before he crossed the main road. The residential block was mostly quiet, with the exception of an elderly man walking a happy-looking golden retriever on the opposite side of the street. Farther down, two middle-aged women sitting on a sidewalk bench were smoking cigarettes and chatting. Contrary to what Dixon had seen on the main road, where small storefront shops were numerous, the side street consisted mostly of tidy single-family homes with nicely trimmed hedges.

A look at the Rolex on his wrist told Dixon it had been seven minutes since he had entered the grocery store. He hurried his pace and made a right turn at the next street. A few pedestrians passed, but a quick glance was enough to rule them out. These folks weren't surveillance operatives. They were regular people minding their own business, oblivious to the game that was being played right in front of them. Dixon used to envy them.

Once upon a time, he, too, had dreams.

Dreams of having a normal life. Dreams of having a real family. A wife. A child, maybe two. But, in the end, when he had to make a choice, when he had to decide between the benign life of an accountant and a life filled with danger and excitement, he'd picked the latter.

He'd chosen Treadstone and had done so willingly, with his eyes wide open.

Approaching the next intersection, Dixon looked to his right and saw the dark blue sedan idling at the curb, facing east. Two men were seated in the sedan. The front passenger-side window was lowered, cigarette smoke was drifting out of the opening, and a man's elbow was resting on the sill. The two occupants seemed to be in conversation, and neither of them was paying any attention to Dixon as he approached the car on the driver's side. The driver's window was also open, and the men were speaking German. The driver was holding a cigarette in his right hand, but Dixon couldn't see what was in his left. Dixon rapped his knuckles on the rear driver's-side window, and the man's head snapped toward Dixon, stunned. Dixon pounded him on the nose with two vicious left hooks. There was the crack of cartilage as Dixon's fist broke the man's nose with his first punch. The second strike rendered the driver unconscious. In one fluid movement, Dixon grabbed the man's collar and pulled him in close and yanked a small kerambit-style knife from a leather sheath that hung from the waistband of his pants. Dixon brought the blade against the driver's neck but didn't pierce the skin.

"You move, he dies," Dixon said in German to the passenger, a man with strawberry blond hair and pale skin. Dixon hoped the man cared enough about the driver not to go for a weapon.

He didn't have to worry. The man was frozen in place by fear, his lower lip quivering. He slowly brought his hands up.

Letting go of the driver's collar, Dixon reached inside the car and pressed the unlock button. He climbed into the rear seat, pulled his pistol out, and pointed it at the passenger.

"Pick his cigarette up and throw it out before the car catches fire," Dixon said.

The man did as he was told, snatching the cigarette from the carpeted floor mat where it had fallen and tossing it out of the sedan.

"Turn off the engine and get the keys out of the ignition," Dixon ordered the passenger, who once again followed his instructions.

"What's your name?" Dixon asked.

"My . . . My name's Karl."

It was clear to Dixon that whatever or whoever Karl was, he wasn't an operator. His body language suggested he was frightened, but also that he was tense and anxious.

"Do you know who I am?"

"Yes . . . You . . . Your name is Raphaël Feldmann," Karl replied. "What . . . Why do you have a gun?"

Dixon ignored the question and pointed his pistol at the unconscious driver. "Who's he?"

"I . . . He's Peter. Are you . . . I don't understand. What is happening?"

Karl was now shaking uncontrollably. Either the man was an exceptional actor, or he was truly scared out of his wits.

"How many vehicles are part of the surveillance detail?"

Karl hesitated, but Dixon didn't. Still holding the blade in his left hand, he brought it back to the driver's neck. This time, though, Dixon pressed hard enough to break the skin, leaving a thin trace of blood.

"No!" Karl screamed, tears welling up in his eyes. "I . . . I'm begging you. Don't kill him."

"How many vehicles?"

"There are . . . three vehicles, but they . . . They don't know anything. I swear it!"

Dixon narrowed his eyes. "Know what? Why are you following me?"

"I'm the one who hired them. Well, not me personally, but the news agency I work for."

A news agency?

Dixon allowed the knife to dig deeper into the driver's neck. More blood poured out.

"Talk, Karl," Dixon warned, "or I kill him and start working on you next."

Karl bit his lip and squeezed his eyes shut. Two perfect

lines of tears fell down his ghost-white cheeks. "Please . . . I'll keep your name out of it. Even better, I'll drop everything. Everything! I promise!"

"Out of what, Karl? You'll keep my name out of what?"

For a moment Karl seemed confused, as if he thought Dixon knew what he'd been talking about all along.

"My investigation," Karl replied, wiping the tears away with the backs of his hands. "You . . . You really have no idea, do you?"

The death stare Dixon threw at him was enough to keep Karl talking.

"I've spent the last six months investigating the hundreds of Swiss bank accounts held by key political figures implicated in corruption scandals all over the world. Dozens of these accounts were handled by you, Mr. Feldmann. Forty-two to be exact. Twelve of those belonging to Russian oligarchs who have been sanctioned by the European Union and the United States."

"You're a journalist?" Dixon asked.

"Yes. I work for the *Süddeutsche Zeitung*."

If there was one situation Dixon hadn't anticipated, it was this. Being caught in the web of a journalistic investigation. Not that the thought had never crossed his mind, because it had on numerous occasions, especially since the Panama Papers had come out in 2016, but he had always believed he'd hear about it well before a reporter came knocking on his door asking questions about his business.

The *Süddeutsche Zeitung* was one of the biggest and

most influential newspapers in Germany. If Raphaël Feldmann was on their radar, there wasn't much Dixon could do about it now. It was already too late. Killing Karl wasn't going to solve the problem. On the contrary, a certain finesse would be needed to turn the situation around, not blunt force.

"The driver isn't a reporter?" he asked.

Karl shook his head. "No. He's private security. A former German state police officer. So are the drivers of the other cars."

"What colors are the other vehicles?"

"There's a white panel van and a silver SUV," Karl said, eager to please. "There's a reporter from the OC-CRP in the SUV."

Shit.

The Organized Crime and Corruption Reporting Project was a consortium of journalists that specialized in high-profile investigations. It was a nongovernmental organization, but one with sharp teeth.

Karl must have sensed a switch in Dixon's demeanor because he said, "Don't worry about him. I . . . I'll convince him to drop the story." Dixon gave Karl a doubtful look, which prompted the German to quickly add, "I know I can. You have to believe me!"

"What is it about today? Why now?"

Karl's eyes moved to the blade against the driver's neck. The driver's left eye was swollen shut and his smashed nose was still bleeding profusely.

"Prague is a setup," Karl said, avoiding Dixon's stare.

"The two men you're scheduled to meet with are reporters."

"Names. Tell me their names," Dixon said. He wasn't about to volunteer information Karl didn't have.

"You think you're on your way to meet with Jakub Svoboda and Tomáš Málek," Karl said. "But you aren't. Svoboda and Málek are legends we created to draw in people like you."

Dixon clenched his jaw with almost enough force to crack his teeth, his mind racing for a solution. Somewhere along the way, he'd made a mistake. He had lost his touch. He'd become complacent, taken too many things for granted and gotten comfortable living the high life.

"What do you want from me?" Dixon asked.

"Nothing. I want nothing from you. Not . . . Not anymore. I just want to . . . you know. I want to get back to my wife," the reporter said. "That's it."

"Do you have your press credentials on you?"

"In my breast pocket, with my driver's license and passport," Karl replied.

"Slowly reach into your pocket and show them to me. I want to make sure you're who you say you are."

"Of course," Karl said.

The passport looked real enough and was German. His ID from the newspaper looked legitimate, too, but Dixon went a step further.

"Google yourself with the name of your newspaper. But if I see you try to make a phone call or send a text . . ."

"I won't!"

A moment later, Karl showed him the results. "See? It is me."

Dixon looked at the screen. Karl's picture was on the official website of the newspaper. It identified him as an award-winning investigative journalist.

Perfect.

Dixon lowered his pistol and removed the blade from the driver's neck, wiping it against the back of the seat.

"Okay," he said. "I'm satisfied you are with the *Süddeutsche Zeitung*."

"I . . . I'm free to go? You're letting me go?" Karl asked, his right hand inching toward the door handle.

"Of course you're free to go," Dixon said. "But you have to know this, Karl. This would never have happened if I had known you were a reporter. You should have called my office instead of having me followed. How was I supposed to know you were a journalist? I've been looking for a way out of this nightmare for years."

"What? I . . . I don't understand," Karl said.

"I thought you were working for one of my clients. They tried to kill me once, didn't you know?"

"I . . . I don't . . . I'm confused," Karl said, but Dixon could tell the man was regaining his composure. His right hand was no longer moving toward the door handle. Karl's initial fear was being replaced with curiosity. "One of your clients tried to kill you?"

"Yes. Some of them are extremely powerful people," Dixon said. "They think I know too much. In a way, they aren't wrong. I could ruin their lives if I was to speak to . . . to someone like you, for example."

"Wait, I'm not sure I understand what you're saying here, Mr. Feldmann. Are you telling me you aren't denying being involved in illegal activities connected to—"

"No, Karl," Dixon said, cutting him off. "What I'm saying is that I'm the one running the entire money-laundering operation for my bank. I've helped dictators, Russian oligarchs, and drug traffickers stash their wealth in opaque jurisdictions using complex financial instruments. And now I fear for my life. Very much so. Can you help me?"

The reporter was staring at Dixon, dumbfounded, his mouth hanging agape.

"I really thought you guys were a hit team," Dixon added. "That's why I reacted the way I did. My apologies."

"You're willing to cooperate with our investigation? Why?"

"Wasn't I clear enough? They tried to fucking kill me, Karl. They threatened to literally crucify me in the lobby of my bank if I didn't do what they asked of me."

"Jesus! I can't believe this," Karl said. "You're serious."

Dixon could practically see the wheels spinning in the journalist's mind.

"Do I look like the kind of guy who makes jokes?"

Karl swallowed hard. "I guess not."

"If you can protect me and keep my name out of your article, I'll become the biggest source you ever had."

"And you'll give me access to all your files? Because for this to work, Mr. Feldmann, I'll need the names, the account numbers, and the dates of all the illicit transactions you've taken part in."

Dixon made a show of thinking about it, as if the decision were tearing him apart.

"If you promise me confidentiality, you'll have unrestricted access to my files and to the accounts. Nothing will be off-limits."

Karl let out a long sigh. "I need to talk to my colleagues," he said. "This isn't a decision I can make on my own. The two reporters you were on your way to meet in Prague started it all. They're the ones who got my newspaper, the *New York Times*, and the OCCRP involved."

"No confidentiality means I'll get prosecuted, Karl. I can't go to prison. I'll be dead in less than a week. You get that, don't you? No confidentiality, no deal. I'll simply disappear into thin air, and you'll have to find someone else to walk you through the multifaceted scheme I've put in place. It's your call."

"No, it's not," Karl pushed back. "As much as I'd love to, I can't make that promise."

"But the two reporters in Prague could?"

The German journalist nodded.

"Who are they with?" Dixon asked.

"UR Real News," Karl said.

Dixon had never heard of them, and he said so to Karl.

"They're exclusively online, and their reputation isn't the greatest," Karl admitted. "In fact, it's shit. But once in a while they get something good, and they're now owned by Mind-U."

This was a company Dixon knew. Mind-U was a social

media conglomerate with more than nine hundred million registered users across their app portfolio. They were big and getting bigger fast.

"I understand. So then, why don't I keep my appointment with your UR Real News colleagues? It's in a few hours anyway. We could stop by a hospital on our way to Prague and drop off your driver. Something needs to be done about his nose."

"Okay," Karl said. "But we all go together. I don't want to be alone with you."

"Fair enough."

As if on cue, in the driver's seat the ex-cop was regaining consciousness. Dixon wrapped his arm around the man's neck and flexed his bicep, applying just the right amount of pressure to keep the man under control without choking him.

"I don't want him to panic or do anything stupid," Dixon told Karl. "Convince him we're all friends here, okay? I'll pay his medical expenses and will transfer ten thousand euros to his account at the end of the day if he behaves."

It took a bit of explaining, but a minute later Dixon released his hold.

"I'm sorry about your nose," Dixon said. "As Karl explained, I thought you were here to kill me."

"Fuck you," the driver said, spitting mucus and blood out the window. "You're a fucking psycho."

Dixon smiled. *You have no idea.*

"Call your friends and ask them to drive over here,"

Dixon said. "Karl will explain to them how we'll proceed, right, Karl?"

"Call them," Karl instructed the driver. "It will be okay. I'll make sure you get paid the entire contracted amount, okay?"

"I want the ten thousand euros, too," the man said.

"I don't make empty promises," Dixon said. "You'll have your money. Now call your friends."

The white panel van was the first to arrive but was quickly followed by the silver SUV. Although the dark sedan driver had told the two other drivers about Dixon's presence, the former police officers appeared stunned to see him standing outside the car next to the reporter. Both the van and SUV drivers climbed out of their vehicles and made their way to Karl, who explained the situation to them. The Organized Crime and Corruption Reporting Project journalist joined them, holding a phone against his ear.

The two former cops didn't look happy. The one who'd been driving the white van, a heavyset man with a shaved head and thick black beard, looked at the dark sedan behind Dixon. He swore.

"This asshole did this to Kevin?" he growled, pointing a finger at Dixon and taking a step toward him.

Karl opened his mouth to answer, but Dixon raised his hands in surrender. "Yes, I did. And I apologized. Like I said, I thought you were a hit team sent by one of my clients. Your friend Kevin will get ten thousand euros for his broken nose. That's more than fair."

The silver SUV driver, a medium-height man with thin blond hair and a slight paunch, looked at Karl and asked, "What do we do now?"

"Mr. Feldmann decided to collaborate with our investigation, and if our colleagues at UR Real News agree to meet with him under these new circumstances, we'll make our way to Prague," Karl said.

"But not before we stop by the nearest hospital to take care of your friend," Dixon added, doing his best to keep everyone calm.

"When will we know if we're going to Prague?"

The OCCRP reporter ended the call he was on and dropped his phone into his jeans pocket. "They said yes," he said, grinning. "They're looking forward to speaking with you, Mr. Feldmann."

Dixon forced a smile. "Likewise."

"Do you mind driving the SUV?" Karl asked his colleague. "I'd like these two to join me in Mr. Feldmann's vehicle."

"No problem," the other journalist replied.

The bearded former cop took two more steps toward Dixon. "I'll drive the Bentley," he said, his lips curling into a snarl. He aggressively reached for Dixon's arm. "But not before I search—"

When the man's hand was inches away from his arm, Dixon sprang into action. With surprising speed, he grabbed the former police officer's extended wrist, twisted it around so that the palm of his hand pointed up, and bent the wrist back hard, in a direction it wasn't supposed to go. The man grunted and fell to his knees but refused to quit. Dixon saw the man's left hand turn into a fist, so gave the wrist another push.

A bone snapped. The man screamed.

Dixon released his assailant's broken wrist and shoved him forward with a low-strength kick between the shoulder blades. The man fell face-first onto the pavement. His colleague didn't move.

Dixon understood.

The man was hired help. He'd signed up to conduct surveillance on a wealthy financier, not to get into a fist-fight with someone who, in the span of three heartbeats, had broken his partner's wrist without even breaking a sweat.

"I'll drive the Bentley," he said, helping his friend to his feet. "No problem."

SIXTEEN

CAIRO, EGYPT

Donovan Wade had a hard time coming to terms with what he'd just witnessed. Diplomatic Security Service Special Agent Steve Cooper was a decorated former marine and the current regional security officer at the US embassy in Cairo. The background check to join the DSS was exhaustive. If anything even remotely suspicious had been red-flagged during Cooper's preemployment screening, he wouldn't have been offered a position with the agency.

So why in hell had Cooper just entered an Internet café allegedly linked to Russia from which classified American intelligence had been uploaded to the dark web?

It doesn't make sense.

There had to be an explanation but, for the time being, Donovan couldn't figure out what it was.

"I forwarded the video of Cooper entering the café to headquarters," he said.

"Good," Helen replied, pushing the now-empty bowl of fruit to the side. "They'll monitor everything coming out of that place. If Cooper uploads something, we'll know about it."

Their waiter arrived and grabbed Helen's bowl off the table, then he looked at Donovan.

"I'm done," he said.

The possibility of a fellow marine betraying his country had ruined his appetite. The waiter removed the half-eaten plates of food and carried them away.

"Any suggestions about how to move forward?" Helen asked.

"I think we can stay here for a little while longer," Donovan said. "I'd like to take a few pictures of who comes and goes while our friend is inside."

"Agreed. What's the camera's range?"

"We're pretty much at its limit," Donovan replied. "Anything farther could jeopardize the quality of the transmission. The feed doesn't get backed up to a cloud or anywhere else. The camera's only link is to my phone. More secure this way, although not as practical."

"Let's order something else so that we can stay without arousing suspicion."

"Feel free to do so, but you don't have to," Donovan said. "You see, service in Cairo is a bit like what you'd experience in Spain or France. It's not the greatest, but the waiters will never ask you to leave your table. It would be ill-mannered of them to do so."

She offered him a smile, but he could see it was absentminded. Her dark green eyes were constantly on the move, scanning her environment for potential threats, while she gently stirred her coffee.

Helen Jouvert was a fascinating woman, no doubt about it. There was an energy about her that couldn't be denied, due in part to her incredible level of fitness, Donovan thought. Oliver Manton had told him all about Helen's many successes with the FBI, but he had never revealed why she had left—not that Donovan would ever have asked him.

Not my damn business.

Furthermore, the last thing Donovan wanted was for Manton to reciprocate the favor and open up to Helen or anyone else at Blackbriar about why the suits at Langley had derailed his career at the CIA the way they had. Not that Donovan had done anything wrong, but in this business, guilt by association was a big thing.

What Manton did make a reference to, though, was that when he recruited Helen, she'd been a professional MMA fighter in Europe competing under the Cage Warriors banner—an Irish-owned mixed martial arts promotion based in England. Intrigued, Donovan had watched her six fights on YouTube.

Four wins, two losses.

Helen's wins had all been by submissions, but her two losses were by knockouts. A few more keystrokes had showed Donovan that Helen was a former Team USA judoka and a fifth-degree black belt who had won silver medals at two different World Judo Championships while she was studying for her law degree at Boston University. He didn't know if she had any siblings or other living relatives, but just by the way she sometimes snapped at him for no reason, he had a feeling she was an only child.

She wasn't married, at least he didn't think so. He'd looked at her finger when he'd first met her. No ring. Not that he cared, but Helen was definitely attractive. Not cover-girl hot, but striking in her own way with a brilliant mind. With her short blond hair and deeply tanned skin, Donovan thought his partner looked more like a Miami Beach lifeguard than the top-level counterintelligence operative she was.

Helen's voice broke into his thoughts. "Don't snap your head, Donovan, but I think I recognize someone who's heading toward the café."

"Okay. Someone I should know?"

"If you read the predeployment package on the plane, you definitely should," Helen said. "All right, take a look at your two o'clock. Tall, broad-shouldered, wearing a business suit."

Donovan spotted him right away. He was a beast of a man. He was as tall as Donovan but had probably thirty pounds on him, not all of it muscle.

"Demian Kirillov," he whispered. "The SVR's Cairo station chief. And he's not alone."

"Yeah. I noticed them, too."

The Russian spy, who was leading the way, was accompanied by one woman, who kept a gap of four to five paces behind him, and one other man. The woman seemed to be in her thirties and about five and a half feet tall, with a pageboy haircut, and wearing a charcoal gray business suit. The second man was smaller and thinner than Kirillov but walked and acted the same way. He, too, was wearing a plain business suit. Both men had their heads on a swivel, scanning ahead, to the rear, and toward the street, and doing so with an economy of motion that indicated they knew what they were doing.

"If I didn't know better, I'd be tempted to say that Kirillov and the other man are acting as bodyguards for the lady," Donovan said.

"Who said they aren't? Make sure to snap good pics of this," Helen said.

Donovan was already on it, his eyes moving from the trio to his phone.

"At this pace they'll be at the café in about twenty seconds or so," Helen said.

All Donovan had to do to take a still picture was to tap the red button at the bottom of his screen. The app would take pictures without stopping the video feed.

"Five, four, three—"

"Shit," Donovan muttered. Without warning, the signal from the camera had turned to static.

"What is it?" Helen asked without looking at him.

"I took one picture, then I lost contact with the device," he said. "I can't take any more photos and the live feed is down, too."

"Handheld jammer?" Helen suggested.

"That's what I'm thinking," Donovan replied. "But I'll try rebooting the app anyway."

Kirillov had entered the Internet café with the woman

while the shorter man had taken position to the left of the entrance.

"I haven't seen a vehicle, but I doubt they walked to get here," Helen said.

"An embassy car probably dropped them somewhere in the city earlier this morning," Donovan said, agreeing with Helen's assessment. "And I'd be willing to bet a few dollars that they've been conducting countersurveillance since, making sure to get here by different means, including taxis, public transportation, and the last leg on foot."

"The three of them together?"

"I don't think so," Donovan said. "They most likely got back together only a block or two away from the café."

"Any luck with the reboot?" Helen asked, tapping a finger on Donovan's phone.

"Nope," he said. "All the apps are working, but I'm not getting the feed from the camera. I can make a pass, if you want, but if I get too close, Cooper might recognize me."

"I'm not taking that chance," Helen said with a shake of her head. "Plus, you don't look like a local. I do."

Donovan raised an eyebrow. "You're going in, aren't you?"

"Get the car," she said. "I just texted you the location."

"I should stick around, Helen, just in case," he said, not liking the idea of leaving her alone with a possible traitor and three likely Russian spies.

"I'll be fine, just get the car and wait for my call. Keep the comms open."

Donovan considered insisting, but Helen was the team leader. She knew what she was doing.

"Understood."

"Well, then, thanks for the lovely breakfast," Helen said, rising to her feet. "But next time, please find a place that makes smoothies."

SEVENTEEN

CAIRO, EGYPT

There was simply too much traffic for Helen to cross the road. Not wanting to get hit by a car, she walked to the nearest intersection, glad to see that her odds of being killed in a hit-and-run had diminished, albeit only slightly. Ten or so other pedestrians were already at the intersection, all of them looking at each other nervously, as if trying to determine who was going to lead the hazardous journey across the road. Helen didn't have the time to wait, so she stepped into the street, dodging and sidestepping fast-moving cars, motorcycles, and trucks alike. She had only one more lane to get through when an irritated truck driver sounded his horn right behind her, its sound so loud it broke Helen's concentration. She hesitated for a second, and only managed to jump out of the way of an oncoming bus at the last moment, missing its front bumper by less than an inch.

My God.

"Good job," came Donovan's voice in her ear. "You made it."

"You had doubts?"

"None. I paid the bill and I'm on my way to pick up the car."

"Good. What's our friends' status?"

"No changes, but two women entered the location while you were playing hide-and-seek with the traffic. Both were wearing blue jeans. One with a white linen shirt; the other had on a light green windbreaker. The bodyguard didn't stop them."

"You think they're with Kirillov?"

"Very unlikely," Donovan said. "Didn't look the part. Not aware of their surroundings, eyes glued to their phones. You know the type."

She did.

Now that the sun was up, the big pair of dark sunglasses perched on her nose weren't out of place. She studied the bodyguard's face as she approached the café. He didn't look like a spy. His spine was too stiff. He wasn't someone used to blending in. He had a stern face, cropped hair, and intelligent eyes. This man was experienced, and potentially dangerous. He wasn't just hired muscle.

Military. Maybe even Spetsnaz.

Helen looked away and grabbed her phone, bringing it to her ear. She felt his eyes on her, but she kept walking, talking in Arabic into her phone. She reached the café's door, pulled it open, and shuffled past the bodyguard.

The lighting inside the café was dim, and Helen estimated the space at less than one thousand square feet. There were four rows of ten computers, a counter behind which an employee sat, and a corridor that led away from the main space. The clerk was a man in his mid-thirties with thick-lens glasses. He was wearing a brown lab coat over a green T-shirt. There were a dozen clients including the two women Donovan had seen earlier, who were sitting side by side, typing on their keyboards. Cooper, though, wasn't there. Nor was the lady who had accompanied Kirillov inside.

"Can I help you?" the clerk asked in Arabic, looking at her over his computer screen, his eyes alert.

"I'd like to buy thirty minutes, please," Helen said.

"One hour is the minimum. Regular Internet or you want to play games? Gaming is more expensive."

"Just need to send a couple of emails. Regular is fine."

"Emails? Really? Why don't you use your phone?" the clerk inquired, his tone slightly accusatory. "Something is wrong with it? I can take a quick look at it if you want. No charge."

It was a given that the clerk was a paid Russian asset. She had to assume that whatever she did inside the café, the clerk would know about it. She hadn't seen any cameras, but that didn't mean there weren't any.

"You're so sweet," Helen said, flashing him her most charming smile. "But there's nothing wrong with my phone. I'm simply running out of data."

She knew it was difficult for a man not to respond to her smile, but this man managed it. He studied her for a long moment, his expression unyielding.

"Is something wrong?" she asked.

The clerk rolled his tongue over his teeth, then said, "One hundred and fifty pounds."

Helen paid cash and walked to the computer the clerk had assigned to her. Aware that the clerk would be able to access her screen with a few clicks of his mouse, she logged into an email account backstopped by Blackbriar and started typing a message to her nonexistent husband in Virginia, explaining why she'd been so late in replying to his last message and that she missed him very much.

She was on her fourth paragraph when Steven Cooper walked past her and stormed out, startling the Russian bodyguard waiting outside. Through the window of the store, Helen watched as the bodyguard grabbed Cooper by the shoulders and yanked him back. Cooper immediately spun one hundred and eighty degrees and swatted the bodyguard's arms away with his right forearm and delivered an open palm strike to the center of the man's chest. The bodyguard staggered back a few steps.

"Back off!" Cooper barked, pointing a finger at the Russian.

Kirillov and the lady walked past Helen's computer station. The SVR station chief quickened his pace, and his movements must have caught Cooper's attention because he looked into the café through the window.

Though Helen didn't catch what it was, Cooper said one more thing to the bodyguard, then he walked away.

Kirillov and the woman exited the café and looked in the direction Cooper had left. Kirillov took a step in that direction, but the woman gently placed a hand on his chest, stopping him. It seemed like the SVR man was taking his orders from the woman. She wondered who the woman was.

Kirillov was clearly not happy. His forehead wrinkled and his lips snarled up like an angry Rottweiler. The woman said something to him, which seemed to calm him down. A moment later, after a brief conversation, Kirillov, the woman, and the bodyguard left in the opposite direction from which they had come.

Helen finished her fake email, sent it to a phony address, then logged out. She waved goodbye to the clerk as she left the store, and slowly made her way back toward the bagel shop.

"Donovan, where are you?" she asked.

"On my way," her partner replied. "I had to make a quick stop. Where do you want me to pick you up?"

"One block east of the bagel shop," she said.

"Understood. I'll be there shortly. Everything okay?"

"I'm fine, but Cooper is neck-deep into something. He isn't happy about it, that much I could tell."

"All right, we'll talk in the car. Give me two or three minutes to worm my way through this traffic."

Helen replayed in her mind what she had witnessed in the Internet café. There was no mistake about it, either Steven Cooper was the mole, or his wife was.

Or both.

But one question remained. What in God's name

could have pushed a decorated marine—or his wife—to betray their country?

Helen wondered if Director Manton would ask her and Donovan to continue investigating or if he was going to pull them out of Egypt and let the FBI handle the investigation. She guessed it all depended on what Manton, or the DNI for that matter, had in mind for Steven Cooper. But was it really their decision? The way Blackbriar worked, she and Donovan, and the other field teams, were like emergency plumbers who were dispatched to fix a specific, urgent problem. They weren't equipped to install the entire plumbing system of a large commercial building, which in Helen and Donovan's line of work meant building a legal case for a potential criminal prosecution against an individual or corporation. This task was reserved for the FBI. On the other hand, Donovan and Helen weren't blunt force instruments, either. Targeted killings were Treadstone's territory, not Blackbriar's. Blackbriar's main purpose was to disrupt foreign intelligence operations.

Something was brewing in the shadows. Helen could feel it. The relations between the United States and Russia were at an all-time low, but she had a hard time believing the Russians would be crazy enough to assassinate the DNI on Egyptian soil. The whole region was a powder keg, barely stable. The murder of a high-ranking American official at the hands of a Russian asset—proxy or not—could light the fuse that would eventually start another world war.

Damn. Maybe that's exactly what the psychopath-in-chief in the Kremlin wants.

The unprovoked, barbaric invasion of Ukraine by Russian forces had been an eye-opener for Helen. Russian tanks rolling uninvited across the Ukrainian border, ballistic missiles striking the heart of Kyiv—a city of three million people—and the killing of unarmed civilians had convinced her that the Russian president was a ruthless despot with a dangerous and very large imperialist agenda.

Before the invasion, she'd always believed that in the end sanity and common sense would prevail, and that a war of such scale in Europe belonged to the history books. Like many others, and despite being educated and more informed than most, she'd been wrong and naïve. She wasn't anymore.

Donovan's voice came in through her earbud. "I see you, Helen. I'm twenty yards behind you."

Donovan rolled to a stop beside her, which earned him a cacophony of blown horns from motorists behind the Mitsubishi Lancer, and Helen slid into the passenger seat. Donovan stepped on the gas and drove away before she had the time to close her door.

"This one is yours," he said, tapping a finger on one of two vibrant green smoothies in the center console's cupholders. Each see-through plastic cup had a bamboo straw jammed into it.

"Where did you get them?" she asked, taken aback that he would stop by a juice bar to pick up something to drink while she was inside the café.

"Bought them at a specialty shop across from the parking lot where you left the car," he said. "There were three fighting-age men hanging about the Mitsubishi when I arrived, so I walked past them and entered the shop. I wanted to see what they were up to."

"You think they placed a tracking device on the car?" she said, worried she had missed a tail when driving around looking for a parking spot.

"No, I don't think so. Two women in their mid-twenties joined them from an apartment building and they all crammed into a powder-blue two-door Volkswagen."

Relieved, she picked up her smoothie from the cupholder and brought the straw to her lips to take a sip. The rich taste of spinach and Swiss chard mixed together with fresh fruits flowed across her tongue.

"Oh, wow." The flavor was spectacular, and it must have shown on her face, because Donovan glanced at her.

"Really? You like it that much?"

"It's delicious," she said. "One of the best. I'm not kidding."

"Guess it's an acquired taste. Feel free to drink mine," he said, smiling.

She rolled her eyes at him and sipped another copious amount of smoothie.

"All right," Donovan said, getting back to business, the grin on his face gone. "Talk to me. What happened in there?"

Helen told him in detail what she had witnessed at the Internet café. "And trust me on this, it was obvious he didn't want to be there," she concluded.

"Then why did he meet with them?" Donovan asked, but Helen knew he was just thinking out loud. "I can't wrap my head around the fact that a man like Cooper works with the SVR."

"You haven't seen him in years, Donovan," Helen said. "People change."

"Yeah, maybe," he said, but he didn't sound convinced. "Anyhow, I spoke with the director while you were inside the cybercafé. I told him about Cooper and Kirillov. I sent him the only picture I was able to take before the camera stopped transmitting."

"What did he say?"

"Not much, but he sounded pissed off and he promised he'd get back to us soon with additional intel."

"Anything else?"

"Yeah. They booked us a room in a hotel not too far from here. That's where we're headed now. If I'm to trust the traffic map on my phone, we should be there in fifteen minutes or so."

Great. She needed to recharge her batteries and grab a few hours of sleep. She was exhausted. They were still ten minutes away from the hotel when her phone vibrated.

"It's the director," she said. "I'm gonna link the call to our earbuds."

"I'm on the line with Donovan," she said a moment later.

"Good. Since Donovan's last update, we've been working nonstop to find something that would explain Steven Cooper's actions," Manton said. "We got nowhere. I've personally reviewed his yearly assessments, his bank accounts, his credit card statements, but Cooper is clean as a whistle."

"What about his wife?" Donovan asked.

"Right. Since she isn't a government employee, it's taking us longer to go through her data. What we know so far isn't conclusive, but my preliminary assessment is that Emma Cooper is an outstanding American citizen. No criminal record, no dubious affiliations. Even pays her taxes on time."

"Where does she work? What's her background?" Helen inquired.

"She studied at the London School of Economics and received a degree in finance. She then moved back to the US and went to NYU for two years to earn a Master of Science in data science."

Helen whistled. "Impressive," she said, meaning it.

"Emma works at Mind-U, a social media conglomerate with almost one billion registered users across its apps portfolio. She's the vice president of business development for the US office," Manton said. "Looking at her online profile, I'm reading that she's in charge of creating strategic business partnerships and driving new revenue sources for the organization."

"But she followed her husband to Cairo?" Donovan asked. "With a job like that, you'd think they would want her to stay in the States, right?"

"Yes and no," Helen intervened. "Vice president of business development is exactly the kind of position one can do from home, at least some of it."

"Correct," Manton said. "Her credit card indicates

she frequently travels back and forth between Dallas, where Mind-U's North American office is located, and Cairo. I'm seeing no less than ten trips in the last twelve months, some of them lasting more than a week."

"Where is she now?" Donovan asked.

"She's in Dallas. That's confirmed," Manton said. "There've been numerous charges on her credit cards in the last few days and we got her on camera withdrawing money from an ATM not far from her residence this morning."

"How do you want us to proceed, sir?" Helen asked.

"I'd usually pass this along to the FBI through the DNI and share enough of our findings to point the investigators in the right direction, but the Russian angle has me worried," Manton said. "Even more so with the picture you sent me."

"Why's that?" she asked.

"Because the woman in the picture is Stanislava Krupin."

"I'm not familiar with the name," Donovan said. "Should I be?"

Manton hesitated, but only for a moment. "Are you familiar with Unit 29155?"

"I've heard of it, but I'm no expert on the subject," Helen said.

"Same here," Donovan added.

"Unit 29155 of the GRU—the Russian military intelligence agency—is an elite unit that specializes in subversion, sabotage, and assassination. As of five years ago, Stanislava Krupin was one of the team leaders," Manton said. "She has traveled extensively around northern Africa and the Balkans, and she's very, very good at what she does."

"Is she an assassin?" Helen asked.

"I can't guarantee she has never killed anyone, but no, Krupin isn't an assassin. She's an intelligence officer through and through. She specializes in blackmail and extortion."

That last bit of intel piqued Helen's curiosity. Rumors had it that Unit 29155 had been operating for at least two decades, but, as far as Helen knew, the CIA had only recently discovered its existence. Manton's statement that Krupin was a Unit 29155 team leader five years ago suggested that the Blackbriar director might have played a role in uncovering the unit. A couple of questions popped into her mind, but she pushed them aside. For now.

"So what are you saying, sir?" Donovan asked.

"Her direct involvement could mean trouble. I'd prefer we keep this operation close to our vest for a little longer. I have a feeling this situation could deteriorate further, and fast. If this happens and we need to handle the situation quietly, Blackbriar is better suited than the FBI to disrupt whatever the SVR and Unit 29155 have going on in Egypt."

"Agreed," Donovan said, the strength of his voice surprising Helen.

"Good. How do you feel about paying Steven Cooper a visit?" Manton asked.

Helen looked at Donovan. He gave her an energetic thumbs-up.

"More than happy to do it," she said.

"Find out as much as you can. Depending on your findings, we'll deal with it ourselves or I'll ask the DNI to bring in the FBI."

"Yes, sir."

"Be careful. Both of you. Krupin isn't to be taken lightly," Manton said.

Something in her boss's voice told Helen the director knew more about Krupin than he had let on. The frown on Donovan's face said the same.

"Anything else we should know about her?"

"No. But I can't stress this enough. Don't underestimate Stanislava Krupin."

EIGHTEEN

Seated in the rear passenger seat of his Bentley Bentayga—something he'd never done before—John Dixon was going through the possible outcomes of his upcoming meeting with the two UR Real News reporters.

He would have to tread carefully. These weren't amateurs.

They had fooled him into thinking they were the real deal, that they had sold their tech start-up Frontal for almost four hundred million euros. Dixon was confident he would have seen right through them the minute he sat down with them face-to-face, but that wasn't the point. By that time, they would have already won, having successfully cornered him. There were many ways the two UR Real News investigative reporters could have obtained Frontal's financial statements, but, if he had to take a guess, Dixon would say that the reporters had also dug up the anomalies he had found in the reports. The journalists had then contacted the real Jakub Svoboda and Tomáš Málek and had threatened to call the authorities on them if they refused to cooperate with the investigation.

In meeting with the two reporters, Dixon aimed to convince them to leave his name out of the article. It was imperative that he succeed. Failure to secure a deal wasn't an option.

Although his cover was solid and could withstand scrutiny, it wasn't perfect. If an entire team of investigative reporters decided to get on his case, they'd eventually find out that Raphaël Feldmann was a fraud. This wasn't a truth Dixon wanted out in the world. If he could remain a faceless, nameless collaborator for a bit longer, it would give him time to put in motion his carefully crafted exit strategy. Dixon had the training to disappear now if he wanted, but doing so without notifying his associates and clients would mean losing most of the fortune he'd set aside for his retirement.

Behind the wheel of the Bentley, the former police officer who'd previously driven the silver SUV had remained quiet since they had dropped his friend Kevin off at a hospital near Hořovice, a small town halfway between Pilsen and Prague. The driver of the white panel van occupied the rear seat on the driver's side, holding his broken wrist with his other hand. He, too, had stayed quiet, though Dixon knew exactly what the man was thinking, his hatred written across his face.

Now that the gig was up, the brunch reservation had been canceled and the meeting had been moved to a small café near the offices of *Hospodářské Noviny*, a Czech newspaper headquartered in Prague with a specific focus on economic news, and the employer of the OCCRP journalist who was tagging along.

By the way the driver wove the Bentley through the narrow and often one-way streets of Prague, it was evident he had intimate knowledge of the city. Prague, with just under a million and a half inhabitants, was spread out into ten sprawling districts that fanned clockwise around a central, historic core. A few minutes ago, they had left the wide, traffic-choked boulevards and had entered a maze of narrow, twisted cobblestone streets. Dixon let his gaze drift to the tiny but fascinating shops that lined each side of the road, their windows showcasing paintings, jewelry, porcelain pieces, and even antique gowns.

There were quite a few people wandering about. Young couples pushing strollers, tourists, shopkeepers, all of them out to enjoy a beautiful sunny morning in one of the most fabulous cities on the continent.

"We're almost there," Karl said from the front passenger seat. "The driver will drop us off at the café and circle around until he finds a parking place."

"Fine," Dixon said. "But this car is in immaculate condition. For each scratch I see, I'll break one of your bones. Fair?"

The driver laughed, but it was a dry, nervous laugh. "I'll be careful," he said a beat later as the Bentley came to a stop next to a fire hydrant. "The café is a few doors down across the street."

As Karl and Dixon were about to exit the car, the ex-cop with the broken wrist asked, "You want me in there, too?"

"Why don't you go find some ice to put on that wrist of yours, my friend? Because you're in no shape to be of assistance to anyone," Dixon said, climbing out of the Bentley SUV and closing the door behind him.

Dixon eyed the café and jogged across the street. The store next to the café was a specialist food shop. It was filled with people lined up at a counter, selecting sausages, cheeses, freshly baked bread, and local delicacies.

"Looks good, doesn't? But don't worry, the café sells some fantastic pastries, too. Trust me, I've had the chance to try many of them," Karl said, patting his stomach.

"Are your colleagues here yet?" Dixon asked.

"As a matter of fact, they are," the reporter said, waving at two men walking in their direction. "My other colleague, the one from the OCCRP, will also join us shortly. I just got off the phone with him. He found a parking spot farther down the street."

"What's these guys' real names?" Dixon asked, studying the brothers' gait, trying to figure out if they were a threat.

"Lucas and William Miller," Karl said. "Lucas is the taller of the two."

"They're Americans?"

"Yes, but they moved to Germany more than a decade ago and they now live in Skopje, North Macedonia, where UR Real News is headquartered."

The Millers were meticulously dressed in dark, and clearly expensive, business suits. But that was where the similarities ended. The contrast between the Miller brothers was stark. Lucas was lean, had black hair, and loomed over his shorter sibling by at least six inches. William had blond hair and was beginning to bulge at the waist.

"Gentlemen," Karl said in English, shaking Lucas's hand and then William's.

The brothers turned their attention to Dixon, studying him with their sharp, highly intelligent eyes.

"Karl told us what you did in Stříbro, Mr. Feldmann," William said, speaking in German for Karl's benefit, his American accent almost gone but still perceptible to Dixon's trained ear. "Impressive, yes, but it does raise questions about the kind of man you truly are."

"What my brother meant to say is that we're not sure we should trust you," Lucas said.

Dixon gave them a confident smile. "I can assure you the feeling is mutual. Shall we go inside?" He opened the café's door and gestured for them to precede him. "After you, gentlemen."

As soon as the door opened, Dixon was assailed by the scents of freshly baked chocolate chip cookies and lightly caramelized coffee beans. As he stepped into the café, he heard car doors click into the lock position behind him. It was the last sound he heard before the bomb hidden under the small Mercedes SUV parked in front of the café detonated.

· · · · ·

The blast was powerful, even more so than the bomb maker had predicted. It was as if the SUV had been hit by a Hellfire missile. The Mercedes disintegrated in the initial explosion. Large chunks of shrapnel from the aluminum body of the SUV tore through the air in all directions while the sound of crunching aluminum and steel echoed among the surrounding buildings. Although the shock wave of the explosion alone would have been enough to pulverize Dixon's organs, it was a large piece of shrapnel from the front passenger door that sawed his body in half and ended his life.

· · · · ·

Half a block south, Gustavo Berganza —previously from the Centro Nacional de Inteligencia, or CNI, Mexico's main intelligence agency—walked away. In his hand he held the phone with which he had triggered the car bomb. In Manzanillo, Berganza's *patrón,* General Ramón Velásquez, had been watching in real time thanks to a cheap, store-bought camera installed across the street from the café.

A quick congratulatory text confirmed General Velásquez was pleased with the latest development, which eased some of the stress Berganza had been under. Mexico's former defense minister wasn't a man you wanted to cross or displease in any way.

Berganza removed the battery from the phone and dropped both into a sewer drain. When the police cordoned off the area ten minutes later, he was long gone.

NINETEEN

Donovan looked around as he walked, exploring the immediate neighborhood around Steven Cooper's four-bedroom home in Zamalek, an affluent district of western Cairo popular with European expatriates and wealthy Egyptians alike. To get to Zamalek from the hotel, Donovan had walked to the second-closest metro station. He had changed metro lines twice before hailing a taxi, which had dropped him three blocks west of Cooper's residence.

The peaceful leafy avenues and nineteenth-century apartment buildings and villas made Zamalek one of the most attractive districts of the city. Donovan had no difficulty understanding why so many countries had chosen its streets to house their embassy.

After their call with Oliver Manton, he and Helen had checked into the hotel and both taken a two-hour nap.

There was no point pushing their luck. For their minds to be sharp and their bodies to be rested, they needed the sleep. They'd been going hard for days, and, as accustomed as they were to the intense lifestyle that came with being a Blackbriar operative, the stress and lack of sleep would ultimately catch up with them and slow their reaction time, which in their line of work could be deadly.

Trying to figure out the best way to gain access to Cooper's villa, Donovan checked for windows and balconies around the property and made a mental note of those that had a direct view of it. The RSO's residence was a three-story end-unit town house in a five-unit building. From afar, Donovan had noticed furniture on the roof, implying a deck of some kind, which confirmed what he and Helen had seen on the satellite photos Manton had forwarded to them. Depending on the type of door Cooper had on the rooftop terrace, it could prove to be an easier ingress point than the main entry door since the terrace was shielded from the view of most passersby. The problem was reaching the rooftop in a stealthy fashion. So far, Donovan hadn't come up with a way. He reached for the transceiver—a tiny gray box—clipped inside his waistband and turned the device on by simultaneously pushing the two buttons on top for three seconds. A moment later, his earbud turned on. Wearing the earbud was an operational habit he had no choice about. Uncomfortable at first due to how deep it was positioned in his ear, Donovan had gotten used to it after a few days. He had to admit the tech was pretty neat. Not only did the volume auto-adjust to the ambient noises, but the incorporated miniature microphone also picked up only the sound of *his* voice and would cut out any other sound.

"Are you on, Helen?" Donovan asked his partner, who had stayed behind at the hotel to do research.

"Yep, I'm here. I searched for real estate listings of similar properties hoping it would give us an idea of the interior layout, but I came up empty."

"Keep looking," Donovan said. "I'm heading back to the hotel. We'll sit down together, and we'll come up with a game plan. I'm sure—"

"Sorry, Donovan," Helen said, cutting him off. "Headquarters is trying to reach me on the sat phone. I'll get back to you."

Donovan turned right into a new street, hugging the corner of a luxurious Art Deco apartment building, and stopped a few steps farther, his back against the stone wall and his eyes ready to scrutinize the face of anyone who followed him. After two minutes, he continued walking on the sidewalk heading east, satisfied that no one had paid him any attention as they walked past.

Donovan was two blocks east of Cooper's residence when Helen got back to him.

"Good news," she said. "It turns out that Steven Cooper's house is owned by the United States government."

"No shit," Donovan said, stunned to learn that the American taxpayers were footing the bill for what seemed to be quite a high-end property.

"And since it's government owned, the analysts had no issues digging up everything we need to enter the property."

"They hacked the DSS servers?" he asked.

"They didn't need to," Helen said. "The director wasn't specific about how he got the intel we needed, but this isn't the first time he's pulled a rabbit out of his hat. If I were a betting girl, which sometimes I am, I'd wager that Manton has backdoor access to these things."

"Makes sense. So, what's the deal?"

"Similar to the ambassador's official residence. Cooper's property is rigged with surveillance cameras, two alarm systems, and a panic button, among other things."

"Yeah, we expected that would be the case," Donovan said, entering an office building through the main doors.

"True, but what we didn't know was that the cameras can easily be deactivated by our friends at headquarters and the alarm system rerouted."

Donovan thought this over as he removed his black ball cap and tossed it in a garbage can. He walked past a bank of elevators, turned left, and pushed through a pair of swinging doors leading into a short hall.

"What time frame are we looking at?" He ducked into a men's room.

"I'd say we move now, before Cooper leaves the embassy. We wait for him at his place."

Donovan took off his light reversible jacket and switched it around, going from dark gray to navy blue. He was surprised Helen wanted to move right away on Cooper. It was only their fourth operation together, but so far she'd seemed to be the careful, if not risk-averse type.

"It's probably the best way," Donovan said as he

exited the restroom. "But don't you think we should wait a few days? It would give us a chance to build a pattern of life on Cooper."

"Duly noted, but no," Helen said. "I saw Cooper almost getting into a fistfight with Kirillov. My gut's telling me they're squeezing him for something specific."

"They want more than what he's already given them, and he's not happy about it," Donovan thought out loud.

"Something's about to go down. We can't wait."

Donovan left the building and looked for a taxi. "Understood. Where do you want to meet?"

"In Cooper's living room. I'll send you the details you need."

TWENTY

CAIRO, EGYPT

Donovan wished he could have waited for night-fall before breaking into Cooper's home, but at least at this hour most of his neighbors were probably still at work.

"I'm two minutes out," he said to Helen.

"You're clear to proceed," she replied. "Alarm notifications are being rerouted to headquarters and the main panel has been deactivated. The alarm is now off. Cooper won't receive any new notifications from his alarm."

"Understood." He crossed the street fifty yards west of Cooper's building.

Donovan scanned the sparse pedestrian traffic. There was a cluster of animated young men farther down the block and one couple lazily walking hand in hand. He approached the townhome, walking confidently as if he lived there, and climbed the porch's two front steps.

If the eight-digit code Helen had shared with him didn't work on the first try, he was to leave without attempting to reenter the code.

But it did work, and Donovan heard the lock slide free.

"Door's unlocked," he said. "Entering now."

He opened the door and silently stepped inside the foyer, closing the door behind him. He drew his Glock 29 and attached a suppressor to the barrel. There were no women's or children's items in the vestibule. The only visible clothing was a pair of men's running shoes under a small wooden bench and a sports jacket hung on a hook on the wall. Despite the alarm having been turned on until two minutes ago and headquarters' assurance no one was inside the property, Donovan didn't take any chances and started to clear the townhome. With Krupin and Unit 29155's involvement, it wasn't beyond the realm of possibility that Russian operatives had quietly gained access to the property and were waiting for Cooper's return.

Leading with his pistol, Donovan continued down the hallway to the living area. The space was open concept, and he rapidly cleared the kitchen, living room, and the small powder room.

"First floor clear," he whispered. "Moving to the second floor."

He moved up the stairs, ascending close to the wall so that the boards wouldn't creak under his weight. He paused at the landing and listened for any sounds that would betray the presence of another person.

Nothing.

The second floor had five rooms spread along the length of the hallway. The doors were all open, allowing enough sunlight to filter through for him to see the hallway was clear. The first room to his right was a medium-size, white-tiled bathroom that consisted of a toilet, a bathtub/shower combo, two sinks, and a large, mirrored medicine cabinet. Towels hung on a rack, perfectly folded with all their edges and corners straight together. The other four rooms on the second floor were all bedrooms, one of them—the primary—had an en suite, but no threats were present in any of them. He edged to a window with a view of the small, gated backyard. A brick terrace occupied half the backyard on which sat a weathered teak dining table and six chairs.

"Moving to the third floor," he said.

"Good copy," Helen said. "Still nothing to report on my end. Outside cameras don't show anything out of the ordinary."

The third floor consisted of a small lounge that gave access to the rooftop terrace through a large sliding door. The door was locked, and a piece of wood was jammed in the tracks to keep it from opening. Donovan doubled back to the stairs and took them down to the ground floor.

"The third floor is clear," he said. "Starting second pass."

Now that he had made sure he wasn't under immediate threat, Donovan began a more thorough search of the house. This time he wasn't looking for another occupant, he was surveying the house for hidden weapons or pieces of intel that would help him and Helen understand the situation Cooper found himself in. Donovan discovered a revolver in a holster rigged under the kitchen sink with Velcro. He pulled it out.

Smith and Wesson Model 19. Donovan unloaded the revolver and holstered it back, pocketing the six .357 Magnum–caliber rounds. The second weapon he found was a SIG Sauer P320 attached to the interior of what Donovan assumed to be Cooper's night table. Donovan removed the magazine and the firing pin. He dropped both into his jacket pocket. He continued his search but didn't find any other weapons, at least none that could be accessed rapidly.

"Give me a sitrep, Donovan," Helen asked. "Are you almost done?"

"I found one revolver in the kitchen and one pistol in the master bedroom," he replied. "But no laptop or computer. I haven't gone through all the drawers yet, but I don't think Cooper's keeping anything that could compromise him inside his house. Is he on his way?"

"Maybe. He's leaving the embassy now. Not sure where he's headed, but if he's going home, it shouldn't take him more than eight to ten minutes."

"Understood. I'll be ready, and I'll leave the back door unlocked."

"Got it. Once he's home, I'll wait ten minutes and join you."

Donovan hadn't seen Cooper in years, but there was no doubt in his mind that his former marine instructor would recognize him. What he wasn't sure about was how Cooper would react.

Awarded a Silver Star for heroism in a firefight on a snow-covered mountain in eastern Afghanistan, Cooper wasn't the kind of man who could be easily wooed into revealing anything he wasn't ready to share. Donovan hoped his former instructor would cooperate willingly, but, if he didn't, Donovan knew a thing or two about how to be persuasive.

TWENTY-ONE

Stanislava Krupin sat in a windowless office in the basement of the Russian embassy, sipping at her jasmine tea and staring at the USB flash drive Steven Cooper had handed her at the Internet café. Assigning her an office barely larger than a broom closet with no windows had been Demian Kirillov's way of making her understand how unhappy he was with her showing up unannounced in Cairo—a city he considered his fiefdom.

She didn't mind at all. Truth be told, she was pleased with it, since her temporary workspace was way out of the traffic pattern. The fewer people who knew about her being in Cairo, the better.

She absently toyed with the flash drive, rolling it between her fingers. She had just gotten it back from the two junior officers of Unit 74455—an elite cyberwarfare unit of the GRU—who had tagged along with her to Cairo. It had taken them a few hours to make sure it didn't contain any malware. Still, to be on the safe side, they had given Stanislava a new laptop that wasn't connected to the Internet. If by some miracle Cooper had managed to hide any malware they had missed, the only computer that would be infected would be Stanislava's new device.

She had yet to fully grasp why she'd been sent to Cairo and why a lowly DSS special agent had become such a high priority for Major General Igor Belousov—the commanding officer of Unit 29155 and Unit 74455. She was used to working with an incomplete picture—it was the nature of the job—but this was different. Her initial mission had been to compromise Steven Cooper. It had taken longer—much longer—than she had anticipated, but she'd done it.

Cooper hadn't fallen for any of the classic honey traps she'd orchestrated. She had then hacked into the American's home network, looking at his browsing history, but she had once again come up empty-handed. By all accounts, Special Agent Steven Cooper didn't drink in excess, didn't smoke, didn't gamble, and didn't cheat or watch porn.

Frustrated, Stanislava had started to dig into Cooper's wife's life. She did find that Emma Cooper had a weekend affair while on a business trip to Paris, but it happened more than a decade ago when Cooper was still in the US Marines. Sadly, Emma admitted her indiscretion the moment she got back to the United States. After days of scouring through Cooper's wife, Stanislava had to call it quits. Just like her husband, Emma Cooper was a dead end. Not enough deep flaws to exploit.

But the same couldn't be said about Emma and Steven's daughter, Britney.

The twenty-one-year-old had two Instagram accounts. The first account had just over five hundred followers. It was the account her parents and family friends could see and comment on. It was the account Britney used to post family vacation photos, holiday memories, and pictures of the food she ate. All of it very boring, Stanislava had thought.

The second account, though, the secret one with more than ten thousand followers, was anything but.

For spies like Stanislava who made a living off finding compromising information about individuals, it took very little work to discover Britney's other account, the one her parents and grandparents didn't have access to. Within minutes, Stanislava had hacked into it. Half-naked pictures of Britney abounded, with some of them quite provocative, even to Stanislava. It didn't take much effort to edit these pictures in a way that would make any future employers or universities think twice before hiring her or accepting her as a student. Going one step further, Stanislava spent an extra thirty minutes to create a video that would make even the most hard-core porn addict cringe.

And it had worked.

Last week, tucked away in a corner booth at Cooper's favorite lunch restaurant a few blocks from the American

embassy, Stanislava had discreetly observed Cooper—
who'd been seated alone at a four-person table—eat his
meal. Before he got up to pay his bill, she had emailed
him the video. The effect had been instantaneous. The
twenty-second video had shaken Steven Cooper to his
core. In fact, he'd become violently sick.

Who are you? What do you want? had been his reply to
her email.

And with her solemn promise that his adorable baby
girl would turn into an international porn star if he
didn't cooperate fully, Cooper's resolve had weakened.
Knowing men like Cooper didn't stay on their knees for
long, she'd immediately trapped him with a request for
information. It wasn't a huge, complicated demand,
but they both knew that if he acquiesced to it, he was
doomed.

*Steven, it's important that you understand how serious
we are*, Stanislava had typed back. *We're watching you.
Right now. At your favorite restaurant. Do as we ask and
save your daughter. Try to reach out to any of your friends,
or try to trick us in any way, and her life is over. We need
what we asked from you in five minutes. So, push that plate
of half-eaten mutton kofta curry away and get to work.
Clock's ticking.*

With Cooper successfully reeled in, General Belousov's demands had been mostly logistical in nature,
including but not limited to the schedules of American
government officials visiting Egypt. Belousov's last request, though, had seemed strange. The general wanted
specific data on media conglomerate Mind-U and UR

Real News, one of its subsidiaries. Had this been the intelligence the head of Unit 29155 had been after all along? Belousov was an excellent chess player, often thinking moves ahead of his adversaries, and Stanislava had come to appreciate the general's astuteness. She could see how Russian intelligence could benefit greatly from unrestricted access to Mind-U's applications.

That was why she'd been caught off guard when she had received a message from Belousov notifying her that a senior Mexican official would be reaching out to her regarding Steven Cooper.

A Mexican? What could the Mexican government want with Cooper?

To get some precision on her orders, she had tried to contact the general on several occasions by encrypted phone calls and by sending him messages, but Belousov's assistant—an army colonel—had told her the general wasn't available to take her call or to respond to her emails.

"You have your orders, Major Krupin. I strongly suggest you follow them."

Stanislava looked at the Omega watch on her wrist. She took a deep breath and let it out as a long sigh. The Mexican official was due to call in thirty minutes, and she had no idea what he wanted. She plugged the flash drive into the laptop and waited for the files to upload. It didn't take long. She clicked on the file folder named "Mind-U/UR Real News" and scrolled through its content.

There they are.

Among other things, the folder contained the codes

someone would need to gain administrative access to the critical Mind-U authentication server—the server that controlled and authorized access to all the Mind-U apps by providing users their authentication and authority level. One of the Unit 74455 officers had told her that with that kind of access they could easily modify most of the Mind-U algorithms.

Everything she'd asked of Cooper, he had delivered. It was all there.

And in alphabetical order, no less.

She placed her teacup next to the laptop and started reading. She'd been at it for less than ten minutes when there was a knock on her door, polite but insistent.

"Come in," she said, closing the laptop.

Demian Kirillov stepped into her office. Kirillov was broad-shouldered, with thick arms and thick legs, and a swarthy round face. He resembled more a wrestling champion than the top SVR spy in Egypt. In theory, Kirillov wasn't part of her regular chain of command. She was a major with the GRU and Kirillov was SVR. Practically, though, members of Unit 29155 could pretty much order everyone around. Kirillov knew that, and he'd sent her to a windowless office in the basement in protest.

"Is the flash drive clean?" he asked.

She looked at him, raising an eyebrow. "I'm not an idiot, Demian Fridikovich Kirillov," she said with a straight face. "I know the SVR officers working the technological desk strong-armed the Unit 74455 officers into talking to them. They told me."

The SVR station chief shrugged, a tiny smile playing

over his lips. She wasn't mad at Kirillov for flexing. It was his turf, and she was doing her best not to interfere too much with his regular activities.

"Anything else?" she asked.

Kirillov handed her a blue paper folder. "Maybe. Someone's waiting for Cooper inside his residence."

She cocked her head to one side. "Inside?"

Kirillov pointed to the folder in her hand. "See for yourself."

She opened the file and looked at the pictures. The first photo was of a tall, bearded Caucasian man climbing the steps of the porch of Cooper's residence. The second was of the same man pressed against the front door, presumably about to open it, and the third showed the man inside the foyer of the townhome and in the process of closing the door behind him. The time stamp on the lower right corner of the last picture read 16:13. Less than five minutes ago.

Since the beginning of the operation, the SVR had kept a static surveillance post on Cooper's townhome. It was the first time someone other than a member of Cooper's family had come over in more than a month.

"An American?" she asked.

"We don't know yet who it is. The technological desk officers are putting the pictures through our facial recognition software."

"Let me know as soon as there's a hit," she said.

"Of course. Should I put together a mobile surveillance team to determine who Cooper's friend is?"

One of her phones rang before she could reply. She didn't recognize the number flashing across the screen, but she knew who it was.

The Mexican.

"I need to take this," she said to Kirillov. "Please close the door behind you."

Kirillov's hand was on the doorknob when Stanislava had a sudden change of mind and said, "Now that I think about it, Demian, why don't you stay and listen in."

The big Russian turned to face her, frowning, and probably wondering why he was being asked to stay. Stanislava wasn't exactly sure, either, but despite Kirillov's initial reluctance, he'd proven himself to be competent.

"Please," Stanislava insisted, gesturing to the metal chair across from her desk. "Sit."

Stanislava took the call, putting it on speaker.

"Yes?"

"Thank you for taking my call, Major Krupin," a man said in excellent, precise Russian, but with a decidedly Spanish accent. "I believe General Belousov notified you of my call?"

"Who are you?"

"Yes, of course. My sincere apologies. I'm General Ramón Velásquez. Is my name familiar?"

Stanislava looked at the SVR station chief. He gave her a brief nod, but she could see he, too, was curious as to why Mexico's former defense minister was on the other end of the line.

"It is," she said.

"Good," Velásquez said. "I believe your government and mine will be working together on a special project."

"General Velásquez, I was told to expect a call from a high-ranking, trustworthy ally from Mexico. That is all. I haven't been read in on any special project—"

"Oh, but you have," Velásquez said, cutting her off. "In fact, General Belousov told me you've been working almost nonstop on Steven Cooper's case. Isn't that so?"

"I'm not comfortable sharing anything with you until I hear back from General Belousov," Stanislava said.

"I see."

There was a long pause, as if Velásquez was debating if he should continue the conversation, but the next person to speak wasn't the former Mexican minister of defense—it was General Belousov.

"Major Krupin," Belousov said, his deep voice easy and unhurried. "I can confirm that for this operation, Moscow's and Mexico City's interests are aligned and that we'll be working closely with General Velásquez's people."

Kirillov showed her a piece of paper on which was written: *Velásquez has no official position within the Mexican government.*

"And who would these people be, sir?" she asked.

"Don't concern yourself with that, Major," Belousov said, his voice flat, but threatening all the same. "Is this a problem for you? If it is, I'll have you replaced."

Stanislava felt the blood drain from her face. She'd asked one too many questions. General Belousov wasn't a man you could mess with and live to talk about it.

"I misspoke, sir," she said, hoping to sound sincere. "It will be an honor to work jointly with General Velásquez's team."

"I'm relieved to hear that, Stanislava," Belousov said. "Now, have you looked at the intelligence our American asset has shared with us?"

"That's what I was doing when General Velásquez called. I'm staring at the data as we speak."

"Ramón's team will handle it from here, Major. There are two things I want from you, though. The first is to copy the data of that flash drive onto a cold storage device. The second is to hand back the flash drive to the Unit 74455 officers."

"Yes, sir. Should we keep the static surveillance we have at Cooper's residence?"

"Only for a little while longer. Once Unit 74455 has full administrative control of the Mind-U authentication server, a GRU Spetsnaz team will visit Cooper's wife in Texas. They will take care of Steven Cooper a few days later. But yes, until then please keep an eye on him. You're to convey any unusual events directly to General Velásquez or one of his associates."

"In that case, sir, I have to mention that the SVR station chief reported someone entering Cooper's property earlier today. We—"

"When?" Belousov asked.

"Five minutes ago. Three photos were—"

"Send the pictures to me immediately, Major."

"Give me a few minutes, sir."

"Hurry. I'm waiting."

Stanislava pressed the mute button and looked at Kirillov. The SVR station chief was paler than she had ever seen him. He'd probably heard about Belousov's reputation, too. Efficient, but not afraid to use brutal methods to achieve his objectives. Displeasing General Belousov wasn't a wise career move.

"Do you have digital copies of these?" Stanislava asked, holding one of the three pictures in her hand.

"Yes. You'll have them in two minutes," Kirillov said, rising to his feet and bugging out of her office.

He had been gone for less than ninety seconds when she received a message with the three photos as attachments. She downloaded them to her desktop, then logged in to the special encrypted instant messaging service Unit 29155 operatives used to communicate with each other. She typed a quick note to Belousov, attached the three pictures, and pressed the send button.

Stanislava unmuted her phone and said, "Message sent."

"Received," her commanding officer replied an instant later.

Kirillov ran back into her office and closed the door, but this time he didn't sit, preferring to remain standing next to her.

"Major, is the man in the pictures still inside Cooper's house?" Belousov asked.

She glanced up at Kirillov, who mouthed to her that he was.

"He is," she said.

"Listen to me well, Major Krupin," Belousov said.

"General Velásquez and I are in agreement about this. Use any resources at your disposal, but you can't allow the man in the pictures to come out of Cooper's house alive."

Stanislava was glad General Belousov wasn't in her office to witness the shock on her face. She hadn't seen this coming at all. Not that she'd never killed before. She had. Twice. But they had been defensive killings. Her or them. This wasn't. She had been ordered to kill—no, to assassinate—a man in cold blood. But she was no fool. In her world—or was it Belousov's world?—one needed to adapt if one wanted to survive.

"I . . . understand," she managed to say.

"I know you're up to it, Stanislava," Belousov said, then added, "I don't care about the collaterals. You do what you must. But don't fail me."

"I will not," she replied, almost like an automaton. "Who's the man you want me to eliminate, sir?"

The Russian general didn't immediately reply to her, but she could hear him discussing it with his Mexican counterpart.

"His name is Donovan Wade. He's CIA," Belousov finally said.

Stanislava was sure she'd heard the name before.

Wade.

"General Velásquez and I believe the Americans have somehow found out Cooper has been turned," Belousov continued. "Under no circumstances can Wade successfully contact Cooper."

Next to her, Kirillov scribbled something. *Too late. Cooper has returned home.*

"What if Cooper returns home before we can hit Wade?" she asked.

"Then it's easy. Kill them both."

TWENTY-TWO

As he entered his eight-digit code into the electronic lock of his townhome, DSS Special Agent Steven Cooper couldn't remember the last time he had been so exhausted, both physically and mentally. His eyes were burning and felt gritty from the lack of sleep. He was heartsick over what he had done, and for the way he'd been played. His entire body felt like a piece of glass, as if it could break into a thousand pieces if he fell.

And the worst of it all was that every time he closed his eyes his mind played the sick video of his daughter these Russian cockroaches had fabricated. When he'd first seen it, he had panicked. For the first time in his life, he hadn't known what to do. The only thing his brain—his heart—told him was to save his Britney.

He kept asking himself how someone could concoct such an awful video about another human being.

Sick fucks!

And for what? Really. For fucking what? The detailed schedules of upcoming visits by government officials? The operational plans? Didn't they know that these plans could be updated? That those visits could be canceled? None of it had made any sense.

Until their last request.

The codes to gain administrative access to the critical Mind-U authentication server. Unlike the operational plans and dignitaries' visit schedules, he couldn't control what was going on at Mind-U. His wife certainly could, at least to some extent, but Mind-U was too big a ship to turn on a dime. If a Russian cyber-warfare unit took control of Mind-U, there could be significant problems on the horizon. Not just for the company, but for a good portion of the world population. Mind-U's apps were mostly used in emerging market economies, but they were gaining in popularity in developed countries, too. His wife, Emma, had shared with him that Mind-U research data indicated that within the next three to five years, Mind-U would have approximately two and a half billion subscribers worldwide, with one hundred million of them in the United States.

The illegal invasion of Ukraine had made people realize how fragile liberal democracies really were. Bad actors controlling Mind-U could destabilize the American-led system of internationalism even more by adding fuel to the rising toxic polarization of politics taking place in so many countries—including the United States.

Cooper couldn't allow that to happen. He might be

just a cog in a big wheel, a peon in an elaborate Russian espionage operation, but he was done being played like a fiddle. The day before, he had thought about reaching out to a lawyer friend in New York City who worked for a firm that specializes in national security law, but he had changed his mind before he dialed his friend's number. Cooper wasn't a coward. His aim shouldn't be to protect himself. His priorities were his daughter, his wife, and his country. His daughter was strong. With her mother's help, she would weather the storm coming her way. And, if Cooper played his cards carefully, there was a chance his colleagues in the government could help demonstrate that the evil video in which his daughter was the star had been fabricated.

Cooper closed the door behind him and punched his code into the panel to disarm the alarm. He removed his suit jacket and hung it on one of the free hooks in the vestibule. He walked to the kitchen and loosened his tie. He opened the fridge, grabbed a bottle of water, and undid the top button of his shirt before letting out a long, audible breath.

Just then, a voice behind him, not twenty feet away, startled him. "Long day, Gunny?"

Cooper resisted the urge to spin around to the voice and draw his pistol from his shoulder holster. For now, whoever was behind him had the upper hand. Cooper didn't want to do anything to give the man a reason to shoot him in the back. Keeping his hands away from his body, Cooper turned slowly.

Standing next to the dining table, a tall man was

holding a pistol in a firm, two-handed combat grip, its muzzle pointed at Cooper's chest.

"How have you been, Steven?" the man asked. "You look tired."

It took Cooper an extra second to recognize the man. *Donovan Wade.*

Wade had once been a marine, and a damn good one. Sergeant Wade wasn't the type of marine an instructor forgot easily. Wade had arrived at the basic reconnaissance course ready to learn, and with the right mindset—the warrior one. Physically fit to the extreme, Wade had enlisted in the Marine Corps after completing a university degree through a boxing scholarship. Most university graduates chose to join the marines by becoming officers through one of the four common paths, including OCC, but not Donovan Wade. Cooper had never understood why, but Wade had quickly gained his respect. He'd never really kept track of Wade after Camp Pendleton, but they had crossed paths a few times in Afghanistan, where they had both served with distinction. Cooper had heard Wade had left the Marine Corps to join the DEA, or the FBI. He didn't remember.

But here he was again, in Cooper's living room, pointing a gun at him.

Cooper took in his surroundings. Wade appeared to be alone. How had he managed to enter the property without triggering the alarm? Were the exterior cameras still operational? Had someone at the embassy witnessed Wade breaking in? Were reinforcements on their way?

Just then, triggered by a memory, every muscle in Cooper's body tensed and his breath grew short.

Wade. Harrison Wade.

Last year, while assigned to the American embassy in Rome, Cooper had read a classified intelligence report about a certain Harrison Wade, a CIA officer operating in Italy who was wanted by the FBI for allegedly selling top secret intel to the Russians. The whole thing had been a bit hush-hush, with the intelligence report not being widely circulated or by way of an Interpol notice. Cooper had read it, committed Harrison Wade's picture to memory, and stopped thinking about it.

Until now.

The resemblance was remarkable. Even more striking, though, were the blue eyes—inquisitive and challenging, but friendly. Was Donovan Wade Harrison's brother?

Shit.

Cooper felt a chill run down his spine. Of course they were brothers.

Russian assets. Both of them.

It all made sense now. There was only one logical reason why Donovan Wade was pointing a gun at him. The Russian bitch he'd been dealing with had sent Donovan to kill him. Cooper almost went for his pistol, but instead forced himself to think this through.

Even under the best conditions it would be almost impossible to get a shot off before a former marine recon like Donovan Wade drilled a hole in the middle of his forehead. And these weren't the best of conditions, were they? His issued pistol was in a shoulder holster. Not good. He'd be dead before he'd even tugged his Glock out of the damn thing.

"Are you here to kill me, Donovan?" he asked, hoping to buy some time. "The Russians sent you, didn't they?"

Donovan's mouth opened slightly, but he didn't speak, a flicker of doubt crossing his face. For the slightest moment, Cooper felt an opening, a way to destabilize the man the Russians had sent to kill him.

"You're Harrison Wade's brother, aren't you? Are you a traitor, too? Just like he was?"

TWENTY-THREE

Hearing his brother's name sent a shock wave through Donovan's body. Did Steven know Harrison? Had they worked together? Did that mean that his brother had really been a double agent working for Russia? Could it be true?

No!

Donovan couldn't let Cooper take charge of the narrative. His former instructor wasn't dumb. Cooper would know that mentioning Harrison would destabilize Donovan, allowing him to make a move, to gain control of the situation. Donovan couldn't fall for it. He couldn't allow the thousands of questions he had for Cooper to interfere with the tactical situation he found himself in. Not now. Not before Cooper was secured. The man was a threat. A dangerous one.

"Keep your hands where I can see them and slowly

move to the dining table," Donovan said. "No sudden movement, Steven."

"Whatever you say, Don. Just keep that finger of yours on the trigger guard. I don't want to die today, okay?" Cooper said, obeying Donovan's instructions. "I'm sure we can work—"

"Shut up! And understand this. It's not up to me what happens to you. You, and you only, decide if you live or die."

"What happened to you, Don?" Cooper asked, making his way to the table, his tone tainted with pity and contempt. "I never pegged you as a cold-blooded killer. Was it Afghanistan that changed you?"

"Do as I say, and there's a chance you'll see your wife and daughter again."

That last bit about Cooper's family earned Donovan a death stare, the special agent's eyes burning with hatred, and, for a moment, Donovan was sure Cooper was about to rush him.

"Don't do it, Steven," he warned. "I'll put a bullet through your heart before you can wrap your hands around my throat. Think about your family before you do something stupid."

"You piece of shit. What do you want?" Cooper asked, now standing next to the dining table.

"Here's what I want," Donovan said. "While you keep your right hand in the air, slowly pull the chair at the end of the table toward you and—"

Despite being at least ten years older than Donovan, Cooper sprang into action with the speed and vigor of a man half his age. Grabbing the dining chair with his left hand, Cooper rotated one hundred and eighty degrees and hurled it at Donovan with an almost superhuman force. Had the chair hit Donovan, it would have knocked him out cold.

But it didn't. The chair sailed two steps to Donovan's right—exactly where he would have been standing if he hadn't anticipated the move—and crashed into the kitchen island, knocking over glass jars filled with uncooked pasta. The chair might have missed, but Donovan knew that for Cooper, there was no going back. He was committed.

• • • • •

The moment the chair left his hand, Cooper knew he had misjudged Donovan. The man had already moved to his left, as if he knew Cooper was going to attempt this exact move. For the second time today, Cooper wished he carried his pistol in anything but a shoulder holster. The extra second needed to pull his Glock out was all it would take for Donovan to double-tap him in the chest. Instead of going for his weapon, Cooper squatted low, using his momentum to charge at Donovan with all his might—half expecting to get one or two suppressed rounds in the head.

He was shocked when the point of his shoulder dug into Donovan's solar plexus and he heard him exhale painfully. With his two legs pumping, Cooper rushed forward, slamming Donovan hard against the fridge, still unsure why he hadn't been shot. Cooper's hand darted upward, just as Donovan was bringing down the pistol, and deflected what would have been a knockout hit to the top of his head.

Cooper was so concentrated on getting control of the gun that he never saw Donovan's left hook coming. It caught him directly on the ear. Cooper felt as if he'd been hit by a crowbar. White lights dazzled his brain and his knees buckled. Cooper was on his way down when a loud crack split the air as Donovan's uppercut connected just under his chin, vaulting him backward and into darkness.

TWENTY-FOUR

CAIRO, EGYPT

Helen looked in horror at Steven Cooper's face. The whole right side of his head was swollen. His lips were split and bloody. "What did you hit him with, for God's sake?"

Donovan showed her his left fist. "You're not the only one who did a few rounds," he said. "Mine weren't in a cage, but in a ring."

"Holy shit," she whispered to herself.

Cooper groaned, slowly regaining consciousness. His hands were cuffed, but in the front instead of behind his back. Donovan had ejected the magazine from Cooper's service pistol and disassembled the Glock, its parts laid neatly on the table.

"Anything I should know?" Helen asked Donovan.

"About what?" her partner replied, his back facing her.

Helen hesitated. It wasn't the best time to talk about what she'd overheard on the comms, but she couldn't help it.

"Harrison Wade," she said.

"Not now," Donovan said, glancing over his shoulder. "But later. I promise."

Helen kept her mouth shut, struggling not to push further. Could she trust Donovan? Was she about to be blindsided?

Again?

Her trust in people had sunk her career with the FBI. She'd been forced to quit her dream job a mere two weeks before becoming the first woman ever to graduate from New Operator Training School—the intensive thirty-two-week course an FBI special agent must go through before becoming an HRT operator. The memory of how it all went down was still fresh, and oh, so painful. Her actions—as justified as they were—combined with a misplaced trust in someone she'd considered her best friend, had torpedoed her law-enforcement career. But a voice in her head told her that with Blackbriar, the price she could pay for trusting the wrong person could be much, much higher than losing a job.

Cooper straightened in his chair and looked around him. His gaze stopped on Helen.

"You . . . You were at the café this morning," he said, his voice hoarse.

"I'm yet to put all the pieces together, but you didn't seem happy to be there," Helen replied, taking a step toward him.

"You're American, too?"

"Born and raised," she replied with a smile. "Spent most of my teenage years in Florida. Dad was a Warthog pilot."

Cooper studied her for a moment, as though he was trying to decide if she was trustworthy. She didn't think it was possible, but the side of his head seemed to be even bigger than it had been three minutes ago.

"How can a nice girl like you work with an asshole like him?" he finally asked, nodding toward Donovan.

"Don't look so surprised," Donovan said. "If you hadn't tried to be a hero, you'd already know we don't work with the Russians."

"But we can't say the same about you, can we?" Helen asked. "Who's your contact with the SVR?"

"Why would I tell you anything? I don't even know who you are."

"Ouch, that hurt, Gunny," Donovan said. "All that quality time we spent together in Camp Pendleton. I really thought it meant as much to you as it did to me."

Helen could see Cooper didn't think it was funny. "If you two were with the FBI, there would have been a bigger team and I'd be under arrest."

"You were distraught this morning," Helen said. "You're not doing this willingly, I'm sure of it. Let me help. Let us help, Steven."

Cooper turned his head to Donovan.

"Harrison Wade. Tell me about him," he said. "He's your brother, isn't he?"

Helen considered redirecting the conversation, but

she wanted to know the answer to that question, too. And if the answer prompted Cooper to cooperate with them faster, even better.

Donovan looked uncomfortable, shifting his weight from side to side, clearly wishing he was somewhere else.

"Yeah, he was," Donovan said. "How do you know?"

"Have you ever stood next to him in front of a mirror?" Cooper asked.

"You knew my brother?"

"You keep using the past tense. He's dead, right?" Cooper said.

Before Helen could intervene, Donovan was on Cooper, strangling him, his face flaring with rage and anger. Cooper kicked at Donovan, but her partner didn't let him go, his powerful hands squeezing Cooper's neck. Within seconds, the DSS agent's face began to turn blue.

Helen was about to yell at her partner to let Cooper go, but Donovan did it on his own. Cooper coughed and massaged his neck with his hands. Donovan grabbed his hair and jerked his head back.

"Harrison killed himself. He hung himself in his cell," Donovan hissed. "Does that make you happy?"

Cooper, who was still trying to catch his breath, didn't reply.

"Now, tell us why you were meeting with the highest-ranking SVR officer in Egypt at the café."

Cooper worked his jaw left and right numerous times, then cleared his throat.

"I fucked up," he said a moment later. "I know my career's over. As it should be. I don't know why you're here, but if we're really on the same side and you were sent to put a bullet in my head, please hear me out before you do."

Seeing that Donovan was about to say something, she raised her hand, hoping he'd take her cue and stay silent.

"Then speak," she said. "Tell us everything."

And he did. Not once did Cooper beg for forgiveness, or for his life. His voice broke several times, mostly when he talked about the video the Russians had made of his daughter, Britney.

"Believe it or not, I was about to talk with Campbell about it tomorrow."

"Nelson Campbell? The Cairo station chief?" Donovan asked.

"Yes."

"Why?" Helen asked, although she had a good idea of the reason behind Cooper's willingness to come clean.

"A lot of folks resent Nelson, but he's a good guy. Hardworking. Honest, I think. Something bad happened years ago, and, since then, he's been working hard to make up for it. I trust him."

"That's not what she meant," Donovan said. "She wants to know why you've had a change of heart. You're feeling guilty?"

"Oh. I know it's cliché, but I couldn't look at myself in the mirror anymore. I should have notified my superiors the same day the Russians made contact, but I didn't. The video . . . it . . . it's appalling. I panicked. I flinched. I lied."

"By the time you came to your senses, you were in too

deep," Helen said with as much empathy as she could muster.

"Something like that."

"Do you know the name of the female SVR officer present this morning?" she asked.

"No. I'm sorry."

"How many times have you seen her prior to today?" Donovan inquired.

"Only once. When she first approached me."

"Okay. What about Kirillov or any other Russian intelligence officer?"

Cooper shook his head.

"You're telling us that every other time you visited the Internet café, there were no SVR officers present?" Donovan asked.

"Correct. At least none that I was aware of."

"Did you know they were going to be there this morning?" Helen asked.

"Yes. Their last request was very particular. They wanted the codes to gain administrative access to the Mind-U authentication server. Emma, my wife, she works there."

Helen looked at Donovan, who seemed as confused as she was. "Did you give the codes to the Russians?"

"Yeah. I put it all on a flash drive. That's what they asked for."

"Is your wife aware of this? Is she involved, too?" Donovan asked.

"No. She has no idea."

"Who gave you the codes, then?" Helen asked.

"No one! I used her login and password to download it, okay? Look, I don't feel good about it. In fact, it makes me sick to my stomach to know I've betrayed her."

"And your country," Donovan said. "You betrayed your country, too. Don't you forget that."

Helen's phone vibrated in her small cross-body bag. She unzipped it and pulled her phone out. She connected the call to her earbud.

"Go ahead, I'm listening."

"Two hostiles are approaching the front door," Manton said. "Both are wearing balaclavas. Marines are on their way from the embassy, Helen, but they won't be there for another ten minutes."

Helen ended the call, then said, "Get ready. We're about to have visitors."

TWENTY-FIVE

CAIRO, EGYPT

By the time Helen opened her mouth to tell them to get ready, Donovan was already on the move. The startled expression on Helen's face had told him all he needed to know. Grabbing Cooper by the back of his collared shirt, he hauled his former marine instructor into the kitchen.

"Not a word, Steven," Donovan whispered, crouching behind the kitchen island. "Or you're the first one to catch a bullet."

In his earbud, Helen's voice came in. "Don, you hear me?"

"You're five by five. I'm in the kitchen right next to Cooper."

"Good copy. I see Cooper from my position. I'm in the living room behind the buffet," Helen replied. "Manton advised two men wearing balaclavas were at the front door. They're probably picking the lock as we speak. Marines are on their way. ETA ten minutes."

In his mind's eye, Donovan pictured his and Helen's locations on a map of the ground floor. If both assailants entered through the front door, he'd be the first to see them out of the hallway leading to the open floor plan of the living area, which covered the kitchen, living room, and dining room.

"What's going on?" Cooper murmured.

"Two of your friends are here to say hi," Donovan said, peeking around the island. "Now keep your mouth shut."

"They're not my friends, Don," Cooper pleaded. "Take these damn cuffs off. I can help. Give me your secondary."

"So that you can shoot me in the back? No, thanks. If you want to get to yours, though, go right ahead. It's disassembled on the table. I can see it from here."

Movement in his peripheral vision made Donovan look toward the sliding doors at the back of the house, the ones that opened onto the terrace. A lone figure, dressed in dark clothes and wearing a balaclava, was aiming what looked like a suppressed MP5 right at him. He had Donovan right and center.

Donovan would never know for sure, but for the rest of his life he would believe that Cooper, who was squatted next to him, had seen the balaclava-wearing figure, too, and had decided to save Donovan's life by forfeiting his. Without saying a word, he propelled himself in front of Donovan just as the figure fired three rapid shots through the sliding doors. There was a crashing of glass as the doors shattered. The first round thumped into the wood cabinet two inches from Donovan's head, but the next two ripped through Cooper's chest, slamming him against Donovan.

Helen, who was less than ten feet away from the shooter, pivoted toward the threat, angled her body to the left, and fired several times. The shooter toppled over, hit center mass at close range by three of Helen's rounds.

Donovan shoved Cooper's body away from him, just as two more shooters emerged from the hallway. The next two seconds seemed to pass in slow motion. One shooter spun left, the other right, each clearing their respective corner. Procedures dictated that Donovan engage the target closest to him—the one who had turned left. But if he did that, the other would have a clear and easy shot at Helen's back, who had just begun rotating toward the new threats. Donovan had one shot, and less than half a second to take down the assailant that was about to splatter Helen's brains onto the thick white rug of the living room. Donovan leaned over, completely out of cover, extended his arms fully in front of him, sighted into the shooter's back, and pulled the trigger once, rushing his shot. The ten-millimeter round hit higher and more to the right than Donovan had intended, but the shooter spun and fell, crashing into a coffee table as he did so.

The other shooter was less than a yard to Donovan's right. He'd only seen Donovan when he'd risen from behind the island, but his gun—a suppressed SR-1 Vektor—had already traveled more than half the way it needed to. The problem for the shooter was that, with the suppressor attached to the barrel of the Vektor, he'd need to take half a step back to successfully point the gun in Donovan's direction. The bad news for Donovan was that the same limitation also applied to him. So, instead of trying to line up an impossible shot, he stepped into the arc of the shooter's arms, deflected the man's pistol upward with his own right forearm, and plowed his left knee into the man's groin with enough strength to almost lift him off his feet. The shooter yelled at the unexpected pain, firing a bunch of suppressed shots into the kitchen's ceiling.

But Donovan was far from done.

He head-butted the shooter full in the face, busting the man's nose under the balaclava. The man was well enough trained to know he had to keep Donovan's body close to his to survive the next blow. Donovan, though, having spent years in the ring, knew how to fight in close quarters. He swung his left fist into the man's exposed side twice, putting everything he had into the punches. Donovan felt the shooter's ribs crack like toothpicks against his fist. Donovan took a half step back, jammed the tip of his suppressor under his assailant's chin, and pulled the trigger. The man fell to the floor, half of the top of his head missing.

Donovan pivoted to his left, gun up. Helen had disarmed the other shooter and used zip ties to secure his hands and legs.

"You okay?" Donovan asked, checking the hallway.

"I'm good, but the exterior shooter's gone," she said. "They're wearing soft body armor under their jackets. I aimed center mass. Sorry, I should have assumed there were more than two."

"Don't worry about it," Donovan said, moving back into the kitchen, satisfied no other assaulters were about to barge in. "Good shooting."

Donovan holstered his Glock and kneeled next to Cooper, who lay on the hardwood floor, shivering in a pool of blood. Cooper's eyes had turned glassy, but he weakly grabbed Donovan's arm and brought his pupils into bleary focus. He opened his mouth to speak, but only produced an unintelligible sound.

Donovan nodded, and clasped Cooper's hand under his own and gave it a squeeze.

"I know, brother. And I'm sorry," he said as Cooper's face grimaced in pain.

At last Cooper stopped trying to form the word and simply closed his eyes, taking one last shuddering breath, and then went still.

Donovan checked the former marine's carotid for a pulse. Nothing. He got to his feet and looked over at Helen. She was holding her phone against her ear.

"Cooper?" she asked.

Donovan shook his head. "He's gone."

Helen said a few more words into her phone, then put it back in her bag.

"Manton wants us to leave before the marines get

here," she said. "But let's pick up our brass and take pictures of these two dickheads before we go."

Donovan pulled off the dead gunman's balaclava, which had become wet with blood from his crushed nose, and used his phone to take a photo of the man's face.

Holy shit. It was one of the men who had been at the café earlier in the day.

"Let me guess," Donovan said to Helen, heading to her. "Your guy is Kirillov."

"You got it," she said as she snapped a few shots of the injured Russian spy. "That means the one who got away might be Krupin."

Donovan had only caught a glimpse of the figure who'd shot at him and killed Cooper, but the height and build of the shooter was indeed similar to Krupin's frame.

"The boss wants us to keep him alive?" Donovan asked, his eyes on the injured SVR station chief.

"Not necessarily," she replied. "But why not? He might give up some useful intel."

"If he lives," Donovan said.

Unlike the shooter who lay dead in the kitchen, Kirillov was still alive, though Donovan wondered for how long. The man was on his back, and he didn't look good. He was in rough shape, shivering, his eyes unable to focus. Helen had done a good job with the zip ties. Donovan grabbed the man by the meat of his arm and rolled him to his side until he could examine the Russian's back. Kirillov grunted.

The entry wound was hard to miss.

"You should have worn body armor like your colleague," Donovan said in Russian.

His 10-millimeter round had hit the SVR officer in the back and shattered his right shoulder blade. By the wheezing sound Kirillov made with each breath he took, and the red foam at the corner of his mouth, Donovan imagined a bone fragment had pierced one of the Russian spy's lungs.

"All right," he said, stepping away from the downed SVR officer. "Time to go."

TWENTY-SIX

Operation Treadstone Director Levi Shaw poured milk over his bowl of sugary cereal and sat down to eat. Not the healthiest choice for the lunch hour, but with his fridge almost empty, his options were limited. It was his first day off in weeks, and he'd decided to sleep in until six a.m.

He'd started the day by watching the news on television but had turned it off after a few minutes. Too depressing.

If it bleeds, it leads. Shaw got it. He'd been an intelligence officer for more than thirty years. He understood how the news cycle worked. Humans nowadays were programmed to love drama, and bad news grabbed people's attention. Bad news drew more clicks. More clicks brought in more revenue. It wasn't complicated.

As the man in charge of Treadstone, Shaw was responsible for running the program's black operations the world over. Bad, disheartening news was part of his daily routine, but today he needed something else.

Peace and quiet.

The last twelve months had been taxing to the extreme. The CIA-sanctioned ambush intended to oust him as director of Treadstone had forced his hand. To stay alive—and to keep control of the program—Shaw had met with General Joseph Mitchell, the chairman of the Joint Chiefs of Staff, and had offered him Treadstone. The transition from CIA to the Department of Defense hadn't been without difficulties, but despite the broader responsibilities given to the program, Operation Treadstone had finally found its footing and was functioning as it was supposed to.

Wanting to escape from the daily grind for a few hours—and hoping to keep the migraines away—he had gone out for a long bike ride on the Mount Vernon Trail. He'd enjoyed it immensely, but he was now paying the price with stiff legs and a sore back.

The encrypted phone next to his glass of orange juice rang. With a sigh, Shaw looked at the number on the screen.

He frowned.

It was the number of the watch officer at the DIAC—the Defense Intelligence Analysis Center. Located on the premises of Joint Base Anacostia-Bolling in Washington, DC, the DIAC was where the Treadstone tactical operation center had relocated.

Shaw considered not picking up, but who was he kidding? Not taking the call wasn't even an option. He pressed the phone to his ear. A double-click confirmed the end-to-end encryption a moment later.

"Levi Shaw," he said.

"I apologize for bothering you on your day off, Director Shaw, but you're needed at the DIAC immediately."

Shaw was puzzled, wondering what could justify his urgent return to the DIAC. None of his assets were presently deployed in a danger zone. "What's going on?" he asked.

"Echelon has picked up chatter about a certain Raphaël Feldmann, sir. He apparently died in the Czech Republic. There's a notice that you're to be contacted in the event . . ."

But Shaw wasn't listening anymore. He felt like he'd been gut punched. John Dixon was a trusted, deep penetration Treadstone agent. He'd been one of the first agents to be permanently deployed overseas—almost thirty years ago. For as long as he could remember, Shaw had never had any issues with John Dixon, something that couldn't be said about many Treadstone agents—Adam Hayes and Jason Bourne coming to mind. True, Dixon was skimming money off the top of the portfolios belonging to the criminals and tax cheats he had as clients, but Shaw couldn't care less. Dixon had proven himself to be reliable and loyal, rare commodities in today's world.

"Sir? Are you still there?" the watch officer asked.

"Yeah. Sorry. Did you say the Czech Republic?" Shaw asked.

"Yes, sir, that's what I said."

What the hell was Dixon doing in the Czech Republic? The only thing Shaw knew with certainty was that Dixon wasn't there on a Treadstone-sanctioned mission. If Echelon—the NSA's listening program—had picked up on conversations about Raphaël Feldmann and not about John Dixon, there was a chance that Feldmann was yet to be exposed as an American intelligence agent.

"Tell me what happened," Shaw said, heading to his bedroom to change clothes.

"Sir, I really think it would be best for you to come—"

"For God's sake, son, tell me what the hell happened in the Czech Republic," Shaw barked, losing his temper.

"Yes, sir. There was an explosion in Prague, next to a café."

"Be precise, dammit! What kind of explosion?"

"Initial reports have mentioned a potential car bomb," the watch officer replied.

Shaw's heart sank. A targeted killing. *Fuck*.

"How many casualties?" he asked, removing a new dark blue sports jacket from a hanger.

"Unknown at this time, but Feldmann is the only body the authorities have identified so far. The others are too severely burned."

Shaw ended the call and dialed his driver's number.

"Where are you?" Shaw asked him. "I need to rush to the DIAC."

"I'm downstairs, sir. Usual spot. I had a feeling you'd call. You're simply unable to take a full day off."

TWENTY-SEVEN

Director Manton strode around his desk, pacing his office with his hands behind his back, anxious to hear back from his team in Cairo. He really craved another cup of coffee—an entire gallon, actually—but he'd probably suffer an acid reflux attack if he swallowed even one more sip.

The situation at Steven Cooper's townhome had turned into a real tragedy. Cooper was dead, and so were two of the three SVR officers who raided his house. Thankfully, Helen and Donovan were unscathed, and the analysts were doing their best to scrub any virtual traces of their presence in the neighborhood. Manton had been advised that the marines had been the first to arrive on scene and had called in the local authorities. When the marines arrived, Kirillov was still alive, but, despite his best efforts, the navy corpsman who had tagged along with the marines had been unable to keep him breathing. By the time the Egyptian authorities arrived at the scene, the SVR Cairo station chief was dead.

Helen and Donovan were on their way to their secondary safe house to grab their surveillance gear and regroup. Manton wanted them out of Egypt as soon as possible and was looking forward to debriefing them personally. Cairo had been their fourth mission together, and Manton was pleased at how well they had handled themselves thus far. Of course, Manton acknowledged that he was looking in from the outside and had no way of knowing the true dynamics between Helen and Donovan, but he liked what he saw.

Both of them were extremely talented, and, in Manton's opinion, complemented each other very well. That said, and through no fault of their own, both Helen and Donovan had been damaged goods when he had recruited them for Blackbriar. After careful consideration, Manton had made the decision not to share between his two operatives too many details about their personal backgrounds. It would be best if they were to share whatever they wanted to on their own terms.

"Director Manton," Faith Jackson said as she poked her head into his office. "The DNI's on line one for you."

"Thank you, Faith," Manton replied.

Manton punched the button to take the call. "Manton speaking, sir."

"Any updates on the situation in Cairo?" Edward Russell asked.

"Yes, sir. There've been some developments," Manton

said, wondering if Russell had received any sort of intel from another source prior to his call. "We're presently working on getting the team out of Egypt as fast as we can."

"Yes, so I've heard," Russell said, confirming Manton's suspicion. "I got a call from the secretary of state. He's confused, and so am I. What the hell happened? The only thing I heard from you about this Cairo operation was that you had rerouted a team to Egypt to investigate a possible threat to my security. Since then, all I got from you is total radio silence. That is not acceptable, Oliver. Do you hear me?"

"I do, sir. I appreciate what you're saying. I really do. But you have to understand that these missions are fluid. Blackbriar operatives have a lot of leeway to accomplish the task we give them, and I myself don't receive situation reports as often as I'd like."

"You haven't answered my initial question," the DNI said.

"I'll have more details later today, sir, but what I can tell you now is that Demian Kirillov, who happens to be the SVR station chief in Cairo, was running an op on DSS Special Agent Cooper."

"The SVR was trying to recruit a DSS agent?" Russell asked.

"And they succeeded," Manton replied. "Steven Cooper has leaked classified information to the Russians."

"You have to be kidding me," Russell said, his voice betraying his anger.

"Earlier today, Kirillov, another SVR officer whose

name we don't know at this time, and Unit 29155 officer Stanislava Krupin met with Cooper at an Internet café in downtown Cairo," Manton said.

"They actually met in person? Why?"

"I haven't debriefed my team yet, so I can't answer your question. What I can tell you is that less than one hour ago, Kirillov, the other SVR officer, and possibly Stanislava Krupin raided Steven Cooper's residence in Zamalek."

"They did what? Have the Russians lost their fucking minds?"

Manton could tell the DNI was pissed off, but he continued anyway.

"During the attack, two Blackbriar operatives were inside the house interrogating Cooper. They killed Kirillov and the other SVR officer. All in self-defense, of course."

"Of course," the DNI growled, clearly unhappy.

"Regrettably, Steven Cooper was killed, possibly by Krupin."

The DNI exhaled loudly. "What about her? You didn't say what happened to Krupin."

"Right. Well, if it was indeed she who participated in the attack, one of my operatives shot her, but she might have been wearing a bulletproof vest because she got away."

"Do we have people looking into hospitals to see if she has checked in anywhere?"

"Yes, sir. But frankly, she wouldn't go to a hospital. The SVR and GRU have doctors on call for such scenarios."

"Okay. When do you expect to hear back from your team?"

"Any minute now."

When the DNI didn't speak for what seemed like a full minute, Manton thought he had lost the connection.

"Sir?" he asked.

"Still here, Oliver. I just needed to wrap my head around what you told me, because, believe it or not, Cairo wasn't the reason I was calling you."

"Oh. What can I help you with, then?" Manton asked.

"Are you aware of an explosion that took place in the Czech Republic earlier today?"

"I briefly saw footage of the carnage on the news. Why?"

"One of the victims is Raphaël Feldmann," Russell said. "He was a senior investment banker with a Swiss bank in Zurich."

"Okay. You want me to look into it for you?"

The DNI didn't answer directly, but continued, "Raphaël Feldmann's real name is John Dixon. He was Treadstone."

Manton had never heard the name. "I don't remember—"

Russell cut him off. "He assumed a false identity thirty years ago. For the last two decades, he invested the money of wealthy Europeans, some of them pretty high up in the underworld."

"You think he got nailed by one of those criminals?" Manton asked.

"I honestly don't know."

"With all due respect, if Dixon was Treadstone, why

are you talking to me? Shouldn't you reach out to Levi Shaw?"

"That's the thing," Russell said. "Shaw contacted me. He had no idea Dixon was in Prague. He's afraid Dixon was the designated target, but he doesn't know why. And he's worried."

With all the problems that had plagued Treadstone recently, if Manton had been in Shaw's shoes, he'd be worried, too.

"Was Dixon on a sanctioned mission in the region?" he asked.

"Shaw told me he wasn't. He's concerned there's another leak within Treadstone. Maybe he's right, but maybe he isn't."

"You want Blackbriar to get involved in this?" Manton asked.

"Cairo is only a short flight from Prague, isn't it?" Russell said, making his intention clear. "I want to know what Dixon was doing in Prague, and who he was meeting with. We need to figure out if it's a case of being in the wrong place at the wrong time, or if he was indeed targeted. Until we know for sure, my recommendation to Director Shaw was to suspend all noncritical Treadstone operations."

"I see," Manton replied, thoughtful.

"What's wrong, Oliver?"

"I have only three teams of two operatives," Manton said. "One is still stuck in Belarus, another needs at least another three to four days in South Sudan, and the team in Cairo just went through a shoot-out with Russian agents."

"And they performed very well, didn't they? Am I wrong in assuming they did exactly what they were supposed to do?"

"No, sir. You're correct."

"All right, then. It's settled. Get your team to Prague ASAP. And this time, keep me in the goddamn loop."

TWENTY-EIGHT

PRAGUE, CZECH REPUBLIC

Donovan climbed the concrete steps of the apartment building—a three-floor quadplex—that sat a ten-minute walk from where the car bomb had obliterated the café. On his shoulder was a nylon duffel bag that would have pushed the weight and size limits at an airport check-in counter.

Headquarters had rented a two-bedroom apartment through an online booking agency using new identities and credit cards backstopped by Blackbriar. Their flights from Cairo to Prague—with a four-hour stopover in Bucharest—had been painful. At least it had been for him. While Helen sat in roomy business-class comfort with free drinks, legroom, and passable food, Donovan was crammed into a cheap, backbreaking economy seat with his knees crushed against the seat in front of him.

Donovan knocked on the apartment's door. There

was the click of a dead bolt followed by the rattle of a chain lock being removed, and the door opened. Donovan stepped into the apartment and placed the duffel bag in the middle of the floor.

"How was it?" Helen asked. "You got everything we need?"

"Yes, ma'am. That's the cool thing about operating in a city in which Blackbriar has set up a weapons cache."

"Show me."

Donovan unzipped the duffel bag and pulled out a pair of CZ 75 pistols with hip holsters, two SureFire suppressors, and six sixteen-round magazines.

Helen picked up one of the pistols. She inserted her finger into the magazine well to make sure it was empty, racked the slide, pulled the trigger. Satisfied the mechanism worked fine, she slammed a full magazine into the pistol and racked the slide to chamber a round.

"What else do you have?" she asked.

Donovan placed two hand grenades, two incendiary devices, and two MP5SDs—an MP5 with an integrated suppressor—and six thirty-round magazines next to the duffel. The communications and audio and visual surveillance gear came next, including two new earbuds.

"What about transportation?" Helen asked while she inserted a fully charged earbud into her ear canal.

"BMW X5 parked in an interior garage a two-minute walk from here," Donovan said, handing her a set of keys. "These are the spare keys for the weapons cache and the X5."

Helen dropped the keys into her jeans pocket and

said, "Come here. I'll show you the pictures I took while you were out shopping."

They spent the next fifteen minutes looking at photos of the area where the bomb had detonated.

"I spoke to a bookstore owner who lives in the neighborhood close to the café," Helen said. "She said that her uncle is with the Czech police, and he believes there were five people killed by the blast and at least twice as many injured. The lady told me one of the injured folks is a reporter who works at the *Hospodářské Noviny*, a Czech newspaper headquartered a few steps away from the café."

"That doesn't sound unusual," Donovan said. "The reporter was probably out for lunch or a coffee break."

"For sure. I'm not disputing that, but the *Hospodářské Noviny* issued a statement that named the journalist as one Andrej Burian, one of their star reporters."

Donovan, who was installing a tactical light on his MP5SD, stopped what he was doing and tried to remember if he had heard the name before, because it certainly rang a bell.

"The name sounds vaguely familiar," he said.

"In journalistic circles, Burian made a name for himself as part of the Organized Crime and Corruption Reporting Project consortium," Helen said. "I checked him out, and he's been involved in a number of high-profile investigations implicating politicians, bankers, and government organizations."

Donovan scowled. In recent years, investigative

journalists had lifted the lid on scandals of gigantic proportions, often accurately reporting about major corruption activities within a government's highest level, but Donovan had also seen the other side of the coin when entire intelligence operations had to be scrapped because reporters had divulged information that should never have been shared with the public.

Had Andrej Burian simply taken a walk and gone out to grab a muffin or chocolate chip cookie at his favorite café, or had he been on his way to question John Dixon about his affiliation with an American black ops unit? Then again, maybe he was looking at this the wrong way. Was it possible that it was Dixon who had contacted the reporter? To talk about Treadstone?

Shit.

Helen's expression told Donovan she'd reached the same conclusion.

"I think paying Burian a quick visit at the hospital should be our first step," he said. "You know if he's healthy enough to have visitors?"

"I think so. He's been tweeting nonstop for the last hour."

"How do you want to play this?" he asked. "Journalists or FBI?"

"Definitely FBI," Helen replied without hesitation. "A reporter like Andrej Burian will recognize another journalist when he sees one, and I mean no offense, but you look like anything but a reporter, Donovan."

Donovan chuckled as he fitted the sling on his

MP5SD. "Agreed. Anyway, getting credentials from a US news organization isn't easily done on short notice."

He dug into the duffel bag and took out two leather FBI credential cases. He opened the first one, looked at the photo, and handed it to Helen.

"These are much easier to acquire," he said. "Bring back any memories?"

Helen took a moment to look at the badge and credentials.

"Holy shit," she muttered. "That looks and feels like the real thing."

"Because it is," Donovan said. "The legal attaché, heck, sometimes even the CIA station chief, keep blank credentials and original badges of different agencies at the embassy."

"I didn't know that. How's that even legal?"

Donovan looked at her funny while checking the spring tension on one of the MP5SD magazines with his thumb. "You're kidding, right?"

Helen shook her head. "Old habits," she said, pocketing the credentials. "I assume these credentials are back-stopped, too?"

"If they made it to the weapons cache, you bet they are. One of the NOCs probably dropped them off. I did it a few times myself when I was in Paris."

Donovan cringed at the realization he'd just shared something that could potentially open a can of worms, or at least a torrent of questions from Helen.

"Tell me about Paris," Helen said, as if she were asking

about his weekend. "I've never really been, but I heard it's beautiful, especially in the spring. Is that true?"

Donovan forced a smile. "Maybe later. For now, let's concentrate on what we need to do to get to that Czech reporter."

"Right. We'll circle back, though. As for our friend Andrej, here's what I think we should do."

TWENTY-NINE

Gustavo Berganza's face contorted in anger.

"I assure you there's no need to send Francisco Abalos to Prague," he said. "I can take care of this mess."

"You had your chance," General Velásquez said. "And you fucked it up."

Berganza grimaced at the rebuke. He was operating on paper-thin ice. He had to be careful not to antagonize Velásquez even more.

"Sir, give me the opportunity to fix my mistake," Berganza said, cringing at the words. He hated admitting responsibility for anything other than successes.

"Francisco's skills are more attuned to what needs to happen next," the general said. "But if you were to prepare the field for him, I might be willing to consider this as atonement for your recent failure. Very few people know that Lucas Miller is still alive, and I'd like to keep it that way. Francisco will meet you at the apartment in a couple of hours, Gustavo, but in the meantime, I want to know who tries to contact Miller."

"Abalos, he's . . . he's already on his way?" Berganza asked, stunned.

The line went dead. General Velásquez hadn't even bothered to reply. Furious, he threw the phone across the room without looking. The device flew through the open door of the bathroom, smacked off the tiled wall above the bathtub, then bounced back into the toilet, where it sank.

Mierda!

He rushed to the toilet and retrieved the phone, thanking God that whoever had last used the toilet had had the decency to flush it.

He dried it with a face cloth, still not believing that General Velásquez had decided to send Francisco Abalos to Prague. Abalos was the general's personal representative in Europe. Words that came out of Francisco Abalos's mouth were as if they had been spoken by the general himself.

And the man is a raving lunatic.

Velásquez's call had been unexpected. Velásquez had been told by a reliable source that one of the two UR Real News reporters had survived the blast. He even knew the hospital room Lucas Miller had been assigned.

Berganza swore out loud. How was it even possible that Lucas Miller had survived?

Berganza had been there. He'd seen the explosion.

He'd seen the devastation. And so had General Velásquez. It was unfair for the general to lay the blame entirely on Berganza's shoulders. He'd done everything by the book. Why should he be held responsible? Surely it was God himself who'd chosen to save the reporter. What else could it be if not divine intervention?

"What's going on, *patrón*?" Salvador asked.

Berganza took a calming breath and looked at his second-in-command. The man had been sitting in front of the television playing stupid video games with a pair of headphones on. At six feet tall, Salvador was two inches taller than Berganza and a good twenty pounds heavier. He had coal-black hair and the sort of face that always looked sad. In his mid-forties, Salvador was ten years older than Berganza, but had climbed as high as he ever would within Velásquez's organization. A former officer with the Cuerpo de Infantería de Marina—the amphibious infantry force of the Mexican Navy—he'd transitioned over to the dark side for the same reason Berganza had.

Money.

Salvador had been a member of the Gulf Cartel for six years before he was recruited by General Velásquez.

"One of the reporters, Lucas Miller, is still alive," Berganza said.

Salvador didn't reply, but his eyes widened. He, too, knew what it meant. A job not done properly, for whatever reason, was a job you didn't walk away from. Not if you wanted to grow old.

"I can take care of it for you, *patrón*," Salvador offered.

Berganza shook his head. "That time has come and gone, my friend. The general is sending Francisco Abalos to take over."

Salvador's eyes bugged out. "We could have taken out the surviving reporter ourselves," he said. "Sending Abalos over is an overkill, *patrón*. Killing a bedridden man isn't rocket science."

"I know, but it's out of our hands now," Berganza replied. "Velásquez wants us to keep track of anyone who's trying to talk to Miller."

Salvador tossed the video game controller on the sofa and got to his feet, eager to get going. He knew his fate was directly linked to Berganza's.

"Which hospital is he at?" he asked.

"General University Hospital," Berganza replied. "Go now, Salvador. Grab a taxi and get to the hospital. Me and the others will get the surveillance gear and the weapons ready, then we'll join you as soon as we can with the SUV."

THIRTY

Helen decided it would be easier and quicker for them to walk from the apartment to the hospital than to take the car. Finding the hospital wasn't a problem, but figuring out which room Andrej Burian occupied would be more challenging. Czech wasn't one of the seven combined languages either she or Donovan spoke.

The energetic lady manning the desk at the main entrance directed them to the emergency room. The ER was buzzing with activity. The waiting room was packed, with not a single free chair in sight. The hurried pace of the staff, the noisy cacophony of phones ringing, crying babies, and people coughing reminded Helen why she hated hospitals. She walked to the receptionist's window and had to wait a good three minutes before the woman behind the glass hung up the phone and looked away from her computer screen.

Before she even said a word, Helen could tell the poor woman was completely drained. Gaunt and drawn, her weary, bloodshot eyes were a sign that she'd probably been on duty for well over sixteen hours.

Helen put on her most charming smile and showed the receptionist her FBI credentials.

"We're here to see a patient of yours," Helen said. "His name is Andrej Burian."

The woman put a finger to her ear and shook her head. "English . . . No," she said, then waved at a uniformed security guard standing at the far corner of the waiting room.

"English," the receptionist said, pointing at the security guard.

Helen turned to face the guard, a man of medium height in his early twenties with an easy smile to go with his green eyes. He wore a pair of black combat trousers, a black T-shirt, black ankle boots, and a two-way radio was clipped to his belt next to a set of shiny silver handcuffs Helen was convinced had never been used.

"Hello," Helen said. "The lovely lady at the reception told me you speak English?"

The man's smile grew even wider than it already was. A chipped tooth was now visible. "Yes. My girlfriend is British, so I had to learn, you know?"

Helen returned the man's smile. "How nice of you.

I'm sure she appreciates it very much. I know I would," she said, teasing him just a bit.

The security guard blushed, his cheeks turning deep red. He cleared his throat, then offered his help. "What can I do for you?"

She signaled for him to follow her away from the crowd, as if what she was about to share with him was of such importance that she couldn't trust anyone but him with the information.

She opened her leather case and showed him her badge. "I'm with the FBI," she said, keeping her voice low.

The guard stiffened, and he looked at her, his green eyes gleaming.

"And do you see the tall, bearded man standing next to the reception desk?" Helen said, nodding toward Donovan. "He's my partner."

On cue, Donovan grinned and gave a little wave.

"What's going on?" the guard asked, his voice suddenly turning shaky. "Please tell me there isn't another bomb?"

"No, we don't think so," Helen said. "But we need to speak with a Czech reporter who was injured in the explosion. We believe he was brought here to this hospital."

"I understand. What is his name?"

"Andrej Burian," Helen said.

"Okay. Wait here," the guard said, heading to the reception desk. He squeezed behind the receptionist and picked up a clipboard. He flipped a few pages, then looked over at Helen and gave her a thumbs-up.

She returned the gesture.

The guard said something to the receptionist, and, to Helen's utmost surprise, she laughed.

He's a good kid.

The guard gently squeezed the older woman's shoulder and hurried back to Helen.

"I found him. He's on the third floor. Room 309. I'll escort you to his room, but then I have to return to my post. You'll have to talk to his doctors. It will be up to them to decide if you can see him."

"Of course. This all makes perfect sense," Helen replied.

"Please follow me. The elevators are this way." The guard gestured to a corridor that led away from the crowded waiting area. "Is your partner coming?"

"Don't worry about him. He'll catch up to us. Lead the way."

• • • • •

Donovan took his time reaching the staircase leading to the upper floors. He wanted to take a few minutes to explore the hospital's layout. If something happened, he wanted to know where the exits were and the quickest routes to get to them. By the time he reached the third floor, Helen was in discussion with a Czech police officer and two sleep-deprived doctors wearing long lab coats and stethoscopes wrapped around their necks. The security guard from downstairs was nowhere to be seen. Donovan assumed he had returned to his post in the waiting room.

"Here he is. This is my partner, Special Agent Jeremy Cross," he heard Helen say.

"How are you?" Donovan asked, joining the group.

"Doctor Shepherd here is an American," Helen said. "She's from Connecticut. Her—"

"No way," Donovan said, feigning interest. "What brought you here?"

The look on Helen's face told him he'd spoken too quickly.

Dr. Shepherd scrutinized him, her dark eyes narrowing in suspicion. She had an olive complexion and long black hair she kept secured in a ponytail. "My husband is the deputy chief of mission at the US embassy," she said. "I'm sure you've met him, right?"

Helen gave him an imperceptible nod.

"Of course. Alan is a fantastic guy. How's he doing? It's been a while."

Dr. Shepherd exchanged a few words in Czech with the other doctor, who then left without even acknowledging Donovan.

"Please excuse her manners. She's been working for thirty-six hours straight," Dr. Shepherd explained. "And so has this officer."

"Is . . . there anything I . . . do for you?" the Czech police officer asked in broken English.

Dr. Shepherd spoke to him, and even though Donovan couldn't understand what was being said, he caught the word FBI a few times.

The Czech officer, who must have been pushing fifty, gave Donovan and Helen each a curt nod and returned to a chair set against the wall across from the elevators.

"I'm not sure who you two work for, though I have

my suspicions, but you're no FBI agents," Dr. Shepherd said, her voice barely above a whisper.

"I'm sorry—" Helen started but stopped mid-sentence when Dr. Shepherd gently, but firmly, placed a hand on her shoulder.

"Let me finish," Dr. Shepherd said, giving each of them a hard, no-bullshit look. "Last night over dinner at our house, my husband's friend, who, by the way, happens to be the *legat*, told us an FBI team is on its way from Quantico at the request of the Czech police. But they won't get here for another two days."

Dr. Shepherd's eyes moved from Helen to Donovan, as though she was challenging them to deny what she'd just said.

Donovan chose wisely. He kept his mouth shut, and Helen did the same.

"Please, I have patients to take care of," Dr. Shepherd said. "Don't waste my time. Just tell me what it is you want."

"Andrej Burian. We'd like to speak with him," Donovan said. "We were told he's in room 309."

Dr. Shepherd let out a dry laugh. "Good luck with that. He won't talk to you, or to anyone else for that matter, without his lawyer present."

Then she cocked her head to one side, and once again looked at Donovan in a way that made him uncomfortable.

"What is it?" he asked.

"It's just that I thought you would have wanted to speak with the American journalist, Lucas Miller," she replied.

Donovan tried to hide his surprise at the mention of

an American journalist, but Dr. Shepherd must have seen the confused look on his face because she added, "You know, the one living in North Macedonia? His brother William didn't make it. The paramedics brought him here, but he died before we could get to him."

"We'd definitely be interested in speaking with him, too," Helen said. "How's he doing?"

"Surprisingly well, considering. Although we removed more than two dozen pieces of shrapnel from Lucas's back and legs, it was his brother and another deceased, a banker from Switzerland, I think, who caught the brunt of the explosion, their bodies acting like a shield for Lucas. Still, he got second-degree burns pretty much all over his back, head, and limbs. But he'll live."

"With what you just said about the gravity of his injuries, I'm surprised he's in good enough shape to talk," Donovan said.

"I didn't say he was," the American doctor retorted. "I'll need to evaluate his condition first."

"I understand, but we would only need a few minutes with him," Helen said.

Dr. Shepherd motioned for a nurse to come over. "Let me talk to Mr. Miller first. I'll assess his medical condition. If he's willing to talk to two FBI agents," Dr. Shepherd said, using her fingers to put the word FBI in air quotes, "and you promise me you'll stay with him for less than five minutes, I'll give you my blessing."

"Fair enough," Donovan said.

THIRTY-ONE

Lucas Miller couldn't remember much of anything. One second he was walking into a café, the next he was hit by a massive, powerful heat wave. Now, lying in a hospital bed and hooked up to an IV drip with pain medicine, anything more than a slow, short breath caused deep waves of nausea. For the first few hours, as he drifted in and out of consciousness, people in surgical gear came and went. At some point, a serious-looking doctor, an American, had told him what had happened. He had asked her about his brother William, but he'd already known the answer.

Still, the confirmation of his brother's death had shaken him like nothing he'd ever experienced. Again, as he thought about his lost brother, his eyes teared up and his chest began to heave, causing him even more physical pain. He started to sob in a subdued, hopeless way.

Deep down, he felt responsible for William's death. They had been playing a dangerous game. There was a reason why Mind-U had been paying them these huge salaries—three times what they used to pull at Politico. For the last month he and William been working on two high-profile but perilous stories. After acquiring UR Real News last year for an undisclosed amount of money, Mind-U's board of directors had wanted to transform UR Real News from a dubious news platform into one of the most reliable sources of international news for emerging markets. One of the first things they had done had been to hire the Miller brothers—with stellar journalistic reputations in the US—who would bring legitimacy to the organization. Knowing they needed their first couple of investigative pieces to be huge, well-researched, and hard-hitting articles, Lucas and William had decided to tackle two trenchant subjects—money-laundering operations performed by private bankers in Switzerland, and the growing influence of Mexican drug cartels in US politics. As the brothers dug deeper into the reach of the cartels, they'd discovered that General Ramón Velásquez, Mexico's former defense minister, had recently brokered an unprecedented truce among the top five drug cartels in Mexico to participate in a joint operation in the United States.

Proyecto de la Verdad. The Truth Project.

He and William had been in agreement that if anything were to happen to them, the Mexicans would be the ones to flex their muscles to scare them out, not the Swiss. From the get-go, they had operated under the assumption that the cartels had only a limited reach in Europe and that if he and his brother stayed away from Mexico and Central and South America, they should have been safe on this side of the Atlantic.

Wrong.

The fact that Raphaël Feldmann and William were dead indicated how badly they had misjudged the influence and power of the Mexican drug cartels—even in Europe. Still, Lucas couldn't shake the feeling that he was missing something. The Swiss banks weren't without teeth. They, too, had the resources to fight back.

Shit.

Either way, Lucas now realized that he and his brother had taken way too big a bite. It was evident that their questions had rankled people who didn't like to be disturbed.

Had contacting Feldmann tripped some kind of fail-safe?

The man was dangerous. There could be no doubt about that. There had been a certain aura of violence about Feldmann. Lucas had felt it immediately. A decade ago, he had spent a month embedded with a team of American Special Forces in Iraq and he'd sensed the same intensity in them that he'd sensed in Feldmann.

Feldmann had outmaneuvered the surveillance team, hadn't he? He'd sent one of the former cops to the hospital and injured another one. Impressive for a banker.

And quite unusual.

Lucas would have loved to have spoken with Feldmann. There had been more to the senior banker than met the eye. But it would never happen. Feldmann was dead, too. His secrets had vanished with him.

"Lucas?"

He forced his eyes open, just barely. The American doctor was eyeing him from the foot of the bed.

"How are you feeling, Lucas?"

He tried to lick his lips, but his mouth was dry. His head was pounding. He needed a handful of Advil and a liter of water, but at least the pain in his back and right leg—which was in a cast and suspended with the help of a sling—had lessened to a constant six instead of the solid ten he'd originally felt.

"Can I get some water?" he asked.

The doctor poured him a glass from a pitcher that sat on the night table. Lucas sipped greedily through the plastic cup's straw, enjoying the lukewarm water.

"Were you able to get some sleep?" the doctor asked, making notes on an electronic device.

"I think so," he said.

"Good. You don't have to if you don't feel like it, but there are two FBI agents who want to speak with you about yesterday's event," she said. "Would you like me to send them away—"

"No! Please don't," he said with too much vigor, which caused him to burst into a coughing fit.

"Are you sure, Lucas?" she asked once he had stopped coughing.

"I want to. I'm fine, Doctor," he said.

She walked over to the edge of the bed and peered at

the monitors. She wrote down some additional notes and made a few adjustments to the drug-dispensing machine.

"I'll get them for you, but no more than five minutes. You need to rest, Lucas," she said, leaving the room but keeping the door open.

THIRTY-TWO

PRAGUE, CZECH REPUBLIC

Helen took one look at Lucas Miller and knew the man was in poor shape. His left arm was wrapped in bandages and his right leg was in a heavy cast supported by a sling. But it was Lucas Miller's face that was the worst. It was a mottled mess of purple bruises mixed with deep lacerations.

She got close to him while Donovan stood at the foot of the bed.

"Mr. Miller, I'm Special Agent Charlotte Johnson. I'm with the FBI," she said, showing him her credentials.

Miller turned his head to her. "Thank you . . . for coming," he said, his voice dangerously weak. "I didn't think . . . you would come so fast."

"Do you have everything you need, Mr. Miller?"

"Lucas . . . Call me Lucas. Yes, I . . . They've taken

very, very good care of me," Miller said. "Did . . . Did you know my doctor's an American?"

"Dr. Shepherd? Yes. I've met her. She's fabulous. You're lucky to have her."

"Water? Please," Miller asked.

Helen grabbed the plastic cup and brought the straw to Miller's lips. When he was done, she replaced the cup on the table and said, "I'm sorry about your brother, Lucas. You have our most sincere condolences."

"Thanks."

It was obvious Lucas was fighting to stay awake. The IV drip feeding him pain medicine was the only thing that kept him from great physical suffering. As for his mental health, there was no doubt in Helen's mind that William's death must be stabbing deep into Lucas's heart and that the poor man must be grappling with an enormous burden of survivor's guilt.

"Lucas, do you mind if I ask you a few questions?"

"No . . . Not at all. Ask me anything . . . Anything you want," he said.

"Thank you, Lucas. Dr. Shepherd was quite protective of you and only allowed us a few minutes of your time. So let me go straight to the point. Is that okay with you?"

"Yes."

"Are you employed by UR Real News? And do you live in North Macedonia?"

"Yes . . . to both questions."

"Why were you in Prague, Lucas?"

"We were . . . supposed to meet with a Swiss banker named . . . Raphaël Feldmann," Miller said.

"Tell me more about him."

"What . . . What do you . . . want to know?"

"Why did you want to meet him? What was he to you?"

"He's . . . a crook," Miller said. "We believe Feldmann laundered millions of dollars for some of Europe's most corrupt politicians. He . . . also deals with Russian oligarchs."

"What else can you tell me about him?"

Miller looked like he might pass out any moment.

"He . . . He somehow found out he was being set up," Miller said, but he was out of breath, and his voice sounded like a low growl. "But Feldmann . . . He didn't do this. They killed him, too."

"Who did, Lucas? Who killed your brother and Feldmann?"

"Powerful people. I . . . I'm not sure, but it's possible whoever controlled Feldmann killed him to shut him up."

Helen swallowed hard. Miller didn't know who controlled Feldmann, but she did.

Treadstone.

But Treadstone hadn't done this. Why would they? Levi Shaw, the director of Operation Treadstone, had personally called DNI Russell and asked for his assistance. For once, Treadstone hadn't shit the bed. Either someone was trying to frame Treadstone, or she and Donovan were looking at this the wrong way.

"Was there someone else you were supposed to meet

with? Any projects you were working on that could have led to you being targeted?" Donovan asked, speaking for the first time.

Donovan had come to the same conclusion she had. Treadstone was a dead end. They weren't behind John Dixon's killing.

"Yes. The Mexicans," Miller said as his eyes fluttered. "The cartels."

Helen looked at Donovan, but the puzzled expression on her partner's face confirmed he was as perplexed as she was.

"Mexican drug cartels? I'm not sure I understand. Can you elaborate?" Helen asked, leaning toward him to make sure she could hear his reply.

Miller let out a long, exhausted sigh and seemed to sink deeper into his bed.

"Lucas, tell me about the Mexicans?"

"Proyecto de la Verdad. The . . . Truth . . . Project," Lucas said, suddenly opening his eyes and grabbing her arm with his right hand. "The . . . cartels. You have to look into this . . . Everything . . . All our . . . research . . . is at . . . my apartment . . . in Skopje."

"Skopje? In North Macedonia?" Donovan asked.

Lucas weakly bobbed his head, then closed his eyes once again. "Yes. Paper files . . . only. Too . . . dangerous. Milan . . . Vel . . . Velkoski. He . . . He knows, too."

"What is Proyecto de la Verdad about? Who's Milan Velkoski?" Helen asked. "Lucas? Lucas?"

She gently shook his shoulder, but she got no response.

"We should go," Donovan suggested. "Let's write this up and send our report to headquarters."

Helen looked at the monitor. Lucas's heart rate was fine. He was just dog-tired, and with the pain medication coming through the IV drip, Lucas wouldn't wake up anytime soon.

"You're right, let's go," she said, heading to the door, nodding at the Czech police officer who was standing by it. "I have a feeling I'm about to visit a country I've never seen before."

"Yeah. North Macedonia wasn't on my bucket list, either."

THIRTY-THREE

PRAGUE, CZECH REPUBLIC

Gustavo Berganza had brought two men with him. Hugo was behind the wheel of their Toyota 4Runner and Guillermo was in the rear seat. Berganza's orders to them were the same he'd given Salvador. Confirm Lucas Miller's exact location within the hospital and find out to whom he had talked since he had regained consciousness.

"*Patrón*, maybe you and Guillermo should continue on foot," Hugo suggested, his eyes on the navigation system of the 4Runner. "The hospital is only two blocks away, but with this traffic, it could take us another ten to fifteen minutes to get there."

Berganza stared out the SUV's tinted window. They had reached the old part of the city, and with its abundance of narrow, meandering, one-way streets, the traffic had slowed to a crawl. All the roads and side streets were

packed with cars, their tires rattling over the cobble-
stones. In front of them, an already slow-moving truck
overloaded with crates came to a stop. Berganza cursed
under his breath as the driver climbed out of his truck
and walked to its tailgate. The driver gave Berganza an
apologetic but friendly wave, then shouted something at
him. Berganza didn't need to speak Czech to understand
what the man meant. He was going to need a few minutes to unload his damn truck.

"Okay, Guillermo and I will walk the rest of the way,"
Berganza said to Hugo. "Drive around the hospital. I'll
call you if I need you, so keep your phone handy."

"Yes, *patrón*," Hugo replied as he unlocked the doors.

Berganza and Guillermo exited the SUV. Berganza
stepped into a puddle of water, remains of an earlier
downpour, and looked up. Dark rain clouds were racing
toward Prague's Old Town, hanging low in the sky. He
zipped his jacket and pulled its collar up in response to a
sudden gust of wet wind.

They were still one block away from the hospital when
his phone rang.

"Yes?"

"Where are you?" General Velásquez asked.

"On our way to the hospital," Berganza replied.

"Lucas Miller is presently speaking with two FBI
agents," the general said.

Berganza flinched at the steel edge in the general's
voice. The presence of nosy FBI agents was never good
news, but their contacting Miller could be a death sentence
for Berganza if he didn't get a handle on the situation.

"I understand," he said. "Salvador is already at the hospital. I'll let him know."

"Get me the names of these FBI agents, Gustavo. I want to know where they're staying and what car they're driving. I'll pass the info to Abalos. He'll have to take care of them, too."

Not for the first time, Berganza was dazed by how precise the general's intel was. Velásquez was well connected and exerted his influence across many borders, but how the general managed to receive current updates about what was going on inside a hospital in Prague while he was in Mexico was a mystery to Berganza.

Before Berganza could punch Salvador's number, he received a text message from him. Attached to the text was a blurry picture of what looked like Lucas Miller's hospital room. Berganza enlarged the photo with his fingers. There were two people standing by Miller's bed. One tall, heavily built man, and one woman with short blond hair.

Berganza texted back, asking Salvador to let him know the moment the agents left Miller's room. Salvador replied with a thumbs-up.

Berganza showed the picture to Guillermo. "These two are FBI agents," he said. "The boss will send Francisco Abalos after them, but he wants us to find out where they're staying."

Guillermo nodded. "Not a problem. I came prepared," he said, patting his right-side pocket.

Guillermo was the only man in Berganza's four-man team not to have any military experience, but that didn't mean he didn't know how to handle himself. Of medium height, burly, and with the crumpled nose of a boxer, Guillermo wasn't a refined man, but he was strong as a bull and was good with knives. Guillermo had joined the ranks of the Sinaloa Cartel when he was still a teenager and had been smart enough to survive and thrive within the organization. With the cartel's blessings, General Velásquez had scooped him up as an enforcer for his special project and assigned him to Berganza's team.

"Salvador will let us know when the agents leave," Berganza said. "Stay here and find a position from where you can keep an eye on the hospital's entrance. Be ready to move in case they depart via another exit."

"*Sí, patrón,*" Guillermo said.

"I'll tell Hugo to stay mobile with the 4Runner and provide backup if needed. Put on your earphones. I'll initiate a call so we can all communicate with each other."

Within minutes, Berganza had found a bench not too far from the hospital's entrance.

"In position," he said.

His three men acknowledged. The next to speak was Salvador.

"Heads up. They've left Miller's room and are waiting for the elevators. They're talking to a woman doctor, a uniformed but unarmed security guard, the same one I spotted earlier standing in the waiting room, and a Czech police officer."

"There's a cop on the third floor?" Berganza asked.

"Yes, but he appears pretty useless. He spends his

time sitting on a chair next to the elevators. His eyes were closed two minutes ago."

"Understood. Let the Americans go, and once you can do so safely, get the doctor's and the security guard's names," Berganza said.

The two FBI agents exited the hospital through the main entrance shortly after. They exchanged a few words, then the woman with the short blond hair headed to a taxi stand just to her left.

Berganza's heart sank. He hadn't thought about that.

"Woman is climbing into a taxi," Guillermo said.

"I'm not blind," Berganza hissed back. "Where are you, Hugo?"

"I'm three minutes away," the 4Runner driver replied. "Sorry, *patrón*, I couldn't find a parking spot."

Berganza felt his blood pressure rising, but he fought to keep it under control. Now wasn't the time to lash out at Hugo or lose his focus. Berganza offered a quiet prayer of thanks when the male FBI agent didn't follow the woman into the taxi.

"Male agent is on foot, moving west," Berganza said.

"I have him," Guillermo replied. "I'll follow from across the street and back from the C position."

"I'm coming out now," Salvador said. "I'll take A."

Berganza rose to his feet, glad to see that his team was on the ball. "I'm B," he said.

With a team of three watchers, the A position was occupied by the man right behind the person being watched. His job was to keep an eye on the rabbit—in this instance the male FBI agent—and call his every move to the rest of the team. The watcher in the B position was responsible for keeping an eye on A's back, making sure not to lose sight of him. The man in the C position usually followed from across the street and slightly to the rear, always keeping the rabbit in his peripheral vision.

"Subject is making a right on Pod Větrovem," Salvador said. "He's heading south."

"Make the turn with him. I'll follow," Berganza said. "Guillermo, you keep going eastbound on Nemocnice and wait at the next intersection. We'll let you know which way the target goes."

After fifteen minutes of wandering around with no clear indication of a destination, Berganza began to wonder if he was being played. Ten minutes later, he was sure of it. The FBI agent was toying with them, strolling without a care in the world. The realization sent his mind reeling as he tried to figure out what to do next.

"We should give him a bit more room, *patrón*," Guillermo suggested.

Salvador, who now occupied the C position, said, "We'll lose him if we do. He's surveillance conscious."

"Quiet! He's already made us," Berganza snapped, then added with a calmer voice, "But he doesn't know who we are or what we want. And I think we should use that to our advantage."

THIRTY-FOUR

PRAGUE, CZECH REPUBLIC

Donovan's hope to be able to go through an abbreviated surveillance detection route went out the window sixty seconds after he stepped out of the hospital. The man sitting on a bench across the street from him seemed distraught when Helen climbed into a taxi. It was a big mistake, one a highly trained operative wouldn't have made. The man looked Hispanic, but Donovan couldn't be certain. He'd be sure to ask him, though. But first, he had to figure out how many of them there were.

He made a right at the first side street east of the hospital and walked south until he reached the next intersection. He then walked north on Lípová and stopped to read the menu at a Chinese restaurant, taking the opportunity to look for evidence of additional surveillance through the reflection in the restaurant's windows. He identified four potential watchers in addition to the one he had already branded. Memorizing their physical descriptions, Donovan continued north.

That was when the rain started to fall. Big, heavy drops, with some of them traveling sideways, carried by the wind gusts and hammering the cars. Donovan didn't mind the rain, but surely his pursuers didn't feel the same way. It was harder to justify one's presence in the streets with such a downpour. After another fifteen minutes of maneuvers, he was sure there were three watchers. He glanced at his watch. He'd been at it for a little less than thirty minutes. That should have given Helen plenty of time to reach their BMW in the underground parking garage and load their gear into its trunk.

"What's your location, Helen?" he asked over their comms system.

"I'm in the X5. I already left the apartment. I'm on my way to you," she replied. "What's your exact position?"

"Walking eastbound on Mikovcova. It's a side street one block south of Anglická."

"Yeah. Got it. I'm three to four minutes away. You have company?"

"Three men. All of them on foot, but I wouldn't be surprised if they had a backup or two in vehicles," he said.

"What do you want to do?"

"I'd like to find out who they are. Is that okay with you?"

"I'm not sure I like the idea," Helen said, sounding

stressed. "You said it yourself, you're alone, and there are three of them. Wait for me. I'm two minutes out. Can you string them a little longer?"

Thirty yards in front of him, one of the men he had identified jogged across the street and stepped onto the same sidewalk Donovan was using, his hands deep inside his jacket pockets. The man was short, with a beaten-up face and a nose that looked like it had been broken several times. Donovan glanced over his shoulder. The two other men were behind him. One was right behind him and closing fast, the other one was still on the other side of the street, probably acting as a blocking force in case Donovan tried to run.

But running had never crossed Donovan's mind. On the contrary, he was exactly where he wanted to be.

"Sorry, Helen," he said lightly, unzipping his jacket and preparing himself mentally and physically for what was to come. "They're moving in on me."

"For God's sake, don't sound so happy about it," Helen said. "Hang on, I'm on my way."

THIRTY-FIVE

PRAGUE, CZECH REPUBLIC

Gustavo Berganza was twenty yards behind the FBI agent when the man did a shoulder check. Instead of the panicked look Berganza had expected to see from the FBI agent when he realized he was cornered on three sides, Berganza had the impression the American was grinning, though it was hard to be sure with the man's beard. Berganza gestured for Salvador to join him and Guillermo on that side of the street.

"Hugo, where are you?" Berganza asked.

"Thirty seconds out, *patrón*," the 4Runner driver replied. "Driving north on Bělehradská."

Berganza's plan was to force the FBI agent into the SUV and take him to their safe house. With luck, Berganza would have a few minutes to interrogate him before Francisco Abalos put a bullet in the American's brain. The trick was to do it with stealth. The street they were on was quiet and the heavy rain had ensured few pedestrians remained on the sidewalks. Still, a bloodbath wouldn't sit well with the general, at least not until they found out what Lucas Miller had shared with the FBI, and where the female agent was.

The 4Runner turned into the street when Guillermo was fifteen feet away from the American. Then all hell broke loose.

• • • • •

Donovan saw the black Toyota 4Runner as it careened into the one-way street the wrong way, taking the turn way too fast. The SUV's rear tires skidded on the wet asphalt, and the driver blasted right over the crosswalk, barely missing two elderly men, who had to dive out of the way.

Were these clowns trying to kidnap him?

A racing-green Mini Cooper sped past Donovan. Its driver, a young woman whose eyes seemed to be on her phone instead of on the road in front of her, only saw the 4Runner at the last moment. Since Mikovcova was a narrow street, with cars parked along either side, both drivers had nowhere to go. Donovan saw the Mini Cooper's brake lights flash red, but it was too little too late. There was a hellish noise of breaking glass and crunching metal as the Mini Cooper slammed into the larger vehicle head-on.

The man walking toward Donovan, not expecting the sudden sound, jumped in surprise and turned his head toward the crash just as his hand was coming out of his coat pocket with a palm-size semiautomatic pistol. The man realized his mistake almost instantly, but Donovan was fast and had already stepped in, wrapping his hands around the small pistol. Donovan wrenched the gun away by spinning around to his right and twisting the gun clockwise. Using the momentum that came with his rotation, Donovan rammed his left elbow into the smaller man's jaw with enough force to incapacitate most men.

But not this one.

The blow didn't have the desired effect and only seemed to piss off the gunman. After an involuntary step back, he lunged at Donovan, who, having completed his one-hundred-eighty-degree turn, had his back to him. Donovan felt the man's powerful arms wrap around his waist and knew he only had a short window to act before the man lifted him up and swung him back down to the cement sidewalk. Due to Donovan's height and weight, the gunman had to really plant both his feet on the ground before he could throw Donovan over his shoulder. Donovan sent his foot back with all his might, the heel of his boot connecting with the gunman's shin, fracturing it. Donovan was rewarded by an inward hiss of breath as the man's arms slackened around his waist.

Before Donovan could release himself fully from the gunman's hold, he was tackled by another attacker. On impact, the small pistol flew from Donovan's hands and landed on the hood of the car parked to his left, before sliding over the side and into the street. Despite losing the pistol, Donovan was able to twist his body in a way that redirected the new attacker's rush and used his hip to trip the man, who flew over his fallen comrade and landed face-first onto the sidewalk.

The third assailant, a man with coal-black hair who looked to be at least six feet tall and on the chubby side, surprised Donovan by lashing out with a perfect flying kick that struck in the middle of Donovan's right thigh. The strike sent a painful shock that resonated through his entire body. Donovan felt his leg go numb and he stumbled backward a few steps until his back hit the wall of the apartment building.

The man hunched into a fighting stance, ready to launch another, even more devastating attack. Donovan was in trouble, and by the way the fat ninja looked at him—he had a large grin on his face—he knew it, too. Donovan transferred weight onto his right leg and slightly lost his balance in the process. The ninja pounced, first with a straight jab to Donovan's face, then with an elbow to his chin. Donovan's vision blurred, and he bracketed his head with his forearms. Seeing this, the man switched tactics, and did exactly what Donovan hoped he would. Trying to pound on Donovan's injured leg, the ninja attempted a powerful roundhouse to Donovan's thigh, but the Blackbriar operative was ready for it. Since he had his back against the wall and had no way of evading the kick, Donovan had only one move. Accepting the pain to his leg he knew would come with moving forward, he stepped in close to his opponent before the ninja's kick could achieved a full wind-up. Donovan absorbed the kick with his right forearm and found himself in the perfect spot. The ninja's head was in line for a left hook, and Donovan let it go with everything he had. His fist crashed into the ninja's ear, rattling his brain inside his skull. The man's eyes rolled back into his head, and he crumbled into a heap at Donovan's feet.

To Donovan's immediate left, his first assailant was holding his broken shin with both his hands, swearing in Spanish. Behind him, though, his friend was getting up. The man's face was scraped and bloodied from taking a joyride on the sidewalk.

"I'll kill you, motherfucker! I'll fucking murder you!" the man shouted, spewing saliva, his eyes wild. Then he pulled a blade.

• • • • •

Berganza had never imagined this simple operation could have turned into this shit show so fast. In less than fifteen seconds, the FBI agent had turned the tide and had forced Berganza into playing defense.

Who the hell was this guy?

It didn't matter. Berganza was going to cut him wide open. He was going to spill his guts all over the sidewalk. General Velásquez would understand. Just like Berganza, he, too, was a proud man.

"Patrón, no!" Guillermo barked at him as he tried to grab Berganza's leg. "I was—"

"Shut up!" Berganza yelled back, and, in a moment of blind rage, launched his foot at Guillermo's face. Berganza felt the crunch of his shoe as it smashed into Guillermo's lower jaw.

"Bravo," the FBI agent said. "You're a real man, aren't you? Kicking your friend in the face when he was just trying to keep you from making the biggest mistake of your life. Not very smart."

"I'll feed you your own balls one at a time, *puto*," Berganza said, brandishing his knife in front of him. "And I'll make you beg for more before I kill you."

"Oh . . . I see. You're a classy kind of stupid," the American said.

Berganza took two steps, closing the distance with the tall FBI agent, but the man didn't move back. On the contrary, he feigned an attack even though he wasn't armed. It took Berganza by surprise and forced him to retreat while slashing the air in vain from right to left.

The man smiled and winked at him, which sent Berganza over the edge. He rushed the American, this time jabbing the knife toward his opponent's abdomen. The man sidestepped, deflected Berganza's arm, then thrust his fist into his ribs.

Berganza grunted, suddenly in immense pain, and staggered sideways, unable to breathe.

The FBI agent grinned again. The man was relaxed, huge, and unconquerable.

"Who are you?" the American asked, advancing toward him with a slight limp. "Why were you following me?"

In his peripheral vision, Berganza saw Hugo carefully heading in their direction. Hugo had his pistol up in front of him, but his forehead was bloodied from the crash with the Mini Cooper. He would have a direct shot at the FBI agent in about ten seconds.

Holding his side, Berganza said, "You have no idea who you're messing with, *señor*."

"Then enlighten me, dickhead," the American replied.

Berganza moved to his right, hoping the FBI agent would follow, which would help Hugo get the proper angle for his shot. It was then that a navy blue BMW SUV sped down the street, aiming straight for Hugo. Berganza heard Hugo's pistol bark three times and saw its muzzle flash. Thinking the American would act like a regular human being and flinch at the sound of gunshots, Berganza attacked, slashing his knife at the man's throat.

But the American did not flinch.

Instead, he dodged Berganza's assault and smashed his iron-hard fist in the center of Berganza's chest. The impact was such that, for a moment, Berganza thought he'd been shot. The knife slipped out of his hand, and he fell to his knees, sure that his heart was about to stop. He didn't even see—or feel—the American's knee as it hit him right under the chin.

THIRTY-SIX

PRAGUE, CZECH REPUBLIC

Helen punched the gas as she cranked the wheel
to the right and turned onto Mikovcova.

"Five seconds, Donovan," she said as the
front bumper of the BMW SUV missed a parked car by
less than an inch.

Helen took in her surroundings. Narrow street. No
pedestrians. Parked cars against the curb on both sides.
She spotted Donovan's head, which was towering over a
white sedan on the north side of the street. The rest of
him was hidden, but she could hear him speak over the
comms. At the opposite end of the street, where quiet
Mikovcova intersected with the busier Bělehradská, a
green Mini Cooper had managed to embed itself into a
black Toyota 4Runner. Gray smoke and white steam bil-
lowed from the crushed hoods. Five yards to the left of

the 4Runner, a man holding a pistol was heading toward the sidewalk where Donovan was standing.

Shit! He's in Donovan's blind spot.

"Donovan! Man with a pistol. Ten yards, at your four o'clock!"

Helen gripped the wheel tightly and gunned the engine, its throaty purr reverberating against the buildings. The gunman pivoted toward the incoming SUV and opened fire. The first round punched through the windshield and smacked against the passenger seat's headrest. The next round spiderwebbed the windshield between the two front seats but didn't penetrate.

Knowing the next bullet would probably find her, Helen ducked down sideways below the dashboard. A fraction of a second later, another round punched through the windshield and pierced her seat where her chest would have been if she hadn't moved.

She had to change strategy. Hopefully she'd distracted the shooter long enough for Donovan to make a move. No longer seeing where she was going and knowing the shooter had undoubtedly moved out of the way, Helen pressed the brake pedal and steered the SUV to the right. The moment the SUV came to a stop, she put the car in park and scurried to the rear seat. She hazarded a quick glance out the window just in time to see the shooter take cover behind a white two-door sports car.

Helen rolled over the backseat and landed in the hatchback. From the duffel bag, she grabbed one of the two MP5SDs and inserted a thirty-round magazine. She opened the tailgate and jumped down, the wail of police sirens reaching her. She heard two gunshots, followed by another—the latter she recognized as coming from a CZ 75.

Donovan's returning fire.

"Donovan, sitrep," Helen said, bringing the MP5SD to her shoulder, hugging the passenger side of the SUV as she took position behind the engine block.

"I'm to your left, north side of the street. About twenty feet from the X5. I saw you push out to the passenger side," Donovan replied. "I have three, I say again, three tangos temporarily down who can come to anytime. I suggest we bug out ASAP."

"Check," Helen replied. "Keep your eyes open. There's one shooter on your side. I last saw him take cover behind the front bumper of the white two-door sports car parked behind the green sedan. Seen?"

"Seen. He took a couple of shots at me while I was taking pictures of his friends. I fired back, but I don't think I hit him. He'll engage me as soon as I break cover," Donovan said.

"Yeah, but to take his shot, he'll have to lean out of his own cover. And when he does, I'll take him."

She heard Donovan chuckle, then he said, "Ready?"

"Ready."

"Okay. Don't miss."

Helen tracked the MP5SD along the white sports car. And, just as Donovan had predicted, the shooter popped his arms and head out of cover to fire at him. With expert precision, Helen fired one round. The man's head snapped back, a bloody mist spraying in its wake.

"Shooter down," she said.

"Never doubted it," Donovan replied, climbing into the driver's seat.

The police sirens were getting louder. Helen slid into the passenger seat and closed the door. "Let's go," she said.

"I'm with you," Donovan replied, executing a three-point turn. "I don't feel like talking to the Czech police at the moment."

THIRTY-SEVEN

It took Francisco Abalos one minute to clear Berganza's apartment. Satisfied it was secured, Abalos toured the apartment once more, taking his time and making mental notes of what he was seeing.

The beds weren't made. The television was turned on, with a PS4 console plugged into it. Abalos refreshed the screen, not surprised to see a first-person shooter game. He shook his head in disgust. Dishes sat unwashed in the sink and on the kitchen counter, cluttering the space. Clothes were strewn about in the two bedrooms. All in all, he wasn't impressed. In fact, Abalos rarely was. But this was beyond carefree. The apartment demonstrated a complete lack of discipline.

Abalos took a seat at the dining table and sent a text message to Berganza and another to Salvador to let them know he'd arrived and was waiting for them.

Abalos stretched his arms and caught his reflection in the mirror resting atop the buffet. People often thought he looked like an accountant or a lawyer. He never understood why. He stood just under six feet tall and was built like a distance runner, even though he hated to run. He always had. In his opinion, running without a specific goal was a total waste of time.

Abalos squeezed his eyes shut and massaged the bridge of his nose with his thumb and forefinger, reflecting on how he'd become Velásquez's top man in Europe.

• • • • •

Born of a Mexican woman and a low-ranking Spanish diplomat, Abalos held dual citizenship. He had joined the Spanish military before he had turned eighteen. Two years later, after completing his first tour of duty in Afghanistan, he had applied and was accepted to try out for the Unidad de Operaciones Especiales, the elite special operations force of the Spanish Navy. By the end of the selection phase, his class, which had started with thirty candidates, had only three men still standing.

Years later, on December 11, 2015, Abalos was in Kabul alongside three other Spanish special operators preparing the logistics for a long-range reconnaissance patrol when the Spanish embassy was attacked by two dozen Taliban militants. The raid had started with the detonation of a powerful car bomb close to the embassy compound's gates. The blast had blown a hole in the outside wall and had allowed the insurgents to breach the compound. The safe house in which Abalos and his team had been stationed hadn't been totally immune from the explosion. The safe house shook, and a large chunk of plaster fell from the ceiling. Bookcases toppled over, and windows were shattered. It was as if the safe house had been sitting right on top of a major earthquake's epicenter.

At the time, Abalos hadn't known it was the Spanish embassy that had come under Taliban attack. Still, within two minutes, he and his team had geared up and were on their way to the embassy—in case they needed assistance. What Abalos hadn't expected—couldn't have predicted—was that more than twenty Taliban militants armed with RPGs and automatic rifles had stormed the three-building compound of the Spanish embassy, even though the official—read redacted—version of the events would only ever mention four insurgents.

Abalos had only realized the true horror of the situation when he and his team had turned into the street that housed the embassy. Wanting to understand what he was about to get into, Abalos had deployed a surveillance drone. After witnessing two Spanish police officers being gunned down by the Taliban, and knowing many more Spanish lives were at risk, Abalos hadn't hesitated. A quick look at the three other operators by his side had confirmed they thought the same way he did.

They needed to go in. Now.

After checking their comms and weapons one last time, Abalos gave the order to retake the embassy. Abalos and his team had killed sixteen enemy combatants, two of them executed by Abalos after they'd shot and killed one of his men. Abalos hadn't cared that the two

Taliban had surrendered and dropped their weapons. He'd put a bullet in each of their heads anyway.

Unknown to him, a hidden camera had recorded the cold-blooded executions.

Twelve hours later, Abalos was taken into custody and sent back to Spain on a military flight. The next day, Abalos's commanding officer visited him at the military prison in which they kept him.

"Between you and me, what you did in Kabul, I would have done it, too. The politicians, though, they want to put you on trial for murder."

"I understand, sir," Abalos had replied.

"To get you out of the very deep hole you dug for yourself, I called in all the favors I accumulated over my twenty-five-year career in the navy. What you and your team accomplished at the embassy is nothing short of heroic. It hasn't gone unnoticed."

"Thank you, sir."

The nondisclosure agreement Abalos had to sign to avoid prosecution was half an inch thick, but he'd taken his commanding officer at his word and had signed the NDA. Forty-eight hours later, Abalos was released from prison, and from the navy.

He had first met General Velásquez while working as a team leader for a well-known private military company operating in Venezuela at the government's request. Velásquez had been Mexico's defense minister at the time, but it was clear to Abalos that the man had other ambitions outside of politics. One evening in Caracas, the general had approached Abalos while he was having a drink by himself at the lobby bar of the hotel he'd been staying at.

Abalos had recognized the man. Velásquez was of medium height, not fat, but on the heavy side, and was in his early fifties. With a single look, Abalos had known the general's expertly tailored, black business suit cost more than most Mexicans earned in a year.

"Can I buy you a drink, Francisco?" the general had asked, signaling the barman to come over. He had then ordered the most expensive bottle of tequila on the menu.

The fact the general had used Abalos's name had confirmed his suspicion that their meeting wasn't fortuitous.

"It's an honor to meet you, General," Abalos had replied, letting Velásquez know he knew who he was, too.

Abalos had quickly gathered that Velásquez wasn't one to waste words, or time, and he'd gotten straight to the point. After they'd both gulped down a shot of tequila, the general had said, "In a few months, I'll no longer be employed by my government. I'm putting together a small group of like-minded individuals who believe in expanding Mexico's reach internationally, and I'd like you to come work for me."

Velásquez had poured Abalos another shot, then pushed a small piece of paper and a pen to him.

"Drink, then I want you to write down how much you think you're worth," the general had said.

Since he'd joined the private military company, Abalos had done a few things he wasn't proud of, but nothing that kept him from sleeping well at night. Saying yes to the general might, or might not, change that, but he knew that once he opened that door, there was no coming back.

The amount of money Abalos had scribbled down was astronomical—about ten times what he was earning as a private contractor.

Everybody has a price. And this is mine, he'd told himself, reckoning the general would simply burst into laughter and leave.

But that's not what he had done. Instead, the general had scratched Abalos's number and doubled it.

"Don't ever sell yourself short, Francisco," the older man had said, rising to his feet. "I'll be in touch. Enjoy the tequila."

· · · · ·

The rattling of a key being pushed into the lock of the apartment's door brought Abalos back to the present. He pulled out his FN Five-seveN pistol and quietly moved into a position of cover, but one that still afforded him a good angle to the apartment's foyer.

Berganza was the first to enter. His lips were cut and swollen. The man looked shaken. Then came in Salvador, Berganza's second-in-command. He, too, didn't look good. His face was a mass of bruises, and the right side of his head was swollen in a way Abalos had rarely seen. It was as if an air pump had been wedged into Salvador's right ear and someone had given it five long strokes.

Something had gone horribly wrong. Holstering his pistol, Abalos stepped into view.

"What happened? And where are Hugo and Guillermo?" he asked.

Berganza jumped at the sound of Abalos's voice. Berganza hadn't even realized he and Salvador weren't alone.

"Not now," Berganza said, once he had regained his composure.

Abalos let it go. Clearly the man wasn't well. Salvador followed Berganza into the kitchen. Both men were unsteady on their feet. Salvador pulled a bag full of ice cubes from the freezer and sat down at the kitchen table. Berganza continued down the hallway and disappeared into a bedroom.

"I'll ask again, what happened?"

Salvador moved the bag of ice away from his head. "I . . . We were caught by surprise."

"Explain."

"We were on our way to the hospital where they'd taken Miller when Gustavo received a call from the general informing him that two FBI agents were already there, talking to him," Salvador explained.

So far, there was nothing in what Salvador said that Abalos didn't already know. When Abalos had learned that one of the reporters had survived and had been sent to the Prague University Hospital, Abalos had arranged for a Czech police officer on his payroll to go to the hospital to keep an eye on things until Abalos arrived.

"Continue," he said.

"We were supposed to find out where they were staying, but one of the agents climbed into a cab and we lost her. The other stayed on foot, and, thinking he was headed to his hotel, we decided to follow," Salvador said, grimacing as he pressed the bag of ice cubes against his ear.

"He made you, didn't he?" Abalos asked Salvador.

But it was Berganza who replied. "Yes, he did."

Abalos turned to face him. Berganza was carrying a laptop in his shaky hands.

"Okay. What did you do, Gustavo?"

A flutter of panic shot across Berganza's face. Before Berganza opened his mouth to answer, Abalos said, "Do not lie to me."

Berganza swallowed and took a seat next to Salvador.

"I thought . . . I thought it would be a good idea to talk to the FBI agent, you know? I figured we could bring him here or to the small warehouse and interrogate him."

"I see. Where are Guillermo and Hugo?"

Salvador shot Berganza a nervous look.

"Hugo's dead, shot by the FBI agent. Guillermo . . . He's—"

"Guillermo is dead, too," Salvador jumped in. "The American broke one of his legs, and, since we couldn't leave him behind, I killed him."

Abalos stared into Salvador's eyes. The man was telling the truth. It was too bad for Guillermo. He'd been a good *sicario*.

"You really fucked up, Gustavo," Abalos said.

Berganza's face turned even paler than it already was. He wiped his sweaty forehead with his sleeve.

"Weren't you specifically instructed to take no direct action? Your poor leadership skills and ill-advised decision cost two of your men their lives. Was your other four-man team on this, too?"

When Berganza answered, his voice adopted a tone of resignation.

"No. Maybe I should have called upon them, but I didn't. I hadn't felt the need to do so. You have to understand that right until we learned that Lucas Miller was still alive, everything, and I mean absolutely everything, had gone according to plan. If it hadn't been for Lucas Miller's luck, Proyecto de la Verdad—"

Abalos had heard enough. He pulled out his Five-seveN and aimed it at Berganza's chest, disgusted with the man.

"Tell me why I shouldn't pull the trigger," he said.

Berganza straightened himself up in his chair but remained silent. Next to him, Salvador seemed to shrink.

"I will not beg for my life," Berganza finally said, with more dignity than Abalos thought the man capable of. "Do what you must, Francisco. But I'll tell you this. I know how to fix this."

"How?"

Berganza opened the laptop he had carried from the bedroom, typed a few words, then turned the device toward Abalos. Abalos's gaze moved from Berganza to the screen in front of him. He recognized instantly what he was looking at.

Abalos sighed, but he brought down the Five-seveN.

"Okay, Gustavo. I'm listening. Tell me everything, and don't leave out any details."

THIRTY-EIGHT

PRAGUE, CZECH REPUBLIC

Francisco Abalos had to admit that Berganza had thought this through. His and Salvador's detailed accounts of everything that had happened at the hospital and during the attempted kidnapping gave Abalos a clear picture of what needed to be done. Back at the apartment, Berganza had reached out to his backup four-man team and requested their assistance. Abalos had done the same with his brother Thiago, who had recently joined him as an outside consultant. Like Abalos, Thiago had served with the Spanish military and had seen some action in Afghanistan. With Abalos's trust in Berganza waning, he wanted someone he could rely on to keep an eye on Berganza's team.

The assignment Abalos had given Berganza was straight-forward, not one Abalos felt the need to participate in, especially since Thiago would be there to represent him.

Berganza and his team were blunt instruments. Abalos wasn't. His delicate use of limited but focused violence made him more akin to a scalpel. He was the man General Velásquez called up when he needed to cut out a nasty infection before it spread. In this situation, thanks to Berganza, it seemed like the infection had already begun to grow, so Abalos's job had switched to cutting off the source of the infection.

Lucas Miller.

Miller was the priority. The main target. But if presented with the opportunity, he'd kill the American physician, too.

Dr. Shepherd.

Abalos had looked her up before leaving Berganza's apartment. Dr. Shepherd's husband was the deputy chief of mission at the US embassy. Because of this new development, he thought he'd better check with General Velásquez before making a move on the good doctor. As far as the general was concerned, killing Dr. Shepherd was worth the additional risks.

No one gave Abalos a second glance when he entered the hospital through the doctor's entrance at the rear of the main building. He'd spent a few minutes online prior to leaving the apartment to familiarize himself with the layout of the hospital. He headed directly to the staircase and went down one level to the residents' lounge. The lounge was large enough, with space for eight six-person round tables and a kitchenette, but it was empty. Abalos took a white coat off a hanger and put it over his blue polo shirt, then grabbed a chrome stethoscope someone had left on the kitchenette's countertop. He draped the medical instrument around his neck and climbed four flights of stairs to the third floor. While he hadn't seen any cameras in the hospital corridors and Salvador hadn't reported any, either, Abalos had nonetheless taken additional precautions. Although he had perfect vision, he wore a pair of silver-framed glasses on his narrow but straight nose, contact lenses that turned his dark brown eyes to green, and a false goatee. A brown wig pulled snugly over his short black hair completed his disguise.

Abalos walked confidently past the nurses' station, which was occupied by a single nurse who was typing away at a report with a phone jammed between her ear and shoulder. One of the housekeeping staff carrying a fresh batch of linen and towels rushed out of a patient's room and almost collided with him.

She apologized profusely, but he kept walking, not wanting to stop and give her a chance to remember him. He strolled by the elevators, spotting the chair Salvador had mentioned, but the Czech police officer's shift had probably ended because the chair was empty.

The door to room 309 was open and Abalos walked right in. He closed the door and locked it. The room was empty but for Lucas Miller, who seemed to be sleeping. Abalos took a good look at him. He had a heavy cast on his right leg and his left arm was wrapped in bandages. His face looked as if someone had pummeled it like a punching bag. Abalos picked up the clipboard hanging at the foot of the bed and read the notes the doctors and nurses had written down.

Miller had been intermittently conscious and wasn't presently sedated with morphine. His next dose wasn't scheduled for another hour. The nurse had picked up his dinner tray ten minutes ago and had helped the patient with a personal hygiene problem, whatever that meant. Of more importance to Abalos, Dr. Shepherd was scheduled to check on Miller in about fifteen minutes.

Perfect.

Abalos pulled out his Five-seveN and screwed a suppressor on the end of the threaded barrel. He lodged the tip of the suppressor hard into Miller's neck. When the man didn't immediately wake up, Abalos pinched his nose with his left hand.

As he woke up and gasped for air, Miller's eyes opened almost as wide as his mouth. Abalos swiftly moved his hand from Miller's nose to his mouth. It took Miller's brain a moment to process what was happening.

"Shhh . . . Shhh . . . Shhh. Calm down, my friend. Calm down. If I remove my hand, will you scream?"

Miller shook his head.

"Okay," Abalos said, offering Miller a smile. "But since we don't know each other well, I'm sure you understand it's a bit difficult for me to trust you, and I'm sure it's the same for you. Am I right?"

Miller nodded.

"Good. So let me explain what I'd be forced to do if you were to break your sacred word," Abalos said, then leaned into Miller until his lips almost touched the reporter's ear. "I'll kill everyone that comes through that door. Then I'll shoot you twice in the abdomen."

Abalos removed his hand from Miller's mouth and said, "I'm glad we came to an agreement, Lucas."

"What do you want?"

Abalos raised an eyebrow. "Really? You're a smart man. Surely you know why I'm here."

"Your . . . Your accent is different from the others'," Miller said.

"Is it, now? You want to know why? I'm from Spain, Lucas. Spain, not Mexico."

Abalos could see this confused Miller.

"You work for the Mexican cartels . . . but you're from Spain?"

"I'm an outside consultant," Abalos replied. "I could explain it to you, but why bother? We both know you'll never leave this hospital room, don't we?"

Miller's eyes began to water.

"It's a bit late for you to realize you messed with the wrong crowd, amigo," Abalos said. "But I'd hate for you to think I'm all stick and no carrot, because that's not true. So, here's the good news. Answer all my questions truthfully, and I give you my word you won't feel a thing."

Miller was trembling now. Tears ran freely down his cheeks.

"But here's the stick, Lucas. There has to be one, yes? Lie to me even once, and I'll take my time with you. That I promise you. I'll then travel to North Macedonia, and I'll murder your wife and child. I might even be tempted to pay a visit to your daughter's first-grade teacher. What's her name again? Help me out here, Lucas. Her name?"

Miller stuttered, trying to find words. "I . . . I . . ."

"I'm disappointed, Lucas. You've been having an affair with her for two years, and you can't remember her name? Color me surprised."

"Liljana. Her name's Liljana."

"Whatever," Abalos said. "You got my point."

"Why? You . . ."

Abalos drove the tip of the suppressor deep into Miller's mouth. "From now on, amigo, the only time you'll speak is to answer my questions. Nod if you understand."

Miller did. Abalos removed the pistol from Miller's mouth and wiped the barrel against the man's chest.

"You had visitors earlier today. Who were they?"

Miller cleared his throat. "FBI. They were FBI agents."

"What did they want?"

"They asked me questions about Raphaël Feldmann."

"Who's Feldmann?"

"He's a Swiss banker who deals with people like you—"

"Careful, Lucas. Don't give me attitude," Abalos warned. "Continue."

Miller's expression was one of pure hatred. Even his eyes glinted with it. But he still answered Abalos's question.

"Feldmann is the reason why me and my brother came to Prague."

"What else did you talk about?"

Miller hesitated, but not for long. "I did mention Proyecto de la Verdad to them."

"I thought you would have," Abalos said. "What did you tell them about it?"

"I . . . I . . . I don't remember—"

"Don't bullshit me, Lucas," Abalos hissed, jabbing the suppressor deeper into the soft tissue of Miller's neck. "Because I'll be on the next flight to North Macedonia to party with your wife and daughter."

"I think . . . I might have told them . . . That I kept a paper file at my apartment."

"In Skopje?"

"Yes."

"What else, *cabrón*? What else did you share with them about Proyecto de la Verdad?"

"Nothing! I'm . . . I'm sorry. Please. I really don't know. I . . . I must have passed out. I don't think I said anything else."

As Miller spoke, Abalos studied his face, looking for a micro-expression that would point to a lie. He didn't see any.

He really doesn't know.

Behind Abalos, someone tried to open the door. Abalos raised his index finger to his lips and motioned for Miller to remain quiet.

"Don't say a word, Lucas. Think about your family."

Whoever was at the door tried to open it again, then knocked.

"Hello? Hello? This is Dr. Shepherd. Open the door. Now."

Abalos held the Five-seveN behind his back and walked to the door. He unlocked it.

"I'm so sorry, Doctor," Abalos said, opening the door,

a warm smile on his lips. "Please come in. Please. I didn't know it was locked."

Dr. Shepherd stepped into the room and looked at Abalos. The American doctor didn't look convinced of Abalos's sincerity. Her eyes moved from Abalos's face to his clothes. She frowned.

"Who are you?" she asked. "And why are you wearing a resident's lab coat?"

"I'm a friend of Lucas. I was just checking up on him," he replied, closing the door with his foot.

"Don't close—"

Abalos brought the FN Five-seveN up and fired one round into Dr. Shepherd's mouth. The back of her head exploded, with blood and bits of brain tissue splattering the medical cabinets behind her.

In the hospital bed, Lucas Miller was sobbing. Abalos walked over to him.

"Please. I didn't lie to you. I beg you. You have to believe me," Miller pleaded.

Abalos shot Miller twice in the heart, and drilled one more round through his right eye.

THIRTY-NINE

Donovan obeyed the voice coming out of the dashboard and made a left turn onto Soukenická, a one-way street that would lead them to the three-level underground parking garage below the Palladium shopping center on Králodvorská Street. Now that the clouds had moved away and the sky had turned to blue, pedestrians strolled on both sides of the street, laughing, chatting, pushing strollers or carrying shopping bags filled with clothes, cosmetics, and who knew what else. Despite the shooting that had taken place just a mile away, Prague was going about its regular business. Traffic was heavy but, with the exception of the occasional jaywalker, quite orderly, with no honking of horns.

A far cry from Cairo.

With more than nine hundred parking spots, their destination was one of Prague's largest and busiest parking garages. A few steps from subway line B, and with different exits, it was a good place to regroup and to think about what they should do next.

The moment they knew they were no longer in immediate danger and that no police cars were chasing after them, Helen had placed a call to Oliver Manton to give him a sitrep. As Donovan backed into a spot, Helen ended the call.

"What did he say?" Donovan asked.

"He wants us to return to New York," Helen replied dryly. "Headquarters is booking the flights as we speak. We'll be leaving from Dresden, with a stop in Frankfurt."

Helen didn't sound too excited about the prospect of traveling back to the US.

"Okay. You aren't thrilled at the idea," Donovan said. "Why's that?"

Donovan considered himself pretty good at putting pieces together, but with the adrenaline that had sustained him during the firefight now gone, it was possible his brain wasn't seeing everything it should. He had the feeling he and Helen had done a good job and had checked all the boxes Manton had wanted them to, with maybe the exception of finding out why Unit 29155 was involved.

"I honestly don't know," she replied, her voice even more shaky than it had been a moment ago. "I guess I'm just tired."

Donovan unbuckled his seat belt and turned to Helen, taking a good long look at her. She didn't turn her head. She kept her gaze fixed in front of her. She was still holding her MP5SD tightly against her. Helen's trigger finger was resting against the frame of the submachine gun, outside the trigger guard. Donovan noticed the speed at which her chest was heaving and the veins in her neck were pulsing.

He gently touched her arm with his hand and asked, "What's wrong, Helen?"

She swallowed hard, then slowly turned her head to him. Her eyes were empty of any expression, her face set. She had the same dazed look he'd seen so many times on young marines who had just experienced combat for the first time. Strangely, he hadn't seen her react that way after the firefight in Cairo.

And then he knew. Before today, Helen Jouvert had never killed a man.

• • • • •

Helen kept replaying in her head what had happened on Mikovcova Street. What unsettled her the most was how shockingly easy it had been to blow out the brains of the raging bastard who had tried to kill her.

And how satisfied she'd been when she saw him collapse.

Despite everything she'd done in the FBI, she'd never had to fire a weapon in anger before Cairo—at Steven Cooper's residence. In fact, she had never in her life killed anything bigger than a rabbit. She had shot thousands upon thousands of rounds during training, but she now realized that popping holes into a paper target gliding toward you in a firing lane, or firing at a synthetic mannequin in a shooting house, was different from taking out another human being. Helen wondered, not for the first time, if it had been on purpose that she'd shot the person in the chest back in Egypt—instead of in the head. Helen had been so close to the shooter that when she'd opened fire, she'd seen the terror in her target's eyes. Had she aimed center mass because she had hoped the shooter was wearing body armor? So that she wouldn't have to take a life?

No. That wasn't it. She had not wavered in Prague. She'd pulled the trigger without a trace of hesitation. She had shot to stop the threat, not to kill. And since center mass was an easier, bigger target to hit, that's what she had aimed for.

End of story.

She felt Donovan's gentle touch on her arm.

"Listen, Helen, for what it's worth, what you're going through is normal," he said.

She looked into his eyes, glad to see there was no pity in them, just understanding. Somehow her partner knew exactly what was going on in her head. And for that, she was thankful. She took a long, deep breath, trying to push back against the gnawing ache that burrowed deep into her stomach.

"Don't fight it. You did what you had to. You're alive, he's dead. That's all that matters."

Images of the man's exploding head popped into her mind, and Helen felt the bile rising at the back of her throat. She closed her eyes and said, "I know. I've trained all my life for these kinds of scenarios. I don't know why I'm shaking like a leaf. I honestly don't. I feel so, so stupid."

"Listen, Helen, I think you're starting to know the kind of guy I am, right? I'm not the best when it comes to saying big words or comforting someone," Donovan said. "My ex-girlfriends would all attest to that, I can tell you that much."

She tried to smile, but it probably looked as if she were simply baring her teeth.

"It's entirely normal for you to have a hard time wrapping your head around the realization that someone you've never met wanted to kill you."

"You still feel the same way?" she asked, willing her finger to stop shaking.

Donovan took his time to answer, no doubt pondering his next words carefully. "Combat isn't pretty, but it does get somewhat easier," he said. "You do what you can to survive and kill the enemy before they kill you. Your training takes over when you're in the fight. Our training is what kept us alive today, but it doesn't do a damn thing once the bullets stop flying."

Donovan tapped a finger to the side of his head, and, for a moment, his eyes seemed hollow and lost. "In there, an entirely different battle is raging."

Then the moment was gone, but for the first time since they'd become a team, Donovan had showed her a vulnerable side. She didn't know why, but it made her feel better. Less alone, if that made any sense.

"We've been at it for weeks now," Donovan said. "The

director is making the right call by sending us home. We've identified and plugged the leak in Cairo, and we confirmed to the best of our abilities that John Dixon wasn't the target in Prague. I think we did particularly well and deserve the break."

It was nice of him to give her an exit ramp, but she knew Donovan was only saying that so she wouldn't feel like shit if she truly wanted to go back to New York.

Helen managed to force a smile this time, though she wasn't sure how convincing it was. "I don't think it's the right call. We should finish this," she said, meaning it. "This isn't over. The UR Real News link should be investigated further. Doesn't Manton understand that Russian intelligence officers have successfully coerced an American federal agent into giving them access to Mind-U's authentication server? I mean, my God! Isn't that reason enough for us to keep digging?"

"I don't disagree, but Blackbriar isn't the FBI," Donovan said. "This UR Real News link you mentioned might very well develop into a thing, maybe even a big thing, who knows? But it's gonna be someone else's problem."

That didn't sit well with Helen. She wasn't used to quitting an investigation halfway. There were still leads they could follow, people they could talk to. Why didn't Manton understand that?

Then Donovan surprised her again. It was as though he could see right through her.

"The director makes the decisions. He knows what's best. Maybe there's another team looking into Mind-U and UR Real News. Maybe there isn't. That's not important. Look at us, look at what we were able to do in so little time. Take pride in that. The FBI, as good as they are, could have never accomplished so much so fast. You're not in federal law enforcement anymore, Helen. Blackbriar doesn't operate the same way. With the FBI, it will always be black or white. With Blackbriar, we're working with different shades of gray. That's the job."

"Doesn't it piss you off?" she asked, wondering why Donovan wasn't as upset as she was about not going to North Macedonia.

"You seem to forget I was CIA. A NOC. This is my world. I never worked in an environment where everything was clear-cut."

"Weren't you a marine? You can't get into an organization more squared away than that," she said.

A sour expression crossed Donovan's face. "War isn't black and white," he said.

"I'm sorry. Of course it isn't," she said, knowing full well she'd just put her foot in her mouth knee-deep.

They didn't talk for a long moment. Helen broke the silence.

"I've never fought in a war," she said. "I never set foot in Iraq or Afghanistan. But my dad did. It changed him."

"How?"

"He was an A-10 pilot in Iraq. He was twenty-six during Operation Desert Storm."

"A-10s, huh? They kept those guys busy, didn't they?"

"My dad was good at killing tanks," she said. "Like

you said earlier, he did what he had to to stay alive. It was only years later that he confessed to my mom how badly it affected him."

"How's he doing?"

"He flies private jets and helicopters for some rich dudes nowadays. I think he's doing well."

"You guys aren't close?"

"My dad . . . he used to drink. A lot. He's sober now. Ten years. But the harm was done."

"I'm sorry."

"Don't be. It is what it is. War sucks."

"Yeah. It does."

Helen's phone vibrated. There was a new email from headquarters.

"Tickets are booked," she said, reading the message. "Same IDs we used to fly in. They've also made a reservation for a new rental. It's only a block away from here. We're to leave this one here. I guess someone will take care of it?"

"That's usually how it works. Someone from the embassy, or a gofer on retainer, will take it away and either dump it in a lake, burn it, or take it to a scrapyard. Text me the address. I'll pick up the new ride."

"Reservation is under my name," Helen said. "I'll go. But before I do, can I ask you a question?"

"Sure. Shoot."

"Okay. It bothers me. Russian intelligence and drug cartels. It's a fucked-up mix, right?"

"Yeah. I'd say that."

"Who do you think is on top?" she asked. "Is there a full partnership going on between the Russians and the Mexican cartels? Or did one of them hire the other?"

"I'm not sure we have enough info to make that call," Donovan replied.

"We don't know much about Proyecto de la Verdad, but can we agree that it's what killed William Miller?"

"Sure."

"Do you think Steven Cooper knew the Russians weren't the only force in play?" she asked. "While you were alone with him, did he say anything about the cartels?"

At the mention of the former marine, Donovan dragged a hand through his hair.

"No. Not a word. I think he would have said something if he'd known. I mean, the guy saved my life in Cairo," he reminded her. "No point in him keeping intel away from us."

"Right," she said. "Hear me out, because I've been thinking about this."

"All right. I'm all ears."

"I could be way off here, but I don't think so. Here's why I believe the Mexicans are running the show," she said. "The economic sanctions have hurt the Russian economy in a way that took the Kremlin completely by surprise. They thought NATO was weak, on life support even, and maybe they were right, but the ill-advised decision to invade Ukraine galvanized the West in a way that no one could have ever imagined. Russia suddenly found themselves cut off from the rest of the world with very limited access to foreign capital and currencies."

"I remember that. At some point, they had half of their gold and currency reserves frozen," Donovan said.

"True, but we have to remember that Russia's intelligence apparatus remains formidable to this day. The SVR, FSB, and even the GRU have their tentacles into hot spots and organizations around the globe. The cartels do not. They're brutes. Unsophisticated, but very dangerous. They're powerful in their own way, yes, and outside of Mexico, their influence is growing, but it's still limited."

"But they have money. Lots of it," Donovan said.

"Bingo. Money. That's the one thing the cartels have that Russia doesn't. Think about it, Proyecto de la Verdad is a Spanish name, not Russian. The Miller brothers must have found something big that somehow threatened the cartels. Either the Russians learned about it first and offered to help the cartels for money or a percentage cut on future earnings, or the cartels found out about the reporters and hired the Russians. It doesn't matter. The drug cartels are running the show."

"There's nothing you said I don't agree with," Donovan said. "But—"

"I know, I know," she said, cutting him off. "Not our problem."

FORTY

PRAGUE, CZECH REPUBLIC

Donovan was fairly confident they weren't being followed. He'd learned long ago to leave nothing to chance and to expect every encounter, road trip, or restaurant outing to turn into a dangerous situation. That's why he'd done a ninety-minute-long SDR coming out of Prague. Now heading north on European Route 55 toward the German city of Dresden, Donovan allowed himself to relax, but just a touch.

In the seat beside him, Helen was snoring lightly. The clouds had returned, and it had started raining again. The constant beating of the windshield wipers had finally gotten the best of her. He knew she'd be mad at herself for falling asleep, but he didn't have the heart to wake her up. Helen was an interesting woman, and Donovan found himself wondering why she'd originally chosen a career in law enforcement. Smart, self-confident, fiercely competitive, and highly driven, Helen would have been enormously successful in whatever field she chose. But whatever the reason, he was thankful she'd had his back today. She'd proven herself to be a true warrior.

Donovan thought about what she'd shared with him about her dad. The former A-10 pilot. Was it because of him? Had she felt the need to prove something to him? Possibly. Family had played an important role in his life choices.

And, for better or worse, it still does. Maybe it's the same for her.

If it hadn't been for his brother joining the CIA, and his father being a cop, Donovan may have become a car mechanic, or an automotive engineer. For as long as he could remember, and even as a kid, when having one of his own had seemed a faraway dream, Donovan had loved cars and motorcycles. One of his best childhood memories was when his dad, who at the time was an officer with the NYPD's Highway Patrol unit, had brought him over to the department's fleet garage to check out the new Harley-Davidsons that had just come in. For young Donovan, the garage had looked more like a small city than anything else.

"These guys' work isn't acknowledged enough," his dad had said, talking about the mechanics working on the fleet. "Without them, the department's nine-thousand-plus vehicles would all fall apart within months."

After showing Donovan around the armored vehicles used by the ESU—Emergency Service Unit—one of the mechanics had gestured for him and his dad to follow him.

"This is your dad's new bike," the mechanic had said, tapping the seat of one of the new Harley-Davidsons with his hand. "I think you guys should check it out, to make sure all's good with it, you know?"

The sixty minutes he'd spent with his dad cruising the streets of Manhattan on that brand-new Harley—a time that would always be seared in his psyche—were some of the most joyful of his existence. From that day forward, Donovan's interest in cars and bikes had expanded from being attracted to the rev of an engine and the jerk of speed when his dad switched from one gear to the other in their convertible Mazda Miata to wanting to learn more about what made them go, how they stopped, and how to make them work more efficiently. Sometimes he pictured himself opening his own auto repair shop but knew, as the years went by, that he'd probably never do it.

He'd have to content himself with restoring the 1973 Corvette Stingray he kept at his father's cabin in Vermont.

Traffic was getting lighter as they drew closer to the German border. Out of habit, Donovan glanced into the rearview mirror of the Škoda Kodiaq, but it was hard to see anything in the heavy downpour.

A big fan of American muscle cars, Donovan hadn't expected he would enjoy driving the Kodiaq as much as he was. Although not a luxurious or fast vehicle in any way, Donovan was impressed with the Czech-built SUV. Acute steering, decent suspension, and a passable seven-speed gearbox would give the Kodiaq's more expensive competitors a run for their money.

Helen's voice broke his reverie. "You shouldn't have

let me sleep," she said, giving him a tired smile. "But thanks."

"It was more like a power nap," he said. "You weren't gone for more than fifteen or twenty minutes."

"Well," she said, stretching her arms in front of her. "It was enough. Where are we?"

"We drove past Lovosice five minutes ago. It's another half hour to the German border. We should be at the airport in ninety minutes or so."

"Plenty of time. Our flight isn't for another four and a half hours. How do you feel about stopping to grab something to eat?"

The mere mention of food made his stomach growl in the most undignified manner. Donovan hoped the rain pounding against the Škoda's windshield had tempered the sound enough that Helen hadn't heard.

"Oh, my God, I heard that," Helen said, laughing.

"Sorry, but you got my answer loud and clear," he replied. "We're coming up to a town called Teplice in a mile or so."

Every muscle in his body was sore, not just the quadriceps the flying ninja had smacked with his foot. Getting some food in his stomach would do him some good. An ice-cold beer would be nice, too. But that would have to wait.

Donovan took the exit off the highway. The exit ramp became a two-lane road that led right into Teplice, which was larger and much busier than Donovan had expected. Donovan stopped at a traffic light while Helen checked her phone, trying to find a restaurant.

He drove around town for a few minutes, admiring its classical architecture. He passed several banks, a couple of hardware stores, a school, and a few pubs, but no drive-through restaurants. Around the town center was a cluster of four-story buildings surrounded by tall hardwood trees next to a beautiful church.

"Did you know that up to World War II Teplice was nicknamed *Small Paris*?" Helen asked.

"Huh . . . No. Did you before you read it on Google?"

"Of course not. Now turn left at the next intersection," Helen said. "There's a family-owned restaurant not too far away with great reviews. Their bean and pig's blood soup is supposedly excellent."

Bean and pig's blood?

"You can't be serious," he said.

"It's good for you. You'll enjoy it."

"A soup, let alone one made with pig's blood, isn't exactly what I had in mind," Donovan said, having a hard time understanding how the two main ingredients could actually work together.

"Right. I forgot. You're a meat-and-potatoes kind of guy. I'm sure they'll have something you'll like on the menu."

Donovan turned on his left-turn signal, looked in his side mirror, and changed lanes. But instead of turning onto the street Helen had suggested, he continued straight past the intersection. Helen was switched on and didn't miss a beat.

"Saw something you didn't like or is it about the bean soup?" she asked, looking into her side mirror.

"White Nissan SUV about fifty yards back," Donovan said. "Could be nothing, but he's been behind us for a few turns now."

"Hard to believe we could have picked up a tail," Helen said. "The SDR we did in Prague was extensive."

Donovan didn't reply but kept an eye on his rearview mirror. Two intersections later, the white SUV turned right and disappeared from view.

"The Nissan just made a right onto a side street," Helen confirmed.

Donovan relaxed. "Maybe we should head straight to the airport. What do you think?"

"C'mon, Donovan. I swear I won't force you to eat the bean and pig's blood soup."

Donovan laughed. "I was serious."

"I know. Just pull over there next to the coffee shop," she said, pointing to a parking space up ahead. "I need to go to the ladies' room, then I'll get us two coffees to go. We'll eat at the airport."

"Sure, but don't tell me you accidentally dropped soy milk into my coffee, okay?"

Helen laughed again—a soft, warm laugh.

Totally addictive.

Donovan parked the Škoda Kodiaq in the open spot just as Helen's phone began to vibrate in the cupholder.

"Text message from headquarters," she said. "They're checking in. They want to know if we'll make our flight."

"They're wondering, without asking directly, why we stopped in Teplice," Donovan said.

"I just told them."

"What did you say?"

"Same thing I told you. I need to use the bathroom."

Helen opened her door and climbed out of the Kodiaq. Donovan caught movement in his side mirror and almost froze when he saw the white Nissan slowly turn onto the street and head in their direction.

You have to be kidding me.

He glanced in Helen's direction. She was already halfway to the café's door, shielding her head from the rain with her hand. Donovan pulled his phone out of his pocket with the intent of snapping a few photos of the Nissan SUV. Not to make his intentions too obvious, he aimed the camera into his side mirror.

The white Nissan had vanished. *What the hell?*

Donovan did a shoulder check. Then his breath caught in his throat.

The Nissan had accelerated and was now almost parallel to the Kodiaq. The Nissan's front passenger window was down, and Donovan recognized the passenger. It was the ninja from the fight in Prague. This time, though, the ninja wasn't going for the flying kick—he had a rifle aimed directly at Donovan. Before Donovan could take cover, there was a gunshot, then the ninja opened fire on full automatic.

Then something slammed into the side of Donovan's head.

FORTY-ONE

TEPLICE, CZECH REPUBLIC

Helen shut the Kodiaq's door and took a few quick steps toward the café, trying to escape the rain.

Shit. My phone.

She pivoted back toward the SUV just as the white Nissan picked up speed. A window came down and the barrel of a rifle poked out. Helen's reaction was lightning-fast. She had her CZ 75 out of its holster and her first shot on target in less than two heartbeats. At the same moment, the shooter fired at the Kodiaq.

And at Donovan!

Incoming rounds tore holes into the Kodiaq, but Helen was undeterred and continued squeezing the trigger as fast as she could. A bullet creased the top of Helen's shirt over her right shoulder and ricocheted off the brick wall of the café. Two feet to her right, a man holding a black umbrella was hit numerous times and toppled backward. Helen's next rounds—she wasn't sure how many times she'd pulled the trigger—shattered the rear passenger-side window of the Nissan as it sped up and swerved down the street, almost losing control as its right rear tire took out two city-owned trash cans, catapulting days-old garbage in all directions. The CZ 75's slide was locked open. Helen ejected the empty magazine and inserted a fresh one.

Her eyes moved to the man with the black umbrella who'd fallen next to her. His body was sprawled on the sidewalk, his blood mixing with the rain draining into the sewers. There was nothing she could do for him. A portion of the left side of his head was missing.

She rushed to the Kodiaq and jerked the passenger door open. At the end of the street, the white Nissan had come to a screeching halt.

They're coming back.

She took a look inside the Kodiaq. Her heart plummeted to the pit of her stomach. Donovan's mouth was open, his eyes set in her direction, and an incredible amount of blood poured from a cut at his hairline.

FORTY-TWO

TEPLICE, CZECH REPUBLIC

Donovan didn't know why Helen had stopped moving after she had opened the door. What he did know was that the white Nissan was coming back for another round.

"Let's go! Move!" he shouted at her. "They're turning around."

She jumped back, letting out a scream, her eyes growing wide.

"C'mon, Helen! Snap out of it. We need to go!"

Helen climbed aboard and slammed the door. She looked at him, confused. "I . . . I thought you were dead."

"Yeah? Well, I thought so, too," he said, pulling out of the parking spot and making a U-turn. "My phone caught a round and exploded in my hand."

"You're bleeding," Helen said.

"Glass shrapnel from a window, or maybe from my phone screen. I don't know."

"You sure you aren't hit anywhere else?" she asked.

Donovan took a sharp right and pressed the gas pedal as far as it would go. "I'm good. Shooter had his rifle on full auto," he said. "That, and the fact that you fired back at him, screwed up his aim."

"Who the hell are these people?"

"I got a good look at the shooter," Donovan said. "He was part of the crew we got involved with in Prague."

"What? How?"

"Don't know, but the rearview mirror is gone," he said. "What do you see at our six?"

Helen shifted in her seat and craned her neck so she could look out the back.

"Shit. The Nissan is on our tail. There's a black Audi sedan, too."

"Maybe I can stay ahead of the Nissan, but there's no way I can outrun the Audi," Donovan said. "Grab our gear and get ready. We're gonna have to fight our way out."

Helen unbuckled her seat belt and jumped into the rear seat, on which sat the duffel bag with their rifles, extra magazines, and plate carriers.

"Stuff as many mags as you can into the plate carrier pouches," he said. "I have a feeling we'll need them."

The traffic light at the next intersection turned red. Donovan didn't slow down—he stepped on the gas pedal, sending the tachometer way past the red line and pushing the 2.0-liter 148-horsepower turbodiesel engine to its absolute maximum. Donovan had to swerve around a delivery truck that had taken an early start on his green light, sending Helen flying against the rear passenger door.

"Shit!" he heard her yell.

He jerked the Kodiaq's steering wheel hard to the right, saving them from spinning out of control, but once again tossing Helen across the entire length of the backseat. He heard her exhale painfully as she plowed into the rear driver's-side door.

A traffic light ahead forced Donovan to make a left into a one-way alley. There was simply too much traffic to chance going through the intersection without stopping. Thankfully, there weren't any cars on the narrow street he'd turned onto.

And he quickly understood why. The alleyway was for pedestrians and only allowed delivery vehicles. He'd missed the sign prohibiting the turn. Helen tossed a plate carrier filled with magazines onto the passenger seat. Donovan was about to reach for it when a pair of little boys, no more than ten years old, shot out into the street right in front of the Kodiaq, running after a soccer ball.

"Hang on!" he yelled to Helen as he slammed on the brakes.

Helen violently thumped against the back of his seat as the SUV skidded to a stop, its wheels almost gliding over the wet pavement. Helen swore and the boys froze in horror.

"The Nissan is right behind us! Fifty yards and closing!" Helen said. "Let's go!"

"I can't!" Donovan shouted back at her, energetically gesturing for the kids to move out of the way.

But they didn't. They were still in shock, immobile in the middle of the alleyway, their eyes as big as saucers.

From the rear seat, Helen opened fire with the MP5SD, her bullets easily punching through the rear windshield of the Kodiaq. Although suppressed, the sounds emanating from Helen's submachine gun combined with the shattering of the rear windshield were loud enough for the two boys to pick up. They ran back to where they had come from, screaming at the top of their lungs. Donovan floored the accelerator and the Kodiaq surged forward. In the rear seat, Helen had already gone through an entire magazine and was reloading.

"Talk to me, Helen," he said.

"I don't know if I hit anyone, but I certainly got their attention. The Nissan's windshield is demolished. No way they'll be able to see through it. They haven't moved yet. Maybe I did get them all. Wait, scratch that. They just kicked the windshield out and . . . Oh, wow. They dumped the driver's body onto the street. The guy who shot at us is now behind the wheel."

"What about the Audi? Do you see it?"

"They're still stuck behind the Nissan. The road is too narrow for them to drive around it."

Donovan made a left at the end of the alleyway and then a quick right, the rear tires of the Kodiaq skidding. He pushed the SUV past thirty miles an hour and tapped hard on the brakes and spun the wheel right, slewing the Kodiaq down another alley and nearly taking off his side mirror on a streetlamp. At the end of the alley, cars zoomed by in both directions.

"Grab on to something, Helen. I'm about to do a sharp right turn at high speed," Donovan warned.

Donovan let go of the gas pedal as he approached the busy street—which turned out to be one of the city's main arteries—but stomped on it again the moment he realized he would arrive at the junction just in time to take advantage of a break in traffic. He merged onto the road too fast and felt the sway of the Kodiaq from side to side, its high center of gravity almost tipping them over. Donovan straightened the wheel and gunned the gas pedal again.

Up ahead was a traffic circle, with half a dozen vehicles waiting for their turn to merge. Donovan scanned the sidewalk to his right. Empty. Praying he wouldn't hit a pedestrian, he popped the two right wheels of the Kodiaq onto the sidewalk and accelerated past the slower moving vehicles. Donovan didn't mind the angry faces of the other drivers nor the beeps of their horns. He took the second exit out of the traffic circle and weaved in and out of traffic for less than half a mile until he made a right onto a two-lane street that seemed to head out of the city.

"See anything?" he asked after a few minutes.

"No sign of the Audi or the Nissan since we left the alleyway. I think we're good."

"We'll need to change vehicles," Donovan said. "If a police car sees this one, we're done for."

"No doubt some civilians have already notified the

authorities," Helen said, consulting her phone. "We definitely need to stay off the main roads."

"Just so you know, we're losing fuel," Donovan said. "A bullet probably punctured the gas tank. We're gonna need that new ride sooner rather than later."

"Take a right at the next intersection. It's coming up in about one hundred yards. It's a rural road that leads to Krupka. There's over ten thousand people living there, so we should be able to borrow a vehicle without too much trouble."

Donovan made a right onto a dirt road.

"Damn," he said. "That isn't even a real road. Looks more like a power-line right-of-way."

"You're right, sorry," Helen said. "Can you turn around?"

"Not a good idea. We might get stuck."

The heavy rain had turned the dirt road into a soft, slushy mud path. Donovan was forced to go faster than he wanted to in order not to get bogged down.

"Keep going. We should come across a paved road in about two klicks."

The sun was dipping low on the horizon and the heavy rain clouds had begun to break up, letting through sporadic patches of long orange streaks of sunlight.

"It's going to be dark pretty soon," he said. "That should help us with what we have in mind for Krupka."

"Maybe, but I still can't wrap my mind around how they found us," Helen said. "It just doesn't make sense."

Donovan had been so focused on driving he hadn't thought about it. But Helen was right. If the cartel *sicarios* had found them once, they would find them again. But how? It was as if they were tracking them. The Kodiaq was a new rental, a last-minute decision following the gunfight in Prague. There was no way the *sicarios* could have installed a tracker in the car. Did they have the technological know-how to hack a car rental agency? Even if they did, how would they know which one to hack or which vehicle to track?

The Russians.

Helen had said it. Russian intelligence working hand in hand with the drug cartels was a recipe for disaster. If Unit 29155 was involved and communicating in real time with the *sicarios*, Donovan supposed it was possible they could have tracked them down. But even that seemed far-fetched. If there was one thing Donovan had learned about Russia's military and intelligence services with the Ukraine invasion, it was their apparent inability to work together as a cohesive unit. Russia's utter failure at combined arms operations was a surprise of epic proportions. If Russia's invading army's engineers, infantry, tanks, attack helicopters, and fighter jets were unable to properly communicate with one another on the battlefield, how in hell was Donovan supposed to believe they could make it work with the cartels?

Cooperation between the two entities? Yes. But running a joint operation together in real time? Absolutely not.

A dark thought entered Donovan's mind. He tried to push it away, but it refused to leave.

No. That can't be it. It just can't.

But the thought lingered, and Donovan felt his heart clench.

Have we been sold out?

Had someone at Blackbriar double-crossed them?

Donovan slammed the palm of his hand against the steering wheel in frustration. "Dammit!"

"What?" Helen asked. "What is it?"

"Could Blackbriar be compromised?"

"What? No. Absolutely not."

"Think about it, Helen. They know where we are in real time, yes?"

"They do, but that doesn't—"

"Blackbriar made the reservation for that rental, and they booked our flights, remember? How easy would it be for them to pass along that intel to the *sicarios*? Didn't you get a call or text message seconds before we were ambushed in Teplice? Maybe it was a way for them to validate our exact location."

Donovan wished he could see Helen's face to read her expression, but he couldn't afford to take his eyes off the uneven, pothole-ridden path. Donovan dodged a large rock and decided to slow down, afraid he would break an axle if he didn't. Helen hadn't replied to his comment, probably digesting what he'd told her.

Helen was smart, but she hadn't been operating deep in the shady side of intelligence gathering as long as he had. Donovan had heard about the problems at Tread-stone. Heck, Levi Shaw had almost been killed by a trai-tor in the CIA. Oliver Manton had told Donovan that

Treadstone was in the process of purging itself of all its bad seeds, and that might be true, but was it preposterous to think that Blackbriar could be infected, too? Donovan had witnessed firsthand what the higher-ups had done to his brother. There was no way Harrison would have ever sold secrets to Russia or to any other foreign nation. Harrison had been a true patriot, a pure soul, and one of the best and brightest covert intelligence operatives the CIA had ever fielded. Somebody had turned on his brother, betrayed his trust, and framed him for treason—there were no other possible explanations.

And now it's happening to me, too, he thought, tightening his grip on the wheel.

"Donovan, did you hear what I said?" Helen asked, leaning toward him.

"No. What is it?"

With the wind gushing in from the shattered windows and his mind having drifted to a bad place, he'd lost his concentration for a moment and missed what she'd said.

"I said that there's no way Blackbriar is compromised. Manton handpicked every single member on the team. No exceptions."

"People can be turned," Donovan replied.

"Yes, they can," Helen admitted. "But not Oliver Manton. I trust his judgment. He's a rough sonofabitch, but he's loyal to us, I guarantee you that. In fact, I'm ready to bet my life on it."

Her tone suggested she was convinced of the correctness of her stance. Helen knew something about Manton that Donovan didn't. She had just made that abundantly clear.

I'm ready to bet my life on it.

This was a strong statement, not one a seasoned operative like Helen would make lightly. Since teaming up with her, Helen hadn't done a single thing that had led Donovan to second-guess her judgment. He'd seen Helen jump in the fight in Prague and risk her life for him. And, just a few minutes ago at the café, she'd once again proven herself to be a top-notch operative.

Lightning-quick reflexes, great situational and tactical awareness. Helen has good instincts.

So, if she was right and Blackbriar hadn't been compromised in any way, where did that leave them?

Donovan grumbled a curse under his breath. He was missing something. He could feel it gnawing at the back of his brain like the name of a former colleague you haven't spoken to in years, but he couldn't quite put his finger on it.

And it pissed him off.

"I think I know how they've been able to track us," Helen said with an edge in her voice Donovan couldn't ignore.

"How?"

"Do you see that farmhouse next to a cornfield on our left?" she asked.

"I see it," he said.

"Do you think our SUV can handle rougher terrain? You'll need to cross that rough patch of agricultural land to get to a dirt road that will lead to the farmhouse."

"It's no Land Rover, but yeah, it should be fine. And now, are you gonna tell me what this has to do with anything? Because you're confusing the hell out of me."

"The *sicarios*, they're not tracking *us*, Donovan. They are tracking *you*."

FORTY-THREE

Helen buckled her seat belt and grabbed the headrest of the passenger seat in front of her as the Kodiaq raced across the farmland, wet clumps of soil churning up from beneath the SUV's tires. Despite the falling darkness, Donovan's face had turned bright red when she'd shared with him that she believed the *sicarios* had managed to tag him with a miniature GPS tracker during the physical encounter in Prague.

If that was indeed the case, it would explain why they hadn't detected a tail during the lengthy SDR they'd executed prior to leaving Prague's city limits. A GPS tracking device would have allowed the *sicarios* to run a much looser tail. When they'd seen the Kodiaq head into the city, they had closed in, waiting for the right opening.

Not a bad plan. It had come very close to working. But it hadn't.

It was only a question of time before the *sicarios* attacked again. If Helen had been running the operation for them, she would wait until her target vehicle was off the main roads, where her assault had a chance not to be noticed right away.

As they closed the distance to the farmhouse, it became clear that the weathered building was a two-story, run-down old barn with a rusty tin roof that looked like it might fall over if the wind blew too hard.

When they were twenty-five yards away from the barn, she told Donovan to stop the SUV.

"I'll grab the gear and update headquarters," she said. "Go inside and drag your right leg behind you as if you'd been shot."

"Brilliant," he replied. "I might even fall once or twice."

Assuming she was right about the GPS tracker, her plan was to simulate that Donovan had been injured and could no longer continue, instead opting to take refuge in a vacant building.

With a single dirt road leading to the barn, Helen and Donovan would have no problem seeing the *sicarios* coming.

But would they take the bait? Helen believed it all came down to how much of a hurry they were in. What kind of pressure were they under to take her and Donovan down? To Helen, it seemed like a tremendous amount. She was no expert when it came to how drug cartels handled their business, but it was plausible to think that the *sicarios* wouldn't get paid if they failed to fulfill their mission. Of course, failure wasn't an option for them, either.

She let her MP5SD loose on the sling and typed a quick message to Blackbriar headquarters, informing them of the latest developments. She hit the send button and dug into the duffel bag from which she took out a small surveillance drone and a remote control. She powered both devices on.

Her phone rang. It was Oliver Manton.

"We don't have eyes on you and Donovan," the Blackbriar director said. "By the time we do, it will be too late."

"Understood. There was a drone in the weapons cache," she said. "We have it with us. Can you connect to it?"

"Yes. Let me know the moment it's in the air. We'll be able to call the shots for you, but you'll have to make sure both yours and Donovan's earbuds are linked to your phone."

"I will."

"Also, we just received word that my request to relocate an air asset to you has been approved by the DNI."

An air asset? This was the first time Helen had heard anything about Blackbriar having air assets. "I'm not sure I'm following, sir."

"For emergency cases only, DNI Russell has given Blackbriar access to the covert fleet of civilian air assets usually reserved for special access programs. When the shit hit the fan in Prague, I sent in my request, trying to plan ahead in case a situation just like the one we're in occurred."

"Okay," Helen said, wondering what it meant for her and Donovan. She asked Manton.

"Means that you're in luck. I'll have a helicopter pick you and Donovan up within the next hour if you want to exfil. Exact ETA is still unclear at this time."

"Pick us up at the barn?"

"Yes, and there's something else you may want to know," Manton said. "We ran the pictures Donovan took of the three twats he knocked out in Prague. One of them is a man named Gustavo Berganza. He's a former Mexican intelligence officer. The DEA has him on file as a suspected member of Los Zetas. Another one is associated with the Gulf Cartel, and the third one is linked to the Sinaloa Cartel."

"That doesn't make any sense," Helen said. "Three cartels that despise each other and spend half their time killing their rivals are now working together?"

"Not three cartels, but at least four," Manton added. "The man you shot was a member of the Jalisco New Generation Cartel. I suspect someone belonging to that same group killed Lucas Miller."

"Wait. Miller's dead? When? How?" Helen asked. "Shit!"

"Not long ago. Shot in the head. Just like the American doctor who was taking care of him."

Helen thought she was going to be sick. "Dr. Shepherd?"

"Yes. These guys aren't messing around, Helen. If I can get that chopper to you sooner, I will. In the meantime, get ready."

"All right. Thanks for the intel," Helen said, still shaken. "I'm deploying the drone in thirty seconds."

"We'll look for it. I'll call back as soon as we have control," Manton said, ending the call.

That was a lot to digest. She wished she knew more about the dynamics of the cartels than she did. But still, she'd never heard of cartels teaming up. Not in this way. Agreements were made in the past, but they usually didn't last very long. Having members of four different Mexican drug cartels working together on an overseas operation was simply unheard-of.

Helen used the remote control to launch the drone, then grabbed the duffel bag and headed to the barn, making sure to walk parallel to Donovan's footprints and a few feet away. It was vital the *sicarios* saw both sets of footprints heading to the barn. Helen noticed a scruffy black cat sitting next to the barn's double doors. It was staring intently at her, its tail curling and uncurling, as though it knew of the impending violence.

Helen pushed open the doors, which squeaked on their corroded hinges. The smell of dirt and wet dust greeted her. The barn consisted of a single cavernous space with a high wood-beamed ceiling. The air was suffused with a dampness that seeped into Helen's bones.

In the middle of the barn, Donovan stood, almost naked. He had kept only his socks and underwear on, leaving his taut abs and toned arms completely exposed. Helen wanted to look away but couldn't. And he didn't try to hide away, either. A blush heated her cheeks. Momentarily distracted, she missed what he'd just said.

"Helen, I found it," he repeated, holding what looked like a black pea between his thumb and forefinger. "You were right. One of them grabbed me from behind and must have dropped it in my pocket. I went through the rest of my clothes and didn't find anything else. I'm sorry."

"I'm just glad you found it," she replied, dropping the duffel bag to the dirt floor. "You can put your clothes back on now."

"Yes, ma'am."

"And you better hurry—they might come at any moment."

Her phone vibrated again. She asked Donovan to pair his earbud to her phone.

"We see the barn and have good visual up to seven hundred yards on each side," Manton said. "It should give you a two- or three-minute warning."

"That's better than none at all. We're about to come out," Helen said as Donovan tightened his plate carrier. "We'll exit through the rear doors of the structure and circle left to take advantage of the slightly higher ground."

"Good copy," Manton said.

Helen turned to face Donovan, who was adjusting the sling of his MP5SD, and shared with him what Manton had told her about the incoming air asset and the men he'd beaten up in Prague.

"That's definitely something else," he agreed. "*Sicarios* from rival cartels working together? That goes against nature for these assholes, though it would explain why one of them had no qualms kicking another one in the face."

"What do you mean?"

"In Prague, just before you made your glorious entrance, one of the narcos punted the head of another as though it were a football. It seemed strange at the time, but now it makes a bit more sense."

"Cartel members usually hate their rivals," Helen said. "They get off on killing members of rival cartels. Whatever Proyecto de la Verdad is, it has to be big. But what's its objective? I'm not seeing it."

"I'm not, either. That's why I hope these crazies will get here before the chopper does," Donovan said, a thin, dangerous smile on his lips. "Dr. Shepherd didn't deserve to go out like that. Let's make this scum pay for what they did."

FORTY-FOUR

Donovan exited the barn from the single door at the rear and took a few minutes to do a quick reconnaissance of the area. Once he understood the terrain, he hurried back inside the barn. Helen had used one of the two hand grenades from the duffel bag to booby-trap the double-wide doors at the front of the barn.

"Good idea," he said.

"I've spent considerable time training how to remove these," she said. "But I haven't had the chance to actually rig a live one."

Donovan checked her work. "Whoever taught you did a great job."

"Do you think I should use the other grenade, too?" she asked.

"No, we might need it for the ambush," he said.

Donovan picked up a wooden stick and used it to draw a crude map in the dirt. He was explaining to Helen what he had observed during his short reconnaissance outside the barn when Manton's voice broke into his earbud.

"Three vehicles just turned onto the dirt road. One of them is a black Audi. No signs of the white Nissan."

"Three vehicles," Helen confirmed. "Good copy."

"Their headlights are off. Unknown numbers of occupants at this time. Their speed is . . . just below six miles an hour. You should get in position."

"Message received," Helen replied.

"All right," Donovan said, using the twig to identify the different parts of his sketch. "This is the barn, and this is the dirt road leading to it."

"Got it."

"Your position will be here, about thirty yards off the barn," he said, pointing to the left of the dirt road and about ten yards back. "There's good concealment and you'll be slightly elevated. If you flatten yourself on the ground, you should have good cover from direct fire coming from the road."

Donovan moved the tip of the twig to another spot on the map. "This will be my position. As you can see, it's on the same side as yours, but twenty-five yards west of you and closer to the dirt road. I'll use the small ditch as partial cover. These two positions will allow for our arcs of fire to overlap over the kill zone," he said, drawing interlacing cones of fire. "Like this."

"Okay. How do we initiate contact?" Helen asked, heading to the door at the back of the barn.

"Two choices," Donovan said. "The first, my preference, is if the front doors of the barn go boom. If that happens, it means they were dumb enough not to check if the doors were rigged."

Helen nodded her understanding. "If they inspect the doors, they'll be sitting ducks," she said.

"You got it. I know I said we had to keep one alive, but let's not take extra risks just to make it happen. Agreed?"

"Yes."

"We're betting the entire farm they don't know we're waiting for them," Donovan said, which earned him a smile from Helen. He followed her outside, then said, "We're going to use surprise to our advantage."

"It might be the only thing we have going for us."

"True, but, in a short engagement, it's huge. To really take advantage of it we need the whole engagement to last less than ten seconds from the time the ambush is initiated till the last round is fired. That's why the violence of our action is vital. There can be no hesitation."

"You've done a few of these before, right?"

"Yes," Donovan replied, without mentioning that all the ambushes he'd taken part in had been conducted by much larger teams armed with weapons punching bigger holes than their MP5SD submachine guns. "You're ready?"

"Let's do this."

· · · · ·

Donovan lay in the long grass. The ground was soggy from the recent rains, and water soaked through his clothes. Donovan dug his fingers, then his palms, deeper into the soil and rubbed them over the backs of his hands and his neck and face to camouflage himself further. He took several long, deep breaths and felt the knots in his stomach loosen. It didn't matter how many times he'd been in combat, the knots were always there, a reminder not to take anything for granted.

Manton's voice once again cracked in his earbud. "The lead vehicle is four hundred yards away. The second one is still following, but its driver is maintaining a fifty-yard gap. The third vehicle has stopped."

Donovan mumbled a curse. "Understood. I was hoping they would all drive directly to the barn."

"Stand by . . . Third vehicle's front doors are opening. Driver and passenger have exited the vehicle."

"What's their distance?" Donovan asked.

"Third vehicle is about five hundred yards away, but the distances I've been giving you are what's left if they stay on the dirt. Because of the gradual bend leading to the barn, the two tangos on foot have only three hundred yards to cover to reach your position."

Donovan brought up the map of the terrain around him in his mind's eye. These guys were maybe not as dumb as Donovan had thought and hoped for. Keeping a fifty-yard gap between the two lead vehicles was good tactics. With two men on foot, there was a chance he and Helen would get squeezed out between the two narcos and the two lead vehicles. Donovan and Helen could cross to the other side of the road, but the situation could get complicated if another set of shooters were to be dropped on that side, too.

"Helen, Donovan," he said.

"Go."

"I'll need to withdraw from my position and move to intercept the—"

"I said go, Donovan," Helen said. "Go take them out."

Donovan was confused, but not for long. Helen was proving once again that even though she'd let him talk when he'd given her the instructions for the ambush, she knew exactly what was going on. She'd probably known the moment Manton had notified them about the two shooters edging their way to the barn that Donovan would move to intercept them.

"On my way," he said.

Donovan left his position and entered the cornfield. "Talk to me, Oliver," he said. "Give me the angles I need."

"I see you," Manton said. "The two shooters are moving fast and perpendicular to you. Turn to your right ten degrees and keep your pace."

Manton continued, "Helen, the two lead vehicles have now come to a stop. They've bunched up. There's no more gap between them. They're two hundred yards away from the barn. Two men are climbing out from each vehicle. They're armed with rifles."

Donovan and Helen both acknowledged.

"The two-man team I'm aiming for is the recon element," Donovan said, moving fast through stalks of corn, his MP5SD raised in front of him. "They might try to get into a position from which they can observe the rear door and set up their own ambush."

"The lead man is pushing to the rear of the structure, Donovan," Manton said. "But the second changed direction and he's now headed straight at you. One hundred yards."

Donovan stopped, took a knee, and listened closely into the light breeze rustling through the cornfield.

"Distance to contact?" he asked, keeping his voice low.

"Fifty yards, and still heading in your direction. If you stay still and he doesn't change course, he'll pass five to seven yards to your right."

"Copy," Donovan replied, inching his way to his right. Seven yards in a cornfield was like five hundred yards in an open field.

"Helen," Manton said. "The four men heading your way are in a V-shape formation and using the dirt road. They're one hundred and twenty-five yards away, but they aren't moving fast."

"Helen copies," she replied. "I see them. They're waiting for their left flank to be covered."

Donovan agreed with her. If the main force was waiting for the support team to get into place before beginning the assault on the barn, odds were that the two men Donovan was after wouldn't be as vigilant as they should be, deciding instead to rush to their positions. That was something Donovan planned to use to his advantage.

As if to confirm Donovan's assessment, Manton said, "The men on the road have stopped and moved to the side of the road, two on each side."

"I saw that," Helen confirmed.

Donovan felt a chill down his neck. He hoped the

narcos weren't about to use the cornfield to conceal the last one hundred yards of their advance.

"Donovan, twenty yards," Manton warned. "He'll be almost on top of you."

Donovan's senses were fully alert, his submachine gun pointed in the general direction where he expected the shooter to pass through, but his eyes never quite locked on anything. Donovan heard the man's hard breathing before he saw him—a fast-moving figure going left to right through his field of vision less than two yards away.

Donovan pulled the trigger, sending a single round into the narco's chest. The man's left hand flew to where he'd been shot, but his legs hadn't stopped moving and he fell forward. Being suppressed, the MP5SD had made only a gentle *puff* when he fired the round, but Donovan was more worried about the louder metallic sound of the cycling of the MP5SD's action. The noise it created didn't belong. It was an anomaly. Odds were that the four men waiting on the side of the road had caught the sound but, without a follow-through shot, they might assume it was something else. That was why when Donovan saw the man he'd shot roll to his side, he let the MP5SD fall against its sling and tugged the knife out of the sheath attached to the front of his plate carrier. He plunged the blade deep into the side of the *sicario*'s neck and twisted the blade hard, silencing the man for good.

Donovan's eyes shifted back and forth, scanning his surroundings. Everything was quiet, but his heart was pounding. He took an extra second to compose himself, then said, "One down. Where's the other one?"

"Approximately seventy-five yards to your east," Manton replied. "He's quickly making his way to the edge of the field."

"Copy. Moving."

Contrary to his four colleagues who had halted by the side of the dirt road, this narco was moving, and if his breathing was as labored as that of the man Donovan had just stabbed to death, Donovan didn't think the narco had heard the shot.

"The main element is back on the dirt road, V-shape formation," Helen said, her voice tense but in control.

Donovan wished he could reply, but he was too close to his new target to chance it. The best Donovan could do was dispatch the lone narco rapidly and hurry back to his initial position.

"Donovan, your target is now immobile and fifteen yards away from you, thirty degrees to your front," Manton said. "It's getting too dark for me to tell you in which direction he's looking."

A few steps later, Donovan stopped to listen. He could feel the other man's presence, and he wondered if the narco could feel *his* presence, too. Donovan was about to take another step when he heard the man talk. It was not much louder than a whisper, but there was certainly tension in the man's voice.

He's calling his partner. He's trying to check in with him.

Donovan chastised himself for not taking the dead narco's radio.

You didn't even look for it. Get your head in the game!

The lone narco was still trying to call his friend, so

Donovan took the opportunity to get closer, choosing each step with care. Donovan could see the edge of the cornfield now. Another five, maybe six yards. He was yet to see the narco, but Donovan could smell him. The familiar odor of tobacco and stale cigarettes emanated from the man's clothes.

The man was close.

Then, slightly to his left, Donovan recognized the shape of a man standing two yards from the edge of the field. For sure an easy shot with the submachine gun but, knowing the four other narcos were advancing toward the barn, Donovan didn't want to risk it. The man's head was turned to the rear of the barn. Donovan pulled his knife out without a sound and took three painstakingly slow steps. Donovan was about to make his move when the man suddenly rose to his feet, bringing a submachine gun to his shoulder.

Something had spooked him. But what?

Then the man opened fire, and Donovan knew he had fucked up.

FORTY-FIVE

Helen glanced up at the sky. It was getting dark, and the moon had taken refuge behind a bank of heavy clouds. She could only see fifty yards in front of her and was having a hard time tracking the four silhouettes leapfrogging toward the barn. She didn't dare look directly at any of them, afraid her gaze would somehow warn the men of her presence.

Donovan had dispatched one of his two targets and was now on his way to intercept the second one. She hadn't heard a gunshot, so she imagined he'd used his knife.

Unless he choked the man to death. That was a possibility, too.

The silhouettes were advancing two at a time. Two moved forward for ten yards, dropped to the ground, their chests flat against the dirt road, and didn't move until the two others had moved past their positions.

Two men approached the Škoda Kodiaq while the others stayed back, covering their advance. Helen was confident that if she was to open fire now, she could take out at least one, maybe two of them, before the survivors returned fire.

Not good enough. Be patient.

Movement close to the barn caught her attention. She slowly turned her head, cautious not to make any sudden moves, and caught a glimpse of something running toward the back of the old barn.

The cat.

She was carefully turning her head back to the Kodiaq when a long burst of automatic fire exploded.

Shit! Donovan!

The four men had been taken by surprise, too. And, for a moment, none of them moved. If Donovan was down, she couldn't wait any longer. Either she engaged the four *sicarios* or she retreated. But there was no way she'd leave without her partner. She picked the narco who was farthest away and aimed the front sight of her MP5SD at his chest. She pulled the trigger once, sending a three-round burst into her target's center mass. At this distance, the man was a dark blur, but there was still just enough light for Helen to see him fall. Helen had sighted her next target when a line of bullets stitched along the ground toward her.

• • • • •

Donovan would never know what had caused the man to open fire, but his decision to favor stealth instead of speed had cost him and Helen their biggest ally: surprise.

Donovan clutched the lone narco's forehead, kicked the back of his leg, and thrust his knife into the man's exposed throat, once, twice, then jammed the blade through his ribs and into his heart. There was so much blood that Donovan's hand slipped from the knife when the man fell forward.

Gunfire erupted not far from him, then he heard Helen scream. His heart sank.

"Helen, talk to me!" he shouted. "Helen!"

But there was no reply. Ignoring his knife, Donovan brought his MP5SD to his shoulder and ran toward the sound of the guns, no longer worried about his safety.

• • • • •

Helen flattened herself against the ground as the rounds poured into her position, throwing up tiny puffs of wet dirt and grass as they impacted in front of her and whizzed above her head.

Donovan's voice buzzed through her earbud, but she didn't hear what he said. And that was when she realized that she'd let out a scream and was unconsciously trying to claw her way deeper into the muddy field.

Get a grip, Helen!

I might be outgunned and outmanned, but I have the slightly *higher ground. And a grenade.*

Now, barely conscious of what she was doing, she rolled to the left, ripped the grenade free from the pouch of her plate carrier, pulled the pin, and tossed it in the general direction of where she'd last seen the shooters.

"Grenade!" she said quietly, knowing her comms

system would amplify it sufficiently for Donovan to hear the warning.

She rolled to her left again and waited for the grenade to do its thing. Two seconds later it did. It exploded with a deafening blast. She pushed herself to her knees, her MP5SD tight into her shoulder, scanning for threats. One shooter was limping toward the double-wide doors of the barn. Knowing what was about to happen, Helen hit the ground again.

"Booby trap about to go off," she said for Donovan's benefit.

One second later, the grenade she had rigged to the barn's doors detonated with a distinctive thump.

FORTY-SIX

Gustavo Berganza was shivering with rage. He had never been so scared, so terrified, and in so much pain his entire life. He'd always been frightened by what he didn't understand, and, at this moment, he couldn't comprehend what had gone wrong.

Hiding behind the Škoda SUV, his back resting on the rear passenger-side tire, Berganza was desperately applying pressure to his stomach wound, but the blood kept seeping through his fingers. To his left, Salvador looked unscathed. The former Gulf Cartel member had escaped the blast.

Fucking Salvador. It was all his fault.

It was Salvador who had somehow missed the two FBI agents at the café. It should have been so easy. How could he have missed such easy shots? Of course, Salvador had an excuse ready. He'd explained his failure by saying that the female agent had recognized the white Nissan and seen their approach. Salvador even had the audacity to add that the female agent had started shooting before he had the chance to align his first shot.

Lies!

How was that even possible? How could they have known about the Nissan? The GPS tracker Guillermo had dropped into one of the tall, bearded American agent's pockets had done its job. The tracker had allowed Berganza and his crew to follow the Škoda Kodiaq out of Prague very loosely, giving the FBI agents plenty of rope. It was only when the Americans had headed into Teplice that Berganza had allowed the vehicles to close in, not wanting to miss an opportunity. When the Kodiaq had found a parking spot next to a café, Berganza had given the order to attack.

Even Thiago—Francisco Abalos's younger brother—had agreed with the plan. Berganza had been furious when Abalos had imposed Thiago's presence and authority over him. He'd never worked with the damned kid!

"My brother, like me and our father before us, was a soldier. A real one. He has seen combat. You haven't, Gustavo. You were an *intelligence* officer."

Berganza's temper had flared up at the way Abalos had portrayed his work for Mexico's intelligence service, but he'd been in no position to argue. After the fiasco in Prague, he had no choice but to walk on eggshells around Abalos. But even more crucial, and something Abalos had made abundantly clear, Berganza couldn't fail. So, if Abalos wanted to send his kid brother so that he could report on him, fine. As long as Thiago stayed out of Berganza's way.

Minutes after the missed drive-by execution in Teplice, Abalos had called him.

"Gustavo, Thiago is telling me you haven't been listening to him and that you've lost another man in Teplice. Is that true?"

"An unfortunate—"

"Enough of your pathetic and never-ending excuses! I've had about enough of you," Abalos had growled.

"Yes, *patrón*," Berganza had said, humiliated.

"This is your last warning, Gustavo. Talk with Thiago and listen to what he has to say. If you follow his lead, you might live another day."

Berganza had listened to Thiago just fine. Berganza had sent two of his men to flank the old, decrepit barn and to conduct a quick reconnaissance.

And for what? They were dead. Ambushed.

Then, as they made their approach, one of his men had cleared the Škoda SUV and advised Berganza of two distinct sets of footprints heading toward the barn. Berganza hadn't even had the chance to respond. Gunfire erupted.

Thiago had been the first to get shot. He was now bleeding to death in the middle of the dirt path leading to the barn. Berganza could see him ten yards away, sluggishly dragging himself with one arm in Berganza's direction.

Upon hearing the muffled shots that had downed Thiago, Berganza had immediately returned fire with

Salvador and another man. He'd been certain they'd killed whoever had opened fire on them. That was until the grenade had exploded and showered him with rocks, dirt, and shrapnel. Berganza hadn't seen the grenade tossed in their direction, though he suspected Salvador might have heard or seen it because the man had suddenly thrown himself to the ground moments before the grenade detonated.

And here I am, hiding behind an ass-cheap Škoda.

Berganza tried to get into a firing position, but the shrapnel that had torn into his side sent hot flashes of pain strong enough to paralyze him.

"We can't stay here," Salvador said, scanning over the vehicle with his rifle. "We need to move, *patrón*. They could be flanking us right now."

Berganza tried to say something but found himself incapable of doing so. He wasn't breathing very well. A volley of fire hit the SUV, raking its side, puncturing steel, and ripping through the interior. Salvador ducked back behind cover, clearly pissed off.

Then, without saying a word or even looking at Berganza, Salvador rose to his feet, emptied his magazine toward the shooter, and took off at a sprint to the barn.

FORTY-SEVEN

Donovan had reached the barn when he heard Helen's warning about the grenade. He dropped flat against the ground but was back on his feet the second after the grenade exploded. He hadn't covered more than a few feet when Helen voiced her second caution.

As he flattened his chest to the ground, Donovan couldn't help but smile. Unless he was mistaken, Helen had already neutralized at least one, but probably two of the four shooters. Helen had more balls than most men he'd worked with at the CIA. The fact that she was still in the fight after the barrage of fire he'd heard coming her way told Donovan everything he needed to know about her. He'd known her only for a few months, but he already felt a deep connection to her.

On his feet, Donovan continued to the front of the barn, his left shoulder hugging the wall.

"What's your twenty, Helen?" he asked.

"Couple yards east of my initial position," she replied. "Two shooters down. I don't know where the other two are."

"Good copy," Donovan replied, approaching the barn's corner.

"Donovan, stop!" Manton shouted over the air. "Two shooters have taken position behind your rental."

"Donovan copies."

"The moment you step out in the open they'll cut you down."

"Understood," he said.

"I have a pretty good firing position," Helen said. "I can't hit them from here unless they break cover, but I can keep their heads down."

"Wait for my word and start sending rounds their way," Donovan told her.

Donovan jogged to the back of the barn and placed his hand on the door handle. "Show them you're still there, Helen," he said.

The shots were muffled, but Donovan heard the metallic pings of bullets hitting the Kodiaq. He opened the door and slipped into the barn. The good news was that the grenade Helen had rigged to the double-wide doors had blown one of the shooters to bits. His upper body lay in the front right corner of the barn while one of his legs had landed right on top of the sketch Donovan had drawn in the dirt. The shooter's other leg had simply vanished. It was too dark for Donovan to identify the dead man, but he hoped it was the guy who'd shot at him at the café earlier. But there was bad news, too. The ladder leading to the mezzanine that gave access to the top front window of the barn had also been blown up.

"I'm in the barn," Donovan said. "I was hoping to get an angle on them from one of the windows but that's not gonna work."

"There's a—" Helen started, but she was interrupted by a long burst of automatic fire coming from an unsuppressed rifle. It was followed by shorter, more controlled bursts from Helen's MP5SD.

"Shit. One of them got away," Helen warned him. "He's running on the opposite side of where you were, Donovan. He might try to enter the barn by its rear door."

"Understood," Donovan said, stepping to the side of the door. He let go of the MP5SD and pulled his CZ 75 out of the holster.

"I can confirm," Manton said. "He's now at the southeastern corner of the barn and heading in the direction of the rear door."

The door opened moments later, and the muzzle of a rifle appeared in the doorway.

Donovan was ready. He wanted this one alive.

He grabbed the barrel with his left hand and pushed it to the side while angling his pistol toward the shooter's legs, but the man surprised him by head-butting him in the face. Donovan's head spun and he saw stars. It was as if he'd been hit by a bowling ball. Donovan felt a powerful hand envelop his wrist, pushing it down. Donovan squeezed the trigger, sending a round into the dirt between the man's legs. As Donovan's vision returned, he recognized the shooter.

It was Ninja.

Ninja let go of his rifle and used his free hand to deliver an uppercut to Donovan's chin. Donovan had taken a lot of hits during his university boxing career, but this uppercut had been perfectly delivered and almost knocked Donovan out. Ninja wrenched Donovan's pistol away and it fell somewhere close to them. Ninja kicked Donovan in the chest, pushing him back a few steps. Ninja rushed him, and Donovan, knowing he didn't have the time to shoulder his submachine gun before his opponent tackled him, moved his hand to the sheath across his plate carrier, only realizing too late he'd left his blade in Ninja's friend's heart.

Shit.

Donovan landed on his back, with Ninja on top. Ninja didn't waste one precious second and began to pummel Donovan's face with punches, a few of them good ones. Donovan threw a fistful of dirt into Ninja's face. Ninja's reaction was immediate, and typical. He closed his eyes, and one of his hands moved to his face. Donovan bridged his hips and threw Ninja off him.

Both men got to their feet at the same time. Again, Donovan tried to level his submachine gun, but Ninja was no fool. He knew the moment he gave Donovan enough space, it was game over for him, so he came at him, swinging, going for the win with a big right hook.

It would have hurt Donovan if it had connected, but it didn't. Donovan easily arched around the punch and swatted away the expected left that followed. This time, though, Donovan delivered a strike of his own. He drilled the left heel of his boot into Ninja's kneecap, driving straight through it. Ninja's leg folded backward, exactly like a normal knee joint would allow, but in the opposite direction. Ninja fell on his ass, but he did not scream. Donovan had to give him that much. The man was tough. He just looked at his fucked-up leg, then at Donovan.

Donovan smiled at the man. "You and I will have a nice, long chat, amigo."

Then, obliterating Donovan's wish, Ninja reached for Donovan's CZ 75, which had ended up only three feet away from him.

"Don't!" Donovan warned, this time having more than enough time to shoulder his MP5SD.

Clearly Ninja wasn't about to listen to his advice.

His loss.

As Ninja was about to swing the CZ 75 in Donovan's direction, Donovan fired. Ninja's hand shot to his neck. Donovan's 9mm round had carved a tunnel to the back of Ninja's throat.

Donovan kneeled next to the dying man. "You simply had to tell me if you didn't feel like chatting. You did this to yourself, asshole. Take that with you to hell. Your stupidity killed you. Remember that."

Donovan could hear the sound of gurgling blood as

Ninja tried to breathe, or speak, Donovan didn't care which. Seconds later, Ninja stopped breathing and died.

• • • • •

Helen let out a sigh of relief when she heard Donovan's voice. She didn't want to celebrate too early, but the overall situation was looking much better now than it had been only a couple of minutes ago.

"I'm good. He's not," Donovan said.

"No changes here," she replied. "Last shooter is still hidden behind the Kodiaq."

"He hasn't moved for the last minute," Manton confirmed. "For your information, the drone is about to run out of batteries. I'm circling one more time around the perimeter before bringing it down. Also, your air asset is on station. The chopper is five minutes out, but I'll need your confirmation the LZ is secured before sending it in."

"Helen copies all. Don, I have eyes on the Kodiaq. I suggest you exit through the rear door and approach the vehicle by the south side of the barn."

"On my way," her partner replied.

• • • • •

Donovan stayed in the shadows, but moved swiftly to the Kodiaq, leaning into his MP5SD in a combat crouch, his boots quiet against the wet grass beside the barn.

"I'll land the drone between the barn and the Kodiaq," Manton said. "Perimeter looks clear but it's too dark to be sure."

"I have a visual on the shooter," Donovan said as he pulled out his SureFire flashlight. "He's still behind the

Kodiaq. He's in a sitting position with his back against the rear passenger-side tire."

"Helen copies. Moving."

Donovan walked past the edge of the barn, his submachine gun aimed at the injured shooter. The man's rifle was next to him, but he didn't make a move toward it. Donovan clicked on his flashlight and pointed the beam at the shooter. Donovan recognized the man from Prague. He was the one who had had the bad idea of attacking Donovan with a knife. Donovan remembered smashing the guy's face with his knee.

The man's face hadn't improved. Not one bit. Donovan would argue it was even worse. It was now gleaming with sweat, fear, and blood. The man's left hand was clutching his side, but he was holding a phone in his right. Donovan almost pulled the trigger, thinking the phone might be an IED—improvised explosive device—but it slipped from the man's hand before he could touch any button. The narco turned his head to look at Donovan just as Helen joined him, but his eyes were empty.

"Nice to see you again, señor," Donovan said, squatting next to the narco.

The blood and gore on the man's shirt made it difficult for Donovan to tell if the man had been shot or if he'd caught shrapnel from the grenade Helen had thrown.

"Let me see," Donovan said, placing his hand on the man's wound.

The narco's body tensed and he let out a faint cry as Donovan roughly explored the injury with his fingers. The man's eyes focused on Donovan's, as if he were seeing him for the first time—then he erupted in a rattling cough.

Donovan shook his head. "That doesn't sound good, amigo, but I have good news for you," he said. "Shrapnel is stuck deep into you, but at least none lodged in your heart. No major arteries were hit, so there's that, too, right? Thing is, you're bleeding to death, and there isn't much I can do about it. Not sure I'd want to anyway."

Donovan moved his fingers to the man's neck and checked his pulse.

Rapid. Weak.

"That little cold heart of yours is working overtime to pump the blood you have left in your body into your pea-size brain," Donovan said. "If we don't get an IV into you in the next ten to twelve minutes, you're done."

The man shuddered.

"Tell us what you know about Proyecto de la Verdad," Helen said. "If you do, I promise we'll drop you at the hospital in Teplice. It's only a couple miles away, so there's time, but you need to start talking."

The narco opened his mouth to say something but only managed to spit out a mouthful of blood. He took a ragged breath, then said, "Fuck . . . you."

"Well, that's disappointing," Helen said. "You must have a truly miserable life for you to prefer dying than to tell us a few words about Proyecto de la Verdad. I almost feel sorry for you."

"You know we'll find out anyway, right?" Donovan said. "So your resistance is quite pointless, to be honest. A waste, really."

The man's phone began to vibrate in the dirt, its screen coming alive.

"Oliver, are you still there?" Helen asked.

"Of course. We're all listening. I'm with Faith Jackson and Teresa Salazar."

"Is there any way for you to track that call?"

"Not if we don't have its number," Salazar replied.

Donovan picked up the phone and said, "I have an idea."

He let the phone ring without answering it. When it stopped vibrating, he refreshed the screen and shined the beam of his SureFire flashlight into the narco's face. The man still had enough brainwidth to understand what Donovan wanted to do. He tried to look away, but Donovan grabbed his jaw and twisted his head back so that the phone could recognize its owner.

The phone unlocked, and Donovan scrolled through its settings until he found the number. He barely had time to share it with Manton before the phone rang again.

Donovan counted to five, hoping it would give the folks at Blackbriar headquarters enough time to do whatever they needed to to track the caller, then he tapped the green button to accept the call.

"*Sí?*" he said.

For a long moment, there was no reply.

"Who do I have the displeasure of speaking with?" a man finally asked in English, but with a thick Spanish accent. "Wait. Wait. Let me guess . . . Is this Donovan Wade?"

Donovan hadn't expected to be called out like that. At the mention of his name, Donovan's brain went into overdrive trying to remember if and where he had heard that voice before. Helen wore a dumbfounded expression.

"Who are you?" Donovan asked. "I seem to be at a disadvantage."

"Even if I was to tell you my name, you wouldn't recognize it," the man said. "I'm surprised the CIA is trusting you enough to let you operate in the field. I wouldn't. How can they be sure you're not a traitor? Like your brother."

Donovan remained silent. The man was talking too much. Donovan understood why the man had gone out on a limb, but by doing so, he'd told Donovan how little he knew. Whoever that man was, he hadn't been kept in the loop.

"Tell me, Donovan," the man said, switching gears. "How many of Gustavo's men have you killed?"

Helen tapped him on the shoulder and showed him the text she'd received from Blackbriar. The analysts had dialed in on the call. The man was in Prague.

"Well, it was fun talking to you," Donovan said. "Hope to meet you real soon, pal."

"Oh, fear not, my new friend, we will," the man hissed. "I promise."

Donovan noted the dangerous stillness in the man's voice. The person at the other end of the line was a predator, a thing of the dark. A stonehearted killer.

"And when we do meet," the man continued, "I'll

slowly peel back the skin from your face, and, just when you start being numb to the pain, I'll push your face into a bowl of citrus juice and I'll—"

Donovan ended the call and looked at Helen. "Well, that went better than I thought."

FORTY-EIGHT

Francisco Abalos removed the phone's battery and returned it to his bag. He would never use that phone again and would discard it later. He then took his personal phone and listened one more time to the voice message his brother Thiago had left him. It only lasted eighty-six seconds, but it was enough for Abalos to feel the immeasurable physical agony his brother had been in when he'd called. Abalos steadied himself against the dining table, resisting the urge to scream as he listened to his baby brother's moans and cries until they became barely audible. In the background, an explosion that sounded like a grenade going off, followed by more gunfire.

Then there was a twenty-two-second pause, but now Abalos wasn't so sure anymore. He closed his eyes, trying to imagine what his brother was doing. There was a faint scraping sound, as if his dying brother was dragging himself on a dirt or gravel road. Abalos had to open his eyes, because he couldn't stomach the images his brain was generating for him.

There.

Abalos tapped the rewind button and went back five seconds. Yes. There it was again. His brother had tried to speak. Abalos heard syllables, but they were slurred, unintelligible. And then, that, too, stopped. It was followed by the harsh, gurgling, and rasping sound of Thiago's last breath. Abalos connected his phone to his laptop and downloaded the voice message. He opened it through a sound-enhancing app and began to clean up the background noise. He then isolated the sound of his brother's voice and heightened its contrast.

He pressed play.

'Cisco . . . Kill . . . k . . . em . . . all.

Abalos couldn't remember the last time he had shed a tear for anyone, or anything, and today wasn't the day he would break the cycle. Crying was not how a warrior avenged his fallen brother. Abalos was going to do it the old-fashioned way. The way his brother had demanded it.

He was going to kill them all, starting with Donovan Wade and the FBI bitch working with him.

FORTY-NINE

Helen looked up but couldn't see the chopper. She could hear it, though. It was close. She could tell by the loud knocking of its blades. Manton had told her it would land on the dirt road west of the barn. While Donovan took mug shots of the dead, Helen took care of their gear, placing it all on the backseat of the Kodiaq. They were leaving it behind, except for their pistols, which they would dispose of at the very last moment.

"We're set," Donovan said, jogging to her. "I collected four cell phones but not much else of interest. I took a pic of almost everyone but couldn't find the first guy I intercepted. I can't remember where he is in the cornfield. Sorry."

"As long as you're sure he's dead and won't start shooting at the chopper."

"A round to the chest and an eight-inch cut deep into one's throat is a one-way ticket to the big guy," Donovan replied.

Helen said something, but it was drowned out by the incoming chopper's rotors beating the air. She showed two incendiary grenades to Donovan. He gave her a thumbs-up. She tossed the two grenades onto the backseat and closed the door. The incendiary devices would completely destroy the Kodiaq, erasing their DNA and obliterating the gear they had left inside the SUV.

They were about one hundred yards away from the Kodiaq when Helen got her first look at the chopper—a sleek black shadow that would have continued to blend seamlessly into the night if it hadn't been for the light emanating from the burning SUV.

A spotlight was suddenly powered on, and the long shaft of its beam sliced up and down the dirt road. It stopped when it reached Helen and Donovan, but they had thankfully already closed their eyes. The pilot powered off the spotlight and made a quick sweep over the barn and the cornfield to the north, once again disappearing from view. It reappeared one hundred and fifty yards farther down the road, dropping out of the night so fast Helen thought it was going to crash, but it flared at the last moment, throwing up a curtain of loose sand, small rocks, dust, and cornstalks.

The helicopter settled onto the road and Helen recognized it as a Bell 407. The pilot, wearing a dark flight suit, a helmet, and a pair of goggles, climbed out of the chopper and signaled for Helen and Donovan to hurry. As they got closer, he opened the rear door for them.

"C'mon! Let's go!" he shouted at them. "Police vehicles are only a mile away."

Helen climbed into the chopper, quickly followed by Donovan. The pilot closed their door and jumped back into his seat. Fifteen seconds later, the chopper took off and bent into a fast, climbing turn. Helen put on her four-point harness and donned one of the pairs of earphones hanging inside the cabin. Donovan did the same.

She looked outside at the emergency vehicles racing to the barn. She pulled the mic closer to her mouth and said, "Thanks for showing up. You have no idea how happy we are to see you."

"Are you, now?" the pilot replied.

Helen gave Donovan a look, but her partner just shrugged and rolled his eyes.

"Let's just say I didn't feel like explaining to the locals what happened," Helen said. "Anyhow, we're glad you picked us up."

"Well, you might not have to explain to the police what you were doing there, but you'll certainly have to clarify a few things for me, Helen," the pilot said.

Helen's heart skipped a beat. How did the pilot know her name? She couldn't believe that Oliver Manton had been so careless. And why should she feel the need to *clarify* anything with the pilot? Who in hell did that twat think he was?

Again, Donovan didn't look too bothered, but he did ask an important question.

"Where are we going?"

"Dresden Airport," the pilot replied. "I'm told you guys have a plane to catch."

"What? Look at us," Helen challenged him. "There's no way they'll let us board looking like this. We don't even have our passports anymore."

"Oh, you guys weren't told?" the pilot said, letting out a light chuckle. "Your boss changed your flights. You'll be flying with me to North Macedonia."

"Awesome news," Donovan said, nudging Helen with his elbow.

Although she was way past the point of exhaustion, going to North Macedonia to continue the investigation was indeed good news. She just didn't get why Donovan's grin was as wide as it was. She opened her mouth to ask him, but Donovan lifted a finger, asking her to *wait for it*.

"Personally, I'm thrilled about this," the pilot said as he removed his goggles and glanced over at Helen. "It will give me time to catch up with my daughter."

Helen's breath caught in her throat, and she felt her jaw drop. She looked at her partner. Donovan had closed his eyes, pretending sleep, but she could still see the tiny smile tugging at the corner of his lips.

FIFTY

Treadstone director Levi Shaw wasn't in a good mood. He hadn't slept well the night before, and now he was being summoned to God-knows-where by the DNI. The only thing Russell had given him was an address.

"Don't write it down, Levi," the DNI had warned him, which had pissed Shaw off. As if he needed to be told.

"And give your driver the night off."

Shaw didn't hold any grudge against DNI Russell—Shaw had heard the man was pretty down to earth and that his knowledge of the world's geopolitical disputes was unparalleled— but it was well past midnight. Couldn't whatever *this* was be done the next morning? Shaw had just spent the last two days negotiating the terms of a lease for two new safe houses in New York with a real estate developer who thought Shaw was representing the interests of an overseas buyer. The only thing Shaw yearned for at the moment was the comfy bed of the five-star hotel he was staying at.

But apparently, even that is too much to ask. I'm so tired of this shit.

"We're here," the cabdriver said in a thick New York accent. "You sure you're at the right place?"

The driver, a beefy man with dark, curly hair, wearing a white shirt whose collar had turned yellowish due to a lack of regular washing, had tried to make conversation. But it had been a one-way exchange, with Shaw's part mostly consisting of throwing in a few *mm-hmms* and *reallys?* Shaw didn't blame the guy for trying, maybe hoping that being chatty would give him a better tip. And it kind of worked. The poor guy was probably looking forward to finishing his shift and heading home to see his wife and kids.

And hopefully take a shower, too.

Shaw paid the man with cash, leaving an extra ten, and climbed out of the taxi. He walked half a block east, hands in his coat pockets, until he saw the four-story commercial building that had been described to him. The building was surrounded by tall trees and a seven-foot brick wall. The only entrance—a ramp leading down to an underground garage—was a bit farther east. At the bottom of the ramp, to the left of the garage door, was a digital keypad. Shaw entered the eight-digit number that had been given to him.

The parking garage was smaller than Shaw had anticipated. It seemed to cover slightly less than half of the building's footprint. Nevertheless, about twenty of the fifty or so parking spots were occupied.

What now?

The DNI had told him he'd receive instructions once he was in the garage. After five minutes, Shaw was beginning to think he'd made a mistake by coming here. Then his phone buzzed.

"Shaw," he said, unable to hide his grumpiness.

"Director Shaw," a woman's voice greeted him. "Thank you for coming. Please make your way to the end of the parking facility and make a left. You'll see the elevator. We're waiting for you."

The call disconnected.

With a sigh, Shaw followed the instruction. When he entered the elevator, there were only five buttons. One for each floor, including the underground garage.

A law office was taking the top two floors, while an accounting firm occupied the second. Next to the first-floor button, a single word was written.

Blackbriar.

I'll be damned.

• • • • •

Oliver Manton sat behind his desk with his eyes closed, his hands behind his head. His feet, crossed at the ankle, were perched on one corner of his bureau. Positioning an air asset had been a good call. The moment the mission in Prague had taken a bad turn, he'd sent in a request. In Manton's opinion, Blackbriar should be given its own air assets. He understood it would be impossible to position choppers for his program's exclusive usage all over the world, but if Blackbriar could at least get its hands on a jet, it would simplify the logistics—at least when it came to transportation—for his teams. Choppers could be chartered at the last minute, just like they'd done in Teplice. He was going to have a serious discussion with the DNI about that.

He'd known for quite some time that Helen's father was one of the pilots for BeachSpray—a covert civilian aviation unit established to support nonmilitary clandestine activities on behalf of the US government. When he was with Treadstone, he had flown a few times using BeachSpray's aircrafts. Despite behind staffed exclusively with civilian aircrews and administrators, BeachSpray's employees mostly came from the military.

Christian Jouvert, Helen's father, was a decorated and battle-tested former air force pilot. He'd once landed his A-10 Warthog attack plane without hydraulics after part of its tail was shredded by enemy fire in Iraq. The man had nerves of steel.

Just like his daughter, Manton thought.

Helen's background investigation had revealed she and her dad weren't close. Manton didn't think it was going to be an issue, but he wondered how she'd reacted when she realized it was her father who'd picked her up from a difficult spot. Manton had sent a quick message to Donovan to forewarn him of the situation.

A knock sounded on the door of his office and Manton opened his eyes to see Faith Jackson step into the room.

"Director Levi Shaw is here, sir," Jackson said.

"Did you leave him in the foyer?" he asked.

"Yes, and he doesn't look happy about it," Jackson replied with a faint smile. "Should I bring him in?"

"Director Shaw is rarely happy, Faith. But yes, bring him in."

Jackson had started closing the door behind her when Manton called her back.

"You know what? Ask security to escort him to my office. I'm sure Shaw's gonna love that."

"Yes, sir."

"And Faith, make sure he gets the pink visitor badge, will you?"

Once Jackson had left, Manton straightened the loose papers on his desk and secured the classified files in his safe. He couldn't wait to see Shaw's face. But as much as he'd been angry at his former boss for pulling him out of operations after Cairo, Shaw was a good, dependable, and devoted man who'd been through a lot recently.

Maybe the pink visitor badge is a bit much, Manton thought, opening his office door.

At the end of the hallway, Faith Jackson was leading the way, followed by Levi Shaw. Mike Houtz—Blackbriar's head of security—closed off the march. Manton retreated into his office and waited for Shaw. By the time Shaw appeared in the doorframe, he had Jackson and Houtz laughing their hearts out.

"Here we are, Director Shaw," Jackson said, shaking the Treadstone director's hand. "And thanks so much again for the tip. It means a lot."

"Don't mention it," Shaw replied, then turned to the

Blackbriar head of security. "A pleasure to meet you, Mike."

"Pleasure was all mine, sir," Houtz replied. "My wife and I will have to check out that restaurant soon."

"You won't be disappointed," Shaw guaranteed him. "Best ratatouille in town, I swear."

If Shaw was surprised to see Manton, he hid it well. In less than three minutes, Shaw had managed to coerce Houtz and Jackson into liking him. The old spy hadn't lost his touch.

As Houtz and Jackson returned to their own offices, Shaw glanced at Manton and gave him a disheartened smile. He tugged free the pink visitor badge Houtz had clawed to his jacket and lobbed it to Manton.

"Really, Oliver?"

"Yeah, a bit overboard," he admitted, closing the door of his office. "Drink?"

"You better make it a stiff one," Shaw replied.

Manton headed to his bar and poured a copious amount of single malt whisky into a pair of crystal tumblers.

He held one out for his guest. Shaw took the tumbler and examined it.

"My Lord, Oliver, you're getting fancy."

"A friend of mine got me into single malt a few years back," Manton said. "It's an acquired taste."

Manton watched as Shaw swirled the liquid around his glass before bringing it to his nose. "Not bad," he said. "What are we drinking to? Blackbriar?"

Manton smiled, tilted his tumbler in silent acknowledgment, and took a sip. He then walked around his desk and took a seat. Shaw eased himself into one of the two chairs facing Manton's desk.

Shaw was the first to speak. "I thought Blackbriar was dead and buried. Apparently not."

Manton could see that Shaw's brain was spinning, trying to make sense of it all.

"Will you give me a tour of the facilities?" he asked.

Manton shook his head. "Not today."

"Is . . . Is Blackbriar set to replace Treadstone? Is that why I was asked to come here? Because you should know that DNI Russell no longer has any authority over me or Treadstone."

"The answer to both of your questions is no. And yes, I'm aware Treadstone now operates under the DoD. Frankly, Levi, there aren't many similarities between our two programs. Though we do our best to be proactive, Blackbriar is mostly defensive, going after whoever wants to steal our government's secrets. This means you don't have to worry, we're not in the assassination business. This field is all yours."

"So Blackbriar focuses on covert counterintelligence and counterespionage work?" Shaw asked.

"Mostly," Manton replied. "We try to mess with our adversaries' intelligence-gathering activities the best we can. Ultimately, though, we serve at the DNI's pleasure."

"A new genesis, then."

"You could say that, yes."

Manton took a sip of his drink, his eyes on Shaw. The man's mind was still sharp as hell, of that Manton had no doubt. Shaw had a commanding presence, but the last few years hadn't been kind to him, and he had aged quite a bit since Manton had last seen him. He had packed on a few pounds, too. The amount of stress Shaw was under was tremendous. Manton, even though he hadn't been at the job for very long, was beginning to feel the pressure. He wondered if he would be able to tough it out for as long as Shaw had.

"What am I doing here, Oliver?"

"Good question," Manton said.

Shaw's eyes narrowed and he moved to speak, but Manton forestalled him with a raised hand.

"I called the DNI earlier today to let him know that what happened in Prague wasn't related to Treadstone. John Dixon was at the wrong place at the wrong time. He wasn't the intended target."

Shaw's expression was a mix of shock, confusion, and relief. But mostly of confusion.

"How . . . Oh, wait. Shit. Russell reached out to you, didn't he?" he said. "He's the one who told you about John Dixon."

"Honestly, Levi, these scenarios, like the one in Prague involving Dixon, are why Blackbriar exists. Treadstone might not be as secretive as it once was, but the government has never, and probably will never, officially acknowledge its existence. When John Dixon was killed, who did you reach out to? The DoD? No. Because you can't trust them. And it isn't like you can call the FBI, either, right? So what did you do? You contacted Edward Russell. And guess what?"

"Russell forwarded my request to you," Shaw said.

"He did."

Shaw nodded. "He trusts you. How could he not after Cairo?"

Shaw looked at his tumbler, realized it was empty, and walked to Manton's drink table to pour himself another. He returned to Manton's desk holding the bottle of single malt in his left hand.

"Top up?" he asked, but he had already tipped the bottle over Manton's glass.

They spent the next few minutes in silence, each working on their drink, thinking. Then Shaw said, "I still don't know what I'm doing here, Oliver."

"Right. Well . . . When I called Russell and told him about Prague, he shared with me that you were in New York and asked if I'd be willing to have you come over to our headquarters."

Shaw finished his second drink, looked at the bottle, but didn't reach for it.

"It makes sense," he said after a moment, his eyes still on the bottle. "Can't say I blame the DNI for putting together a program like Blackbriar. The FBI's hands are full, and they can't get anything done quickly anyway." Shaw continued, "I'll even go a step further, Oliver. I think you're the perfect man for the job."

"I appreciate that."

"Now can you tell me what the fuck happened in Prague? Targeted killing or not, John Dixon's dead and I want to know why."

Manton's glass was empty, too, but, like Shaw's, it

stayed that way for the next thirty minutes as he talked Shaw through Helen and Donovan's investigation.

When he was done, Shaw scratched his head and said, "I can't say that I'm surprised to hear the Russians are now working with Mexican drug cartels. After the horrors the Russians have committed in Ukraine, nobody wants to be associated with them anymore. Unless you're the scum of the earth, or a drug cartel. But Proyecto de la Verdad, that doesn't ring a bell. I wish it did, though."

"Same here. And believe me, we looked hard. My analysts ran it in six different languages in all the federal databases we have access to. Nothing."

"What do you think this has to do with Mind-U?" Shaw asked. "Is it possible that this goes beyond UR Real News?"

"I'm wondering the same thing. Why was Russian intelligence, especially Unit 29155, and possibly Unit 74455, interested in Mind-U?"

"Mind-U is a powerful corporation," Shaw said. "For the last couple of years, it's been growing by a factor of two every freakin' year. Within two, maybe three years, they'll be the largest social media conglomerate in emerging markets and will hold a commanding presence in the United States, too. Every month they're growing more influential, not just for their dating apps and games, but in all spheres of society."

Manton thought about what Shaw had said. "I see it. That's why they hired Lucas and William Miller, two highly respected American investigative journalists. And they haven't stopped there. We were able to find out that six more well-known European reporters had joined the fold in recent months. Mind-U wants to be taken seriously. They want to be listened to when they speak."

"Exactly. And it's working. The question we need to ask ourselves is why? Who's behind Mind-U? What do they want? Is it just money, or is there a darker, more dangerous motivation? By the way, last time I checked, four of their apps were among the top ten most downloaded worldwide. Mind-U is fast approaching one billion users. Twelve to eighteen months from now, it could be two billion. That's power, Oliver. That's real power. It scares the shit out of me."

"All valid points," Manton conceded. "We'll see what my team digs up in Skopje. They left Dresden aboard a Cessna Citation CJ3 about ninety minutes ago, so they should land in North Macedonia in about . . ."

Shaw beat him to the punch. "Twenty to twenty-five minutes," he said. "Did Helen know it was her dad who was going to fly her and Donovan out of danger?"

"No. What would be the fun in that?"

"Uh-huh. For what it's worth, I've never met the guy, but I know who Christian Jouvert is. Balls of steel, or so I've heard. Anyhow, what's the plan once your team gets there?"

Manton shrugged. "It's their plan, not mine. I'm only here to support them, not to micromanage every aspect of their investigation. Everything you and I talked about, they know."

Shaw chuckled. "So, what you're really telling me is that you have absolutely no idea what they're gonna do in North Macedonia?"

"I'm a retired assassin, Levi, not an investigator. Helen will figure it out."

"Anything I can do to help?" Shaw asked.

That was Levi Shaw, all right. Always ready to help, or at least that's what he wanted you to think. But Manton wasn't fooled. With the confirmation that John Dixon's Raphaël Feldmann deep cover persona hadn't been blown, Manton had removed a major thorn in Shaw's side. In Manton's book, the Treadstone director now owed him a favor for Blackbriar's operation in Prague.

"You know what, Levi, I think I'll keep that chit in my back pocket for now," Manton said.

Shaw rose to his feet, and, after a moment of hesitation, he offered his hand to Manton. "Till next time, then."

FIFTY-ONE

MANZANILLO, COLIMA, MEXICO

General Ramón Velásquez rushed through the opulent living room and walked to the large floor-to-ceiling windows that covered the entire length of the rear of his seven-thousand-square-foot oceanfront villa. He opened the doors and stepped onto the massive terrace facing the Pacific Ocean. Built to his specifications, the property was positioned to maximize the spectacular view of the ocean. The sun was bright and strong, with not a cloud in the sky, but the gentle breeze coming off the water made for a perfect temperature. Major General Belousov, wearing a pair of long khaki trousers and a white short-sleeve shirt that accentuated his thickly veined, muscular arms, was leaning against the glass railing. He glanced over his shoulder, gave Velásquez a polite nod, and resumed staring at the open sea.

Velásquez was far from being a choirboy. He'd committed his fair share of atrocities, but he had never willingly hurt women and children. Had there been incidents in which some of them had died? Of course. A few occasions, here and there. But only as collateral damage. Never because they were specifically targeted.

That alone differentiated him from men like Belousov. Belousov was a savage who had never made any distinction between enemy combatants and civilians. A few weeks after the beginning of the invasion of Ukraine, Major General Igor Belousov, then a colonel with the Spetsnaz GRU, had ordered the destruction of a pediatric hospital. More than fifty children had perished that day. Belousov was a war criminal.

Velásquez felt dirty just being in the Russian general's vicinity, but the cold, sad truth was that he needed him. In order for Proyecto de la Verdad to succeed, he needed access to Belousov's Unit 74455. Contrary to the other special program Belousov commanded, Unit 29155, which specialized in diversionary operations and occasionally dipped its toes in the assassination business when it fitted its needs, Unit 74455 was an elite cyberwarfare program that employed the Russian military's best mathematical minds. Without Unit 74455, Proyecto de la Verdad would grind to a halt. The cartels, as rich as they were, simply didn't have the expertise to launch a complex campaign of disinformation across the United States the way the Russians could. The Russians were simply the best. No one could even come close when it came to destabilizing a country by spreading misleading information.

Velásquez had watched with interest—and quite a bit of admiration—the significant effects of Unit 74455's multi-pronged operations in the United States over the last decade. It had been a thing of beauty. Velásquez honestly believed that if they had kept at it instead of switching their focus to Ukraine, Russian intelligence could have set the United States back an entire generation. Within only a few years, Unit 74455 had successfully divided American society more than any conventional war could ever have.

The cartels had loved it, too. While the Americans fought among themselves, they weren't paying much attention to what was going on south of their border with Mexico. When they had finally realized that the cartels had swept into practically all spheres of their society and had started to wield their influence, the Americans had fought back—as if their survival depended on it.

Velásquez knew that it did. And, unfortunately, so had the president of the United States.

In a bold, provocative move meant to appease the citizenry, the American president had publicly declared his intention of designating the cartels as foreign terrorist organizations by year's end—establishing the base for future US military interventions in Mexico. The cartels had pushed back hard, forcing the politicians they controlled at home and abroad—and there were many of them—to tell their American counterparts that moving ahead with the president's strategy would put an immediate end to the newly signed US–Mexico security agreements and economic cooperation deals.

But this time, it hadn't worked. To the cartels' horror, the American president hadn't backed down.

During his years as Mexico's secretary of defense, Velásquez had gained the trust of the cartels by making sure that as long as they remained in their lanes and kept civilian casualties to a minimum, the Mexican government wouldn't interfere with their activities. He had never broken his word, and, under his six-year tenure, the cartels had continued to flourish. By charging one-fifth of a percent from the net income of each cartel for his pacifying services, Velásquez had become extremely wealthy. And with the cartel's protection, he had become untouchable.

By wielding the specter of military operations in Mexico, the Americans weren't only threatening the cartels, they were also coming after Velásquez's income and security. That was when he had reached out to Igor Belousov, who, after being flown in a private jet to Velásquez's mansion in Manzanillo and treated to all the best things in life for a couple of days, had been more than receptive to Velásquez's proposition.

Velásquez, using his influence, had invited the heads of all the important cartels to his house for a two-day convention to propose Proyecto de la Verdad. Present at this meeting was General Belousov.

When asked by the head of the Sinaloa Cartel how Proyecto de la Verdad could force the American president to abandon his idea to designate them foreign terrorist organizations when all other previous efforts had failed, Velásquez had said, "We will destroy their will from within, my dear friend. We will plant the seeds of doubt deep into their mind, and they won't even know we have done it. Slowly, but surely, we will convince them of the disastrous effect such a designation would have on their society. We will also display for everyone to see the terrible repercussions this would have on poor, regular, hardworking Mexicans. And believe me when I say this, the American public doesn't have the stomach for it. They will be the ones who will convince their representatives to fight against the president's proposal."

"How, Ramón?" the head of Los Zetas had growled. "Stop with your political speeches! You haven't explained to us what you're planning to do. The majority of Americans aren't as dumb as we used to think. They have a tendency to gel together when confronted with a common enemy. And right now, that enemy is us. That needs to change!"

"I'm not disputing that, but I will tell you how we can weaken their will to fight us. But first, let me remind you that we are at important crossroads, gentlemen," Velásquez had said. "What we decide today at this table will drive us into the future. I don't pretend to have all the answers, and, although I believe you will all agree with me on the path we must take, the last thing I want to do is to force upon you a decision you don't want to make. With that in mind, here's how we can come out of this stronger than ever."

At its core, Proyecto de la Verdad was a group effort. Every cartel signing on to the operation would have to provide Velásquez ten *sicarios* and pay an initial fee of fifty million in United States dollars, a weighty sum for sure, but not overly expensive considering the billions of dollars each cartel was bringing in every year. Velásquez would keep a hefty fee for his trouble, which he was smart enough to disclose from the get-go. Fifteen million dollars. The rest would be used to pay the salaries of the men he had requested, and the substantial amount General Belousov demanded for his services.

Challenged about the one hundred million Belousov had requested up front, Velásquez had given the floor to the Russian general, who had seemed completely oblivious to the danger he was in. Velásquez had known that if Belousov failed to convince the cartels, chances were he'd never return to Moscow. At least not in one piece. But Belousov had handled himself well. More than well, in fact.

Truth was, Igor Belousov was a force to be reckoned with. The cartels' leaders had quickly understood that. Belousov, although polite and respectful, was no pushover. He had clearly explained his strategy and had done so in flawless Spanish.

The cyberattack would unfold in multiple stages. It would begin with Unit 74455 infiltrating an audience, then influencing it by using kompromat obtained by Unit 29155 to drive narratives against American politicians supporting the US president. These steps would be controlled by Belousov and administered through a combination of media actors, including Mind-U, which was quickly gaining popularity in the United States. The operation would be backed twenty-four hours a day by troll factories and hackers based in Moscow.

"This kind of attack works because we seek to form an early narrative and we repeat it using a wide range of outlets," Belousov had explained. "My top software engineers have told me they've detected a structural vulnerability they could exploit on the Mind-U platform. We're presently working on acquiring the necessary codes to begin our exploit."

"I assume you've been working on this vulnerability for a while, haven't you, General Belousov?" a cartel boss had asked.

"We have. This exploit would allow us to control the algorithms of most of Mind-U's apps. In order not to tip our hand, the changes would be subtle at first, but, over time, it could be a game changer."

"And you would be willing to share all of this with us?"

"For the fee mentioned by Ramón, I would."

"And you're confident this will work?"

"Based on the results of similar operations we ran in the recent past, I know it will," the general had replied. "You have to understand that once we've decided on a narrative for the target audience, it gets repeated and echoed through different traditional actors and also on social media. That gives it an appearance of truth. Since all they see are multiple news and social media sources with different perspectives reaching the same conclusion, how can they fight back? The average American social media user is simply overwhelmed with the sheer amount of repetition."

Velásquez had promised the cartels that with this kind of relentless multichannel propaganda machine, Belousov's team would be able to pump out a tremendous amount of damaging information in a very short period. The meeting had lasted more than eight hours, but, in the end, the cartels had bought into Velásquez's Proyecto de la Verdad.

But with that newfound power also came responsibilities. And accountability. Until today, Proyecto Verdad had gone according to plan. The loss of Berganza's team was an important, if not fatal, setback. Velásquez understood he couldn't afford too many of those. The alliance between the cartels was a fragile thing. To preserve that cooperation, Velásquez would have to show the cartels positive results soon.

Velásquez eyed the two naked girls lounging on the sun bed, sipping champagne. Their warm, inviting smiles morphed into a stoic expression as they deciphered his mood. He put them off with a wave of his hand. They pushed off the sun bed and hurried past him, disappearing into the mansion, but without forgetting to sway their hips while doing so.

At his request, lunch was laid out on the long wooden table, which was surrounded by stone pots planted with cascading flowers. A selection of grilled meats, pastas, and salads was presented family-style. A bottle of premium vodka sat next to a wine decanter filled with an exquisite pinot noir, but the news Velásquez had just received from Francisco Abalos had ruined his appetite and put him in an irritable temper.

He joined Belousov at the railing.

"Thank you for organizing that fishing expedition this morning, Ramón," Belousov said. "I'd never caught a sailfish—"

"I don't care about your fishing expedition, Igor!" Velásquez spat, his hands tightening on the railing. "I've lost eight good men in the last twenty-four hours."

Belousov's head jerked in his direction. "How?"

"I don't have the details, but Abalos told me his brother Thiago was killed, too."

"By the two Americans? Donovan Wade and the female FBI agent?" the Russian general asked. "Eight, well, nine, isn't it now? Nine of your men against two lousy Americans? And you manage to lose them all without inflicting a single enemy casualty?"

Velásquez's blood was beginning to boil. He didn't appreciate Belousov's condescending tone.

"Is there something you haven't told me about the CIA officer?" Velásquez asked, because he, too, had a hard time believing two American federal agents could have taken out Gustavo Berganza's entire team.

"Why would I keep anything from you, Ramón?" Belousov asked, making it look like he was deeply offended by Velásquez's question. "All I know about Donovan Wade, you know, too. I have nothing else to share with you about him. But tell me about the reporter. Lucas Miller, is he dead?"

Unhappy with the way Belousov had brushed off his question about the American spy, Velásquez considered pushing back. He couldn't shake the nagging feeling that the Russian general hadn't being totally truthful. In the end, though, he let it slide. He had a favor to ask Belousov and needed the Russian to be receptive to his request.

"Abalos did his job, and he took care of Miller's doctor, too," Velásquez said.

Belousov crossed his arms over his chest. "That means the Americans are on their way to Skopje," he said.

"I assume they are. We'll know if they make contact with our man," Velásquez said. "But I'll need you to send a team to assist Abalos."

Belousov nodded. "Major Krupin is recuperating well and should be able to travel very soon," he said. "She made it clear she would love to have another crack at the Americans."

Velásquez resisted the urge to remind Belousov that if Krupin and the SVR operatives in Cairo had done what Belousov had promised him they would, Velásquez wouldn't be short eight men and Abalos's brother would still be alive.

Though, in the back of his mind, Velásquez wasn't sure that Thiago's death was such a bad thing. Abalos wasn't one to forget and forgive easily. There wasn't a thing Abalos wouldn't do to avenge his brother. That was fine with Velásquez. In normal times, Abalos was a terrific operator—Velásquez's top operative in Europe—but now he would be driven by the most powerful source of motivation known to man.

Revenge.

"Major Krupin proved herself quite useful as a spy," Velásquez said, using as much diplomacy as he could muster, "but I'd be more comfortable if you were to send . . . real killers to Skopje."

"I do have a GRU Spetsnaz detachment available," Belousov replied. "The same that took care of Steven Cooper's family in Texas. Most of them have already left the United States and are on their way back to Russia."

"Could they be diverted to North Macedonia?" Velásquez asked.

"I could have the entire eight-man team in Skopje within the next twelve hours, ready to go. If I was to give them the order, that is."

A small electric shock passed through Velásquez's body. He cocked his head to one side and slowly turned to face the Russian general, hoping he was wrong and that Belousov hadn't just passive-aggressively threatened not to send the Spetsnaz team to Skopje.

Unfortunately, the expression of arrogance on Belousov's face was on full display.

The bastard isn't even trying to hide it.

"A highly trained Spetsnaz detachment with recent combat experience and a proven track record is a rare commodity nowadays," Belousov explained, his voice way too patronizing for Velásquez's taste. "An additional twenty percent on top of the original agreed-upon fee would go a long way toward convincing me to release such a team of . . . real killers, yes?"

Taking a deep breath, Velásquez willed himself to

relax. He had ordered men killed for much less. At the moment, though, slicing off the general's body parts and putting them in a grinder wasn't an option, so there was no point losing his temper. It would only further empower Belousov.

It was no secret that the economic sanctions imposed by the Western powers against the Russian Federation had pushed Russia to the brink of collapse. The ruble was now worth less than a penny, and the purchasing power of ordinary Russians had eroded sharply. Even high-ranking officials like General Belousov—who were usually immune to such unpleasantness—were feeling the weight of the sanctions. Despite all of this, and the fact that Russia was once again about to default on an interest payment on its foreign debt, Russian intelligence still remained a force to be reckoned with, particularly Unit 29155 and Unit 74455, and with both of them answering to General Belousov, Velásquez had to tread with caution.

He had to remember that his own neck was on the line, too. The cartel leaders expected results.

"I'm curious, Igor. What makes you think you're in a position to make any demands? I thought we were partners. Have I missed something?"

Belousov straightened himself. He was tall, and a rather physically imposing man. His dark eyes, filled with barely contained anger, were set on Velásquez.

"Don't take me for a fool. I know what I'm worth. I know what I'm bringing to the table. If you could accomplish your objective without me, you would have."

"I think you greatly overestimate your value," Velásquez said.

"Is that so? In that case, the price is now fifty percent more, not twenty."

Velásquez felt the blood drain from his face. "You're fucking suicidal, Igor," he hissed. "If you think—"

Belousov's right jab to Velásquez stomach came fast and furious and drove the air out of him. Velásquez didn't have time to fill his lungs before the Russian's hands wrapped around his neck in a viselike grip. Belousov's fingers squeezed, digging deeper into his neck.

I can't breathe!

Velásquez desperately tried to break free of the grip, but he just couldn't loosen the hold. The edge of his vision began to fade. Then, as if he were being dragged like a puppet, he felt himself being pulled closer to Belousov. The Russian weakened his grip, but only enough to allow a limited quantity of oxygen through.

Belousov was in perfect control. Clearly, he had done this before.

"Listen to me, you little fuck," the Russian said in Spanish, his lips touching Velásquez earlobe. "You might have the upper hand now while my country's economy is getting rebuilt, but Russia isn't as broken as you think it is. Do not underestimate me, and do not underestimate the will of my president. The only reason I'm here, doing business with you, is because he agreed to it, and you've been paying on time. You want my Spetsnaz team to perform work outside of our original agreement? Fine. I will provide this team to you, but at a fee."

In his anger, Belousov had once again tightened his hold on Velásquez's throat, blocking his oxygen intake. Velásquez's legs were like two strands of cooked spaghetti.

"If it was up to me, I'd knock you out right now, place my thumbs in your eyes, and squeeze your head until I split your skull like a melon. Then I'd throw your overweight and disgusting body over the railing and watch you crash into the rocks one hundred feet below. But it's your lucky day. I—"

Then a shot rang out. Then another. For a moment, Velásquez felt himself falling, and he wondered if Belousov had changed his mind and thrown him over the protective glass railing of the terrace, but his head hit the ground almost immediately and he realized that the Russian had simply released his hold.

Velásquez heard someone yelling behind him. It sounded like a woman. He squinted, trying to see, but his vision was blurry. He tried to get up but managed only to get to his knees.

Then his vision cleared, and he looked in horror as General Igor Belousov hurled a naked woman over the railing. There was a scream, similar to the one he had heard seconds ago.

Dios mío! *He's thrown both of them over the railing and into the sea!*

Armed men belonging to Velásquez alerted by the women's screams, rushed to the terrace, rifles up, pointed at Belousov, who was slowly raising his hands. But they didn't shoot. Belousov was unarmed. A pistol lay at his feet. That was when Velásquez saw that Belousov had been shot in the left arm. A bullet had gone through his bicep, just above the elbow.

"*Patrón?*" one of his men asked.

Slowly, carefully, Velásquez stood up, not convinced his legs would support him. But they did.

He looked at Belousov, not sure what to say. But Belousov, surrounded by armed men, with blood snaking down his arm from a bullet wound, surprised him again.

"You have two options, Ramón. The first is instant gratification. You can kill me now. Easy, yes, but you'll die before the week is over. That I can guarantee. Your second option is to order your men to stand down, so that we can continue our business. But hear this, the price is now double the very first amount we had agreed upon, and it needs to be paid immediately. It's your choice. I don't care either way."

"*Patrón?*" his man asked again.

Velásquez tried to swallow but couldn't. His throat was raw, and his neck hurt like hell, but he fought back the impulse to touch it. He stared into Belousov's icy blue eyes. The Russian didn't flinch, although a cold, calculated smile appeared on his lips.

Velásquez gestured to his men to lower their weapons. "That's fine. You can go," he said to them. "Ask the doctor to join us so that he can attend to the general's wound."

"And my money, General. Don't forget my money," Belousov said, bringing down his hands.

Velásquez pursed his lips, not sure how he was going

to justify the expense to the cartels' bosses. But this was a problem for another day. Today's objective—apart from staying alive—was to ensure the two Americans wouldn't gain access to the notes Lucas Miller had left behind. Failure to do that could jeopardize the entire operation. So far, the cartels had given him free rein on how to run Proyecto de la Verdad. But what the cartels gave, they could take back. With interest.

"Get my laptop and bring it to me," Velásquez barked to the *sicario* still standing next to him. "Now!"

The man scurried back inside.

Velásquez walked to the dining table and pulled out a chair, signaling Belousov to do the same. "Let's eat."

FIFTY-TWO

SKOPJE, NORTH MACEDONIA

Helen reluctantly got out of bed and turned on the bedside lamp. She looked at the pull-out sofa bed where Donovan had slept for the last two nights, but he was gone, and the sofa bed had already been made and set back in place.

Slipping on a terry-cloth robe, she went to the curtains and parted them. Sunlight spilled into the room. She slid the glass door to the right and stepped onto the small balcony. The noise and floral smell of the street below greeted her, and so did the view of the River Vardar—as long as she craned her neck to the right.

Not bad. Considering what she'd read about the city, she expected worse.

Due to Skopje being nestled in a valley between mountain ranges that edged the city from the north and the south, that specific landscape often created a blanket of smog that settled heavily over the valley, trapping the polluted air emanating from the communist-era power plants and factories on the city's streets—and in its residents' lungs. But today wasn't bad. A few mothers with their small children played in the park across the street, laughing.

The room door opened, and she turned to see Donovan enter the room, holding a coffee tray, a plastic bag, and two small paper bags. She tightened the belt around her waist and greeted him with a smile.

"Breakfast?" she asked.

"Blueberry muffins and buttered toast for me," he said, placing the two paper bags on a small round table, then handed her the plastic bag. "And for you, a cucumber and tomato salad with feta cheese."

"You got me a Greek salad for breakfast?"

"Not at all. Greek salad has onions, this one doesn't," he said.

"Really?"

"You almost bit my head off when I brought you a baklava and a piece of sweet bread yesterday," Donovan said. "I thought you'd be happy with a salad. It's low carb."

She gave Donovan a wry smile. They sat down and ate in silence. It was sweet of him to have gone out to pick something up to eat, but she was still pissed at him. A little. Even after two days. He should have warned her about her dad. It was a strange thing to learn that your father had been lying to you for years. Not that she and her dad talked much. They barely exchanged Christmas cards. But still. She felt that she should have known her father was working for a covert aviation company.

That goes both ways, Helen, she told herself. Her father must have been flabbergasted when he had seen her jogging to the helicopter.

"For God's sake, Helen, put yourself in the poor man's shoes!" Donovan had told her. "He picked up his only child, who he thought was safe back home in the US, in the middle of a war zone, with dead bodies all over and a burning vehicle. He must have freaked out."

Shit! Now she felt guilty for having been such an ass with her dad during the night flight to Skopje.

"Hey. You okay?" Donovan asked her.

"Yeah. Just thinking about my dad," she said, stabbing at a piece of feta cheese with her plastic fork.

"Try to focus on the good things, you know? Like the fact he didn't lie to you about being sober for ten years. That should count for something."

"Uh-huh," she said, munching on a piece of cucumber and reaching for her coffee.

"And when you really think about it," Donovan continued, "he did tell you he was flying jets and helicopters for a private aviation company. Chris might need to work on his transparency—"

"'Chris'? Oh, I see. So you guys are best pals now, is that it?" Helen said, looking at Donovan over the rim of her coffee cup.

"I like the guy, Helen," Donovan said. "What do you want me to say? Just the fact he was flying A-10s gives him a lifetime membership into the cool club."

Helen slowly chewed on a piece of cheese. Donovan was right, of course. She should be proud of her dad. He had turned his life around and was once again doing something he loved. Once they had this operation wrapped up, she would carve out some time to spend with her father. Helen brought the steaming coffee to her lips and inhaled, closing her eyes as she tentatively took her first sip.

"Your meeting with Milan Velkoski is in four hours," Donovan reminded her between mouthfuls of blueberry muffin.

"Did headquarters dig up anything new about him?" she asked.

"One thing, but I don't think it's relevant. As you know, Milan is forty-eight years old, born and raised in Skopje, and he lives in a condo not far from the UR Real News offices. What we didn't know yesterday was that he studied journalism at Cardiff University in Wales."

"Cardiff U, huh? He comes from money?"

"Not at all," Donovan replied. "Government grant. At least that's what headquarters thinks for now. But they're looking into it. Anyhow, when he came back, he got an offer to work at the *Nova Makedonija*, North Macedonia's oldest daily newspaper."

"And now he's the editor-in-chief at UR Real News. How did he end up there?"

"Unclear. But he's been there for four years, and his track record is far from stellar. Under his management, UR Real News has gotten a reputation for publishing the kind of political hit jobs favored by the conspiracy theorists. To be fair, though, they did publish a few outstanding articles about women's interests, the environment, and lifestyle that garnered quite a bit of attention."

"The hit jobs, were they published before or after Mind-U purchased them?"

"Before, but I think these articles are what got Mind-U interested in them in the first place. They got a lot of attention. I'm talking millions of clicks. For a digital-only media enterprise, UR Real News's international reach is pretty good, especially in the US. Due to its mixed reputation, I have a feeling that UR Real News's acquisition cost was low for a behemoth like Mind-U."

It all made sense to Helen. UR Real News had a large and growing readership in the United States, so by acquiring it, Mind-U also grabbed all the customer data UR Real News had accumulated over the years. For a media conglomerate like Mind-U, whose top priority was to get a foot in the American market, the customer data alone was worth the purchase price. And, if hiring a few distinguished American investigative journalists like Lucas and William Miller helped them become more mainstream, even better.

Somehow, though, everything had turned to shit. Unit 29155 had become interested in Mind-U, and two of the renowned reporters UR Real News had hired had been assassinated.

Because of Proyecto de la Verdad.

"Did Manton get back to you regarding the backstop of our new covers?" Helen asked.

"As a matter of fact, on my way back this morning

Faith Jackson sent me a message to confirm that they've been ready since yesterday. So far, it doesn't appear like Velkoski tried to call the *Globe and Mail* to verify our identities."

"Either that or they weren't able to intercept the call," Helen said.

"I don't think there are too many calls to the *Globe and Mail* originating from Skopje on any given day. I'm confident the analysts wouldn't have missed it."

"We'll know soon enough, but you're right, I don't think Milan Velkoski has any reason to dig too deep. Maybe he's already done an online check to see if there is indeed a Lisane Averill and Gabriel Hudson working at the *Globe and Mail*. Anyhow, we don't need him to believe we're Canadian reporters for very long. We just need him to give us Lucas Miller's address."

"It's hard to imagine that in this day and age, a man like Lucas Miller, or even his wife, aren't listed anywhere," Donovan said. "How can our analysts not find a single clue about them since they moved to North Macedonia?"

"Yeah, I wondered the same thing. Given they have a teenage daughter, it's highly unusual. Most kids nowadays are incapable of going through life without social media."

Donovan took a long pull from his coffee. "Exactly."

"But wait, I've thought this through," Helen said. "Here's what I came up with. When Mind-U hired him to join UR Real News, Miller knew exactly what kind of investigative pieces he'd be doing for them and, to protect his family, he's following a strict protocol that probably looks like what the US Marshals Service uses for their witness protection program."

Donovan tapped his coffee cup against hers. "All right, you did think this through," he said. "That makes sense."

Once they were done with breakfast, Helen unfolded a map of downtown Skopje and said, "I want us to go over the op one more time."

"Here's Velkoski's condo," Donovan started, tapping his finger on a blue-green circle on the map five hundred yards east of the old town. "The green circle just north of our hotel is where the UR Real News offices are located, and the black circles are the three vehicles we positioned yesterday."

"And they're all within a ten-minute walk of the meeting point in the old town," Helen added, putting her index finger on the red circle.

Helen grabbed a brown marker and circled two locations on the map. "These are the two Airbnbs headquarters got for us in case of emergency."

Helen and Donovan spent the next hour discussing how they were going to conduct their respective SDRs on their way to meet with UR Real News editor-in-chief Milan Velkoski. They had already established that Helen would see Velkoski by herself while Donovan provided cover.

They looked at Google Maps to familiarize themselves with Skopje's old town and to select the different routes they could take to get to the two Airbnbs. Three hours before the scheduled meeting with Velkoski, Donovan exited the hotel room. Helen sent a sitrep to headquarters and stepped out of the hotel twenty minutes after Donovan, with no way of knowing that her cover was already blown.

FIFTY-THREE

SKOPJE, NORTH MACEDONIA

Until the night before, Major Stanislava Krupin hadn't slept with a man in quite a while. Since the death of her husband—an armored brigade commander—in Ukraine, her libido hadn't been the same. But the moment she'd set her eyes on Francisco Abalos, she had felt a tingle in her chest that had spread down to her belly.

Even now, as she stood to the side of Lucas Miller's apartment door, gun in hand and only moments before breaking into the apartment, Stanislava's eyes moved to Abalos, who was busy picking the old door's dead bolt and knob lock. He was tall and lean, with a handsome, angular face and dark, intense eyes. She especially liked the smirk that seemed to be permanently settled lightly on his lips.

A man at ease with dangerous situations, but also a

man who knew how to be kind and caring, and, if she was honest with herself, quite an expert when it came to the pleasures of the flesh. A shiver ran down her spine as she remembered how gentle his fingers had been while they had explored every inch of her body, including the bruises she had on her chest and ribs.

She'd been lucky to survive in Cairo. The FBI bitch had fired center mass, hitting her three times. Thankfully the rounds hadn't penetrated her light body armor. She was looking forward to seeing the FBI agent again.

Next to her, Abalos replaced his lock-picking kit in his backpack.

"Ready?" he whispered to her in Russian.

She took three short breaths, then nodded. "Yes."

The Spaniard turned the handle and eased the door open. He went in first and immediately angled right to the large living room. She went left, clearing with one sweep the small but well-furnished dining room. Satisfied there were no immediate threats, she closed the door and pushed farther left to the kitchen. A woman in a maid uniform was wiping the counter. She had a pair of earbuds in, a thin white cord trailing down to a pocket Stanislava couldn't see. The woman was in her midtwenties and was bobbing her head to whatever music she was listening to. She never saw Stanislava and didn't hear the muffled pop of the suppressed shot. Stanislava's round hit her a fraction of an inch above her left eye. The maid disappeared behind the counter, leaving a spatter of blood mingled with slivers of pulpy matter on the fridge's door behind her.

A moment later she joined Abalos at the entrance of the hallway that led to the three bedrooms. He indicated to her that he had heard something coming from the second door on the left.

She nodded, signaled she was going to take the lead, and took a few cautious steps. She'd only advanced a few feet when she heard a toilet flush. She stopped and hugged one side of the wall while Abalos took the other, their pistols pointed down the hallway. The second door to the left opened, and a woman came out, wearing a white bathrobe. She was in her forties. Her long black hair, flecked with gray, had been messily clipped on top of her head. She was sobbing, with mascara dripping down her cheeks. Stanislava recognized her from the intelligence brief she'd received from General Belousov.

Lucas Miller's wife.

The woman locked eyes with Stanislava, an expression of utter shock on her face. She heard Abalos's pistol bark once. The woman sucked in a breath, a spot of red appearing in the middle of her stomach. Her hands went straight to the spot where she'd been shot, then she fell on her knees, but Stanislava missed that as she was already on the move, clearing the room to her right.

Fifteen seconds later, with the bathroom and the three bedrooms cleared, she unscrewed the suppressor and holstered her pistol. Abalos had put a piece of tape over the wife's mouth and was now zip-tying her blood-soaked hands. She writhed on the floor, moaning, her eyes clenched in agonizing pain.

"Sit her up," Stanislava said.

Abalos grabbed the woman under the armpits and sat her up against the wall.

Stanislava squatted next to her, looking at her tear-drenched face.

"I'm aware of how much pain you think you are in," Stanislava said, stroking the woman's hair. "But believe me, it can get much worse."

The woman fought to breathe through her mouth, but it was an impossible task with the duct tape pressed over it. "Calm down and breathe through your nose," Stanislava said. "We'll remove the tape in just a few moments, once we're sure you understand the rules. For now, try to relax and focus on your breathing."

It took a few moments, but the woman did it, though her entire body was now shaking. She was going into shock, which was fine. They didn't need her to stay alive for much longer.

"Okay. Good job. So, here's the deal. Your husband Lucas and his brother William were working on Proyecto de la Verdad. A big, very dangerous assignment. We already know that. There's no point in denying it. If you did, you'd only prolong your agony.

"He didn't trust many people at UR Real News and, for that reason, he only kept paper files. He told us he kept them here, in this apartment. I need those files. If you tell us where they are, we'll take them, we'll call you an ambulance, and we'll leave your apartment. In this scenario, your chances of survival are better than fifty-fifty."

"Nod if you understand," Abalos said.

The terrified woman's eyes flicked in Abalos's direction. Since she was shaking so badly, Stanislava had a hard time assessing whether she'd nodded, but Abalos gave her the benefit of the doubt.

"If you refuse to tell us where they are, we'll make your life even more miserable than it already is. And, as a bonus, we'll wait patiently for your daughter's return. You can't even imagine what we'll do to her. I truly hope you know where your husband kept his files, because if you don't, the consequences will be the same as if you had refused to cooperate with us."

Abalos turned to Stanislava. "Was I clear?"

"Yes. Very clear, I think."

Abalos ripped the tape from the woman's mouth. "Speak."

"They are . . . in our closet. Master bedroom. A . . . brown shoebox."

Stanislava rose to her feet and headed to the bedroom. She opened the closet door. A neat row of business suits, skirts, dresses, and blouses hung from a metal rod. Above the clothes, shoeboxes sat on a wooden shelf. Stanislava stepped deeper into the closet and grabbed the shoeboxes one by one. The third one was brown and heavier than the others. She opened it and looked inside. Under a dozen newspaper clippings was a blue file with PROYECTO DE LA VERDAD clearly written in bold, black letters across the dossier. She quickly scanned through the fifty or so pages inside the file. Some were handwritten notes, but many were typed. Lucas and William Miller had done a pretty good job researching Proyecto de la Verdad. She was yet to be fully briefed by General Belousov on what Proyecto de la Verdad was, and Francisco had assured her he didn't know, either. She wasn't sure if she should believe him, but, in any case, this file would certainly enlighten her. For good measure, she checked the other boxes, but found nothing else useful.

She sent an encrypted message to General Belousov to let him know she'd found the file. He replied quickly with a message of his own and very specific instructions. She read it twice, then a third time to make absolutely sure she understood the meaning of her orders, then pocketed the phone.

It was time to share the good news with Abalos.

FIFTY-FOUR

SKOPJE, NORTH MACEDONIA

For Donovan, using the SDR techniques he'd been taught at The Farm—the CIA training facility at Camp Peary, Virginia—had become second nature. Donovan had spent months practicing how to blend in to a crowd while maintaining situational awareness. On one occasion, a few weeks before he was due to graduate, he'd fucked up on an SDR. The worst was that he had felt—known, really—that someone was onto him. But he hadn't listened to the little voice in his head begging him to abort. He hadn't followed his gut. His failure to do so had cost his team the mission.

In real life, though, it could have killed them all.

After the long debrief in which he had chewed Donovan's ass in front of the whole class, the chief instructor had pulled him from the group.

"Don, you're one of the strongest recruits I've ever

trained, but sometimes you're just plain reckless, or over-confident. Some of the instructors think it's because you're a natural prick, but I was in the marines, Force Recon, just like you. So I know what's going on in there." The chief instructor tapped a finger on the side of Donovan's head.

"Marine Recons like us are trained to go at it one hundred percent all the fucking time, right? We've been taught to push our fears aside, to work through them and to persevere no matter what. If we have to charge through an open field as rounds kick up spouts of dirt around us, we'll do it if that's what it takes to complete the mission, yes?"

"Yes, sir."

"Okay, good. But you're not Marine Recon anymore, Donovan. Forget you ever were. As an intelligence officer, if you do your job right, you'll never have to fire a gun again. Your tradecraft is everything. It's your bulletproof vest and your weapon at the same time. Your survival will depend on how proficient you are at executing it. And out there in the field, it needs to be fucking flawless. Always assume you're being watched, and that the enemy knows exactly who you are and what you're doing and why. But, even more importantly, and listen carefully, because this might save your life one day, always assume that they're going to push you into a van and put a bag over your head any second."

Donovan had never forgotten that lesson. In fact, it had probably saved his life in Prague. And right now, after spending two hours doing an SDR on his way to the old town, he was hearing that same little voice again. He couldn't see the impending threat to his safety, couldn't hear it, but he could feel it. He'd notified Helen the moment he thought he was being watched and they had automatically switched to running aggressive counter-surveillance techniques. They had tried all the tricks in the book to identify potential watchers, but, unlike in Prague, where it had been easy to uncover the three amigos, so far both he and Helen had been powerless to isolate even one watcher.

While they had been able to top up their magazines in the Citation jet, he and Helen had no weapons other than their pistols and knives. Their stealth and the cover Blackbriar had manufactured for them were their main means of defense, just like the chief instructor at Camp Peary had told him. If they had to go to their guns, something had gone terribly wrong.

As a last resort, Donovan had decided to stop at one of the numerous terraces to grab a bite to eat. He wasn't hungry, but ordering something would give him an excuse to stop and keep an eye on the passing crowds as he ate. He had tried to catalog in his head as many faces and vehicles as possible during the last two hours. Now was the time to cross-reference them with the ones he was about to see while seated at the table. The table he had selected gave him a good view of the traffic driving through Boulevard Krste Petkov Misirkov and the pedestrians browsing the shops on Kiril Percinovik.

Sipping his Coca-Cola Light, Donovan couldn't shake the unpleasant feeling that a sniper some one hundred yards away had him in the crosshairs of his scope. His lunch arrived, served by a squat, round-bellied waiter who smelled of cooking grease and cigarettes. Donovan looked at his plate. It was huge and loaded with enough stuffed cabbage rolls and beets to feed a small army. But if its smell was any indication of its taste, Donovan wasn't even sure he'd be able to swallow a single bite. He cut into one with his fork and played with whatever poured out. Since he couldn't identify a single ingredient, he didn't even bother tasting it. They didn't look—or smell—anything like the salmon and rice ones his mother made him each Thursday night when he was a kid.

I should have ordered the borscht or the boiled pierogies.

Donovan took his time finishing his Coke, keeping his eyes moving, studying the crowd. After ten more minutes, he peeled off enough denars to cover his meal and a generous tip, then left the terrace.

"Helen, what's your twenty?" he said, heading toward the meeting spot.

"I'm walking south on Pokriena Charshija, about three minutes away from the meeting point at the Old Bazaar hotel," she replied. "You?"

"I'm north of the hotel, too, but on Samardziska, which runs parallel to Pokriena Charshija," he said. "I have a bad feeling about this. I say we abort and postpone to tomorrow."

"Have you identified a specific threat or is it just a gut feeling?" she asked.

How could she so easily dismiss his legitimate concern for their security?

"Nothing specific, but I'm—"

"Then we keep going," she replied, cutting him off without hesitation. "We've done everything by the book. We're clean. I'm doing the meet. Just make sure you get my six."

Donovan gritted his teeth, not happy with her decision. Was he making a big deal out of nothing? Was it possible that his nerves were playing tricks on him?

No. Something's not right.

Donovan was about to challenge Helen when her voice buzzed in his ear.

"I spotted Velkoski," she said, her excitement pouring out of her voice. "He came out of a restaurant . . . the restaurant name is . . . Palma. He's now heading south on Pokriena Charshija. He's going to our meeting point. We're doing this, Donovan."

Fuck.

FIFTY-FIVE

SKOPJE, NORTH MACEDONIA

It wasn't that Helen didn't trust her partner's instinct, but she felt he sometimes overcomplicated things. They had spent the last two hours doing SDRs and they hadn't been able to spot any hostiles. They had two safe houses nearby, and three getaway vehicles. Surely they were okay to conduct a five-minute meeting with the editor-in-chief of UR Real News?

Worst-case scenario, if Milan Velkoski was a no-show, they could try to pinch him at his condo later in the day or simply set up surveillance on him and make contact at another time. Still, Donovan had been playing this game longer than she had. During their first mission together, he had said to her, "In this line of work, a healthy dose of paranoia is what will keep you alive long enough to have gray hairs."

Maybe she'd dismissed him too quickly.

With that in mind, she was about to acquiesce to his demand and postpone today's meeting when Velkoski cut right in front of her, exiting from a small restaurant not even twenty yards away.

"I spotted Velkoski," she said, doing her best to remain calm, but knowing she was failing. She glanced at the restaurant's name as she walked by, but the name was so washed-out she had a hard time reading it. "He came out of a restaurant . . . the restaurant's name is . . . Palma. He's now heading south on Pokriena Charshija. He's going to our meeting point. We're doing this, Donovan."

"Copy," he replied, sounding not too happy about it.

Helen slowed her pace a touch and let a few other pedestrians walk past her so that they could act as buffers. The majority of the streets in Skopje's old town were closed to motor traffic, which was nice, but, except for the narrow streets, there was nothing in common with the beautiful open squares and parks she loved so much in the rest of Europe. It didn't matter where she was, it seemed that everywhere she looked there was a weirdly designed and very ugly concrete building standing tall, in blatant disrespect of any human-scale landscaping. Most of the public spaces she had walked through had been poorly maintained, and so were the buildings. She had seen some occasional gems here and there— like an elegant arch or elaborate stonework—among the inescapable litter, but most of the alleys were graffiti-ridden and carried a scent sourer than the average politician's soul.

"Still going south on Pokriena Charshija, but approaching the T-junction with Bojadziska and Kujundjiska," she said.

Having studied the map with Donovan, she knew that, from Velkoski's location, he had two options for reaching the meeting point. The fastest would be to make a slight right onto Bojadziska, then a left onto Bozhidar Adzija. His other choice was to make a slight left on Kujundjiska, which would lead him farther south. He would then need to make a sharp right onto Bozhidar Adzija.

"Okay, stand by," Helen said as she watched Velkoski head south. "He took Kujundjiska. I guess he's in no hurry."

"Copy, Helen. He's walking south on Kujundjiska. Keep calling it."

Their meeting wasn't scheduled for another fifteen minutes, so it was possible that Velkoski had decided to make one or more stops on his way to the small square in front of the Old Bazaar hotel.

Wanting to keep Donovan updated on her progress and location, Helen glanced to her left to read the name of the shop she was walking by. It wasn't a big shop—it was tiny and rather shabby—but the window display showcased an attractive tiered cake, a selection of blueberry and strawberry tarts, and smaller, but well-decorated, cupcakes and pastries. But what really caught her attention was the man standing behind the display. Young, clean-shaven, with eyes the color of polished steel. He was about six feet tall, very fit, and holding a small tart in his left hand. He was wearing a pair of jeans, a black leather jacket, and a dark blue baseball cap, with one earphone connected to a device in his jacket's pocket. He tried to look away, but it was too late. She'd seen him, and she'd seen the spark of recognition in his eyes.

Helen's stomach knotted, but she continued walking. She did her best not to appear bothered, but her heart was pounding in her chest.

"Donovan, I believe we have unwelcome company," she said.

"Give me the description, whenever you can," Donovan replied, his voice calm and soothing. He was all business.

"About six feet tall. Caucasian, wearing blue jeans and a black leather jacket. And a blue baseball cap," she said.

"Location, Helen," Donovan said. "What's your location?"

Then, taking her by surprise, Velkoski made an abrupt right into a small alley. She had expected him to continue another fifty yards before making a right onto Bozhidar Adzija. She tried to remember where that alley led. She checked over her shoulder, trying to keep it as casual as possible, and was surprised, but mostly relieved, to see that the man she had spotted wasn't following her.

"Helen, talk to me," Donovan said, this time with more insistence.

"Velkoski made a right into an alley," she said.

"Don't follow him into the alley, Helen. Disengage," Donovan said. "Keep going south till you reach the next intersection and make a left, then make your way to the emergency vehicle we positioned in the parking lot in front of the Hotel DOA. We'll regroup at safe house Bravo."

"Copy," she said through gritted teeth.

Donovan had been right. She should have heeded his warnings.

Helen quickened her pace, mad at herself. Though she had no intention of going after Velkoski, she nevertheless looked down the alley into which he had turned, now remembering that it was one of the two entries leading into a courtyard, the other entry being just east of the Arasta Mosque.

For a moment, she couldn't see him. Then she saw a body, not even thirty steps away, facedown on the pavement but still moving. She knew the right move was to keep on going, to ignore Velkoski, but it didn't mean it was the right thing to do.

"Velkoski's down. East side entrance of the courtyard," she said, then rushed to Velkoski's side, her eyes scanning for threats.

She was five strides away from Velkoski when the first shot rang out. She threw herself to the ground, but the shot hadn't been fired at her. She dragged herself with her elbows until she reached Velkoski. There was an exit wound at his back. She rolled him to his side until he rested against the curb. A round had caught him two inches above his heart. By the amount of blood that had pooled underneath him, Velkoski wouldn't last much longer. His eyes were glassy, and his breathing was coming in gasps, but Helen thought Velkoski recognized her.

Just like the nice-looking, clean-shaven man she'd seen at the bakery had.

"Velkoski's been shot," she said to Donovan. "But he's still breathing."

More shots echoed through the alley, but no bullets were coming their way. For now.

"I'm on my way, Helen," she heard Donovan say. "Talk to me. Keep the comms open."

"Copy," she replied.

Velkoski had closed his eyes. Helen took his pulse. Weak. At the touch of Helen's fingers on his neck, the reporter opened his eyes.

"I'm Lisane Averill, Milan," she said to Velkoski. "I'm the Canadian reporter you were supposed to meet with."

Velkoski's mouth opened, but the words that formed on his lips were hardly perceptible. Helen had to lean down closer to him to make them out.

"You . . . FBI," Velkoski rasped.

His words shocked her to the core. If Velkoski had known she wasn't a Canadian reporter, why did he accept the meeting with her?

Because they lured you into a trap and you fell for it.

"Who told you, Milan?" she asked. Velkoski was dying, there was no point in her continuing to pretend she was a journalist. She waited for him to say something, but he kept quiet, defiant even.

Bursts of automatic fire resonated against the buildings. *Shit!*

"Whoever told you I was with the FBI used you, Milan. They tricked you. Who did this to you?"

Velkoski rolled his eyes up to meet with hers. "Aba-los . . . Francisco Abalos," he said, then closed his eyes and stopped breathing.

Before she could reply, a couple ran past her as more shots were fired close by. The firefight was getting more intense. She had to get out of there.

Helen got to her feet, her hands sticky with Velkoski's blood, and started to the courtyard's exit, looking be-hind her shoulder to make sure she wasn't about to get shot in the back. Forty yards across the courtyard, several men armed with rifles were moving from west to east. Two were dressed casually, but she did spot one wearing what looked like a police uniform.

"Donovan, armed men—"

That's when she saw him, just as she turned around. He was right in front of her, the man from the bakery. He had an expression of utter disbelief across his face, but his pistol was halfway up, with his finger already on the trigger.

FIFTY-SIX

Captain Alexei Lebedev smiled at the pretty baker and paid for his lemon tart and coffee, leaving her an extra-large tip. The young woman blushed, returning his smile, a twinkle in her eyes. If the operation continued to proceed as planned, Alexei didn't rule out returning to the bakery later in the day to ask her out. With luck, he'd be able to stay in Skopje for a few more nights and take her to a nice place for dinner.

Maybe this unexpected trip to Skopje wouldn't be so bad after all. But whether he hooked up with the baker or not, being in North Macedonia certainly beat the alternative, which for him and his seven Spetsnaz would have meant traveling to Belarus to train with members of the 5th Spetsnaz Brigade in Marjina Horka, a town located thirty-seven miles south of Minsk.

With a round trip to Texas thrown in, it had been a

long, tiring week for him and his team. The tempo of operations had certainly gone up threefold since his team had been assigned to Major General Igor Belousov. But Alexei wasn't about to complain. The general was a legend, and it was an honor to serve under him. Alexei wondered if his team had been selected for its proven track record in Ukraine and Syria, or the transfer was due to the last name he carried. Perhaps a little of both, but in his opinion his team was the best Spetsnaz detachment of the Russian Armed Forces. Deployed in Syria's northwest region, his team had fought valiantly in al-Ghab and directed air strikes against enemy positions for almost fifty consecutive days without sustaining a single casualty. More recently, his team had deployed to Ukraine. Despite operating behind enemy lines for more than thirty days without the support it had been promised, his team had met all the military objectives it had been given. And, when the chopper sent to carry them back to Russia was shot down on its way to their location, he and his team had walked nearly a hundred miles back to the Belarus border, losing only one man to an enemy sniper. Alexei had carried him for ten miles, refusing to let someone else carry his fallen teammate.

An elderly couple neared the entrance of the bakery and Alexei placed his coffee and lemon tart on a high-top table next to the window display and moved to the front of the store to open the door for them. The woman thanked him with a curt nod.

"Alpha One, from Three," a voice came through his earphone.

"Go for One," he replied.

Alexei and the elderly couple were the only patrons in the shop, but he kept the volume of his voice low anyway. Although the baker and the older folks probably didn't speak Russian, there was no point attracting unwanted attention.

"Three is in position," his sniper replied.

"Understood. I'll let our friend know."

Alexei took a bite of his lemon tart, then tugged his encrypted phone out of his pocket.

"Alpha One, from Five."

"Go."

"Male secondary target just passed my location."

In his mind's eye, Alexei visualized Five's location on Samardziska.

"Understood, Five. Stay in position."

Alexei's phone buzzed in his hand. A message from General Belousov. Alexei entered his four-digit code and read the message with interest.

> Initial objective has been reached. Asset is now primary objective and needs to be immediately taken out of the game. Secondary targets have now become targets of opportunity. Disengage and follow exfil protocol once asset has been eliminated.

As a combat veteran and GRU Spetsnaz officer, he knew no operation was ever one hundred percent airtight. As the commanding officer of his Spetsnaz unit, it was his responsibility to leave room for the unexpected.

But this? This was beyond unexpected. This was a total reorientation of the mission. At least it was for him. He was starting to understand how General Belousov operated, and this option had probably been in play from the beginning. Alexei had simply not been told about it. He was still a lowly captain. He understood.

"To all call signs, this is One," he said as casually as possible. "Be ready for a change of our primary objective."

Once his seven operators had confirmed they were ready to copy, Alexei said, "It appears that our primary objective has been achieved by the other team. This means that our primary target is now our Skopje asset. I say again, primary target is now our Skopje asset. Our secondary targets are now targets of opportunity only. We are to withdraw from the area as soon as our asset is down. Three, acknowledge."

"Three copies. New primary target is Skopje asset."

"All other call signs acknowledge," Alexei said.

Alexei glanced at his watch, then typed a message to their Skopje asset.

Schedule change. We need you in position now.

The asset's reply came a moment later.

On my way.

Alexei took another bite of the lemon tart and looked behind him. The cashier was chatting with the elderly couple at the far corner of the store. The cute cashier was looking at him, and so was the older woman, who waved at him. The cashier's face turned bright red.

Alexei sighed, truly disappointed. It looked like he wouldn't have the chance to ask the baker out after all.

He turned to face the street again, startled to see their Skopje asset walk in front of the bakery. Milan Velkoski must have been waiting close by. Alexei didn't know what the man had done to warrant his execution. Only the general and Major Krupin were privy to this information, but Velkoski had somehow lost Belousov's trust.

And it's up to me to make sure he pays the price.

"All call signs, from One. Our asset is heading to the meeting point. He just walked past my location, heading south."

Alexei's eyes flickered right, attracted by the striking woman with the confident stride and short blond hair who was walking by the bakery. Before his brain clicked and Alexei realized he was looking at one of his targets, the woman's green eyes met his. It was only an instant before he averted his eyes, but he felt as if he'd been hit by lightning.

Shit. Had she made him?

No. It was impossible. How could she? They'd never seen each other before, and he'd only looked at her for less than a second.

Stop being paranoid.

"Huh . . . To all call signs, this is One. Female target of opportunity is following our primary target to the meeting point. She passed my location ten seconds ago. Three, be ready."

"Three's ready. Can I take her, too?"

"Affirmative, but only if the primary target is down and it's safe for you to do so. Remember, the Americans aren't a priority. Killing the asset is."

"Three copies."

"Alpha One, from Five. Permission to move to the meeting point."

"Five, One. Permission granted."

"One from Four. I'm with Six," called in another of his men. "We'll approach the meeting point from the west and cover Three's withdrawal."

"Four, One copies. Okay for you and Six to move in from the west," Alexei said, then continued. "Alpha Two, stay in position and cover the area north of Three."

"Two copies."

"Alpha Seven and Eight from One, I want you guys close by and ready to move," Alexei said, talking to the two Spetsnaz driving their exfil vehicles.

Alexei had been so busy visualizing all the moving parts in his mind that he hadn't noticed that the elderly couple were standing right behind him.

"Who are you?" the old man asked, speaking Alexei's language.

The old man's wife was clearly upset with him. She was tugging at his jacket as if she wanted him to leave. Alexei looked over at the baker. She was still smiling, but definitely wondering why the old man was angry with him. He gave her a wink and an exaggerated shrug.

"You speak Russian, I see," Alexei said, returning his attention to the man.

"We're Russians!" the man barked at him, his eyes fierce and unafraid. "Of course we speak Russian, you idiot."

"Come on, Maksim, you old fool, we should go now. Leave this young man alone," his wife begged him, pulling harder at his jacket now. "I apologize for my husband's behavior, sir. He was an artillery officer during the Soviet–Afghan war. His ears aren't what they used to be, I assure you."

The old man gave his wife a dirty look. "What are you talking about? My ears are as good as new!"

"No, dear. No, they're not," she replied, pushing him to the door.

"Listen to your wife, old man," Alexei said. "For your sake, and hers."

The man was clearly yearning for a fight, and that made Alexei smile. His wife was right about calling him an old fool.

In his earpiece, Alexei's sniper's voice came in.

"Alpha One, this is Three. Primary target is in sight. He's entered the courtyard. I have a clear shot."

"Take it," Alexei said.

"Primary target down," the sniper said a moment later.

Before Alexei could give his next order, Alpha Two shouted a warning. "Three! Behind you!"

Through his earphone, Alexei heard a gunshot. Then another. Both unsuppressed. Without giving the pretty baker another look, Alexei rushed out of the shop and ran toward the meeting point.

"Three, this is One, sitrep," he said.

"One from Two, Three is down. I say again, Three is down!"

"What? How? Two, what happened?" Alexei asked, slowing his pace as he reached the entrance to the courtyard.

Another series of gunshots echoed through the old town. People in the alley had stopped moving, looking around them, trying to figure out what was happening.

"This is One. Someone give me a fucking sitrep!" he shouted, stopping just before the corner of the alley leading into the courtyard.

More gunshots. It was then that the panic began. And it was contagious. People started running in every direction, parents scooping small children into their arms as they bolted away from the sound of the guns.

Two short, controlled bursts of automatic fire rang out.

"I'm hit! Two's hit! Fuck!"

"Who's shooting at you?" Alexei growled, just about ready to lose it.

"I . . . I don't know! There are maybe four, maybe five of them. They . . . I got the one who nailed Yuri."

"Alpha Four and Six, get in there and tell me what's going on," Alexei ordered.

Five more gunshots followed by another short burst. Alexei heard one of his men yell in pain through the comms system, but he didn't know who it was.

Fuck this.

Alexei pulled out his pistol—an SR-1 Vektor—and turned the corner, keeping his weapon close to his leg. A middle-aged couple coming out of the courtyard at a sprint bumped hard into him, their momentum shoving him to the side. The man screamed and fell face-first to the ground, but immediately jumped back to his feet and resumed his sprint, doing his best to catch up to his wife, who hadn't bothered to stop to help him out.

Movement in his peripheral vision made Alexei snap his head to the right, instinctively raising his pistol. The striking woman with the short blond hair was four feet away from him. Before he could even blink, the tip of her right shoe connected with the interior of his right wrist. A sting of pain shot up Alexei's arm as his pistol flew away from his hand. He had never seen someone move so fast and with such agility.

If her left foot hadn't slipped in the pool of blood draining slowly from Milan Velkoski's body, the fight might have ended differently. But her foot did slip, and she lost her balance. Not for very long, not even a full second, but for someone with Alexei's training, it was all the time he needed. His pistol hadn't yet hit the pavement before a knife appeared in his left hand, drawn from a sheath in a single, fluid movement. To her credit, the female American agent saw exactly what was about to happen. Alexei could tell by the way her eyes opened wide in fear and shock a fraction of a second before it happened.

Not that it changed the outcome.

He still thrust his blade deep into her.

FIFTY-SEVEN

As Stanislava rampaged through the Millers' closet in search of the paper files the reporter had allegedly left there, Abalos covered Miller's wife's mouth with his hand, tired of her nonstop moans and sobs. Curious about how the other part of the operation was going, he used his other hand to pull out of his pocket the earbud he had stolen—well, borrowed—from the spares the Spetsnaz had brought with them at the briefing. He had already encoded it to the right frequency prior to leaving the safe house so that he could listen in to the back-and-forth chatter between the eight-man Spetsnaz team General Belousov had flown in.

As far as he could tell, the Spetsnaz hadn't made contact with the Americans yet. Since the meeting location was known, they hadn't bothered following the two American agents. Six out of the eight Spetsnaz had moved to static positions, with the other two standing by in the exfil vehicles. There was no point in rushing the job. They just had to wait for the Americans to fall into their trap.

True professionals.

The day before, Abalos had spent more than four hours with them and Stanislava going over the ops plan and its contingencies. It was the first time since Kabul that he truly felt like he was part of an exceptional team. Working for General Velásquez had certainly proven to be financially rewarding, but he had never felt a brotherhood-like connection with any of the cartel members. Although some of them had served with the Mexican military, none of them had demonstrated a level of abilities that matched Abalos's.

That was why he'd brought his younger brother Thiago into the fold.

And now Thiago's gone.

Abalos's throat tightened, and his spirits momentarily dropped as he thought about his brother. He couldn't wait to meet Donovan Wade and the female FBI agent face-to-face. He'd talked to Stanislava about the loss of Thiago. She had seemed to feel genuine empathy at his loss and had shared something very interesting with him. Until very recently, Donovan Wade's brother Harrison was said to have been one of Russia's most prized intelligence assets. Although his death hadn't been independently verified by any of Russia's intelligence services, it was believed that Harrison had killed himself shortly after being arrested for treason.

To Abalos, this was an important piece of the puzzle as he tried to understand how Donovan Wade operated. He and the female agent had eliminated, no, slaughtered Berganza's entire team.

And my Thiago.

Having to live with the shame of Harrison's treasonous actions meant that Wade wasn't only fueled by patriotism or a paycheck, he was there to prove to the whole world that he was better than his traitorous brother. It explained Donovan's behavior and intensity.

As a bonus, it was obvious to him that Stanislava held a solid grudge against the female FBI agent. Stanislava had exhibited the same fervor Abalos had for seeing the two Americans punished for what they'd done. On a more personal level, to say that Stanislava had swept him off his feet would be an understatement. For the first time in his life, he had felt an instantaneous connection with a woman. Within two minutes, he had recognized it for what it was.

Lust.

He didn't know what the future held for him, but, after last night, he had already made the decision that no one else but him would ever touch Stanislava.

She was his, and his only.

Having her by his side dulled the pain his brother's murder caused him.

"I have it," Stanislava said, showing him a shoebox as she walked past him, heading down the hallway toward the dining room. "I think you've killed her."

Abalos's eyes moved to Lucas Miller's wife.

Well, shit. She *was* dead. He'd accidentally asphyxiated her by blocking her airway. He rose to his feet, took a step back, and shot her in the side of the head. He removed the suppressor, dropped it into his inside jacket pocket, and holstered his pistol.

In the dining room, Stanislava had started to spread out the contents of the file onto the table. Included in the pages were 8×11 color copies of General Ramón Velásquez and various other high-level Mexican government officials. Stanislava pulled her phone out of her pocket and took quick snaps of the photos. A sense of dread grew in the pit of his stomach. Abalos's hand moved to his holster.

"What are you doing?" Abalos asked in Spanish, knowing from the night before she spoke the language fluently.

"Insurance policy," she replied without even bothering to turn around. "Don't worry, Francisco, I'll send you the link."

Abalos was taken aback by her honesty, and, for a moment, he wasn't sure what to do.

"Why do you need an insurance policy?"

Stanislava stopped what she was doing and jerked her head in his direction, her eyes moving to his hand, which was still resting on top of his holster. She gave him a quizzical look.

"Oh, my, Francisco, you made love to me, and now you want to shoot me?" she said in Russian, her voice a throaty, sexy whisper.

A look of disappointment crossed her features, then it

was gone. She took what remained in the shoebox and started scanning the typed pages and the written notes with her phone.

"Right now, maybe you feel that all is going well between you and your general, but in our world, my love, one needs to take precautions, guarantees, leverage, and insurance policies, don't you agree? You never know when the person standing next to you will want to put a bullet through the back of your skull," she said without looking at him.

Abalos knew she was asking him to make his choice. He moved his hand away from his holster and joined her at the table. He took a pen and a piece of paper and wrote something on it.

"My address. For the link," he said, pushing the paper toward her.

"Smart move, Francisco. I'll send it to you as soon as I'm done."

Still passively listening to the chatter between the members of the Spetsnaz team, something the team leader said caught Abalos's attention. He was about to mention it to Stanislava but refrained from doing so. His Russian was pretty good, but it wasn't perfect. He had probably misunderstood. A moment later, though, when the team leader repeated the instructions, Abalos knew he had heard it right the first time.

Done with taking the pictures, Stanislava typed something into her phone and said in Spanish, "Sending you the link now."

"Great. By the way, have you told General Belousov we've found the file?" Abalos asked.

Stanislava turned and smiled at him. She took a step toward him, closing the distance between them. Abalos felt the muscles in his stomach involuntarily tighten. Her eyes met his and held them.

"Not yet," she said.

She cupped his face in her hand as a lover would, then she let her fingers move slowly down the side of his jaw. He could easily picture Stanislava standing next to him on a beach near Mallorca, wearing a simple dress, with some flowers in her hair, maybe. A look of pure, unconstrained love in her eyes . . .

But it wasn't to be.

His right hand snapped out and he struck his palm hard against her chest. It was a quick, impersonal shove, as if he were reprimanding a dog. The knife in her left hand cut through the fabric of his shirt and sliced through his forearm. Her eyes widened in panic as she realized she had lost the upper hand.

Despite his wound, which he knew would start hurting seconds from now, he drew his pistol.

"Stop!" he shouted.

But Stanislava was committed now. There was no going back for her. They both knew it. Still, he waited a millisecond more than he would have if it had been anyone else. Then he pulled the trigger. Twice.

Both rounds punched into Stanislava's chest. She staggered back a couple of steps, as though she were drunk, then her legs deserted her, and she fell. Abalos holstered his pistol and kicked the knife away. By the sucking noise she made with every breath she took, Abalos knew at least one of his rounds had punctured a lung. She looked at him, her eyes moist. He stood over her, calm, watching her with a certain curiosity.

He chuckled, but it was mostly at himself. She'd almost had him.

He sighed and kneeled next to her. He took her hand in his and bent at the waist. He pressed his forehead against hers.

"I could seal the breach in your lung, you know?" he whispered in Russian. "I could save you if I wanted to. But I won't. Die, bitch. Die."

FIFTY-EIGHT

F rancisco Abalos felt Stanislava's last labored breath on his cheek, and then she went still. He was surprised at how long she had clung to her life, refusing to die. It wasn't as if she'd had any hope of survival. She had to know that, right? So why had she refused to simply let go?

Then he understood.

She had wanted to prolong her misery and suffering to punish herself. She wanted to show him how much she regretted betraying him. It was her way of telling him that she was sorry for trying to take his life.

What else could it be?

Abalos sighed and let go of her hand. He gently caressed her hair back with his left hand.

"I understand. It's okay."

He closed her eyes with his fingers and went to the

bathroom, looking for something he could use to fix his forearm. It was still bleeding pretty badly, and it hurt like hell. He found a well-stocked first-aid kit below the sink. That was all he needed for now. He would see a doctor once he was back in Spain or Mexico. If he cleaned the wound and packed it well enough, he'd be okay. He sanitized the wound with an antiseptic solution and a bacitracin ointment. He then placed four pads of absorbent cotton along the length of the cut and wrapped gauze around it, keeping a steady pressure on the wound. He then went to the kitchen, stepped around the body of the maid, and took the roll of duct tape he'd left on the counter. He wrapped the gauze with the duct tape several times and as tightly as he could.

Satisfied he wasn't about to bleed to death, he grabbed Stanislava's phone, put all the papers back into the shoebox, and went to the living room fireplace to start a fire. Their original plan had called for them to secure the apartment, retrieve the documents, and wait for the two Americans to show up in case the Spetsnaz missed them in Skopje's old town. But now that there had been two unsuppressed gunshots, waiting inside the apartment didn't seem like such a marvelous idea. Once he got the fire going, he started feeding it with the contents of the shoebox. It didn't take very long to go through the entire box. By the time he was done, the fire was roaring and crackling. A spark flew out of the grate and landed on the hardwood floor, which gave Abalos an idea. He hurried back to the kitchen and picked up two bottles of lighter fluid. He squirted the liquid onto the hardwood floor, on the beds, and on the living room sofa. He lit a match and threw it on the sofa. It caught fire immediately.

Abalos exited the apartment and headed for the BMW sedan parked across the street.

Then something the Spetsnaz team leader said stopped him dead in his tracks. Abalos raised the volume of his radio.

He couldn't believe it.

Not only did it seem like the eight-man Spetsnaz team had run into some unforeseen resistance, but the Americans were still there, too, although the female had been stabbed. A full-on gunfight was now raging in the old town.

Maybe that's why the police are yet to show up here.

As he climbed into the BMW, Abalos shook his head. Why did the Russians always seemed to run into *unexpected resistance*?

It's for the best, he told himself.

Wasn't that the perfect opportunity he'd been waiting for?

Abalos started the car, then sped toward the old town. Every second counted.

FIFTY-NINE

As soon as Helen told him Milan Velkoski was down, Donovan quickened his steps in the direction of the courtyard. He knew Helen wouldn't be able to simply walk by and continue to the closest of the three emergency vehicles they had positioned nearby.

For better or worse, she was not that type of person.

The last couple of weeks he and Helen had spent together had been quite intense, and, if he was honest, much more dangerous than he had anticipated. He was starting to know her better now. Definitely not enough to finish her sentences and predict her next move the way he'd been able to with his Force Recon teammates, but he felt he and Helen were slowly earning each other's trust. That was why he was still irritated by how fast she'd simply brushed him away when he had suggested postponing the meeting. Maybe she didn't trust him as much as he trusted her. They'd have to talk about that at the debrief.

Donovan glanced casually around, his gaze constantly moving as he continued toward the courtyard at a hurried pace. The early afternoon sun radiated down and warmed the back of his neck. Residents and tourists pulled out their wallets to make purchases at bookstores, cafés, and bakeries. The shops weren't upscale, but the people seemed happy, and many were smiling. It was business as usual.

The calm before the storm.

Donovan could feel it. The shit was about to hit the fan. Hard.

Helen's voice came in through his earpiece.

"Velkoski's been shot," she said, "but he's still breathing."

Donovan was still one hundred yards away from the courtyard when the first shot rang out. While most people who heard the shot froze in place, wondering what had just happened, to Donovan the gunshot had the same effect as if he had been a one-hundred-meter Olympic sprinter at the start line. He pulled his Glock 29 from its holster, not bothering with the suppressor, and raced toward the courtyard. By the time the crowd realized that the gunshots weren't firecrackers, Donovan had already traveled a quarter of the distance.

Since he hadn't heard the shot that had downed the UR Real News editor, it meant there was more than one group operating with guns in the area. Differentiating between the bad guys and the good guys was going to be a challenge.

Or maybe they're all bad guys.

"I'm on my way, Helen," he said. "Talk to me. Keep the comms open."

Coming from somewhere west of his position, several bursts of automatic fire split the air, but Donovan kept running, listening to her as she questioned Milan Velkoski. From Samardziska, Donovan turned left onto Bozhidar Adzija.

Fifty yards to his right, in the square between the Old Bazaar hotel and the south side of the Arasta Mosque, two North Macedonian police officers were exchanging fire with an unknown number of shooters too far west for Donovan to see. All around him, scared shoppers were trying to hide wherever they could, giving Donovan concerned looks as he raced past.

Bursts of automatic fire mixed with single gunshots continued to push people in Donovan's direction. He did his best to dodge them as they zoomed past in the opposite direction. Sudden, panicked shouts behind him had Donovan glancing to his rear. Twenty yards behind him, coming out of Samardziska, a bald man stopped running and brought a black pistol up, taking aim at Donovan.

Donovan threw himself to his left behind a newspaper stand as two gunshots cracked in the tight confines of the pedestrian street. A young man fell holding his chest, his mouth agape in surprise. Donovan aimed his pistol in the shooter's direction, but the man had disappeared.

Shit.

Just as he was about to resume his sprint, the bald man reappeared from behind an alcove. Donovan, who had his pistol aimed that way, squeezed two shots, but the man had already ducked back behind cover. Donovan didn't waste one more second. As soon as he realized the bald man had retreated, he dashed across the street, effectively restricting the shooter's angle, and ran as fast as he could toward the courtyard, doing his best to keep his weapon out of sight. The last thing he needed was to be fired upon by scared police officers who misidentified him as a threat to their safety.

The firefight on his right suddenly grew in intensity, with multiple shooters using automatic weapons. Donovan looked behind him to see if the bald man had given chase. He hadn't, but what happened next caused Donovan to pause. A police officer, flanked by two men dressed in civilian clothes, who Donovan presumed were also police officers, rushed out from Opincharska—a small street just south and west of Samardziska—and ran to where Donovan had last seen the bald man. Surprising Donovan, and catching the three officers completely off guard, the bald man left the cover of the alcove in a rolling dive that carried him into the street. He leveled his pistol and fired three rounds in quick succession, downing the three officers. The bald man fired a fourth shot into one of the fallen cops, then scanned his surroundings. He briefly locked eyes with Donovan, then leaped back to his feet and sprinted out of Donovan's sight and toward the firefight.

What the hell?

"Donovan, armed men—" Helen started. And then nothing.

But it didn't matter. He was almost at the courtyard. Five more yards.

Donovan sprinted into the courtyard, leading with his pistol. He spotted Helen at the other end. She was standing next to a tall man wearing a black leather jacket and a dark blue baseball cap, as if she was giving him a hug.

At their feet lay a man. Milan Velkoski.

Tall man. Black leather jacket. Blue baseball cap.

It took Donovan's brain half a second to put two and two together. *Shit!*

The world around him suddenly seemed to move in slow motion, and Donovan experienced a moment of paralytic disbelief as he watched Helen's legs give way beneath her.

No!

Donovan rushed forward, his pistol up, not caring if a police officer or another shooter saw him. Helen started to fall, and Donovan had to stop to align his shot, not confident of hitting his target while running at full speed. With Helen close by, and scared pedestrians in the background, Donovan couldn't afford a stray round.

SIXTY

Alexei spotted Donovan Wade when the American was halfway across the courtyard. He spun the female FBI agent around, holding the tip of his knife under her chin, which Alexei thought was a nice and easy way for him to remind her to remain on her feet. She yelped in pain.

Alexei figured the woman wasn't faking it. She had to be in excruciating pain. She'd somehow managed to twist her body just as he had thrust his knife into her, hitting a rib instead of her heart. Alexei had never been stabbed, but it had to hurt like hell, right?

Wade was looking at him, unflinching, holding his pistol in a two-hand grip.

"Drop the knife, asshole!" Wade shouted. "Do it now!"

The American was an imposing man, and his eyes left

no doubt in Alexei's mind that he would have no qualms about pulling the trigger if given the slightest opening. Alexei's pistol lay out of reach, two feet to his right. He thought about shoving the American agent forward and risking it, but Wade looked like the kind of guy who'd be able to pump three or four rounds into him before he even reached his pistol. His secondary was in a holster at the small of his back, but there wasn't a scenario in which he pictured himself able to draw and fire before getting killed.

Patience, Alexei. Patience.

In his earpiece, the news coming from his men wasn't much better. Alpha Two and Three were down. Shot by police officers. Four and Six were still engaged, but were in the process of withdrawing to the vehicle driven by Alpha Seven. Alpha Five, who had called in his short firefight with Wade, had done what he could, but hadn't been able get to Alpha Three in time. He was now on his way to meet with Alpha Eight.

How the police had known they were there, Alexei couldn't be certain. But he had a few ideas. Milan Velkoski had always been an asset of Francisco Abalos and the cartels. Could they have betrayed General Belousov? There would be hell to pay if they had.

Idiots. Didn't they know what Belousov was capable of?

Then again, maybe it was Velkoski. The little shit may have feared for his life and called the cops, telling them about a possible high-risk situation. Whatever the reason,

Alexei promised himself he'd find out. Alpha Two and Three deserved it.

Life was unfair, wasn't it? Two and Three had survived the worst of the shithole that was Syria, only to die in a place as insignificant as Skopje, North Macedonia.

Fuck me.

"One from Alpha Eight. What's your position?" the Spetsnaz driving the second vehicle asked.

"Courtyard. Southeast of the meeting point. The two Americans are here."

"One, this is Five, I'll make my way back to you."

"Negative! Meet up with Eight now!" he ordered his man while shuffling back and dragging the female agent with him.

"Alpha Eight copied your last, sir. On my way to pick up Five. We'll wait for you at the end of Pokriena Charshija."

"One copies. Two minutes," Alexei replied, slowly making his way to the end of the alley.

"One from Four, Six and I are out of here. Six took a round, but he'll be fine."

"One copies."

While Alexei talked to his men, Wade had inched closer and was now sidestepping to his right, trying to get an angle on him.

"Move one more step and she dies!" Alexei yelled at Wade. To make his point, he pushed the tip of the blade a bit deeper until he felt the FBI agent's flesh pop. Blood seeped on both sides of the steel blade.

Wade stopped. His eyes filled with the purest hatred Alexei had ever seen.

"She's hurt, Wade. She's hurt bad. Only you can save her now. It's your choice. You can come after me. Or you can save her."

He was about to thrust his knife into the FBI agent's right kidney when, catching him by surprise, she pushed herself hard into him, forcing him to take a couple of steps back. Alexei caught movement to his left, and he realized that part of his body was no longer in the alley, his entire left side exposed to anyone heading north on the pedestrian street running perpendicular to the alley. A man wearing a cheap two-piece business suit with a police badge clipped to his belt was aiming a pistol at him.

Alexei cursed.

He should have seen this coming. The FBI bitch had probably seen the cop slowly making his way toward them and had timed her push perfectly. He tried to spin in time to shield himself with the FBI agent's body, but the plainclothes police officer fired first, his round punching Alexei high on the left shoulder.

Alexei spun and fell, which saved his life as the officer's next two rounds sailed inches over his head, ricocheting off the stone wall of the building behind him. Alexei rolled to his left, his right hand moving to his secondary weapon. The police officer fired his fourth round at the same time Alexei squeezed the trigger. Alexei felt a sharp slap to his right thigh, followed immediately by a searing pain. At least the cop had gone down, too, although Alexei had no idea where he had hit him.

To his right, the female agent was dragging herself toward Alexei's SR-1 Vektor. The only thing going his way was that Wade, instead of engaging him, had rushed to his partner—who was now directly in Wade's line of fire.

Alexei scurried back behind the wall, propelled awkwardly by his left heel and right palm. He then extended his right arm into the alley and fired five shots without looking. Alexei pushed himself to his feet. Pain shot through his shoulder and thigh.

"Alpha One from Eight. One minute out."

"Yeah. I'll be there," Alexei said through gritted teeth as he half jogged, half limped north on Pokriena Charshija.

Alexei glanced behind him and was thankful Wade hadn't started after him, or maybe he'd been hit by one of the five shots he'd fired blindly into the alley, but he still sent a couple more rounds at the courtyard's entrance to make sure Wade didn't change his mind.

Alexei couldn't feel his left arm anymore, and his right leg was oozing blood at an alarming rate. The closer he got to his rendezvous point, the dizzier he felt. He had to fight to remain alert.

I'm losing too much blood.

"Alpha One, where are you?"

Alexei looked around him, disoriented.

There.

Twenty yards north and to his right was the bakery

where he had met the pretty blond baker. He wondered what she would say if she were to see him all bloody like this. Someone yelled something behind him. He turned, almost losing his balance, and, holding his pistol one-handed, fired twice at the two cops behind him, his bullets zipping past as they ducked to cover.

He continued north, both his wounds burning viciously. He fell to his knees.

Get up! Come on. Let's go. Don't quit. You're almost there.

He was still in the fight. His mind was. He'd been through worse, right? So, why was his body not responding? He summoned the rest of his energy and got up, forcing himself to put one foot in front of the other. When he reached the bakery, two more police officers emerged from a side street. Alexei brought up his pistol, which was much heavier than it should have been, and pulled the trigger until his pistol ran dry.

"Alpha One, Alpha One, this is Eight, where are you, sir? We need to get moving."

It took pretty much everything Alexei had left to open his mouth and say, "You guys go. Now. I'll—"

A bullet fired by one of the officers behind him struck him square in the middle of his back. Another hit him at the base of the neck. As he fell, he saw the pretty baker standing by the window display. Lying facedown in the street, unable to move and bleeding out, he swore he could still taste the lemon tart he'd eaten not five minutes ago.

SIXTY-ONE

SKOPJE, NORTH MACEDONIA

Donovan saw the pistol appear around the corner and jumped on top of Helen, shielding her with his body as the man with the blue baseball cap fired five rounds into the alley. None of the bullets came even close, but when Donovan pushed off from Helen, he could see she was injured.

"Go!" she yelled at him. "Go get that fucker!"

Donovan looked at the plainclothes police officer. He'd been shot, but he was still moving.

"For Chrissake, Donovan, go!"

Just as he was about to turn the corner, two more gunshots echoed into the pedestrian street. To his right, the cop moaned.

Shit.

Donovan rushed to him, grabbed him under his armpits, and pulled him to safety. The officer had been hit in the chest, but the light body armor he was wearing under his shirt had caught it.

"You'll be fine, my friend," Donovan told him. "Don't worry."

He returned to the corner and peeked into the pedestrian street, looking north. The man with the blue baseball cap had disappeared, but he had left a long smear of blood behind him. The blood loss was impressive, and Donovan thought it was possible one of the cop's bullets had nicked an artery. There was no point in chasing after the man. Whatever his objective was, he wasn't going to make it.

Donovan holstered his weapon and returned to Helen, who was holding her side. The front of her shirt was sodden with blood.

"He's gone, isn't he?" she asked, her voice strong despite her injuries.

"He won't go far," Donovan assured her, gently plying her hands away from the cut she had sustained.

She grimaced in pain but didn't cry out as he examined her wound. The skin all around the cut was purple, while the wound itself was open and raw, with blood seeping out of it. Helen needed medical care, but for now, Donovan's priority was to stop the bleeding.

"I'll carry you to the car," he said. "I need to stitch you up until we can get you to a doctor."

The sirens of emergency vehicles were getting closer. Not just police cars, but ambulances and fire trucks, too. Donovan could only imagine how many people had been caught in the crossfire of the violent gunfight that had raged on for more than five minutes. Donovan was going to use the confusion to get Helen out of the old town. Then, in the distance, through the cacophony of the sirens, Donovan heard a multitude of gunshots.

"Ready?" he asked Helen, but he didn't wait for her answer. He picked her up, folded her over his shoulders, and took off with her in a fireman's carry, heading toward the parking lot of the Hotel DOA.

SIXTY-TWO

A balos had a hard time keeping track of what was going on, but he did know that for the Spetsnaz team, everything had turned to shit and that the two Americans were in a courtyard close to the original meeting point.

But the sheer number of emergency vehicles converging to the old town was staggering and had slowed down Abalos's approach considerably. It had also confirmed that absolute chaos now reigned in Skopje's old town. Like all the other nonemergency vehicles, Abalos's BMW hadn't been able to escape the congestion as he traveled eastbound on Boulevard Goce Delchev.

General Velásquez had tried to call him multiple times, but Abalos needed time to think. He still couldn't comprehend why the Russians had double-crossed him. Or did it go higher than that? Was there a rift between

Velásquez and General Belousov? If there was, maybe it would be wise for Abalos to take a step back and wait in the shadows until the situation cleared up.

Or retire. On my own terms.

He had enough money set aside to do pretty much anything he wanted. Velásquez was a powerful man in Mexico, but that was because the cartels supported him. If Proyecto de la Verdad failed, that could change in a heartbeat. The dynamics between the drug cartels was forever changing in Mexico, and Abalos wasn't sure he wanted to be part of the next evolution. Being on the side of the losing team had consequences. Europe being his area of expertise, he was somewhat immune from the wrath of the cartels, since he'd been the one managing the accounts for Velásquez on this side of the Atlantic, but that didn't mean they couldn't find him if they really wanted to.

The more he thought about it, the more convinced he was that it was time for him to move on, to pull the plug. But what about the two Americans who'd slaughtered his brother?

That, he couldn't let go.

In his ear, Abalos could still hear the chatter between the surviving members of the Spetsnaz team. They were now just north of Skopje and traveling northbound on E-65, apparently racing to the Stenkovec Brazda Airfield, where a Russian twin-engine light turboprop Antonov An-28 was waiting for them.

The traffic light at the crossroad of Boulevard Goce Delchev and Philip II of Macedon switched to red, and

Abalos brought the BMW to a stop, thinking about his next move. It was going to be difficult to find Donovan Wade and the FBI agent in the old town. If the Russians were already out of the downtown core, odds were that Abalos had also missed the Americans by a few minutes. His plan had been to get to the closer parking lot southeast of the meeting point, since this was where the Russians had mentioned their last sighting of the Americans.

Abalos wasn't so sure anymore. With all the emergency vehicles, it would be prudent to revise his strategy.

At least he knew one name. Donovan Wade. How difficult was it to find someone?

His phone buzzed.

Velásquez. It was time to make a decision.

Then, just in front of him, crossing his field of vision from right to left as it made a left turn on Boulevard Goce Delchev, a black Kia Sportage caught his attention as it accelerated through the intersection.

Behind the wheel was his least favorite American.

This couldn't be Lady Luck smiling on him. It was Thiago who'd sent his killer into Abalos's path, daring him to honor the promise he'd made.

SIXTY-THREE

Donovan sped through the intersection, glad to see that the traffic out of the old town wasn't as bad as that trying to get in.

"We're less than three minutes away, Helen," he said. "Keep putting pressure on the wound."

Donovan had looked at the wound once more before they left the parking lot. As ugly, painful, and bloody as it was, the blade had missed the vital organs. Donovan had called Manton to brief him on the situation, and the Blackbriar director had given him two options. Donovan could either drop Helen off at a hospital and hope that her Canadian journalist cover would hold, or they could get back to the Skopje airport, where Manton promised him that two NATO doctors would be in attendance inside the jet by the time they got there.

But the airport was eleven miles away, and Donovan

feared Helen would have lost too much blood by then. Still, Helen had been adamant. She didn't want to be stuck in North Macedonia, especially since they couldn't be sure that whoever was behind Milan Velkoski's murder was gone. And they had known Donovan's name, too, she had reminded him. She was right: North Macedonia wasn't safe for them.

Donovan ended up agreeing to go to the airport, as long as they could make a stop at one of the safe houses to stop Helen from bleeding to death.

From Boulevard Goce Delchev, Donovan made a left onto Grigor Prlichev and an immediate right into an alley. He parked the Kia SUV a bit farther down and turned off the engine. He hurried around the car and opened the passenger door.

"I can walk," she said. "Help me up."

She draped her arm around his shoulders and Donovan wrapped his arm around her waist.

"Let's go," he said. "It's not far."

They entered the fenced-in backyard through a four-foot-high wooden gate and walked past several overgrown flower beds. Donovan entered a six-digit code into the electronic lock and pushed the door open. The safe house was a small, sparsely furnished one-bedroom apartment on the first floor of an old two-story house whose yellowish stucco walls had seen better days, but it had a great medical kit.

Donovan helped Helen onto a red velvet sofa.

"All right, here we go," he said once he had grabbed everything he needed.

He unscrewed the cap off a bottle of rum and handed the bottle to her.

"Rum? I'm more vodka than rum, but okay. I guess vodka is harder to get these days, right?" she said, then drank four healthy gulps directly from the bottle. She winced. Drank four more.

"Oh my God," she said, licking her lips. "Okay. I'm ready."

"It's gonna sting a little," Donovan said.

"Yeah, I figured it would," Helen replied. "Don't enjoy it too much, okay?"

He cleaned the wound the best he could with several pads he had doused with alcohol, then started with the stitches. It took twenty to sew the cut to his satisfaction. After cleaning the wound again, he applied a dressing and secured it with medical tape.

"That should do it for the bleeding. I think we're good until we reach the plane," Donovan said, but Helen had passed out, or fallen asleep. He wasn't sure which.

He took her pulse. Strong, steady, but a touch too fast.

He looked at Helen's face. She was a tough girl. Not once had she complained when he'd navigated the needle through her flesh. Not a single peep. Her eyes were screwed shut. She'd burned through the entire adrenaline dump. Her body needed to rest.

Soon. But now they needed to get to the airport.

He grabbed Helen's phone and sent an update to Oliver Manton. He then walked out to the Kia and opened the passenger door. He returned to the apartment, scooped

Helen up in his arms as if she weighed half a feather, and carried her outside.

Her eyes fluttered open. "I . . . can walk, Don."

"You drank too much," he replied with a smile.

"Isn't that the title of a James Arthur song?" she asked, a tiny frown marring her forehead.

"Almost. The song's called 'Say You Won't Let Go,'" he said without hesitation. "And the lyric is '*we* drank too much.'"

"Uh-huh . . . So you're a fan?"

"Huge," he said, easing her into the seat. He reached for her seat belt and pulled it across her lap.

She gently touched his forearm. She seemed to hesitate for a moment, then said, "Thank you."

He looked at her, and that's when he caught movement through the rear window of the Kia SUV. And then he saw the gun.

SIXTY-FOUR

SKOPJE, NORTH MACEDONIA

Francisco Abalos had no problem following the Kia SUV to its destination. At first, he had been afraid that Donovan Wade would go through a long, painful SDR, but no. He drove slightly above the speed limit but didn't do any of the maneuvers Abalos expected him to.

At some point Abalos even wondered if he wasn't being led into an ambush. How could someone who slaughtered his way through Berganza's entire team and killed his brother Thiago be so stupid? It didn't make sense.

Unless . . .

Could Wade or his FBI partner be injured? If so, then why weren't they going to a hospital or a medical clinic?

Because he's CIA. He's here on a non-cover assignment.

But how could that be? The FBI and CIA didn't really

work together, did they? Was it possible that the woman Abalos had always believed to be with the FBI was in fact working with the CIA? An NOC officer like Wade?

She had to be.

And now, one, maybe even both of them, had been injured in the firefight with the Spetsnaz and were on their way to a safe house.

Abalos grinned, feeling the adrenaline rush through him once more. He took long, deep breaths to steady his mind and body in anticipation of the competition ahead of him. When the Kia made a left on Grigor Prlichev, Abalos feared for a moment he might lose them, but then the SUV made a quick right into an alleyway.

They must be getting close.

Abalos turned onto Grigor Prlichev but drove past the alleyway without tapping the brakes. As he crossed the intersection, he looked to his right and saw Wade climb out of the SUV next to a pale, dirty-yellow building surrounded by a wooden fence. Abalos continued straight but the road transformed itself into a gated and secured parking lot for a learning facility. Abalos turned around and found a parking spot in front of a Greek restaurant fifty yards south of the parking lot entry. From the backseat he grabbed a small black duffel bag. He pulled out a few additional items and dropped them in his coat pockets.

General Velásquez had called two more times, but Abalos hadn't bothered answering. He was yet to make a decision about his future. Either way, what he was about to do next was personal. Abalos left his phone and the one he had taken from Stanislava Krupin in the car.

The throbbing coming from the cut on his forearm the filthy, treasonous bitch had inflicted was still there, but not nearly as bad as it had been. It was manageable.

Abalos climbed out of the vehicle and started toward the ugly two-story house Wade had pulled up next to.

• • • • •

Squeezed between two vehicles—a red Opel Astra and a beat-up sedan at his back—Abalos had found the perfect spot. From his position, he could see through the windows of the Opel and another vehicle—a decade-old pickup truck—that were parked nose to nose in front of him and get a clear view of the Kia Sportage and the wooden gate next to it. Although he couldn't be sure into which of the houses Wade had gone, the yellow one made the most sense. Abalos had located six windows from which he could be seen, but three of them had their blinds closed, and the other three didn't have a good angle on his position.

Abalos's FN Five-seveN was out with its suppressor attached. He had been in position for less than fifteen minutes when Wade came out of the wooden gate. Abalos was ready for him. He raised his pistol, leaned out from behind the cover of the red Opel just enough to get into a solid firing position, and waited.

He would take his shot as soon as Wade crossed over to the driver's side of the vehicle.

Abalos estimated the distance at fourteen, maybe fifteen yards.

An easy shot for him.

In fact, easy enough that Abalos would cripple Wade first. Why kill the prick quickly when Thiago had agonized for eighty-six seconds?

No. Wade would suffer, too. A thousand times more than what Thiago had to endure. And Abalos would do the same to Wade's pretty partner.

After a few seconds, when Abalos hadn't seen Wade appear, he returned to his original position to reassess. He looked through the windows. Wade had vanished into thin air.

Where is he?

Then he noticed that the front passenger door of the Kia was open.

What is Wade doing?

Abalos wasn't about to underestimate the American. He scanned his surroundings, taking his time as he checked the windows, the balconies, and the roofs of the nearby buildings.

Abalos heard them talking before he saw them.

How cute.

Wade was carrying his injured partner in his arms. Given how blood-soaked her shirt was, Abalos guessed she'd been shot. But she was alive.

It was time to change that.

When Wade's body was half into the SUV, Abalos made his move. He came out from behind the red Opel and quietly approached the Kia in a combat crouch, his Five-seveN up and on target, his right shoulder hugging the pickup truck. His finger had moved from the trigger guard to the actual trigger when the rear window of the Kia exploded.

Abalos crouched lower and returned fire from over the hood of the pickup truck, pumping rounds into the Kia as fast as his finger could pull the trigger, aiming at the passenger seat.

SIXTY-FIVE

Donovan's right hand moved from Helen's seat belt buckle to his Glock 29.

"Get ready, contact rear," he said, calmly but with an intensity that couldn't be denied.

Holding his pistol with his right hand, with his body bent at the waist over Helen, Donovan knew he was far from being in an optimal shooting stance, but he didn't have the extra second and a half he needed to get into one. He jerked the trigger once, sending a bullet through the back window of the Kia. Donovan didn't wait to see if he had hit his target before grabbing Helen and throwing her out of the SUV. She landed hard on her ass, her head whipping back violently against the wooden fence as incoming rounds shattered what remained of the Kia's back window. A piercing din could be heard as bullets punched through the thin metal of the SUV's tailgate and ripped through the inside of the vehicle, showering the interior with metal fragments, torn plastic, and glass.

If the shooter wasn't yet out of ammo, at this rate of fire, he was going to need a fresh magazine soon. Donovan could either charge and hope to surprise the man while he was changing magazines or move Helen—who was in a disheveled heap against the fence—away from immediate danger. If Donovan charged and got it wrong, or the shooter was already in the process of repositioning, Helen was dead.

Donovan fired two rounds at the windshield of the pickup truck parked behind the Kia, hoping it would spiderweb the window enough that the gunman wouldn't be able to see through it. He scooped an unconscious Helen in his arms for the second time and ran through the still-open gate that led into the backyard.

• • • • •

Abalos, who'd taken cover behind the front left tire of the pickup truck, had no way to know if his rounds had hit anyone. But Donovan had probably counted the rounds Abalos fired and would know he was almost empty. Abalos grabbed a fresh magazine from his pouch, ejected the spent magazine, and inserted the new one. He was about to pop his head above the hood to assess the situation when two rounds pounded against the windshield to his right.

Mierda!

Abalos ducked back behind the engine block of the pickup truck, his heart hammering high in his chest. Somehow, the cut on his forearm had reopened, and blood was seeping through the bandages. Abalos flattened himself on the pavement and looked under the chassis of the vehicle.

He saw Wade run into the backyard carrying the limp, bleeding body of the FBI agent. Abalos pulled the trigger, only having the time to fire once, but he made it count.

· · · · ·

Donovan felt the bullet go through his right calf. He knew he'd been hit, and he tried to push through the pain, but it was excruciating—as if a professional golfer had smacked his driver into the back of his shin. He lost his balance and fell to his left side, dropping Helen onto the unkept grass. He rolled toward her, making himself as big as possible, doing his best to shield as much of her as he could. He aimed his pistol at the wooden gate, expecting the shooter to barge through at any moment. But he didn't. Donovan glanced at his wound.

Through-and-through.

Keeping his gun trained on the gate, Donovan got up, glad to know he could still use his right leg. He and Helen were sitting ducks. They couldn't stay in the middle of the backyard, but they couldn't go inside their apartment, either, since the entry door was in direct line with the gate.

Donovan kept his pistol aimed at the gate and used his left arm to drag Helen farther away from the gate. That was the best he could do. With the exception of a decaying picnic table set against the fence, an even older barbecue, and a few rusty gardening tools, the backyard was empty with absolutely no cover. Then something sailed over the fence and landed with a thud five yards to Donovan's left. He recognized what it was instantly.

Fuck me.

$$\bullet \bullet \bullet \bullet \bullet$$

Abalos knew he'd hit Wade, but he also knew the big American wasn't down for the count just yet. The right move would be for Abalos to withdraw. The authorities could be on their way, but with what had happened in the old town, including the deaths of several police officers, Abalos was ready to take the gamble that he still had a few minutes.

Nevertheless, he was aware of the tactical situation. But he couldn't simply let it go, could he now? His brother's killer was less than ten yards away from him. He wished he could simply rush into the damn backyard and kill the Americans, but that wouldn't be wise. The advantage always went to the defenders.

Unless one has the proper tools.

Abalos dug into his coat pocket, grabbed the stun grenade, pulled the pin, and tossed it over the fence.

Game on, Mr. Wade. Game on.

Abalos crouched behind the vehicle so that he would be protected from the flash and most of the concussion. He opened his mouth and closed his eyes anyway. The moment after the stun grenade exploded with an extra-loud bang, Abalos was on the move. He had already visualized exactly what he would do. What he had never planned for, though, was Donovan Wade's reaction.

· · · · ·

The instant he heard the stun grenade land next to him, Donovan was on the move. He knew that if they stayed in the backyard, he and Helen were dead meat. At least now he had a fighting chance. If the shooter was as good as Donovan thought he was, he would take cover until the stun grenade detonated, leaving Donovan a minuscule window of opportunity. Praying his leg would hold, and leading with his pistol, Donovan rushed through the gate just as the grenade exploded. The concussion shook him more than he thought it would, and he briefly lost his bearings. Then to his left, less than three yards away, popping out from behind the pickup truck, he saw the shooter.

The utter shock in the man's eyes was like nothing Donovan had ever seen. Donovan, who was still at a half sprint, had the time to pull the trigger three times before his right leg gave and he fell forward, cracking his head against the asphalt, his pistol clattering away from his reach.

Dizzy, Donovan knew he had to get up. He couldn't stay down. He got to his knees, feeling sick to his stomach from the pain in his leg and the blow to his head. He looked over at the shooter, having no idea how many times he had hit him. The shooter was still moving.

No, he's getting up!

Donovan grabbed his knife, but the man was already on him and kicked it away. Before Donovan could put his arms up to defend himself, the shooter swung his pistol against the side of Donovan's head. It connected with a sharp crack that sent Donovan onto the pavement. The shooter sent the toe of his boot hard into Donovan's ribs. Donovan grunted and rolled onto his back, still seeing stars in front of his eyes. He tried to scissor the man's leg, but he was too slow, and the shooter brought his foot down hard onto Donovan's injured calf.

Donovan screamed in agony.

The shooter pointed a suppressed pistol at Donovan's head, but he was holding it with his right hand only. His left arm hung loose and useless at his side, bleeding from at least two bullet wounds.

"Do you know who I am?" the man asked.

Donovan's ears were still ringing from the gunfight and the stun grenade. He had heard this voice before, but it was the man's eyes that told Donovan the true story.

"Yeah . . . I know who you are," Donovan said, fighting through the pain. "You're the citrus juice guy, right?"

The man cocked his head to one side, then nodded. "Ah, yes. I'm glad you remember our conversation, Mr. Wade."

"Do you have them?"

"The citrus fruits?" the man asked, chuckling. "Hmm . . . Unfortunately, I do not. But please, don't let that oversight bother you, Mr. Wade. I'll find other imaginative ways to entertain you, I assure you."

"Okay, I get it. But seriously, you have the wrong guy, buddy," Donovan said. "I didn't kill your brother."

"I did!" shouted Helen.

The man was fast. Donovan had rarely seen someone move so damn quick. If Helen had hesitated, even for a fraction of a second, the man would have drilled a hole in her chest before she could pull the trigger. But Helen did not hesitate.

Her three shots were fired so close together that Donovan could have sworn she'd fired a three-round burst from an MP5.

The shooter collapsed, hit three times in the heart. Tight grouping.

But Helen didn't take any chances and walked to the shooter and shot him in the face.

"You okay?" she asked Donovan as she squatted next to the dead man.

Donovan forced himself up to his knees and waited a few beats before standing up. His calf was killing him, but it would have to wait.

"You find anything?" he asked Helen.

"Car keys. BMW. Spare magazines, a knife, and this," she said, showing a small black box to Donovan.

"Check his ears," he said.

"Yep," she said a moment later. "Earbud."

"I think we're done here. Time to go, but we need a vehicle."

Helen held the BMW key over her head and gestured for Donovan to be quiet. Not far away, a car alarm blared.

"Wait here," Helen said. "I'll pick you up."

SIXTY-SIX

BLACKBRIAR HEADQUARTERS, NEW YORK

They left Ramstein an hour ago, Director Manton," Teresa Salazar said. "They'll be in New York later this afternoon."

One of the screens at the front of the room turned on and a blue dot appeared over the Atlantic Ocean. Standing behind Teresa, Oliver Manton was tired and caffeine jittery. But he was relieved. By the end of the day, his three field operations teams would be back stateside. To his right, Faith Jackson let out a long sigh. She'd also been under a tremendous amount of pressure, and Manton was proud of her. He was proud of his entire team.

"You know they could have left Germany two days ago, right?" Jackson asked him. "The doctors cleared them."

"Yeah, I know," Manton replied, "but Helen wanted to spend some time with her dad."

"How did it go?" Teresa asked.

"You'll have to ask her yourself," Manton said, then turned to Jackson. "Have you looked at the data Helen sent you?"

"Yes, sir. My team and I have a preliminary report ready for you. We were also able to crack into Major Krupin's phone. The folks in IT have been at it nonstop since we got it three days ago."

Manton had seen the potential value of the intel stored on Krupin's phone. The moment Helen had mentioned what they had found in the BMW, he'd ordered her to turn off the phone and remove its battery. He had then contacted DNI Russell and asked for a favor. A big one.

Hours later, a navy jet had landed in the US with Major Krupin's phone aboard.

"What does your report say?"

"It's pretty straightforward," Jackson said. "Major Krupin took pictures and videos of the Miller brothers' research and sent it to Francisco Abalos, who we believe represented the Mexican drug cartels' interests in Europe."

"Through General Ramón Velásquez, yes?" Manton asked.

"Exactly. It seemed that Velásquez has been acting as a freelance adviser to the cartels for many years, well before he was sworn in as Mexico's secretary of defense. His tenure boosted his power and influence to another level. Very few people have been able to successfully navigate the troubled waters of an alliance between several cartels. But he did."

"What's Russia's angle in all of this?" he asked.

"As I said, this is only preliminary, but it appears that Velásquez has put together a plan to penetrate our defenses by using specialized Russian cyberwarfare units to gain access to several leading American and European app development companies."

"Like Mind-U," Manton said.

"Yes, and after going through Lucas and William Miller's research about Proyecto de la Verdad, we strongly believe that they are doing so to influence American public opinion by manipulating the algorithms of these companies."

"The cartels or the Russians?"

"Both," Jackson said. "The cartels are terrified that the US assigned them a designation of foreign terrorist organizations."

"So, they're lashing out at us through social media?" Manton asked, skeptical. "Come on now! Isn't that a bit far-fetched?"

Faith Jackson looked at him as if he hadn't been listening to her. Even Teresa gave him a weird look.

"Okay, dammit! What is it that I'm not seeing?"

"With all due respect, Director, I think you don't fully grasp how powerful social media and other online entities have become in recent years," Jackson told him.

Manton could see Jackson was doing her best not to use a patronizing tone, but she wasn't particularly successful.

"Okay. Make your point."

And she did. For the next fifteen minutes, and with

Teresa jumping in from time to time, Jackson brought forward arguments Manton had a hard time refuting. Social media and cyberwarfare weren't his forte, but he was glad Blackbriar had people like Faith Jackson and Teresa in the fold who understood the dynamics at play better than he ever would. Manton had a feeling Teresa and Jackson could have kept talking about the subject for many more hours.

"You're telling me General Belousov is backing out of the deal he made with the cartels?"

"We can't be sure about that. Helen and Donovan's actions in Cairo, Egypt, and then in North Macedonia truly messed up their operations."

Teresa cleared her throat. "Can I add something?"

"Don't ever ask me this question again, Teresa," Manton warned her. "Always speak your mind. If I weren't interested in what you have to say, you wouldn't be working here."

Teresa nodded, then said, "I've looked at the data, the text messages, and the notes stored on Krupin's phone, and it's my belief that Belousov tried to sabotage Proyecto de la Verdad."

"Okay. I'll bite," Manton said.

"We all agree that Belousov is a murderous sonofabitch with a huge ego. If he felt crossed in any way by Velásquez, who we know is a pompous ass, Belousov would be the kind of man who'd go over the top to assert his dominance."

"And lose his deal with the cartels?" Manton challenged. "I'm sure he's charging the cartels a pretty penny for the services of the specialized units he commands."

"We think he could have been paid as much as two hundred million dollars since the start of Proyecto de la Verdad," Teresa said.

A pretty penny indeed, Manton thought.

Teresa continued, "That's why he tried to do it quietly by asking Major Krupin to take possession of the Miller brothers' research."

"To give him the opportunity to blackmail Velásquez if he felt like it," Manton said. "Okay. I'm seeing it. Correct me if I'm wrong here, but if no one knows he's backstabbing Velásquez and the cartels, it also allows Belousov to continue selling his services to other criminal, governmental, or terrorist entities."

"Yes, you're right," Jackson said. "I haven't explored this angle yet."

"This means that if we could find a way to disseminate what we found on Major Krupin's phone to potential clients of Belousov, we could really rattle his cage," Manton said, thinking out loud.

"But would they believe it?" Jackson asked.

"That's the thing, Faith," he said. "They don't need to. We just need to instill doubt in their minds."

"I guess we can look into it," Jackson said. "I like the idea."

"What do you think Belousov will do in the meantime?" Teresa asked.

"He'll stay on the sidelines until the cartels figure out

what they want to do. He's not interested in sticking around if the alliance is about to blow," Manton said.

Manton's phone buzzed in his pocket. It was the DNI.

"Yes, sir," Manton said, walking to his office.

"How's your team, Oliver?" the DNI asked. "On their way back?"

"They are. They left Ramstein and should be in New York later today."

"Great to hear," the DNI said. "I thought you'd like to know that I was speaking with Melissa Hutchinson over at the DEA before I called you."

Though Manton had never met the woman, he knew she had recently been appointed administrator of the Drug Enforcement Administration by the president— after Russell had recommended her. If what Manton heard about her was true, she was a brilliant attorney with a proven track record of getting things done.

Russell continued. "Melissa told me the DEA has noted a significant increase in chatter between the cartels and some high-level Mexican government officials they already had on the radar. Do you know anything about that?"

"I don't," Manton replied, closing the door to his office.

"You're telling me you're not aware that several cartel leaders will meet up in Manzanillo three days from now?"

Manton sat behind his desk and leaned back in his seat, closed his eyes, and massaged his forehead. "I'm tired, Edward. If you want to say something, please say it."

"One of the calls the DEA intercepted mentioned the death of a Spaniard named Francisco Abalos, who, by the way, was suspected of being General Ramón Velásquez's emissary to Europe. Are you curious to know where Abalos was killed?"

"Let me guess . . . In Skopje," Manton replied.

"Three neat holes in his tiny black heart, and one more in the middle of his face. A thing of beauty if you ask me," the DNI said.

"I assume this isn't a problem?"

"Far from it. In fact, it appears that the fragile equilibrium between the cartels Velásquez had managed to hold together is about to break at its seams. The recent success of Blackbriar's operations in Cairo, Prague, and more recently in North Macedonia have pushed the alliance to the breaking point. That's why they'll be holding an emergency session at Velásquez's mansion in Manzanillo. Mistrust between the cartels has never been so high since Velásquez assumed the role of pacifier. A little push could drive them into the abyss."

That got Manton's attention. "What do we know about this meeting?" he asked.

"Not much more than that for now. Why?"

Manton shared with the DNI what he had just discussed with the Blackbriar analysts.

"If we could break the alliance between the cartels and mess with Belousov's reputation, that would be two big wins for the good guys," Russell said.

"Do you think Belousov is on the up and up with the Russian president?" Manton asked. "That could be an interesting angle to work on."

"I like how you're thinking, Oliver, but since the invasion of Ukraine, Belousov is one of the Russian president's brightest stars. The man has his president's ear and full support. I'm not saying there won't be cracks we might exploit in the future, but it's not an option right now.

"That said," the DNI continued, "the NSA is already in talks with its Canadian and British counterparts over at the Communications Security Establishment and GCHQ to figure out how to minimize the impacts of Belousov's Unit 74455 on Mind-U and its affiliates. Thanks to your team, we have a good chance at interdicting Russian intelligence's access to the authentication server."

When Manton didn't reply, the DNI asked, "Are you listening to me, Oliver?"

"Yeah . . . I'm sorry, sir. You know the little push you mentioned earlier? I have an idea."

EPILOGUE

As he stood behind the upper helm station of the Galeon 800 Fly, Donovan wondered what kind of profession he should have chosen if he had wanted to be the owner of such a marvelous object of desire. With his current Blackbriar salary, which was more than he thought he'd ever make, he doubted he could even afford the eighty-two gallons of diesel the beast asked for every hour in exchange for its cruising speed of twenty knots.

Tastefully decorated with elegant furniture worthy of a design magazine, the eighty-two-foot long four-stateroom yacht was a head-turner. But what really got Donovan going were the two MAN V12 engines, each delivering 1,920 horsepower. Donovan pushed the throttles fully forward, knowing he'd probably never have the chance to play with an expensive toy like this again. The big yacht slowly gained speed as it plowed through the four- to five-foot waves as if they were pebbles. They were running parallel to the coast of Colima, about seven miles out at sea. The cove they were heading to was located a mile west of Espinazo del Diablo—the Devil's Backbone—a road near the port city of Manzanillo.

Donovan's right calf was still tender, and would probably remain so for several weeks, but it could have been much worse. As long as he kept changing the dressing twice a day, the risk of infection was minimal.

"Why are you smiling, Admiral?" Helen asked as she lounged on a large sun bed next to him, sipping her Pellegrino.

"I wasn't aware I was smiling," he said, doing his best to keep a large grin off his face. "I'm sorry, ma'am. My mistake. Won't happen again."

She got off the sun bed and stood next to him at the helm, looking at the horizon. They didn't speak. They didn't need to. They were solid. A good team.

Twenty minutes later, a man in his late thirties with wavy, sandy-blond hair and laughing blue eyes joined them on the flybridge. He was quite a few inches shorter than Donovan, with a glowing tan that never seemed to fade, and a laid-back surfer vibe that hid the fact that he was a hard-core operator who'd served fifteen years as a Navy SWCC—Special Warfare Combatant-Craft Crewman. His name was Raymond Garrison, and for the last two days, he'd let Donovan drive *his* boat.

"Having fun?" he asked Donovan.

Donovan eased the throttles a bit. "Got carried away, I guess."

"I'll take it from here, brother," Garrison said, taking Donovan's place behind the helm. "I want to get to the coordinates and set the anchor at least two hours before showtime. Weather's turning."

Helen said, "I'll get everything ready down below."

Donovan looked west, toward the ocean. Garrison was right. Big, black, almost opaque clouds reached down from the sky and into the sea. It could get ugly. And it could screw up their mission.

• • • • •

Oliver Manton had hiked to his position the day before after being dropped from Garrison's yacht five hundred yards from shore. He could have made the hike at night, but despite studying the topography on maps and satellite imagery back at headquarters, he wasn't familiar enough with the terrain to risk twisting an ankle or busting his knee. He had moved slowly, making sure to always stay concealed from his target's house. The house, which sat across the cove on top of a rocky cliff four hundred and fifty yards away, was huge, and, Manton had to admit, spectacular. The views of the Pacific Ocean from the large terraces and balconies must have been sublime.

Manton doubted he'd ever be invited to see for himself.

Manton had spent hours working on his sniper's nest. It had to be perfect. Four hundred and fifty yards wasn't an easy shot. A lot of things could influence the trajectory of the bullet at this distance. While the sniper rifle's bipod was firmly planted on the black waterproof carrying bag, which also doubled as a shooter's mat, the back of the rifle was supported by beanbags. With the rifle being supported on both sides, Manton's aim would be steady. Confident he had the right angle, he allowed himself a few gulps from his water canteen.

Seven hundred yards away, he recognized the sound of Raymond Garrison's boat.

Right on time.

Manton wasn't surprised. Garrison's reputation within the Naval Special Warfare community was beyond reproach. During his career as an SWCC operator, Garrison had taken part in dozens of high-risk missions in which he and his teammates had facilitated the insertion of SEALs into enemy territories. Three years ago, Garrison had won fifty million dollars in the lottery.

And, just like that, his life had changed.

Now he was living alone on his yacht near Puerto Vallarta, spending his time chasing fishing tournaments on Mexico's west coast, and begging his former SWCC teammates and SEAL friends to come and visit him down in Mexico on all-expenses-paid trips—which they often did, not because Garrison footed the bill, but because he was a genuine and likable guy.

But the man was bored, and he was ripe for recruitment into Blackbriar. Manton knew that for a fact.

Manton glanced at his watch. It was time.

He concentrated on his breathing and listened for anything out of the ordinary that would indicate something other than wildlife moving around him. Manton's senses weren't what they used to be, but they were still sharp, and they registered nothing atypical. There was the occasional deep hum of a sportfishing yacht heading out to sea, or the high-pitched sound of a motorcycle's exhaust heading to town, but nothing else.

He peered into the scope of his rifle. General Velásquez's oceanfront mansion was filling fast, as more and more of his guests arrived. A feast of some sort had been set up on a large table, but no one had dared touch the food yet. Though he was too far away to hear the conversations, Manton had no difficulty reading the atmosphere. It was tense. He'd spotted a couple of cartel leaders who tried to appear casual, but their bodyguards were anything but.

That's right, guys, keep your fingers on the triggers. Let me be the spark that will start it all.

The wind was light, but had started to pick up, and Manton prayed it wouldn't start to rain. That could really screw things up for him.

Seconds later, the first raindrop—cold, thick, and flat—landed on the back of his neck. Another followed, smacking against his left hand. The raindrops picked up force and fell faster and harder.

Dammit! Not a single fucking drop for the last two weeks, and now this? You gotta be shitting me.

That was a major setback.

Just as Manton was about to let out another curse under his breath, there was movement on the terrace. For an instant he thought the house staff had been sent out to cover the food or to bring it inside, but he was wrong.

There he was in Manton's crosshairs. The man himself. General Ramón Velásquez.

Another man joined him. Manton instantly identified the newcomer as the Sinaloa Cartel leader. Behind them, standing at a respectable distance, were four bodyguards. The cartel leader didn't look happy. His screwed-up face told the story, and his clenched fists confirmed it. Velásquez was trying to calm him down. The general placed the palm of his hand on the cartel leader's shoulder, but it was immediately swatted away.

Manton took a long, full breath, paused, and released. He steadily pulled the trigger. Despite the suppressor, the crack of the rifle was surprisingly loud, but at four hundred and fifty yards, odds were that the cartel members didn't hear it. Manton briefly lost sight of his target as the recoil pushed the muzzle of the rifle up. He reacquired his target an instant later.

Velásquez's body was sprawled on the terrace. Men were shouting at each other. Velásquez's bodyguards were aiming their rifles at the Sinaloa cartel leader while *his* bodyguards were pointing theirs at them. But, to Manton's dismay, no one else had begun shooting.

You guys need another push to completely lose it, don't you?

Manton's second shot, which came five seconds after the first one, ripped through the cartel leader's neck, severing his left jugular. As a bonus, the round angled down and deviated left, ending its trajectory deep into the cartel leader's bodyguard's abdomen.

The surviving bodyguard, seeing his boss and his fellow *sicario* fall, opened up on Velásquez's bodyguards on full automatic.

By the time Manton hit the water thirteen minutes later for his swim to Garrison's boat, the firefight was still raging in Velásquez's mansion.

• • • • •

Donovan's eyes were glued to his binocs when Manton's first round punched through Velásquez.

"Hit!" Donovan called for the benefit of Garrison and Helen.

Helen was seated at the dining table, but ready to move to the outside deck to cover Manton's retreat if needed. Several rifles and spare magazines were on the floor of the living room for that purpose. Garrison was at the lower helm, ready to move the boat if required.

"Hit! Again!" Donovan said. "And . . . here we go, the party has started."

"My God," Helen said after a loud explosion was heard coming from Velásquez's home. "Are they shooting at each other with rocket launchers?"

Exactly thirty-two minutes after the first shot was fired, Oliver Manton climbed aboard. Helen and Donovan helped him up and grabbed his gear while Garrison maneuvered the yacht.

• • • • •

At cruising speed, it took them five hours to reach their next destination, a quiet bay near the coastal area of Costalegre. Along the route, with an abundance of caution in case they were stopped by a Mexican Navy patrol boat, they had thrown overboard their equipment, including Manton's sniper rifle and the three M4s they had on board, but held on to their pistols, which were now locked in the master cabin.

Once the anchor was set, Garrison joined the three Blackbriar operatives on the flybridge, holding four ice-cold beers in his hands.

"I kept browsing through the local radio stations on our way here, and who would have guessed? Not one peep about the big party going on at the general's place."

"Can't say I'm surprised," Helen said. "The police, the politicians, and even the reporters will wait to see who's still standing before they commit to saying anything."

"We did our bit. Cheers," Manton said as they all clinked their bottles.

"What's the plan for tomorrow?" Helen asked.

"If the weather clears like it's supposed to, it shouldn't take us more than eight to ten hours to reach Puerto Vallarta," Garrison said, then took a long pull from his beer.

"We really appreciate your assistance," Manton said. "Let me know how much we owe you, okay? Total everything, double it, then tell me what the number is."

Garrison dismissed Manton's request with a wave of his hand. "Nah. My treat. George vouched for you. He told me you were good people."

Donovan looked at Manton and narrowed his eyes. "Our George?"

Manton nodded.

George, a former Navy SEAL, was one of the six Blackbriar field operatives currently on staff.

"What else did George tell you about us?"

Garrison leaned forward. "That's just the thing, he didn't say very much. But please, enlighten me, because this was the most fun I've had since I left the navy."

Around the world, Treadstone agents are being hunted down and murdered. Someone high up in the U.S. government is erasing all evidence of a shocking mission from Jason Bourne's past known as Defiance—including trying to erase the existence of Bourne himself. Staying one step ahead of a team of killers, Bourne follows a global trail that leads him to one of the government's darkest secrets—and brings him face-to-face with his archenemy, the assassin known as Lennon, for a final deadly confrontation.

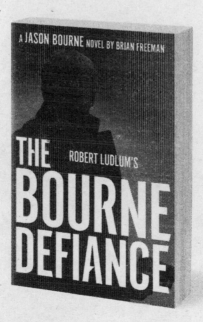

The five-day war between Russia and Georgia had taken place years earlier, but the Treadstone agent known as Cain still saw the aftereffects of the conflict around him. He passed abandoned farmhouses with their roofs caved in by mortar fire. Tall grass grew around bombed-out rubble, and the stone walls of a lonely Orthodox church bore the pockmarks of bullets. The area felt emptied of people. Many of the refugees of the region had fled south to Tbilisi and never come home again, leaving ruins of their old lives behind them.

Cain knew he was on the right path. He could follow the trail of blood and footprints. His target was wounded, probably dying. Initially, there had only been a few tiny red drops in the white snow, but the evidence of blood came more frequently now, the stains larger. Abel was slowing down, losing strength. He couldn't be far away.

The pursuit had taken Cain north out of the town of Gori. Abel's left rear tire had blown near Tergvisi, and since then, he'd proceeded on foot through the rural countryside, making a run for Russian-occupied territory. Cain had gotten close enough to him in one of the empty farm fields to land a bullet in the man's back, but then Abel had struggled to his feet and disappeared into the trees again.

Cain and Abel.

Holly Schultz, who'd assigned the code names, had a malevolent sense of humor. She'd teamed them on Treadstone missions for years. They'd saved each other's lives often enough that they were almost like brothers. Cain had thought he knew the man well. He'd trusted him. But under the jokes, under the disguises, under the Beatles songs he whistled before a kill, Abel had been an agent with a deadly secret.

Abel was a traitor. A Russian asset.

And now Cain had been sent to kill him.

He stopped in the forest, listening to the hiss of November wind and feeling the wet flakes of snow on his eyelashes and inside his heavy boots. The snow made the whole world quiet, and in the silence, he heard movement—branches snapping—close by. It wasn't Abel. The blood trail didn't lead in the direction of the noise. He was more concerned that it was a Russian soldier. He wasn't sure which side of the border he was on, and the Russian base at Eredvi was just a few miles away.

Cain leveled his Makarov, a Russian pistol he'd acquired upon arrival in Georgia. The assassination needed to be done with a foreign gun; Holly had been clear about that. There could be no evidence of American involvement. He snapped his shoulders from side to side, his eyes hunting for movement in the trees. Then he saw a tiny face, and lowered his weapon. It was a boy, no more than nine or ten years old.

The boy came out of the trees, not looking scared. He had a dirty face, greasy brown hair that was raggedly cut, and intense blue eyes. He wore a pullover shirt that resembled a burlap sack, plus torn jeans and red rubber boots that were caked with mud. The boy took note of the gun in Cain's hand.

"You hunt that man?" the boy asked in Georgian.

Cain nodded.

"He is Russian?"

Close enough, Cain thought, so he nodded again.

The boy pointed through the trees. "I saw him go in a farmhouse over there. He's bleeding, but he has a gun, too, like you. Be careful. You kill him, okay? Shoot him dead. Kill the fucking Russians."

Cain dug some coins from his pocket and handed them to the boy. Then he nodded his head for him to run in the opposite direction. The boy thumped his chest twice with his fist in a gesture of solidarity, then vanished silently through the snow.

The farmhouse was close, not even a hundred yards away. The wooden front door was open, hanging from one hinge. It was a small structure, mostly destroyed by bombs, and he circled the place to confirm that there were no other doors, just the one way in and out. Cain smelled the smoke of a fire and the stink of boiled cabbage. As he neared the door, he heard singing from inside.

"Back in the U.S.S.R."

Abel wasn't hiding his location. He knew Cain was out there. Between the lyrics, his voice broke in alternate fits of laughing and coughing. Then he called out, his words slurring as he got weaker, "Come on in, Cain. We might as well get this over with."

Cain led with the Makarov. He moved fast, expecting a battle, but there was no gunfire as he spun through the door. Instead, he saw Abel sitting in the corner of the main room, lost in the shadows on the wooden floor. He wasn't alone. His legs were spread wide, and he had one arm around the waist of a black-haired teenage girl sitting in front of him. With his other hand, he held his pistol to the terrified girl's head.

"Hey, Cain. This is Tatiana. Say hello, Tatiana."

When the girl said nothing, Abel shoved the gun hard into her dark hair and repeated in guttural Russian, *"Say hello."*

"Hello," she gasped.

Tatiana was undernourished, her arms and legs skinny. Her plain face was winter-pale, and tears leaked from her dark eyes. Her whole body trembled. She couldn't have been more than fifteen.

"Let her go, Abel," Cain murmured, aiming the Makarov at the man who'd once been his friend. But he didn't have a clean shot, not without risking the teenager's life. "Hurting her won't change how this ends."

"Oh, I think you're wrong. See, I know you too well, Cain. You're always a hero when it comes to women. It's your fatal flaw."

"Let her go," he repeated.

Abel managed a laugh. He leaned forward and kissed the back of the girl's head, keeping his face barely visible. It was clear that Abel had a wary appreciation for the accuracy of Cain's shooting, even with a foreign gun.

"So here we are," Abel said. "You and me. Brothers in arms."

"Here we are."

Cain studied the man's features in the shadows. Abel was a master of disguise and rarely looked the same way twice. He could be young, old, blond, redheaded, dark-haired, and have blue eyes, brown eyes, or green eyes. About the only thing that gave him away was his walk when he thought no one was looking, a strange way of gliding so that his shoulders seemed to float above his hips. But here, at the end, he was simply himself. Tall, strong, blond, blue-eyed, smart, and arrogant when he smiled.

Yes, Cain thought, seeing the truth for the first time. *He's Russian.*

Abel had been a Russian mole from the beginning. A graduate of Putin's charm school, designed to blend in like a native and infiltrate the U.S. intelligence services. He'd played them all. Fooled them all. Cain included.

Tatiana struggled in Abel's grasp, but the man held her tight. Staring back, he seemed to read Cain's mind.

"You think they want me dead because I'm a traitor, don't you?"

Cain didn't answer.

"Well you're wrong," Abel went on. "Think about it. Why kill me? If that's what this is about, Holly would want me in a cell somewhere, so they can sweat out every secret I've given away. When they'd bled me dry, they'd trade me, use me as a bargaining chip. But send you out here to shoot me? No. They're scared, Cain. Somebody wants to shut me up. Make sure I don't talk."

More games. More *lies*!

But Cain couldn't stop himself from playing. "Talk about what?"

"*Defiance.*"

A flash of puzzlement ran through Cain's eyes. "Defiance? That was a Treadstone mission."

"That's right, but what was the mission really about? Who ordered it? What was it covering up?"

"Are you saying you know?"

"I know enough for them to want me dead."

Cain shook his head. "You're stalling. It's too late for that. You've run out of time. Do you think the Russians are coming to save you?"

Abel's blue eyes glinted, as if laughing at a joke only he could hear.

At that moment, Cain felt a rumble under his feet. Vibrations traveled through the ground and under the floor like an earthquake. He knew what that meant. The lonely woods around the farmhouse were located near the road to Eredvi, and heavy vehicles were thundering down that road. The Russians *were* coming. Soldiers would already be in the woods, zeroing in on their location.

"You activated a tracker," Cain concluded, thinking furiously, assessing his options.

"Of course I did. See, you're the one who's running out of time, Cain. Get out of here while you still can."

Cain tightened his grip around the Makarov. He tried to send a message to the girl, Tatiana, with his eyes, telling her to jerk sideways and give him a shot. But the teenager's face was flushed with panic, and he couldn't trust her not to swing back into his line of fire. Abel recognized his predicament. They knew each other too well.

"Go, Cain. Save yourself. You can't kill me without killing her, and I know you won't do that. If you stay, you're dead."

The thunder on the road deepened and got louder. The throb of engines carried to his ears on the still air. Through the open door, he heard men trampling noisily through the forest. There were shouts in Russian. Cain endured a moment of paralysis—*stay or go*—but then the decision was made for him. A man's body filled the farmhouse doorway. It was a soldier dressed in olive gear, with an AK-12 rifle braced against his shoulder.

The man didn't see Cain at first, and Abel shouted in Russian, "Left! Left! Left!"

In that fraction of a second, Cain swung the Makarov and fired a single shot that took down the Russian soldier between his eyes. At the same moment, he dropped to the ground, watching as Abel threw the girl sideways and aimed his gun at Cain. Abel squeezed off a shot but missed high, and Cain fired back, hurrying, choosing the fattest target. The bullet landed squarely in Abel's chest.

A fatal shot; it *had* to be fatal.

Wasn't it?

Always confirm your kill.

Treadstone.

But there was no time to do that. The cursing voices outside got louder. More soldiers were coming. Cain took three steps forward and dragged Tatiana from the floor, where she was huddled in a fetal position, and slung her over his shoulder. Together, they burst through the farmhouse door, and Cain saw another young soldier running toward them through the snow, drawn by the gunfire. The man froze, startled by their sudden appearance, and his hesitation let Cain get off a wild shot that hit the man's knee and took him down, screaming.

Cain bolted into the woods, where the trees gave him cover. He was barely aware of the weight of Tatiana draped over his shoulder. He ran, dodging around thick pines, hearing more shouts as men joined the hunt from the road. They hadn't brought in a helicopter, but he doubted he had more than a few minutes before the search headed to the sky. He reached an open farm field where there was no protection, and he sprinted across the frozen land, chased by weapons fire crackling from behind him.

One bullet seared his leg, but he didn't slow down. Another whistled past his ear. As he neared the next grove of trees past the field, the firefight intensified, and he zigzagged, feeling another near miss that sprayed blood from his neck. When he finally reached the shelter of the trees again, he sagged to his knees, letting the girl slump to the ground next to him. He expected to hear the voices closing on him, expected to see dozens of soldiers converging on his location through the snowy field.

Instead, the gunfire stopped.

The Russians all withdrew.

At first he was puzzled, but then he understood. He'd crossed the border. He wasn't in the South Ossetia province; he was back in Georgia, in unoccupied territory. The Russians weren't ready to start another war over a single spy.

"We're safe," he told Tatiana as he exhaled in relief. "They won't come for us now."

The girl didn't answer. He looked at her for the first time since they'd reached the trees, and he saw that her eyes were open and fixed in a look of scared surprise. Her trembling had stopped; her body was motionless. When he turned her over, he saw that a single bullet from one of the Russian rifles had landed in the back of her skull. Her black hair was matted with blood. She was dead, killed instantly.

If he hadn't been carrying her, that bullet would have killed him.

Cain got to his feet. He stared down at the lifeless teenager and felt a crushing wave of exhaustion, the weight of the world slumping his shoulders. His blood was warm inside his clothes. He needed to go, but he found he couldn't move; he couldn't leave her, not yet. He shook his head in bitter regret, and not for the first time, he hissed out a curse against the life he led.

• • • • •

One week later, Cain waited outside a cargo hangar at the airport in Antalya, Turkey, on the Mediterranean coast. The weather was unseasonably hot, almost eighty degrees. He wore a black formfitting T-shirt and cargo shorts as he waited for the arrival of the Treadstone jet. Sunglasses covered his eyes. By habit, he examined the faces around him, but he concluded that he wasn't being watched.

His wounds were healing now. At least the ones the doctors could treat.

Cain pressed the secure satellite phone to his ear. The signal was crystal clear. Holly Schultz, who was in Washington, could have been standing a few feet away.

"You haven't checked in about the mission," she chided him. "I had to hear from Nash that you called for the jet."

"I've been busy staying alive," Cain told her.

That silenced her complaints, but the truth was, he'd deliberately put off making his report. He'd taken three days to make his way south from Georgia, and then he'd spent the last four days at a Turkish beachside resort. He'd swum out in the sea until the land was just a smudge on the horizon. He'd drunk a lot of raki. He'd paid a prostitute to do nothing but sit in his room for an entire day and talk to him, even though he didn't speak the language. That was how Cain ran from his troubles.

But he couldn't run forever.

"Anyway, I'm back," he went on.

"And Abel?"

"I shot him."

"He's dead?"

Cain hesitated. "I think so. I didn't have time to check as the Russians moved in."

"That's unfortunate," Holly said.

"I had to act fast. I didn't figure you'd want an American agent captured in Russian-occupied territory."

"True enough," she admitted in a grudging voice. "We'll need to do a full debrief when you're back. I'll have someone meet the plane."

"Fine. Whatever." He didn't hide the hatred he felt at that moment. For her. For himself. For the whole world.

"Are you all right, David?" she asked, injecting a forced bit of sympathy into her tone. When she wanted to pretend she cared, she used his real name. David Webb. But he had been Cain for so long that his birth name had little meaning for him. There were days when he didn't even remember it.

"I'm fine," he replied, "but I had to take over one of Abel's covers as I made my escape."

"What identity are you using now?" Holly asked.

Cain squinted into the hot Turkish sunlight. "My name is Jason Bourne."

ONE

When Sam Young spotted the blond woman in the *Norwegian Jewel* sweatshirt coming into his gallery, he knew they'd found him. Yes, she looked like any of the thousands of other tourists streaming off the cruise ships every day. Her eyes went to the cheap framed prints of Mendenhall Glacier, not the handcrafted Native sculptures. She carried a plastic bag stuffed with Chinese-made T-shirts from a discount gift shop near the port. If he took her in the back and searched her, he was sure he'd find a valid cruise ship ID and a matching passport with her name and photograph. Spies didn't make obvious mistakes like that.

But she was a fake.

Cruise passengers came and went every day, but once their ship left for the next port, they were gone for good.

In by eight a.m., out by four thirty p.m., depending on the tide. But this woman had been here before. Not in the gallery. She was smart enough not to kiss the dog more than once. However, Sam had learned to study and remember faces, and he was certain he'd seen this same woman outside the shop in the last couple of days.

He'd know for sure if he got a buzz on his phone. Sam's tradecraft specialty was as a computer hacker, and even though he'd been inactive for Treadstone for two years, he still kept his hand in the game. That was partly for his own protection, because when it came to Treadstone, you were never really out. He kept surveillance cameras inside and outside his Franklin Street shop, as well as on the road near his house on Black Wolf Way. He'd written an app to isolate faces from the video feeds and maintain them in a database, and with each new entry, the program ran facial recognition to look for duplicates. When it found one, it sent the information to his phone.

Buzz.

Sam felt the vibration in his pocket. He took out his phone and examined the side-by-side photographs that appeared in the notification from his app. One was the thirtysomething woman standing in his shop right now, pretending to study a display of colorfully painted Russian nesting dolls. The other was a woman with dark hair and an oilskin jacket who'd passed on the sidewalk outside the shop three days earlier. Although the second image was less focused, and she'd changed her hair in between, it was definitely the same person.

Studying the picture again, Sam was also certain that he'd seen her at a table at Mar y Sol when he'd had dinner there on Wednesday. She'd been watching him for a while.

Sam slipped his hands casually into his pockets, one hand curling around the grip of his Hellcat pistol, as he approached her. "Can I help you?"

The woman was good. A pro. She looked up with a false smile, but he could see her eyes take note of his hands, then flick up to the corner of the ceiling and spot the positioning of the security camera. He assumed there was a weapon hidden inside her gift bag. If she went for it, the question would be which one of them was faster. Sam didn't like his odds. There was something about the hawkish look in her blue eyes that made him think she'd be the better fighter.

But she was the advance scout, not the shooter. There was too much risk going after him in the middle of downtown.

"Oh, no, thank you," she replied pleasantly. "Just browsing. You have beautiful things here."

"Thank you."

"I suppose most of your business comes from the ships. It must get so quiet off-season. Do you close up for the winter?"

"No, I'm open all year, but you're right. Most of the crowds disappear as soon as the cruise season ends."

"How did you come to be in a place like this?" she asked him.

Sam shrugged. He was sure she knew exactly where

he'd come from. "I don't know. How does anyone end up anywhere?"

"Oh, well, I guess you're right about that. Anyway, I wish I could afford to buy something, but you know, the family's always on a budget. T-shirts for the kids and not much else."

"That's okay," he told her. "Take your time and look around."

"I will, thanks."

She spent another five minutes in the shop, just to make it look good. As she was leaving, she called out to say goodbye, and her eyes shot another glance at the ceiling camera. Then, as the bell on the door chimed, she headed out to Franklin Street and turned toward the harbor. She didn't look through the window again. That would be the last time he saw her. But others would come soon. Tonight, most likely. She'd probably report that she'd been blown and that the assault team needed to assume he'd be waiting for them.

She hadn't fooled him, and he hadn't fooled her.

As soon as she was gone, Sam closed the shop. He assessed his options but decided there was only one thing to do. Get the hell out of Juneau right now. Whoever was after him, he'd be outgunned and outnumbered. He didn't know how they'd found him—there were no more than half a dozen people who knew that the Arizona hacker with the Treadstone code name Dax was now gift shop owner Sam Young in Alaska—but he didn't have time to worry about how his cover had been blown.

He'd had an escape strategy in place from day one. It was time to put it into play.

Sam emptied the cash from the register. There wasn't much, just a few hundred dollars. He thought about stopping at the bank to withdraw the money from his accounts, but he assumed if they were watching the store, they'd have someone watching his bank, too, to see whether he was making a run. It didn't matter. His bank had a branch in the town of Haines. Once he was clear of Juneau, he could stop there on his way into the backcountry.

He locked the shop and hiked up the Franklin Street hill. He always parked several blocks away, which gave him time to identify any surveillance that might be waiting for him. It was a cold September day, gray and ominous, with low clouds clinging to the steep green hillsides. Drizzle spat on his face. He kept his hand around the Hellcat in his pocket, but his shoulders were hunched, just a man trudging along in the rain. His eyes took a close look at each parked car and each doorway. If they were watching him, they were keeping it under wraps. He saw no one.

Sam debated whether to go home. He had his go bag, his laptop, and more money hidden under the floorboards in his living room. He could be in and out in ninety seconds, and then he'd be on the way to Statter Harbor, where he kept his Exhilarator speedboat gassed up and ready to go. As he'd developed an escape plan—knowing a day like this would come sooner or later—he'd thought about using a floatplane. That would give him more range and speed, but the flying weather around Juneau was too iffy day by day to guarantee he could get out of town on short notice. With the Exhilarator, he could head to Hoonah or race up the channel to Haines or Skagway. Once there, he could hide out in the woods or take an SUV over the Rockies on the Alaska Highway.

He found his red Honda parked at the top of the hill near 6th Street. From there, he could see the dark water of the harbor through mist and fog. The *Jewel* was the only cruise ship docked there today, and he knew it would be gone in less than two hours. Everyone in Alaska retail knew the port times of the ships. Sam made a show of dropping his wallet, which gave him a chance to check the undercarriage of his Accord, in case anyone had planted explosives or tracking devices. He also noted the tiny red threads he'd secured across the gaps of each car door. They were still there; no one had broken into the vehicle during the day.

Even so, he held his breath when he started the engine. It caught. He didn't blow up.

Sam headed north on the Glacier Highway. He watched the mirrors and didn't see anyone following him. He decided to stop home to grab his go bag, but ten minutes later, he changed his mind. A shrill alarm went off on the phone in his pocket, which was the signal that someone had broken one of the invisible laser barriers guarding the windows and doors of his house. There were people inside. Sam pulled onto the highway shoulder near the bridge at Lemon Creek, where wooded hilltops and snowcapped mountains went in and out of view through the clouds. His breath came quickly; adrenaline surged through him.

When he dug out his phone, he activated the cameras located in the house's ductwork, which gave him sound and video of the interior. He spotted four men, all dressed in black, all armed with semiautomatics and suppressors. The faces of the men were unfamiliar, but who they were didn't concern him. What mattered was that they would take him down as soon as he came through the door.

"Should we check the computer?" one of them said through the video feed.

"Don't bother," another replied. *"He's a hacker. He'll have it secured. We'll take it with us and let the pros crack it. But keep your eyes open. He's bound to have backups. Maybe electronic, maybe print."*

"What are we looking for?"

"Anything about Intelsat."

On the shoulder of the Glacier Highway, Sam closed his eyes and swore. Now he understood. Now it all made sense.

Intelsat. Of course.